PRAISE FOR
SANDY NATHAN

I have been following Sandy Nathan's writing since her very first book, *Stepping Off the Edge: Learning & Living Spiritual Practice*. Then came her novel, *Numenon*. Being a sci-fi fan, I have always been leery of new writers. Sandy put the lie to that for me. *Numenon* definitely had what I was looking for: a good story, imaginative ideas, and good writing. When I got to the end I was both sad and happy; sad because I was so invested in the story that I wanted to know what was going to happen next and happy because I was assured this was only the first in a series and I would be able to spend more time with these great characters down the line.

Then *Lady Grace* came along and I found that Sandy had reached new heights in her story-telling and her craft. I told her I thought it was the best thing she had written. But then I read *The Headman & the Assassin*. Out of the ballpark! It's a terrific story with wonderful characters – both the good guys and the bad guys – in all kinds of wild situations.

I think what makes Sandy's writing so powerful is that her stories originate from her real-life experiences. *The Angel & the Brown-eyed Boy*, first in the Earth's End, for example, came out of processing the grief over her brother's death. So her stories are charged with the authenticity of what she's going through.

If this is your first experience of Sandy Nathan's writing, prepare yourself for a wild ride. And give thanks that there are Sandy Nathan books already in print and even more on their way.

Laren Bright
Emmy-nominated television writer

THE
HEADMAN
& THE
ASSASSIN

ALSO BY SANDY NATHAN

Stepping Off the Edge: Learning & Living Spiritual Practice

Numenon: A Tale of Mysticism & Money (Bloodsong Series I)

Tecolote: The Little Horse That Could

The Angel & the Brown-Eyed Boy
(Earth's End 1)

Lady Grace & the War for a New World
(Earth's End 2)

THE HEADMAN
& THE ASSASSIN

EARTH'S END 3

SANDY NATHAN

VILASA
PRESS

SANTA YNEZ, CA 93460

ISBN-13: 978-1-937927-04-2 (Trade Paperback)
ISBN-13: 978-1-937927-05-9 (ePub Version)
LCCN: 2011941268

Editor: Melanie Rigney
Interior design: Lewis Agrell
Cover design: Damonza Book Covers

First Printing: 2012
Printed in the United States of America

Publisher's Cataloging-in-Publication Data
Nathan, Sandra Oddstad.
   The Headman & the Assassin / Sandy
Nathan.
     p. cm.
   ISBN: 978-0-9762809-6-5 ISBN: trade paperback: 978-1-937927-04-2
eBook: 978-1-937927-05-9

   1. Man-woman relationships—Fiction. 2. Multiple
personality—Fiction. 3. Future life—Fiction. 4. Nuclear
warfare—Fiction.   I. Title.
Ps3614.A864 S26 2012
813—dc22

2011941268

To my husband, Barry Nathan, the Sam in my life

INTRODUCTION
A NOTE FROM SAM GOOD MAN

My name is Sam Good Man. By rights, I could use the name Sam Baahuhd. I can claim that name because I am the oldest descendant of the original Sam Baahuhd, the headman of the village when we had to go underground to escape the atomics. I am the headman now, one hundred and five generations later.

Legends are told of lives like mine, but my life doesn't seem legendary to me. It seems normal. Even ordinary.

Well, perhaps a bit more than that.

I was born in the underground shelter and escaped from it in its darkest time. I was badly wounded when I escaped and am alive only because Jeremy Edgarton—known by my people as the Great Tek—and his mother, the lady, Veronica Edgarton—saved me.

We found ourselves living on a great stone cliff over a river valley. We were joined by those who had gone to the angel Eliana's planet to escape the great atomic war: Jeremy the Great Tek, Eliana herself, Henry and Lena, and Mel and James. We had many adventures. The battle for the underground when we saved the children was the greatest. I'm not going to talk about those times. I'm going to talk about what started it all.

To understand this book, you need to know that I have another name. I am Sam of Emily. I am the last of the line of Emily born in the underground shelter. Emily is the woman Sam Baahuhd carried into the shelter just before the bombs went off and sealed us down there forever. I carry inside of me Emily and Sam Baahuhd and Arthur Romero and so many more of the first ones. They sing in me, telling their tales.

Every story has a story behind it. This book has one, too.

After the battle for the underground, we went back to the cliff by the river with the children we'd saved. When we got things squared away so that no one was near dying, we started having campfires every night. We laughed and had fun—the best times I'd ever had.

At the campfires, the children sang the way we did underground, humming and warbling deep in our throats. The lady said our songs reminded her of the way the monks in Tibet sang. I don't know about that. It's just how we sing. Our voices sounded good in the shelter, bouncing off the cement walls. The sound carried a long way, too. You could put different meanings into the sound, if you wanted to sneak a message past the Bigs who enslaved us down below.

The first time I told a story, I started at the beginning, telling about Sam and Emily and Arthur and all the first ones. I didn't think it anything special until I looked up and saw that everyone had tears about to spill out of their eyes.

When I'd been telling a little bit every night, Mel Abrams started teaching me to read. Mel was a teacher and a revolutionary before the world blew up. He was Jer the Tek's teacher and friend. He teaches everyone here, whether they like it or not.

After I had told stories for few weeks, Mel got the "wonderful idea" that I should make the stories into a book.

"How can I write a book?" I said. "I cannot write."

"This is what we're going to do," Mel said. "I'm going to record your stories and transcribe them. When you can spell the words from hearing the sounds, you'll do it yourself. Then we'll start polishing."

I would write a chapter or two, and then he would read it and say, "Yes, but your POV"—that means "point of view"—"jumps here, and this goes on too long. You need to watch your punctuation. This doesn't move the story forward."

Somewhere along the way, I learned to use a computer. That made it easier. Then I wrote this story on the computer, instead of telling it at the campfires at night.

I'm glad of that, because I didn't want to tell parts of this story around the children. There's nothing wrong with people knowing that their ancestors were real people and went to bed with each other and made mistakes. But the kids ought at least to grow up enough to read about it, rather than hearing it by accident at a campfire. Some bad things happened down there. I'd just as soon not tell anyone about them, but a record should be kept. Maybe people will learn from it.

In the end, I wrote this book because my ancestors wanted me to do it. They'd come to me, raucous like a flock of crows, and flap around in my head until I wrote what they wanted. Whatever Mel thinks, I expect that my stories and this book will die on this ledge with me. But, even if they do, those who came before want those who came after to know what happened.

I offer you this story with love in my heart and gratitude that I have the life I do. I survived when so many others didn't. This is the story of my ancestors, Sam Baahuhd and Emily, who loved each other beyond death.

Sam Good Man

Who is also Sam of Emily, the last Sam Baahuhd, the headman of the village and the people who live on the cliff by the river. I am the man who wed the lady and will love her forever.

Part 1:
The First Year
Underground

1

"**G**ET OUTTA MY WAY, YE DUNG-EATIN' NINNIES!" Sam took the stairs down to the lower level of the mansion two at a time, clutching the naked girl to his chest. He had thought everyone would be safely in the bomb shelter by that time, but they weren't. The huge room outside the shelter's round steel door swarmed with villagers who'd snagged one last treasure from the big house.

A long sofa with a hump in its back was stuck in the shelter's doorway. Two men carrying a grandfather clock screamed for someone to move the sofa so they could get through. Others holding fine wooden tables with curved legs bellowed, "Hurra up! Hurra up!" Women clutching clothing and dishes shoved each other.

"Drop that shit and get in the shelter!" Sam cried. "Yer s'posed to be down there *now*."

"Ye weren't here, Sam. We didn' see ye nowheres. Everyone thought ye'd gone up in the ball o' light wi' Jeremy an' Henry and them. Gone to anuther world. We thought we better get it all," said Cooty Gill, the barrel maker.

"Ye couldna think to save yer ass, Cooty. Ah did *not* go up in the ball o' light. Get inside! We have to get to the bottom before the bombs go off!" Sam threw the girl over his shoulder. "Get in the shelter, y' idjits!"

No one responded. Then the image of Jeremy Edgarton appeared on the wall, bigger than in real life. His family owned the estate and he had created the fallout shelter. The image screamed, "The bombs are going off in three minutes! Get in the shelter!"

Sam leapt on top of the sofa in the doorway, ducked his head under its round steel lintel, and jumped over the arm on the other side. He was inside, but couldn't get far. The first of the six staircases leading to the shelter's depths was clogged with more villagers and their booty. Shouting and kicking, he shoved the girl and himself past the people and furniture.

"Get outta ma way!" Sam roared, scrambling through another door and sprinting down the steps on the other side.

That did the trick; if *Sam Baahuhd* was running for his life, the villagers knew this was for real. They dropped their treasures and bolted.

"Clear the doors so they can shut!" Sam yelled over his shoulder. "If even one door canna close, we'll fry."

They cleared the doorways and ran. Once the rout began, the villagers followed on Sam's heels, but being careful not to touch or push him. They held back as though jostling him would cost their lives, which it might. Sam was headman of the village because his father had been headman, yes, but mostly because of his ferocity and cunning. He would kill any who interfered with him.

He galloped down all six levels, the girl bouncing on his shoulder and the looters following closely. When he got to the bottom, Sam stepped aside so the others could run past him.

They weren't able to run very far; the area just inside the door was jammed. They'd been transferring the contents of the mansion to the underground since before dawn and had done a pretty good job of emptying the place. Piles of household goods and furniture were dumped where villagers had left them as they sprinted back for another load.

His people pressed around Sam, pushing each other and howling. The reality of their situation was dawning on them.

"Shut up! Get away so ah can think!" Sam felt like a cornered bear.

He saw Arthur standing by the bottom door, waiting for him.

"Art'ur, shut 'er down!" he screamed.

Arthur was from New York City—the only one down there, besides the girl, from outside the village. Arthur had been Jeremy Edgarton's protector for years, a commando masquerading as a driver. His presence was crucial: Arthur was the only person there who could read. He was also the only one who knew about computers and could run the systems for air and water, waste disposal, solar power, and all the rest.

And he was the only one who could close the shelter's steel doors.

"Shut 'er, Art'ur." Sam was almost hysterical. Arthur had shown him a number of things the night before. One was how to read a digital clock. Sam stared at one on the wall in front of him.

The bombs were supposed to begin detonating at 7:35. It was 7:35.

2

They heard the muffled sound of metal against metal as the foot-thick steel doors twisted shut. After the doors were tight, the reverberation of bolts sliding into place struck home. All six levels were locked. They were sealed in.

The people of the village stood before Sam, too horrified to speak. They were ninety-three strong, counting him. Ninety-five, adding in Arthur and the girl. Sam didn't know numbers or math. Anything more than he could count on his fingers, he had to reckon with a mark on a stick. Arthur had told him how they counted out.

Sam was as mute as he had been when Jeremy had showed him the underground city the night before. How could he explain that the living world they knew would soon be destroyed? That the atomics would make the world outside lethal for two thousand years? How could he tell them they were *lucky* to be there?

He shifted the girl on his shoulder. She hung limp. Being in the river all night would do that to anyone. She was covered with muck and bruises, and looked beat to hell. Even so, she was prettier than any woman in the village, except maybe his third wife,

Winnie. The way the girl was hanging, her bare ass was pointed at the crowd. That saved Sam from having to make a speech; the village rowdies filled in for him.

Ronny Nahyuhn played his usual role. "Who's she, Sam? Somethin' to while away the hours?"

"This's Em'ly, ma wife." He used the broadest village dialect, hoping she wouldn't hear or understand until he'd had a chance to warm her to the notion of her new marital state. "Found her in the field." She hadn't been naked when he found her; she had been wearing the black uniform of an FBI agent. He had told her to shuck off her clothes and throw them into the sea. The villagers would kill her for sure if they knew she was a fed.

His four other wives stood at the front of the crowd and scowled when he announced the new addition to the family. Their eyes narrowed, but there wasn't a thing they could do about it. Men in the village took as many wives as they could support.

"Ye gonna share her, bucko?" Ronny Nahyuhn, grinning broadly, piped up again. His cronies guffawed.

Sam shifted the girl so she was lying across his arms, thereby removing her buttocks from view, but the new position was even worse. Her arm flopped so they could see her titties and belly. That prompted a chorus of catcalls.

"Look here," Sam shouted. "A buncha things're gonna change real soon. How we do things in the vil' is gonna be different. Jeremy left us Commands that ah'll tell ye about. But first ah need to put her down." He raised the girl a bit, causing her breasts to jiggle. Jeers followed.

"Art, get me into ma room," Sam said. Only Arthur knew how to open the locks. "Ru"—Sam turned to his oldest son, Rupert—"keep 'em down until ah get back."

Sam bolted for the VIP corridor, originally planned to house the lady, Mrs. Edgarton, who owned the estate and the village, too. Her son, Jeremy, would have been there along with Arthur;

Sam and his oldest son, Rupert; a few members of their families; and a whole bunch of genius scientists. Mostly scientists. Instead, the way things had worked out, the VIPs were Arthur, Sam and Rupert, and their wives and kids. The geniuses hadn't made it. Neither had the lady.

His room was the first one on the right, and meant to be the lady's. The space was grand enough to be quarters for Veronica Piermont Edgarton, owner of the village and the big house and the estate and who knew how many other estates and homes around the world. But the lady and her lover, the general—a stone-cold killer and the real ruler of Russia and the United States—were dug into a bunker in Siberia.

"OK, Sam. Here's the pattern of the lock's combination." Arthur stood before a panel outside Sam's door. It had buttons on it, each bearing a number. "I know you can't read numbers well, but memorize this pattern and it will get you in." Arthur pushed the buttons, one by one.

The door swung open and Sam walked into a chaotic jumble of furnishings. He'd made a momentous decision early that morning. He'd told Rupert to bring everything in the lady's rooms in the big house to this room. His room. He wasn't going to stay in the quarters set up for his family.

Rupert did as he was told, but Sam had had no idea how many rooms the lady had or how much stuff. All of it sat where Ru or his boys had put it down. A forest of tall chests, tables, chairs, bureaus, and carpets covered the floor. Paintings were stacked against the walls. A pile of clothes reached almost to the ceiling, furs, satin, and lace peeking out. The bed had been taken apart. The main part of it, where you slept, filled the middle of the room. Long spikes of ostrich plumes were tossed on it, along with metal rods and poles.

Sam looked around for some place to put the girl and finally sat her on the bed. She was awake and looking around blankly.

"Ye got to get cleaned off. Pick yerself some clothes." He indicated the pile.

"There's a bathroom over there." Arthur pointed to the top of a door mostly obscured by furniture.

"Ah'll be back when ah can. Stay here," Sam said to her, patting her shoulder. She continued staring vacantly as he and Arthur left the room.

Sam's hands were shaking so badly he could hardly punch in the code to lock the door.

"Sam, are you OK?" Arthur looked concerned.

"Yeah. Ah can fix 'er. Gimme a minute by myself. Go out there with Rupert. Show the folk around. Ah'll be there directly."

"OK, but, if you need me, use the phone on your belt. I'll come."

Sam waited until Arthur had disappeared into the main hall before heading deeper into the VIP corridor. The corridor formed a very large U, the legs emptying into opposite ends of the main hall. His room was the first one on the right leg. Arthur's room was down the corridor next to the big one for Rupert and his family. In the middle of the U was a huge space for Sam's family. Empty rooms for the scientists who were supposed to be there dotted the corridor, along with a gym and a library.

When he'd gotten as far from the main hall as he could, Sam put his back to the wall and leaned against it. He was gasping, his heart pounding, lungs reaching hard for air. The trembling had gone up his arms. He could feel it shuddering in his gut. He wrapped his arms around himself and rocked from side to side. A moan escaped him. "Ah'm gonna die right here."

It was the hooch. He'd quit drinking the day before, when he figured out that the big things that had come up in the fields were atomic weapons goin' to detonate the next morning—which was now. Jeremy had told him that he was an alcoholic and shouldn't quit that fast. If he did, he might see things that weren't there or fall on the ground, shaking. Sam already knew that. Those who had newly quit the hooch had been shaking and puking all over the Hamptons as long as people had lived there.

Sam figured he could control all that with his Power. But he could have used a slug right then. Maybe a big one. The shaking was harder to handle than he had thought it would be.

But he wouldn't take a taste, even if he had had a bottle. Jeremy had given them the Commands the night before. They said no hooch or anything that made ye high. He'd had to promise Jeremy that he would keep the Commands and make sure everyone else did, too. Even though Jeremy had gone off to Ellie's world in a giant ball of light and would never know a thing about what happened in the shelter, Sam intended to keep and enforce the Commands. A promise was a promise. Knowing what the old village had been, he had a feeling that the new village would do better dry.

Sam had always partaken of the hooch. The whole village did. Kiddies did. Mas gave their babes a taste to quiet 'em down. Das gave 'em a taste the first time they killed somethin' out huntin'. Not only did the villagers slug it down, the lady and her guests led the way, but with fancier stuff. Brandy and champagne. They staggered about the lawn, pawin' each other and laughin'.

The hooch was nothin'. The previous year, he'd stayed as loaded as one of the lady's guests all the time.

It had been the cover Jeremy and Arthur had worked out for him, something to keep the feds off his trail. Things had gotten bad in the Hamptons along with everywhere else. Sam knew the smoke rising in the distance meant a war was on. The front moved along the horizon with the smoke. As isolated as the Hamptons were, no one had sent them news about who was fighting or why. Arthur said their isolation didn't matter; the feds wouldn't tell them anything anyway.

Sam knew about the prison camps and people disappearing. The feds had built a camp not far from Jamayuh. Sam had ridden out there to see it, an evil, ugly place reeking of death. There were others dotted around the Hamptons.

People escaped from the camps, and others ran away from the cities. They formed bands of marauders that roamed the hills looking for food and shelter. He and the villagers had driven them off when they had attacked. He'd managed to hold the estate for the lady. Many of the old places had fallen to the marauders and were pirate dens, pure and simple.

When Jamey Stulhmahn had disappeared out of his own field, Sam knew the feds had started going after the village headmen. Sam had heard of other headmen disappearing, but always far away. Jamey ran the village two days north.

Jeremy told him that the feds had found out about the Power and the Voice. All the headmen had the Power and the Voice to some degree. They'd been isolated in the Hamptons for so long, marrying among themselves, that some things that everyone could do had been intensified.

Everyone had mental powers. People could tell when someone they loved was coming home; others could predict events in the future or had visions. Everyone could put a tone in his voice so that what he said was more compelling.

The villagers had more of those abilities than people in the outside world, and the headmen had more than their people. Sam had more than anyone. He had the Voice. He had the Power. He had them stronger than any headman, ever.

Using his Voice, he could talk people into doing what they didn't want to do. Into being peaceful and honest and working hard. The villagers would do the right thing with just a little hint of Voice. He could tell the people tales around the fire that would have full-grown men weeping. He could move them and shape them with a word or a sigh. He could give their lives meaning and happiness, and he did.

And he had the Power. He could heal. He could set bones and cure ordinary diseases. He could heal broken minds and hearts.

He had the Power and the Voice stronger than anyone had seen or even heard about. Sam Baahuhd was a legend all over the Hamptons.

"The feds found out what the headmen can do," Jeremy had told him. "They want them to work in the camps and for the police.

Headmen don't have to torture or interrogate prisoners. They use the Voice and the prisoners tell them whatever they know. They could use their Power to heal soldiers.

"The feds get the headmen to work for them by taking their families hostage and torturing *them*. They've caught a bunch, Sam. You have to stay below the radar. This is serious."

No one in the Hamptons would turn in a headman, but feds were crawling all over the woods. They had developed machines that told them when a headman was working his magic. "It's your brain waves," Jeremy said. "Your electromagnetic frequencies are different from regular people's. They've got instruments that pick them up.

"Booze will cloud your brain waves, Sam. They won't even know you're around."

Sam had stayed drunk for a year. Now he was paying for it.

Sam's stomach heaved and he thought he might puke. He forced the sickness down. Somethin' wavered at the edges of his vision, a boogie that wasn't there. He focused his eyes, willing the mirage to oblivion. It took all he had to keep himself in the real world of the cement hallway.

"Oh, lady," escaped his lips. He'd loved the lady his whole life. He and Veronica Piermont Edgarton were the same age, the two of them: forty-one. They'd been pals since they were tots. He'd loved her all that time. Sam wished she were there. He wished he could lay his head on her soft breasts and have her stroke him. Comfort him. Take up some of the load.

But that had never happened and never would.

He wanted to be from the city and read like he'd been born knowing how. He wanted to be like Arthur, wearing clothes that were new and made of soft cloth, not hides or canvas. He wanted to have a sharp haircut and not have the itches.

But he was of the village and would never be anything else. He was an ugly sucker, and big. Sam was as tall as the meeting hall's door. His arms spanned almost that distance. His dark red hair, now streaked with gray, was matted and plastered down where his hat sat on his head. The hair on his chest was mostly white. His nose had been broken so many times, it sat on his face like a potato. He crawled with bugs. The itches were part of the village. The bugs probably had kept the lady away from him as much as anything.

He gritted his teeth. At least he still had all of them.

3

"Sam Baahuhd! Sam Baahuhd! Sam Baahuhd!" The voices reverberated from the main hall. Sam shoved himself off the wall and stood tall.

He walked out of the far end of the U-shaped corridor and into the main hall. The villagers were facing away from him, toward the hallway into which he had disappeared. Ronny shouted as though Sam were hiding just out of sight. He leaned forward slightly, a huge man, half a head above the rest, though still shorter than Sam. He raised a massive forearm and pointed at the corridor.

"Where're the 'splosions, Sam Baahuhd? Where's the fire an' hell?" Ronny Nahyuhn bellowed. "Why're we locked down here? Huh? Sam Baahuhd! Where're ye hidin'?" The others nodded their agreement, their voices forming a muttered undertone. "We shud be home in bed!" He moved his hips as though he were fucking. People laughed.

"Ah'm here, Ronny. What's the trouble?" Sam said softly, moving toward Ronny from behind the crowd. They spun to face him, crying out in surprise.

"Sounds like *yer* a 'splosion, Ronny. Or do ye jus' like to hear yerself squawk?" Sam spoke quietly, but the chamber amplified his words.

"What're ya doin', Sam? Sneakin' up?" Ronny jeered.

"The day ah need to sneak up on such as ye will ne'er come, Ronny. What d' ye have to say to yer headman, man to man?" Sam approached Ronny and his henchmen. He saw that his first wife's brother Lester and several of his own first cousins were among them.

He stood close to Ronny, relaxed and ready, more menacing relaxed than they were in their agitated bravado. "Or have ye forgot yer manners total'?" Addressing Sam as Ronny had was a grave breach of village protocol and a challenge to Sam's authority.

"Well, *some* say a 'tomic war is coming," Ronny spoke mockingly. "S'posed to start at 7:35, sharp. But it didn't happen. For that on the wall"—he nodded at the digital clock, which said 7:51—"tells a time later than 7:35, or ah don't know nothing." He spoke to Sam, but glanced around for support. "Mayhap the war is *bullshit*, made up by that little fart Jeremy to see us locked in hell." Ronny stuck his chest out and strutted. His cohorts jockeyed around him.

"Ye want to go out, Ronny? Ah'll let ye out. Ye an' yer gang of idjits. Ah'll tell Art'ur to open 'er up now, so's ye can go back to pretendin' to work in the fields when ye're buggerin' yerselves." Sam gazed steadily into his opponent's eyes, the rage building inside him showing in his glare. "G'wan. Get over to the door. All o' ye. Ah'll call Art."

"OK! Ah'll go. See ye at supper, Sam, when ye get tired o' hidin' down here." Ronny spit out his words. The other villagers pulled together, muttering.

"C'mon, Carly, get the kids. We're goin' home." Ronny called to his wife. "C'mon, everybody, let's get some sleep."

"No. Just you," Sam said. "An' yer frien's." He indicated Ronny's cronies. "Ye can leave. We'll take care of yer wives and kids."

"What? Leave ma wife to ye? Don' ye have enough nookie, Sam, with the new one ye added today? How's an' ol' man like you gonna foock 'em all?"

Sam took one step toward him, fists clenched.

"Gawd! What's that?" someone cried. The side wall of the hall had lit up. People turned toward it, exclaiming.

The main hall was a huge room with built-in tables and benches at the far end. The floor was tiered, so that the area farther away from the now brightly shining wall was raised a foot or two. The hall's ceiling rose higher than the rest of the underground, perhaps fifteen feet at the topmost point.

The elevated ceiling should have made the room less oppressive, but it couldn't offset the effect of all the cement. The high ceiling simply allowed a grander scale of depression.

Sam had seen another flat white wall like the one now shining. They'd had one in the ballroom of the big house. They would open the curtains on the stage and behind them was one of these picture-viewing walls. The lady and her guests had watched movies on them. He had watched them, too, from the bushes outside the ballroom windows. They had been strum interesting, though not being able to hear the sound made them hard to understand.

He looked behind him and saw a glass pane in the back wall. Light streamed from it; a picture-making machine was up there.

He'd just figured that out when Jeremy's head and shoulders covered the middle section of the wall, which was really a very big screen, bigger than in the mansion. Jeremy looked more real on the screen than in life. Sam could see the computers of his lab shining behind him, making his hair look like a curly halo.

"Hello, everyone. This is Jeremy Edgarton. I'm recording this from my lab in the Hamptons. I don't know exactly where I'll be when the party starts, but I wanted to say good-bye to everyone more personally than I'll be able to when the action begins."

The villagers were silent. Jeremy looked very different from the skinny little rich kid who had wandered around the estate talking to himself. On the screen, he had a ferocious intensity.

"I'm sorry for what's happening, everyone. We gave it our best shot." He smiled stiffly, and his eyes looked misty—for an instant.

"I'm so glad I was able to know you, even if it was only over the 'net.

"If you've got your screens set up, you'll see yourself on this map. We cover the earth." The third of the screen to Jeremy's left lit up. A flat map of the globe filled the newly illumined area. Bright dots were all over it, hundreds of them.

"This is *us*. Each light is one of our shelters. We've got a lot of good people dedicated to rebuilding a righteous world when this is over.

"Your shelter has a module hooked up to a satellite. Even if everything above ground fries, the module will let you get broadcasts in the Hamptons. That's how you're seeing this.

"The broadcasts will continue as long as the satellites do, maybe thousands of years. My programming will track radiation levels, air quality, everything, all over the world. You'll be able to tell when it's safe to come out. That's if we survive . . . what's coming in the next few days."

Sam watched, arms trembling and starting to itch. He clawed at his forearms, glad that what Jeremy was saying was keeping anyone from looking at him.

He knew Jeremy wasn't just talking to them. He was broadcasting to all those lights, all over the world. Sam had seen a map of the planet like that once. He'd hung it in the barn for the lady. She wanted him to know where she'd been when she went wandering around the world.

That map had also been flat, and cut in ragged pieces at the top and bottom like the one on the screen. The world was supposed to be round. He didn't know how big it was or how many people Jeremy had touched. Even as sick as he was, Sam realized he'd known someone almost like God and hadn't recognized it.

The villagers now grabbed each other and began glancing around, looking for him to shore them up. Sam stood straight and stared at the screen, hoping he was fooling them.

"I'm right here, at the estate," Jeremy continued. One of the lights flashed on and off. "That's on the Connecticut shore in the Hamptons. The Atlantic Ocean is a few hundred yards to my east.

When I recorded this, I had a live hookup—some of our people called in to say hello, and good-bye."

Jeremy nodded at the camera and said, "Buenos dias, amigo." Then he introduced the person he was addressing. "Este hombre es mi amigo bueno, Rodrigo. Es un físico." He then paraphrased in English, "A very good physicist, who helped with the design of the shelters. My good friend, I welcome you."

A dot of light flashed on and off brightly, showing them where the speaker was. Sam didn't know the place, a country that stuck out into a dark area of the map. Sam knew that darkness was the sea. But which sea? He didn't know how many seas there were, or how many different lands.

A man with shoulder-length hair, a thin mustache, and a goatee filled the final third of the screen. He spoke sincerely and with great emotion. "Jeremy, mi amigo, qué una día buena cuando te aparecido in mi vida."

The camera panned around a cement room like the one they were in, but much smaller. Faces stared at them; a few people waved. The screen went blank and then Jeremy's face was back.

More people appeared like that, speaking in different languages. Sam didn't know so many existed. He recognized Russian, from when the general and his men had come to the estate. Lights in different places on the map flashed, showing where they were from. Jeremy looked progressively more serious. Sam marveled at all the languages he could speak and how much people loved him.

Jeremy's face filled the center of the screen again and the others dropped away. "I have 100 percent accurate intelligence that the general has his own cells set up, cells dedicated to taking over the planet when the radiation clears. He will stop at nothing to take over. He's got viable cryogenics—that's 100 percent certain, too. He'll be frozen until it's safe to defrost and then come for us."

Jeremy smiled and waved. "That's it, my friends! Live well and die well." He kissed his hand and blew the kiss at the camera.

The center screen went blank for an instant, and then Jeremy was back.

"OK, this is for you, Sam, and everyone in the village. This video is playing in all the major living areas and the main hall.

"You are in the biggest shelter and the biggest cell. The other cells didn't have the funds to do the job we did where you are. You probably will be the only one that survives. You are the hope for the future of the planet."

He glared from the screen, lips tight. He seemed to be collecting himself before speaking. When he did, his words erupted from the speakers.

"I *know* you. I know how you operate. It's us against them, and also us against *us*. Cheat whenever you can and stay drunk forever. *That is over.*

"Stop playing games like idiots. This is real! You're going to have to change the way you live in so many ways you won't believe it—just to survive!

"And, if any of you do survive and claw your way out of there in ten generations—or a hundred—the general will find you so fast you won't believe that either. He wants to kill you. Do you understand?

"So stop the fucking games with Sam and get that he's the one who's going to keep you alive!" Jeremy bellowed.

"I left Sam some Commands that he'll tell you about. But, right now, I'll give you one of the most important. I dissolve all marriages between cousins or closer and forbid you to make new marriages with anyone as closely related as that. You've got runaway birth defects because of marrying your relatives.

"I'm starting with Sam's family. I'm sorry to break it to Sam's wives this way, but that's how it is, ladies. You're no longer married to him—he's your first cousin. The rest of your marriages to cousins are over.

"I've authorized Sam to do *anything* he has to do make you follow my rules. He can kill all of you if he has to, to make you"—Jeremy waved his fists and looked as if he might roar—"act like *grown-ups!*

"Sam is the law. Get used to it.

"By the way, the show has already started in other parts of the world. I told you it would start at 7:35 because I knew you would never get in the shelter in time. On the east coast of the United States the detonations should begin at 8:25 a.m."

Sam looked at the clock. It turned to 8:25, and they felt the ground shudder; the lights flickered.

"You'll need to get settled with blankets and mattresses for padding. The party will take two to three days, maybe more. It won't be too bad if the bombs don't detonate close to you. If you take a direct hit, the shelter probably won't handle it. In that case, it will be over. I'm sorry. But, if you survive, the real struggle begins.

"You've got as many months of Russian army rations as I could cram into the storage rooms. They should last a year, maybe a little more if you're careful. Then you'll have to rely on the gardens and animals you brought.

"That's it. Hole up until the blasts stop. Satellite broadcasts will show you what's going on, out on top, around the world. The detonations started almost twelve hours ago in Russia. Retaliatory strikes are programmed automatically. The pattern will continue all over the world until the last nuke has exploded.

"The big screen will come on from time to time. I've set up messages to broadcast at various times and places in the shelter.

"Sam, my man, you are *on*." Jeremy made a high five with his hand into the air and the screen went blank.

Sam turned to Ronny Nahyuhn. "Ronny?"

When Ronny turned toward him, Sam slammed his fist into his belly. He loaded his entire weight into the punch. Ronny doubled over. As he did, Sam kneed him in the face. Blood splattered on the floor. Ronny dropped to the cement, struggling to breathe. Sam kicked him in the ribs. Bones cracked. Ronny groveled, gasping.

"That's a warning, Ronny. Talk to me like that again and ye're a dead man." Sam stood, fists clenched.

4

"Get yerselves tied down tight. This here's real," Sam said. "Put these beds around the floor like Jeremy said. We're in for a rough one." He moved around the main room, comforting people and helping them settle in. They looked at him in fear and trust.

"Ah, Sammy! We're los' forever!" old Maddy Ewancth wailed, reaching for his hand. "What're we to do?"

"We'll get through 'er, Maddy. Don' worry." He patted Maddy's white head and held her hand before moving on. "This here place is built to last. We'll be fine."

When he'd done as much as he could, Sam headed for his room. He beckoned to Arthur to follow him and gave his oldest son Rupert a look that told him to stay there and keep the hall under control.

He was holdin' the shakes down, but just barely. He didn't want to lose control and have to run from the hall in front of everyone. When he passed Ronny Nahyuhn, lying on the floor with his wives and family clustered 'round, Sam nodded, but didn't stop.

What he had done to Ronny didn't bother him; he'd probably end up killing him soon enough. Ronny was a troublemaker and a braggart who'd been out of line since he was born. And he would take over Sam's position if he could—by killing Sam. That was the village way of changing headmen. Sam had fought wars against his own cousins since his da had died. Ronny was biding his time, looking for somethin' to start a war over. Sam would oblige him when he found it. And Ronny wouldn't be able to keep any of the Commands. Sam intended to enforce them, if it killed Ronny and half the village. Which it might.

What bothered him was the fact that he'd had to use force at all. Before he came into this place, he wouldn't have had to touch Ronny. He would have walked up to him and said, "Eh, Ronny, havin' a bit of a bad day? Is a bad day for us all, but don't mean we need to get het up. Now, calm down, man. We'll settle in for a rough bit, an' then we'll figure it out."

He would have said that in the Voice, which was not so different from his usual voice, except in its effect. Ronny would have hugged him like a brother and grabbed a cushion to sit on. The mess he'd have to fix because he beat Ronny wouldn't exist.

But his Voice didn't work. He'd tried it when he'd walked into the hall. Nothing. He didn't know if it would ever work again. Sam rubbed his chest. It was this place. It properly frosted him the first time he had entered it the night before, and that was with all the doors open and Jeremy himself there.

But now, with everything shut tight? He could barely breathe. Was it taking his Power, or was he a rum coward not worthy of doing the job he had? He'd been thinking womanish thoughts in the hallway. Was he becoming weak?

Jeremy's picture show had made it possible for him to begin carrying out the Commands. Jeremy had told Sam's wives, and all the others married to close relatives, that their marriages were over. But he wouldn't have needed Jeremy's help before. He could have walked into his family's room, with all his wives and their warring broods, and said, "Ah, me darlin's, a sad day has come. We've lost our old home, an' we have new Commands to live under. Ah've been told by Jeremy the Tek himsel' that cousins canna marry. An', ma beauties, we are all first cousins. Ah didn't know that until Art'ur tol' me what a cousin is."

He would have used the Voice, and his wives would have understood. He might have had to explain several times; there might be tears. But that would have been it.

He had settled problems with violence only when nothing else had worked. For instance, the Voice didn't work on the village's disease, the cause of the most dangerous malady his people carried. It ran from generation to generation, like a curse.

His first wife, Mollie, had it. She had to be tied up when it was on her. She once had taken an ax to the women near the chopping block in one of her rages, killing three and maiming more. Her status as the headman's first wife was all that kept her alive, that and her brothers, who would have killed any to lay a hand on her. Sam worried about his children by Mollie, including Rupert, his oldest and favorite. He had no way of knowing if Rupert might go berserk one day.

But he hadn't needed to use violence to run the village—until now. He felt ashamed.

Sam reached his room, remembering the pattern of the buttons on the lock. He let himself into the room with Arthur tailing him.

"Good, Sam. You remembered the code," Arthur said cheerily.

Sam's guts were heaving. He put a hand over his mouth while his ribs pumped.

"Oh, shit!" Arthur shoved him into the bathroom. "Do it there, Sam."

Sam puked until he was empty. Arthur flushed it away. "Rinse your mouth." Arthur went to a basin and worked some handles. Water came out and Sam cleaned himself up, hands shaking like the aspens the lady had planted to screen the barn. It was the first time he'd been in an indoor bathroom. He wasn't in a mood to appreciate it.

Arthur took his arm and guided him to the bed. "Tell me how bad it is."

"Bad enough. But ah can handle 'er."

"Yeah, right."

The girl sat in a chair by the bed. Her hair was wet and she wore a soft, shiny robe. She looked liked she'd washed herself. The gray of her skin was a couple of shades lighter than Sam's. Black circles ringed her eyes. "Look," she said, pointing.

The wall had lit up the way the one in the main hall had. Jeremy's head and shoulders filled it, and he began to speak.

"Sam, I've recorded messages for you in case I don't end up in the shelter. They'll appear on this screen when I think you'll need them. You can replay them. Arthur will show you how.

"Stuff you need to know: There's an entrance to the main computer lab from your room—which was supposed to be my mom's room. I figured you'd end up there. Mom isn't too good at making it home." Jeremy shrugged. "The entrance is through the back wall of the closet. It's hidden. The door will take you to the lab and to the munitions stores you saw last night. There are also entrances from the room next to you, and the next. Make sure that only the most trustworthy people get those rooms. Arthur, basically.

"My mom left you an encoded message on a memory cylinder. She wanted to say good-bye to you privately. It was hidden somewhere in her room. I hope you got all her stuff." Sam looked at the mounds around him in despair. Did they bring it? How could he find it in all this?

"The most important thing is the laptop in your room. Arthur knows the passwords and can teach you how to use it. It has all the plans for the place, how to work everything, special step-by-step instructions. Everything.

"Now I'm going to patch you in on a feed that will show what's happening around the world. On one side of your screen, I've got the map with the lights where my cells are.

"So, my friend, even if we weren't very friendly when I was with you, I care about you and wish you luck. Mom and I were glad to spend all we had on the shelter if it saves you."

The feelings rolling over Sam were like the flood that had risen from the river ten years before, rising and rising until it seemed as though it would wipe out the village and the big house, too. He didn't know if he could take any more, yet the flood inside him was still coming. Even the shakes had backed off in the face of it.

The screen went blank for a moment, and then images of a city filled half the screen. They could see a lacelike building with high spires, scaffolding all around it.

"It's Barcelona," Arthur said. "I went there with Jeremy. That building is a church by Antonio Gaudi. It's ancient. They were restoring it."

A boom resounded and the screen showed the confection-like structure being blown away. Whoosh—the scaffolds and building were gone. The camera panned around the city. Smoking ruins.

The image changed. It was night wherever it was. "That's Tokyo, Japan," Arthur said. A street busier than anything Sam could imagine swarmed with life. Big signs made of moving colors ran along both sides of the road. Then, another whoosh, and everything was gone.

"Tokyo is gone! Oh, my God," Arthur cried.

A dozen cities, a dozen more. Lights indicating Jeremy's cells disappeared all over the globe.

"Oh, no! That's New York City!" Arthur wailed, looking at the familiar streets and landmarks. The Chrysler Building, still there after so many years. The Trump Towers. Antique structures from the city's Golden Age. And the big, new buildings—the Russian embassy, and the Chinese trade centers.

"Don't . . . they can't . . ." The girl squeaked, staring at the screen.

The camera caught it from the air: a circle of nuclear explosions ringing the metropolitan area.

"That was the idea of how to do a nuclear war after the year 2000," Arthur managed to say. "Before that, nuclear strikes used huge bombs, aimed at destroying an entire city. They discovered later that many small bombs, going off in the air, would kill the people but leave most of the buildings intact. And without much fallout, so the city would be habitable pretty soon."

The city looked quite normal after the blast; most of the buildings were still there. Only a ring of small mushroom clouds around the boroughs indicated anything had happened.

And then the huge blasts came, a volley of them, destroying the center of the circle, and then the rest of the metropolis. New York City was rubble.

"Oh, no," the girl moaned.

Sam couldn't comprehend what he was seeing. He'd never seen a big city, or even the towns closer to New York. The lady sometimes sent a picture-screen out to the barn and let them watch films on it. This was like one of those moving pictures, something that couldn't be real.

When the screen focused on the estate, Sam sat up straight. The camera showed the mansion's stone façade and the lovely banks of windows along the front. The balcony where the lady liked to walk.

The manor house had been built in 1863. The numbers were carved into the stone on one corner. Jeremy had told him that was more than a thousand years before, long before the Second Russian Revolution of 2097, when Tsar Yuri put himself in charge. Long before the world was run by lies and secrets and torture.

Trees and lawns surrounded the magnificent stone building. Acres of gardens. The screen showed it all, even the village out back and the barns behind that. He could see the cattle and horses.

Why was the screen showing the estate?

Sam knew. The cameras focused on the heat and motion of the missiles.

And then they struck. Sam, Arthur, and the girl clutched each other as the shelter rocked. Its concrete groaned and shimmied, but didn't crack. Sam looked at the wall and saw that the mansion was gone. Everything was gone. Fire filled the screen.

Sam cried out, holding the other two even tighter. Howling filled their ears as whatever was happening above tried to work its way down to them. Would the fire reach them? The shelter was dug in as deep as the cliff by the ocean. Was that enough?

The noises went on for a long time, or maybe it only seemed like a long time. The screen showed more flames, as though it were reeling out pictures of hell. All the while, they clutched each other. With each sound, their bodies jerked as if they were whores of the devil himself.

The doors and walls of his room were thick enough that they couldn't hear the others in the main hall. His family and children were alone and he couldn't help them. The ground heaved so that he dare not move.

Sam had never known fear, not really. As big as he was, only a grizzly could hurt him, and they were scarce. Or maybe a haunt might scare him, but he'd never seen one that proved real. He'd never imagined anything like this, the whole world coming apart.

Something happened as Sam looked up at the screen and watched the mansion disintegrate. When all he could see were the burnt shards of what had been his world, he became aware of something vicious flying over them. Malevolence circled the wreckage. Its eye caught him and it dove through the earth as though cement and clay were air. It lit on him where he cowered.

Black wings embraced him. The vulture turned its head so its glittering eye could watch. It held him down and began to feed. Hunks of his flesh were pulled away, strips of skin and organs. Death consumed him. When he was gutted, the beast unfurled its wings. It beat them, filling the room, knocking down the walls. It rose again, flying over the ruined Hamptons with Sam's heart its mouth. His arteries dangled, spewing blood over the dead land.

Sam's mouth formed a silent wail. He clenched his fists and closed his eyes. He'd had visions all his life, but not like this.

When he opened his eyes, the room appeared unchanged. The others didn't seem to have noticed that his heart was gone. He had no Power, no Voice. No way to stop the flood.

Sam stared at the wall. The surface of the concrete rippled; something was moving under it. Snakes as big around as ponies rolled up from the floor and burst from the cement. Their mouths opened, hissing and exposing jagged fangs. They exploded from the wall, making straight for him.

He jumped back. Something bit his forearm. He looked down to see bugs crawling under his skin. They were all over his body, moving up toward his neck. Sam screamed and tore at them. Then he was on the floor, convulsing.

His back arched, and everything turned black.

5

Maddy Ewaneth lay on the mattress where Sam had put her, shawl wrapped tight. She drew her legs up, curling in a ball on her side. Her knees pained where they touched, as bony as they were. An old stick woman, that was all she was. White hair an' six teeth. Seemed like she'd welcome dyin', but, when it got close, turned out she didn't want to die atall.

At first, the 'splosions hadn't been too bad, but then one came that felt as if it was right on top of them. The cement above groaned and she heard it cracking.

Moans arose from the people, echoed from the hard gray walls. This place was like the wide-open mouth of a bear, somewhere you'd go in and never get out. The lights flickered and almost went out.

She had never thought to go like this, in a tomb already dead and cold. She had thought she'd die in the village and be laid out with the people all around to see her done proper. Maybe raise a glass to see her off.

When the really big 'splosion came, she was tossed off her mattress like a bag of rags. Maddy screamed and didn't stop. "Sammy!

Where's my Sammy? Ah'm gonna die all alone. Sammy, *help* me."

No one answered her; the rest were busy holding on to their own. Maddy didn't have anyone. Her kids had died from the spots before they had had any babes to care for her when she got old. Her Jimmy had left long before, from the cancer.

"Sammy! Oh, Sammy." He didn't answer. Was he leavin' her to die? She pulled herself back on the mattress and lay there, shivering as if she had the ague. "Sammy, Sammy," she whispered. She trusted Sam Baahuhd more than anyone she knew. He was a hard one an' she wouldn't want to be his wife, but he took care of her better than any other had. Always checked on her, got her what she needed. "Sammy. My Sammy. Help me."

She was drifting off, tears dried on her face, the terrible room shuddering. The screens up there showed the dots disappearing like someone was swatting flies.

A hand touched her, and then someone was slipping his arms under her and lifting her up.

"Sam!" she exclaimed.

"Nah, it's me. Rupert." His voice was deep and slow, a voice ye'd trust, rumbling in his chest. "Ah heard ye screamin' an' thought ah'd come get ye."

"Oh, Rupert, such a good boy." She raised her hand with its clawlike joints and petted his cheek. "Ye thought of me, Ru."

"Yeah, Maddy. Yer like a ma to me."

He brought her to his room and laid her down on his bed with Jennie and the kids. Rupert held them in his strong arms all night long, and in the days after.

"Where's Sammy, Ru?" she asked when the rumbles and thuds had died down.

Rupert drew in a breath and said, "He's with her, Maddy. In a room with her."

"With *her*? The naked one he brang down here? Lef' his own people to be with *her*?"

"Well, ye know how he is, Maddy." Rupert blushed.

"Yeah. Dragged ev'rywhere by the thing 'tween his legs. Can't say no to any o' 'em."

"That's right, Maddy. That's how he is. But ah'll take care of ye, an' see ye safe."

"Oh, Ru. You are such a good boy." She patted his cheek. "Yer gonna be a rum fine headman when Sammy passes. Rum fine." She gazed at him lovingly and then drifted into sleep.

Maddy Ewaneth had known all about that naked stranger from the first moment. She was a witch. Witched Sam complete. A pretty witch would get him good. The old lady held her hand so as to ward off the evil eye. Well, she would make that witch sorry for keepin' her Sammy from comin' to her.

6

"Sam, it's Arthur. Can you hear me?"

He moved and then struggled in panic when he felt himself tied down.

"I've got you in restraints. I had to make sure you didn't roll off the gurney when I had to leave." Arthur's voice came from behind him.

Sam opened his eyes. He was lying on his back in a room he hadn't seen before. It was all white, with flat lights in the ceiling. Tall cupboards ran along the walls. Tight straps held him onto a bed. He remembered that he was in the underground and the bombs had gone off. His eyes closed.

"Sam, are you awake?" Arthur came around to where Sam could see him. "Don't move. I'm doing a rapid detox on you. I've got an IV in your arm. You've got a few more hours until you'll be OK to get up. I had to strap you down; you were in rough shape."

Arthur took out a small light and shined it in Sam's eyes. "That was a close one. Rupert noticed something was wrong with you in the main hall and followed you to your room. If he hadn't been out in the hall, I wouldn't have been able to get you in here and on the bed."

"What happened?"

"DTs. You were convulsing and bit your tongue. I had to take some stitches." Arthur busied himself, putting something on the end of Sam's finger and punching something on a computer pad. He listened to Sam's heart and put a cloth around his arm, squeezing it tight and releasing it while watching a dial. "Your vital signs are good. I'd like to keep you here another couple of days, but it's crazy out there." He jerked his head to the left, in the direction of the main part of the shelter.

"What? What's goin' on?"

"Ru and I have kept the village down as well as we could, but we're not you. They wanted you. The blasts freaked everyone out." Arthur looked at Sam. "God, I've been so worried about you." He put his hand on Sam's head. Sam's eyes widened when he felt Arthur's hand on his bare scalp.

"Oh, I shaved your head and treated you for bugs while you were out."

"The itches?"

"Yeah. You had about every kind of external parasite you could have. And some internal ones, too. But no more. How do you feel?"

"Like ah'm mostly dead. Ma head feels like a drum's beatin' inside. What happened?"

"Severe withdrawal from alcohol. Hallucinations, convulsions, everything. Your blood pressure was so high, I thought I might lose you. I put you under with drugs and did a rapid detox to get the booze out of you. Your system is clean now, but you can't ever drink again."

"Ah don't plan on drinkin' again, Art'ur. Ah'm keepin' Jeremy's Commands. That's why ah quit drinkin' to start."

"But you quit too fast. You'll be OK now. I want this last round of medication into you, and then we begin getting you on your feet." Arthur indicated a clear bag with liquid hanging from a stand. Tubes fed it into a needle taped to the back of Sam's hand. "Don't try to pull it out. I'll take it out when you're ready. Rest awhile and then we'll talk."

Arthur turned around and busied himself with someone on another bed. Sam could see a figure under a sheet when he turned his head.

"Who's that?"

"Emily, or whatever you want to call her. She passed out a few minutes after you. Lucky for her, Rupert went back to lock your door. He found her on the floor of your room, convulsing."

The girl lay in a bed next to him, utterly still. Arthur wrapped the cloth around her arm and pumped it the way he had with him. Sam craned his neck and looked at her. Arthur had her trussed her down like she was a man-eater fixing to bust loose. She had two of the needles attached to the medicine bags stuck into her arms and a tube coming out from under the cloth covering her. She looked dead, her skin whiter than Sam had ever seen anyone's.

"She's way worse off than you, Sam. We need to talk about her. I don't know if she can be saved or if she's worth saving." He moved around the girl. Emily, Sam remembered. He'd given her that name when he brought her into the shelter. He thought she'd be his wife.

"What's wrong with her?"

"She's addicted to combat packs. I'm detoxing her. I don't know how long she's been on them, probably a long time. They're supposed to be used in combat situations where a guy has to stay awake for five days. But they're so addictive that almost everyone who uses them gets hooked. They'll kill you. They wreck your kidneys and liver, in addition to making you a killer.

"The packs have pretty near every type of drug you can name in them. Steroids—look at her arms." Sam did. They were roped with muscle. He'd never seen a woman's arm like that. "The packs also contain heavy-duty painkillers—narcotics—and speed, lots of that. Mood-altering drugs to cut fear and make people feel like they can handle anything. You've seen feds on them; you know what they do."

Sam *had* seen federal agents on them. After a big escape from the camp or when someone high up enough had complained about a country estate being taken by outlaws, the feds would rage through the Hamptons, killing anything in their paths. They were more dangerous than the marauders. The drugs made them fearless predators who would die before quitting.

"Ye know who she is?"

"Yes. I've done a workup on her. I'll show it to you. But first we have to get you going again and take you to see your people. They're about to riot, thinking something's happened to you."

Sam moved quickly, then put a hand to his head and grimaced.

"You'll have a headache for a while."

"How long have ah been here?"

"It's been five days, Sam. You've been very sick."

"*Five* days?"

"Yep. That's about two days short of what you really need, but I don't think they'll buy what Rupert said much longer." Arthur cracked a smile.

"What did he tell 'em ah was doin' for five days?"

"He said you were fucking her brains out and would come out when you were done."

Sam laughed. And kept laughing. "What did they say?"

"That you were a cunnie-lovin' fool, but they laughed, too. You have a reputation."

"Aye. Ah earned 'er, too. That's a good'un. Get me up, Art. Ah'm ready to go back."

"You better put something on then. I incinerated your clothes. You'd never get the bugs out of them. Here. Wear this."

Sam pulled on the black uniform of the tsar's elite guard.

Arthur looked him up and down. "Well, that should scare the crap out of them. We've got several lifetimes' supply of Russian uniforms, courtesy of the general."

7

Sam walked into the big hall. Things looked different now that he was sober.

He knew he had neither the Voice nor the Power, nothing to manipulate the people with, and nothing to use to shade the truth. He'd left his people alone during the greatest calamity they'd ever face. He'd been drunk for a year, spreading his seed wherever he wanted. And they thought he'd been swagging the girl for five days, leaving them to their fates. How could he face them?

People fell silent. Not even Ronny Nahyuhn said a word. Sam walked to the middle of the wall where the pictures had shown, squared his shoulders, and began to speak.

"Well, we lost it all." He looked at his friends and family, making eye contact with as many as he could. "Ain't nothing left of what we had. Ah watched it on the screen, same as you. It's all gone. The big house, the village, all the animals. All blown away. We're stuck down here forever."

Sobs broke out from the crowd.

"If we go out, or even open the doors, we'll get a sickness that will rot us from the inside. We'll puke blood and our skin will fall off. Every one of us will die.

"We need to start whole new lives, with new ways of doing everything. Jeremy the Tek gave us some Commands before he rose up into the sky. If we follow them, we'll live, and, if we don't, we'll die. Ah'll talk about them tomorrow. Ah'm a little short now." He felt shaky on his feet, but stood strong.

Ronny Nahyuhn took that opportunity to break in, still smirking, though sobered. "Yeah, Sam. Tell us how she was."

"Rupert and Art'ur told you that, not me. Ah wasn't with Em'ly. Ah was sick." Eyes opened all over the crowd.

"We got a proper hospital down here. Ah was in it. The hooch got me. Ah was seein' snakes and feelin' bugs under ma skin. Art put me out cold for five days, with medicines workin' the booze out of my body. Otherwise, ah would have been with ye, and helped ye as much as ah could."

Sam squatted and held his arms out to them. "Come to me."

And they did—women and children first, then the men. He embraced them and said what they needed to hear. "We'll get through 'er, Maddy. We'll figure 'er out." Something to each of them, even Ronny Nahyuhn. "Sorry to be so hard on ye, Ronny. Ah couldn't let you say what ye did."

"Ah know, Sam. Ye were right about the atomics, about it all. Ah'm sorry for what ah said."

They accepted everything he said as though he were the Sam of old. Some looked at him with shining-faced admiration. He was mystified. When he got back to the sick bay, Arthur explained it.

"It's the uniform, Sam. And the shaved head. You look like the general." Arthur chuckled.

"The general? Nah."

"Yes. And I'll say something else, Sam. You really know how to work a crowd."

He worked everyone but his own family. His wives didn't come to his arms. All four turned away from him and kept his kids away, too. But they weren't his wives anymore, were they? Little Winnie had bruises on her face. Had his other wives been beating on her again? How could she get along without his protection?

8

"I need to tell you what I've found out. *You* need to make a decision about her. I know what I would do, but it's your call." Sam and Arthur stood over the girl in the sick bay. "She's bad, bad news."

Emily was unconscious and waxy pale. Her hair was dark, not quite black. Arthur had her covered with a sheet. She might have been beautiful, but for all the bruises and looking dead.

Arthur regarded her coolly. "She's from New York City, for sure. You can't get a haircut that good outside Manhattan. She had a ring on that is worth a fortune."

"Where'd ye put it?"

"In the drawer over there." Arthur pointed, then pulled black sheets out of a large orange-yellow envelope and stuck them up on the wall. "X-rays. Fortunately, we've got a well-stocked clinic down here, and Jeremy's computer lab. I could figure out who she is.

"Bad news first. She's a serious addict. If she kicks this time, she may go for the drugs again. I do have painkillers here, and we don't need any junkies trying to steal them.

"I took her fingerprints and searched the federal records in Jeremy's data bank. Her name is Valerie Zanner. She's 26. Actually, she's 24, but I'll get to that. She was a lieutenant in the FBI's Anti-Terrorism Unit. She's a breaker. You know what that is?"

"Yeah. They torture people until they give 'em what they want." Sam's forehead crinkled. This pretty girl? But he'd seen her hold a gun on him.

"She had the highest break ratio on the force. I don't know how many people she's killed. Hundreds, more likely thousands."

Arthur walked over to the wall where he'd stuck the black sheets and flipped a switch. The wall lit up. "We've got a complete medical setup down here. X-ray equipment, a lab, everything but a doctor. I'm a medic. I can do some procedures, like taking X-rays."

Sam turned toward the wall, but his attention was taken by something other than the X-rays. Next to the dark sheets Arthur was displaying was a map of the world showing all Jeremy's cells. The map he'd seen before had had more lights on it than he could count. This one had three.

"What's this?" He pointed.

Arthur exhaled. "That's what's left. We're here"—he pointed— "this one's in India, and this one's in France."

"Three lights!" Sam felt like he'd been slugged. "Only three left?"

"Yeah. And I don't expect the others to last." As they watched, the light in India went out. "Jesus!" Arthur exclaimed. "Eighty people there."

Sam stood staring, his jaw slack.

"We'll probably end up the only cell left. That's on our side. The general has his own cells, but I don't think they will do any better than we did. He's dug in here"—Arthur indicated the entire northern region of Russia and China—"somewhere. And his son is somewhere else, underground. They're probably the only ones that will make it when all this shakes out. They've got cryogenics, so the people in their bunker will defrost and come back to life. Our *descendants* will come out of here."

Sam's mind wouldn't hold the information. "*All* of 'em are gone?"

"All but us and France."

He staggered to a chair and plopped down, staring at the map.

"Do you want to wait on the report on the girl? We can do it later?"

"Yeah. Can ah see what it looks like up top?"

"Yes. I can get a satellite view." Arthur tinkered with a piece of equipment and a blackened plain appeared on the screen. No trees, not a blade of grass, nothing above the ground, not the shadow of a building. No life. "That's where the big house was."

Sam slumped. He'd seen it when the bombs went off, but not like this. Quiet. Final.

"Why don't you lie down, Sam? I've had days to get used to this. There's a bed behind that curtain."

But, after Arthur left, Sam went back to the map and touched the two bright spots. He punched the controls on the wall the way Arthur had and looked at the ruined land above him. Staggering backward, his hand caught a chair and he collapsed into it, back in the vision he'd had when the bombs were still exploding. A monster flew high above the estate, clutching his heart, blood falling from it like water from soaked clothes.

"No!" he cried, facing the wall with its pair of lights. "*Don'* let the devil get me! Not that!" He held up his hands, blocking the view of the map. He whispered, "Ye said Ye would watch out for me every minute. Ye said Ye would help me. Ye said that, out in the field when ah found Em'ly. Don' Ye *remember*?" He was face-to-face with something, but he didn't know what.

"Don' let the devil get me." Sam believed in the devil. He'd seen the devil as he looked into Mollie's eyes when the disease was on her. He'd seen the devil in men gone on the hooch, or the weed and mushrooms. And, certainly, what had happened to the earth was the work of the devil.

Was God abandoning him to that?

What Sam knew about formal religion came from the snake men. Those black-clothed doomsayers roamed the Hamptons preaching hell an' damnation and waving snakes. Sam thought everything the snake men said was bull crap. Theirs was a vicious God, seeking revenge. They preached about Jesus Christ, but their Jesus was the same as the devil, ready to pop back any minute and send people to hell.

Sam knew God wasn't the nonsense the snake men scared people into believing. God was something that came to him and showed him what to do. Sometimes. It was usually silent and never acted the way he wanted it to. But when it did act, things turned out right. *That* was what he called God. The clearest evidence that God existed came when an unmistakable voice had spoken to Sam in the field.

"Ah *heard* Ye say Ye loved me an' would help me," Sam wailed. "Why did Ye let 'em blow up the world? *People're* the bad uns. Why not jus' kill 'em and leave the rest alone? The horses never done nuthin', nor the grass or trees.

"Ye take ma Power. Ye take ma Voice. Yer gonna *help* me? How're Ye helpin' me? Showin' me bein' taken by the devil?"

He sat, listening for an answer. Nothing.

He was stuck in the underground with nothing. The girl made a little moan. Sam looked over at her. He wasn't stuck with nothing. Ninety-four other people depended on him, and a bunch of them would do anything to get in his way, even if it meant killin' all of them.

Was the devil more powerful than God? Was that what happened? God and the devil fought, and God lost? Was God just another force, like the wind or the ocean? Not the strongest one of all?

"Ah don't want that! Ah want a *good* world. Ah want everythin' to be *good*. Ah want the world like it was, but with no bad. *That's what ah want!*"

An awareness came from somewhere, like the voice in the meadow, but with no words. He knew what God wanted. God wanted a good new world, too. They weren't s'posed to come screamin' out of the shelter one day to "take over the world," like Jeremy said in the Commands.

God was giving him orders as he sat. He, Sam Baahuhd, was to create a good world, where no one would ever blow up God's creation again. A kind world. A better world. Sam couldn't move.

"How the *foock* am *ah* s'posed to do that? *Ye* couldna do 'er!"

9

"You don't need to be a doctor to read these." Arthur beckoned Sam to the lighted wall to look at the dark squares
several hours later. "She has scars on her lower back, so I did an
X-ray. She's had multiple surgeries, which is probably why she's an
addict." Arthur indicated a spot. "She must be in constant pain."

Sam looked at the picture and gasped. "That's a screw!"

"Yep. Three of them, through the vertebrae." Arthur continued, "She's lasted quite awhile with that hatchet job. Valerie Zanner didn't exist until eight years ago; her fingerprints appear out of
nowhere at a military hospital. She went into the army when she
recovered—with that back. Her age is given as eighteen, but other
things I've found suggest she was sixteen. Somebody got her in
using influence. The army wouldn't take her any other way.

"But that's not the big problem. She's going to be a paraplegic
in a couple of weeks if she doesn't get help. She's losing sensation in
her legs—I tested her reflexes."

Sam looked at the girl. He remembered how she'd leveled her
pistol at him when she ambushed him out in the pasture. But when
he got the gun away from her and she relaxed against him, she

acted like every other woman in his arms. Could he heal her? He
didn't think so. The Power had deserted him.

"The good news is, she's the *perfect* wife for you." Arthur
snorted. "I did some DNA tests on her. We've got a state-of-the-art
DNA testing lab, along with every data bank and bit of software
that exists for comparing genes. She's clean of every genetically
transmitted disease we have markers for. And wait until you see
her parents."

Arthur went to a desk and pushed a button on the writing
board of a computer. Sam had never been so close to a computer.
He pulled away.

A screen above lit up and two faces appeared. "These are her
real parents. They were processed into a federal facility about eighteen years ago. We lucked out there; the feds weren't detaining
masses of people back then. They kept records, including DNA."

Sam looked at the images. They were nothing like the people
the lady brought to the estate. They had serious faces. He could see
the girl in them: the dark hair and fair skin and the shape of her
face. The woman had fine features. She was very . . . not pretty. Too
serious for pretty. Beautiful.

"This is Dr. Judith Asher, a professor of mathematics at NYU. Her
husband is Dr. Daniel Asher, a professor of astrophysics at Harvard, the
Manhattan campus. They had three children, Joshua, Eli, and Shira.
She's Shira." Arthur indicated the unconscious girl. "Shira means *poetry*
in Hebrew, by the way. The parents were detained as intellectuals.
They were also Jewish. The feds picked up Jews wherever they could."

"What happened to 'em?"

"I'm sure they were killed, except Shira. They were the sort of
geniuses who would have been picked to come down here." Arthur
clicked a few times and brought up pictures of the Ashers.

Sam looked at several images of the serious parents, and one
with the kids teasing each other and laughing.

"She should be brilliant, Sam. It's in her genes. Shira was six
when they processed her into the state orphanage. They gave her

the name Stella Brown. Stella Brown was adopted from the orphanage at age nine, a private adoption managed very high up in the government, with records only Jeremy's computer hacking could get.

"This is the man who adopted her." Arthur punched another button and the face of a paunchy, scowling man appeared. "Jeffrey Bouldine, one of the richest men in America. He didn't make news when he was adopting the girls, but he did later."

"Girls?"

"Fifteen years ago, Jeffrey adopted six little girls, all beguiling and beautiful, all with very high IQs. He kept them in a pink room under his mansion."

Sam looked at Arthur. "Kept them?"

"He kept them in a room in his basement and did whatever he wanted to them. Homeschooled them. And taught them to kill any way they could."

"Is that where she hurt her back?"

"Yes. He threw her off a balcony. She hit her spine on a railing before landing on the cement. She had been sparring with her sister and accidentally killed her. A kick to the temple.

"He had targeted the girls for specific hits. They were supposed to marry and kill very prominent men, doing it so it looked like an accident or natural causes."

"That's crazy." Sam pulled away, crossing his arms over his chest and shaking his head.

"Very crazy. But it worked in one case. One of the girls did carry out her 'assignment.' She married a rich guy; he choked to death two months after the wedding. She inherited and went back to daddy."

"It don't make sense. How'd he do it?"

"You remember our world before it blew up. It was a crazy world. It was nuts out here in the country, but the city was worse. Bottom line is, Jeffrey's plan went bad. He was bringing the girls out, introducing them to society and the men they were supposed to marry.

"Except that one of them emptied an automatic pistol into him in the lobby of a major New York hotel. The other girls were there. The police couldn't suppress the crime: too many people saw it." Art nodded at the unconscious girl. "The police questioned the sisters and found out about the scheme. Do you know what the girls were most upset about?"

Sam could only shrug.

"They wanted to know what had happened to their sister, Pearl. She was a hero to them. They said there had been six of them at the start. Then Pearl accidentally had killed Pink and disappeared.

"The girls gave the date Pearl disappeared—the exact date Valerie Zanner was admitted to the military hospital." He indicated the unconscious form on the bed. "Meet Shira Asher, Stella Brown, Pearl Bouldine, and Valerie Zanner."

Sam approached her. Her face was smooth like wax. She had fine features like the lady's, dark lashes lying against pale skin. She was beautiful. And doomed.

"Valerie was in big trouble. The feds had figured out who she was, too. They had decided to send her back to the front. They were putting her down."

"They were gonna kill 'er? But ye said she was a genius an' perfect an' all. Kill 'er?"

"She's too damaged, Sam. Her back, for one thing. And no one could withstand what she's been through without being a mental basket case. Not only the abuse, but what she was trained to do. She's a killer."

Sam shook his head and looked at her pretty face. She had felt so right when she was in his arms. "Puttin' her down."

"That might be the best thing to do with her, Sam."

10

"Can you heal her?"

Sam didn't answer Arthur. He continued to study the girl's features. Her nose had been broken; the bones were setting crooked. Her face looked like Ronny Nahyuhn's wife's did most of the time—beat to hell.

"Ah can't heal nuthin', Art. Ah've lost the Voice and the Power."

"It's trauma. They'll come back when we get settled in, don't you think?" Arthur spoke a bit too fast.

"Ah don't know. Ah've had 'em both since ah was a babe. Now ah'm alone."

"But you moved the crowd so well today. You were great."

"That was jus' me. Wait an' see what happens when a fight starts or some bullyboy breaks the Commands. Wait 'til then an' see how ah do."

"Shit."

"Aye, shit. This girl, now. Let me have some time with her. Ah'll see what ah can do. Ah'll stay the night here."

Sam lay on his bed. The sick bay lights were turned down low.

Shadows gathered in the corners and the place felt damp and sticky. He could just hear the girl's breathing. She seemed like one of the shadows, barely there.

He got up and walked around the room. An all-white room. Nothing fancy about it. Still, it almost paralyzed him, speakin' as it did of medicine he'd never seen. Instruments and machines. The map was lit on the wall. France and their place were hangin' in there, bright as ever. He went back to bed.

The girl was over there with tubes in her arm. Arthur had saved her life. Saved his, too. Sam owed him plenty. Arthur was at home in this white room and this underground world. Sam felt a stab of fear as he realized how dependent they were on him.

Sam didn't really know Art. He'd been to the estate often, guarding Jeremy, teaching him to shoot and fight. He'd been around the village for years, watching everything they did. The old ladies loved him. He was polite and said, "How do you do?" But he didn't go in anyone's house or share a meal.

He and Sam had downed a canteen of the lady's best bourbon the night before the planet exploded. Arthur was trying to be friends. But *was* he a friend? Sam had heard what he'd said once about the village to a Russian soldier, back in the days before the world blew up, when they came out with the general. "Do they think ah'm deaf *an'* stupid?" he'd thought.

But everyone in the big house had thought the villagers were just above animals, and had expressed it in dozens of ways. Could he be friends with someone who felt that way about him and his people?

Could he be friends with anyone? Sam had had to bust heads whenever they needed it, so he didn't have any real friends in the village either. He'd try with Art. He'd make himself believe they could be friends.

Sam thrashed around. He hadn't slept alone since he was fourteen years old and married Mollie. She was a good one when they'd wed. They'd torn up the village for years, until she got the disease.

Sally became his second wife when he was seventeen. Another good'un, though Mollie kept her running scared. Sally still was a friend he could count on. She was his one true friend.

His da died when Sam was nineteen and he had become the headman. Winnie's father, the headman from a village far out in the Hamptons, gave Winnie to him as his third wife and a gift for the occasion. She was twelve and the most beautiful girl anyone had seen, with her white-blond hair and big blue-green eyes. He'd always had to watch out for his other wives with her. They'd scratch Winnie to death if they could, both because of what she looked like and the fact that he visited her more than either of the others. She was his favorite.

His fourth wife, Fannie, was a mistake; they'd only been wed a year. He taken her in because her husband died. Fannie was a sow-faced brawler who caused nothing but trouble.

But the four of them were always there, offering comfort every night. If he wasn't with one of his wives, he was with some other woman out in the village. Being alone came hard. He sighed and thrashed.

How could Jeremy say that his marriages were over? What were they supposed to do? Walk away as though those years hadn't happened?

He groaned and turned over again. The numbers on the clock on the wall kept changing. 1:30. 2:30. The shadows grew deeper and more threatening. The hollowness of the place made his chest seize up. Breathing became hard. Something fell from his eyes to the sheets. He wiped them. His hand was wet.

Sam jumped out of the bed, wiping his hand on his leg. He made a circle of the room, including a look at the map.

France was gone.

Now only one light shone—theirs. They were the only people left on earth. Except for the general's killers.

He backed away, bumping into the girl's bed. "Oh, sorruh." He looked back at the map with its light for their shelter glowing. He turned to her, as though to say, "What do you think of that?"

Without thinking, he ran his thumb and forefinger down the sides of her nose. The flesh followed his fingers, molding to his will. When he was done, her nose was straight and the bones set hard.

His eyes widened. The Power *hadn't* left him. He laid his hands on the cuts and bruises on her face. They disappeared. Could he do more?

He looked at her, strapped down like a dangerous animal. If he moved her over a little, could he . . .?

Sam carefully undid the restraints and moved the stands with the bags of medicine out of the way. He was shaking, that single spot of light on the map seeming to fill the room.

"Ah'm sorry, Em'ly, but ah need ye tonight, maybe as much as ye need me." He was able to fit on the narrow bed by lying on his side and squeezing between her and the bed's railing. "Won't bother you any. Don't worry." Whether he could heal her or not, he needed to lie next to her.

It was like lying next to a bag of bones and rope. Corded muscles wrapped around her legs as well as her arms. She was so skinny he was surprised she had titties at all. She did, though. Nice ones.

Sam laid his arm over her body and jerked as if he'd been hit. She was screaming inside. Outside, she was drugged and unconscious, and inside she was screaming. The sounds ricocheted in his soul. Panic. Terror. Pain. All banging against him. It was as though the terrible cement hell around him had a voice.

He kept his arm over her, resting his hand on her wrist. He hummed a little, the way he did when he was curing people. He entered her. Sam had never tried to describe what he did when he healed; he did it naturally and without a thought. He went inside his own body and mind. A lot went on in there: he could see streams of colored lights and feel his life force, strong as a river. When he touched people to heal them, he went inside them. Maybe just a little, maybe a lot. His soul touched theirs and that's how they got better.

Her soul was a big space of white mist with bright white light shining through it. No memories, no images. The screams shot around, one wave followed by another. He let them wash over him, absorbing her pain and terror. He felt her, a white light in front of him, a soul in mortal agony. Behind her, he could see the forest. The tall uprights of the trees. The sun shining through, the white beams of light.

He took her agony and moved it through himself, letting it dissolve in the light. She was finally quiet and still.

Sam began to doze off. He jerked awake. Something was calling to him. He opened his soul's eyes. The dark outline of a child gazed back at him. A tiny girl with enormous eyes. Her eyes burned into his heart.

"Shira," he whispered. She was the little girl who was supposed to die, but didn't.

11

"Oh, shit. Sam, I'm sorry." Arthur walked into the sick bay in the morning and found a naked Sam wrapped around the girl. He quickly turned his back.

"Weren't nuthin'. We weren't doin' nuthin'. Ah always sleep like this." Sam got up and put on his uniform.

Arthur studied the still form on the bed. "Her face is fixed. You healed her!"

"Got a start on it, anyway. Ah'll finish 'er up tonight."

"You've got the Power back!"

"Don't know. Ah can heal *her*, anyway. Ye got a bruise or a cut? Ah'll try 'er out."

"I've got a bruise on my leg."

Arthur pulled up his pants leg and Sam put his hand on the wound, trying to summon up his healing energy. When he took his hand away, the bruise looked exactly the same.

"Well, that's it. Ah can heal her; no one else."

"You're supposed to explain the Commands today. How will you get them to go for them without the Voice?"

"Ah got an idea. Ye got the Book?" Arthur nodded. "OK. Think of some good things about Jeremy. Things that ye will 'member forever. Then tell 'em when ah tell ye to."

Before they left for the main hall, Arthur set up the bags of medicine for the girl and started to strap her down.

"Oh, ah don't think ye need do that. She's a nice lil' thing."

Arthur looked at him as if he were crazy. "I'll put only half the straps on. That's as far as I'll go."

Sam walked into the hall like a king. He moved to the center of the big wall where Jeremy had broadcast his message and everyone had watched the world be destroyed. The villagers gathered in front of him, sitting on the tiered floor. They were silent and seemed cowed, their eyes focused on him.

"Ah'm here to tell you about the Commands." Sam appeared even bigger than he was. His black uniform gave him the look of a snake man, the scariest snake man anyone had ever seen. Lights came on from the projection box in the wall at the back of the room. Other lights appeared behind him. The lines on his face grew craggier. A harsh shadow fell on the wall behind him, moving like a specter. Arthur slipped up and stood next to him.

"All o' you remember Jeremy, the little *punk* around here, the *lady's* son?" Sam spoke in a cadence known all over the Hamptons. "What we *thought* was a little punk. You remember, don't you? Answer me!"

"Aye, we remember!" the villagers responded, schooled to reply at the meetings the snake men held in the hollow.

"Well, we was wrong about him. Wrong as could be. For, on the night before the end of the world, Jeremy took us down here, me and Art'ur, and Henry and all o' them you seen go up in the sky in the ball of light. Remember that? Remember the light?"

"Oh, yeah. Oh, yeah. We remember!"

"Jeremy showed us what he really was that night. He stood in front of his computers, an' the computers' lighted up his hair, makin' him look like a sanctified thing. What was he? What was he really, under the punk we thought?" Sam glared at the group. "What was he?" They were silent, so Sam roared, "He was a Tek! The Great Tek! We were lucky to have known him! Tell me!"

"We were lucky!"

"How lucky?"

"*Verra* lucky!"

Sam turned to Arthur. "Tell 'em, Art'ur, what happened the night we come down here."

"Well, Jeremy gave us a tour of the shelter and pointed out the features—"

"That's right," Sam cut him off. "He pointed out the *features*! What features, Art'ur? Tell 'em!"

"Um, he showed us the water reclamation system, and the waste recycling system. The air recycler and computer labs—"

"Tell how he looked in front of the computers!"

"Scary as shit, I'll tell you. The light of the screens behind him. That kid was intense."

"Scary as shit! You hear? Tell me!"

"Scary as shit, so scary!" the village responded, terrified and enthralled.

"What did Jer the Tek do best, Art'ur?"

"Well, he was brilliant at writing code."

"He wrote code! He wrote code! *Hear* me now! What did he do?"

"He wrote code!" they shrieked.

"What is code, Art'ur?"

"Well, it's computer programming. Writing computer language to implement systems and—"

Sam was getting annoyed with Arthur's responses. They would have bored a slug. "What do you do with code, Art?"

"Well, make this place, for one thing. All this is the result of Jeremy's—"

"The Great Tek wrote *code*—and he made this place. The Great Tek made this place from *nothin'* but dots and lines! Tell me!"

"He wrote code and made this place!" Cries went up. Sam could hear a tinge of hysteria in their voices. Good.

"He made this terrible place! This place that saved our lives when the atomics come! HE SAVED US AND HE PUT US IN HELL, BOTH!"

"WE'RE IN HELL AND SAVED! MERCY! HAVE MERCY!"

Sam raised his arms and the noise stopped. Families clutched each other and stared at him.

"Show 'em what he gave us, Art'ur. Bring 'er out!"

Arthur pulled the Book out of his shirt. It was a portion of the notebook the extraterrestrial visitor, Eliana, had carried, a book written in light. The Book glistened, throwing sparkling beams around the hall. Arthur ruffled the pages and the Book lit up the room. The villagers gasped.

"Yes! This is what Jer the Tek left us. Would he leave us a reg'lar book? A paper book?"

"No," they moaned.

"That's right. He left us a book of light, given to him by the angel, Eliana. You remember her, prancin' around the lawn with her little hooves? Her that called the light to come from heaven to carry them away? Eliana the *angel*? You remember her?"

"Oyez, oyez, oyez!"

"Jer the Great Tek gave us the Commands in this book of light, right before he went up in the heavens in the great golden ball. Remember?"

"Yeah!" they shrieked. The whole village had seen it. The golden ball of light had filled the eastern sky and landed by the cliff by the ocean. Everyone had seen it, and had seen it take Jeremy and the others away.

"Do ye know why they got to go up in the heavens to the golden land and we got stuck down here in hell? Tell me!"

"We are sinners! We are sinners! We are *sinners*!"

"Yes, we are sinners. Filthy sinners. We would sooner do *wrong* than *right*. And that's why Jeremy gave us the Commands. So that when the world changes again, and we've done our time down here, we can come out of this hell-place and take over the world!

"That is the Number One Command." He turned to Arthur, who opened the Book, releasing cascades of light. "See, it's right there, #1. WHEN YOU GET OUT OF THE SHELTER, TAKE OVER THE WORLD!"

The crowd sat stunned for a moment, and then cried out with joy.

"See, the Commands ain't no terrible thing. They's what we want to do anyway." Sam looked around, beaming. "We always wanted to take over the world. We knew we were best. Not the folks in the big house, not the folks in the cities: us, right here in the village. We're the *best*!"

They erupted with joy.

"*But*! Let me tell you the but part—the general's out there. You know him, him that stole the lady? Him that shot up the pastures with guns so big no one should have 'em? Him who would have whipped Ronny's back clear off for mouthing him that time? Do you remember? Tell me!"

"Yes! We remember!"

"He's out there, hiding. An' he's gonna come for us when we get outta here. Sure thing, he'll be on us fast."

"Oh, no! He'll get us!" They moaned and writhed in terror.

"So what do we do? The Great Tek gave us the Book and the Commands to protect us. So we can win when we get out. So we will be smarter and tougher than the general. So we can live down here and make it."

"We have the Book! We have the Commands!" The crowd stomped and whistled.

"Here are the Commands." Sam couldn't remember all of them. They were in the Book, which he couldn't read any better than anyone else in his audience, so no one could contradict him. "First, we take over the world when we get out." He raised his arms in triumph. "Second, the headman—me—has total power over the shelter, including the power to kill all of you if you don't do what ah say.

"Do you understand? The Great Tek says *ah* run this place! And, when ah die, my oldest son will run it. That's Rupert. And it will be that way as long as we're down here. Ye ken?"

"We ken. Oh, yeah, we ken."

"We have to live like warriors. We gotta train to be commandos, every one of us." He swung around to face every section of his audience. "Arthur will help with that.

"And no hooch, mushrooms, weed, or anythin' else. Nothin' to make ye high atall. The Tek forbids that.

"Ye gotta learn to read. All of us have to read in six months. We got a library to teach us. And we gotta talk reg'lar English, like they did in the big house. We can do that, easy." Sam looked around, beaming.

"An' the Tek said what he already tol' you jus' before the atomics went off: no marryin' cousins or anythin' closer. Arthur and the Tek did up charts on us to tell who's what. Mos' of us is married to our cousins. So we ain't married no more. Tha's a hard one, but we'll figure 'er out.

"Oh, an' each man can have only one wife. No more tradin', pile-ons, or runnin' around—one man, one wife, only." That was as many Commands as Sam could remember.

"So, tell me why we are down here? Why didn't we get to go up in the ball of light?"

"We are sinners!"

"We are sinners, so we got stuck in this hellhole. How do we get out?"

"Follow the commands!"

"WILL YOU FOLLOW THE COMMANDS?"

"YES! YES! YES!" Pandemonium broke out.

Sam stood still as emotion rocketed around the room. When it was almost spent, he raised his arms for silence. "That's the Commands. We'll follow them, and ah'll enforce them. Hail to the Great Tek!"

"Hail to the Tek! Hail to Jeremy, the Great Tek!"

"The Tek commanded one more thing: we got to get rid o' the itches. We're gonna do that right now."

Sam and Arthur spent the rest of the afternoon supervising the removal of lice and other crawly things from the ninety-two villagers. They used the communal shower out by the indoor fields. Before being doused with parasiticide, the men had to shave their beards and heads. The women got to keep a bit of hair.

Sam could not remember doing a more difficult thing.

"Don' take ma beard! Don' take 'er." They pleaded to keep every shred of their old existence.

"Nah, ye cannot keep yer hat, Billy. Put that on yer head and the itches will come right back. That's right, all o' ye; ye gotta give up all yer clothes. In return, ye get these"—he held up a black Russian army uniform—"that's what we wear from now on. Like what ah'm wearin."

When it was over, the villagers slunk back into the main hall, chastened and raw. Some cast murderous looks at Sam and Arthur.

12

"I can't feel my legs." The girl was awake and struggling with her bonds when they returned to the sick bay. "I can't feel them at all."

Sam raced to her. He kneeled by the bed, slipping one hand under her lower back and putting the other on her abdomen. "Let her loose, Art; she's not gonna hurt anything."

Sam felt himself wrapped around her spine, surrounding the shattered vertebrae, soothing the frayed nerves, coming to grips with three steel screws that were damaging everything they touched.

Sweat broke out on his back and dripped off his face.

"Can I help you?" he heard Arthur say. Didn't answer. Couldn't.

"Sam. Sam, wake up." Arthur shook him. "Wake up. My God, what happened?"

Sam was lying on the floor next to her bed. Felt like he was at the far end of the universe. He shook his head and pushed himself up on an elbow. "Ah dunno. How long have ah been out?"

"I don't know. I was watching you heal her, when I felt so sleepy

I couldn't hold my head up. I lay down on the bed over there and fell asleep. It's been hours. Is she OK?"

"Lemme see." Sam sat up and grabbed the edge of the bed, starting to pull himself to his feet. Something was in his hand. He opened it.

Three screws lay in his palm.

He scrambled up and looked at her. She was sleeping peacefully. Her face was pale, but rosy. Her lips were parted into a tiny smile.

He showed Arthur the screws.

"Ah'm a bit tired maself, Art. Think ah'll take a nap."

When Sam woke up this time, he could hear her moving in her bed. He went to her, and she sat up, then looked directly into his eyes.

Her eyes were brown with lighter streaks that made them look gold. He had never seen eyes that color. She had a sharp, quick way about her. She studied him, her eyebrows pulled together as though she was remembering something.

"You were in the field."

"Yes, lass. Ah was."

Arthur walked into the sick bay and stopped dead at seeing her sitting up.

"You were in a field. There was a big house. I had a gun. I was pointing it at you." She looked mystified. "Why would I have a gun?"

"Do you remember anything?" Arthur asked.

"Just that. I remember him. He saved me. He picked me up and ran."

"Do you remember your name?"

"No."

"Her name's Em'ly," Sam said.

"Emily? I don't remember that." The girl seemed bewildered. She looked down at her hospital gown. "Where am I? In a hospital?"

Arthur interjected, "You're in the sick bay of the underground shelter on the Piermont estate in the Hamptons."

Her face was blank. "Why am I here?"

"Ye were sick, lass. Verra sick," Sam answered.

"I don't remember." She shook her head, looking at Arthur. "Who are you?"

"I'm Arthur Romero. He's Sam Baahuhd, headman of the village. He runs things here."

"Why are you wearing the uniform of the tsar's elite guard?" she asked Sam.

"How do you know that?" Arthur asked sharply, as Sam listened carefully for her answer. The elite guard was seldom seen out of Russia. Almost no one in the United States would have known what the guard's uniforms looked like. Sam knew how they looked because the general and his guards wore them.

"I don't know. I just do." Her eyes were wide, her lips slightly parted. She was so beautiful that Sam couldn't stop staring at her. Her eyes darted around the room. "This is a hospital. What happened to me?"

Arthur began, "You were detox—"

"Ye had a fall. Down some stairs," Sam cut in. "Ye been out for a long time."

"I feel fine now. Where are my clothes?" She indicated the hospital gown. "I must have had clothes."

"Don' worry about that. Ah've got some in ma room. Ah'll take ye there."

"No! We need to keep her here. Run some more tests, make sure she's all right. I've got a room for her down the hall where she can't get out." Arthur's eyes flashed. "No, Sam. You can't do that."

"Ah'll take her to ma room. She can have the lady's clothes."

"Sam, I need to talk to you. Come over here." Arthur led him into a supply room and closed the door.

"You can't take her to your room. She's killed more people than anyone I know. I can put her in a room where she'll be safe and we can contain her. We can watch her and see how this amnesia crap works out."

"Amnesia?"

"Not remembering anything. Except I think she does. How did she know about your uniform? Very few people have seen the elite guard's uniform."

"Ah dunno how she knew. She's all right, Art'ur. She's fine. Ah can—"

"What if I come to your room one morning and find you with your head cut off? What if she goes to work on the rest of us next? Sam, she's so dangerous, she makes Ronny Nahyuhn and those guys look like pussies."

"She will not do nuthin."

"She's the most dangerous thing down here by a long, long shot. You can't take her to your room."

"Ah can do anything ah want," Sam spoke quietly, but with an edge.

"Sam, do you want to know what they say about you in the village?"

"What?"

"They say you think with your dick."

"Who says that? Who?"

"Pretty much all of them. They say it in different ways, but that's the message. Your dick runs your life."

"How d'yuh know that?"

"Jeremy had the village hooked up to a satellite system. He could sit in his room in New York City and hear what was going on in your living room."

Sam flushed. "What? That's . . ."

"Illegal? Yeah, sure it is. It's also pretty damn rude. But Jeremy needed to know what was going on. And he made sure he did."

"But ah'm the best headman ever. The crops—"

"I'm not saying you aren't a good manager. I'm saying that you need to take a look at certain aspects of your personal life. When you go after every female that moves, you may put others in jeopardy. Especially down here."

Sam huffed, "Ma *personal* life is ma business. What ah do is ma business. An' ah will keep the Commands!" He glared at Arthur. "AH AM THE HEADMAN."

"OK, Sam. You're the boss. I've got some pictures of what the feds did to people that you might want to look at, though. Demos of your girlfriend's line of work."

"Em'ly is *fine*. Nothin's wrong with her. She won't hurt no one— ah'll see to that."

Sam kept a close lookout as they moved down the corridor. His family's room was up the hall to the right, his room was down to the left. He didn't want to run into any of his kids playing in the hallway. He wanted to see his wives even less. They said he thought with his dick. How could anyone say that about him? Everyone did the same thing in the village; he just had more opportunity.

"OK, Em'ly, this is ma room." He punched the combination into the lock, looking down at her. Emily wore her hospital gown with a blanket wrapped around her shoulders and the boots from Jamayuh she was wearing when he had found her. Her eyes were enormous in her thin face.

"I'm not any good at it," she said.

"Wha', lass?"

"Sex. I'm not good at it."

"How do ye know that?"

"I just know. I don't feel anything and I don't come. That's what this is about, isn't it? You give me a place to stay and I give you sex?"

That brought Sam up short. "Well, not quite like that. Why don't we get to know each other and see how it is?" She'd pretty much told the truth of it, though Sam hoped she might turn into more. He wanted something better than he'd ever had. He couldn't say exactly what.

She walked through the door with a resigned sigh.

"This place is a mess!"

It was. Sam hadn't been to his room since the day the world blew up and he and Arthur and Emily had clung to each other.

"D'ye remember this place, lass?"

"No." Furniture was jammed in every way, along with piles of clothing and draperies. Paintings and everything else needed to furnish a palace filled the spaces in between. She wandered through the piles, marveling. "Look at these things. They're beautiful. They look like they came from a museum."

"They're the lady's, lass. Veronica Edgarton's. She owned the estate we're under."

"Veronica Edgarton. I've heard of her. She's famous."

"Was famous. She's gone now."

"Did she die?"

"In a way. She's under the ground in Siberia, frozen."

"Oh! That's awful."

He could see she didn't remember anything, including the earth coming to an end.

"Do you have anything to eat? I'm hungry."

"There's some stuff over here. Ah don't know how to use that thing." He pointed to a box on the wall in an area intended to be a small kitchen. It didn't look like any kitchen he'd ever seen.

"I do."

In short order, they were at a table eating heated Russian army rations in plastic wrappers.

"This stuff is terrible," Sam said, forcing a bite down. "All we got, though."

"This is what they eat in the military," she replied. "You get used to it."

How did she know that? What Arthur said to him came back. How did she know some things and not know others?

Yet, he felt no danger with her. He was certain he had healed her, not just her back, but all of her. He was sitting with Shira, the little girl who didn't die.

13

"I don't have a nightgown," she said.

"Ye can prob'ly find one in the pile." He pointed to the mound of clothes.

She pulled something out and disappeared into the bathroom with it. Sam looked around. She'd been there only an hour and had already gotten to work, moving things so they could walk around, putting lamps on each side of the bed, and neatly stowing the big bundles of feathers and metal rods that had lain on top of it.

"It's a canopy bed. These pieces fit together to make the frame. The ostrich plumes go on top. I can't imagine having things like these."

"Ye've got 'em now, Em'ly, if ye and ah get along and ye want to stay."

She jumped.

He added, "Art can give ye a room by yerself if ye want, but, ah promise, ah won't bother ye here."

Now he got to see if he could make good on what he had said. She came out of the bathroom with wet hair and wearing one of the lady's silk gowns. He hid a smile. The lady was four times as big as Emily on top. The gown flopped down and the girl kept pulling up the straps and trying to hide herself. No matter what she did, the front and armholes hung to her waist. He could see her just fine. She was a lovely thing, even if she was too skinny and covered with muscles. She snuck into bed as far from him as she could get and turned off the light on her side.

He dropped his pants and pulled off his shirt. His lamp shone on him, highlighting his muscular form. The reddish gray hair on his body glowed.

She stared at him hard, and then looked away fast, embarrassed that he'd seen her looking. He didn't know that he wasn't as embarrassed as she was.

"Ah know ah'm an ugly old man. Ah'm forty-one years old."

"That isn't old."

"Ma da died at forty-three. An' look at me—ah'm an old gray bear." He ran his hand over the salt-and-pepper mat on his chest.

"Generals haven't even started their careers at forty-one. You haven't reached your prime." She kept stealing glances at him, as though he were something to see.

He got in bed. "Ah'll leave ye alone. Don' worry."

She went to sleep right away, but Sam lay there. No one had ever told him he hadn't reached his prime. Or looked at him the way she did. Like he was beautiful. Sam felt as if he had a rock in his gullet he couldn't swallow or spit out.

Sam turned toward her. She was so neat and trim, from her hair to her toes. She knew things, he could tell. More than how to read and so on. She was educated, like the lady. She was above him, but not so far above him that the distance couldn't be bridged.

He had never wooed a woman. His wives had been given to him. All the women he'd had either piled on top of him or were coaxed with the Voice. He didn't want to use that on her. He wanted her to come to him fair an' square, because she wanted him. He wanted something he'd never had and couldn't name.

What? And how could he get her to want him?

He woke up hard as a tree trunk with the girl wrapped around him.

"Sam! Sam! We've got to get going!" Arthur was at his door yelling into the intercom.

She raised her head, looking around sleepy eyed. When she realized where she was, she jumped off him as if he were a red-hot poker.

"Ah didn't do nuthin'." Sam put up his hands. "Ye were on me." He pulled on his clothing as fast as he could and went to the door.

"Here." Looking very disapproving, Arthur handed him a black bundle. "These are for her. Russian army standard issue. It's what everyone else is wearing, though they're not too happy about it. She shouldn't get preferential treatment if she's going to go out there."

He realized she hadn't been out in the main hall since he carried her down the stairs. "Should we take her out today?"

"Maybe. You need to see something first. Come to my room. I have to show you something."

Sam handed the uniform to Emily. "Here Em'ly. Ah gotta go to work. You wear these. Ah'll be back as soon as ah can."

Arthur's room was around the corner from his. "OK, this is your introduction to handling the life-support systems down here—and a little wake-up call."

Arthur's bedroom was spotlessly clean and sparsely furnished. A single bed, the blanket folded down so tight it looked like it might split in half, sat in one corner. A rack held a few items of clothing. An almost bare desk had a computer on it. It was a soldier's room.

"Here." Arthur hit a button on a little control on his belt. A panel in the cement wall moved out and then slid to the side, exposing a small computer lab. "I've got this so I can keep a round-the-clock eye on the instruments without going into the main lab. Monitors for all the life-support systems are here, plus these . . ."

Screens on one wall displayed different parts of the underground. The growing fields. The place where the rabbits and chickens and sheep were kept. The main hall. Seven specific areas of the main hall. All the little rooms Sam had thought were cells in the beginning. His family's room. Everything but Arthur's room and his own. The images changed constantly, giving different perspectives on each scene.

"Jeremy set this up. It's like the system he had for spying on the village. Jer was brilliant. Also a little paranoid. But we'll know what's going on. The sensors are undetectable. Your room doesn't have sensors; it was supposed to be Jeremy's mom's room. No way he'd stick his nose in her business! And I put my foot down. I've got to have some privacy.

"Look at this. I'll show you the most dangerous person in the underground, apart from your girlfriend." Arthur smiled, but it wasn't a happy smile. He panned one of the screens from the main hall.

The hall looked like nomads had inhabited it. Sam could see that different clans had staked out their turfs.

"It's not Ronny Nahyuhn or your cousin Lester either. Look." Arthur zeroed in on a tiny old lady with white hair. She looked ridiculous in her Russian army uniform. She had a group of women around her.

"Maddy Ewaneth? She's a sweet ol' thing."

"Like hell she is. Listen . . ." Arthur clicked the sound on the monitor up and pulled the focus back to include more people. Sam's breath caught. Maddy was talking to three of his four wives. The sound was very clear.

"She's witched him. She's a witch pur' and simple. Ah knew it from firs' sight when he brung her down here bare-ass naked. She's witched him away from ye. Ye know that Sammy would ne'er leave ye. Not ye that he loves. She's witched him away. She's castin' spells on him right now." The old lady put her hand to her forehead. "Ah can feel 'er, righ' in ma middle eye. It's sore and tender."

His first wife, Mollie, peevish and argumentative even when the disease wasn't on her, burst out, "Ah knew it. Ah knew it. She was prob'ly waitin' out in the field for my Sam, ready to witch him. Ah knew it." Mollie cast her head around the way she did before she blew. "Ah'll get her. Mind me."

"Have a care, girl," said Maddy. "She'll witch ye, too. Be curful and wait 'til the right time."

"Ah'm gonna talk to my brother Lester. He'll know what to do." Mollie got up and lumbered off. Sam was more than alarmed. She took on that gait a few days before going berserk.

"He's left us alone, Maddy," said Sally, his second wife. "Ain't come back wi' even a glass of water. We'd be daid if it weren't for Les and Ronny bringin' food. An' the kids canna understan' where their da's gone."

"Bad witchin', Sally. The worst kinda witch can do that to a man. Make him leave his fam'ly." Maddy nodded as though intoning a gospel truth.

"OK, Sam. You get the picture?"

"She's stirrin' 'em up against Em'ly."

"Yeah. Emily's got a problem if she goes out on the floor. But it's not just Emily. People come to Maddy the way they came to you. She's undermining everything we're trying to do. You need to get out there and hold court, hold hands, whatever you need to do. And you need to see your wives."

Sam nodded, appalled. "Have you seen Winnie?"

"Not out on the floor. Here's their room." He fiddled with a screen covered with static. Arthur adjusted the monitor, then the computer powering it. "It's not working. It must be a programming malfunction.

"I haven't seen her outside the room, though. I have seen them hassling her in the room."

Sam wanted to go across the hall right then. He took a step toward the door, but Arthur pulled him up.

"Wait a minute, partner. Nobody's going to die in the next few minutes. I have to get you going on running these systems right away. If I get sick, we're screwed."

Arthur moved to a computer on the other side of the room. "OK. The systems consist of two parts. There's the physical equipment, including ducting and pipes, the actual machinery and valves. And then there are the computerized controls. Both have to work for us to live.

"The most important system is air. No air, we die. Jeremy used air scrubbers like on the old submarines, but his are way better. We have a beyond-state-of-the-art air purification and filtering system."

Sam kept nodding, trying to keep up.

"The problem is, of course, that we breathe the O_2 in the atmosphere and leave the CO_2. The growing fields are the source of the O_2 . . ."

Sam felt his ribs tighten. What was Arthur talking about?

"The O_2 is picked up by the system and recycled back into the air supply with the scrubbed air, fixing the O_2/CO_2 balance. Of course, if the plants die, so do we." Arthur chuckled.

"The really ingenious part is the use of surface oxygen—the oxygen outside the shelter. As soon as the radiation levels go down enough for the exterior ports to function, we'll be able to mine the exterior air safely."

Sam's mouth dropped open. "Uh, Art, uh . . ."

"When the exterior ports open, the radiation outside will still be high enough to kill us, but low enough for the radiation filters Jer stole from the government—you know, QASA2—to work. We should be able to pull in fresh air created from the radioactive atmosphere, so we'll be able to breathe even if the crops fail. Of course, we'll die of starvation."

Sam felt dizzy. What was Arthur talking about? How could Sam ever learn it?

"The most important thing down here is NO FIRES. Not even a spark. Fire uses up oxygen like crazy. Anybody lights a campfire, we all die.

"Next, water. We've got huge holding tanks of water built under what used to be the mansion's lawn. We get to shower and wash now; later we'll probably have to curtail that. But that's just until the surface water system gets going. Then, we'll be able to funnel rainwater into our purification system. When there is rainwater, that is." Arthur laughed again. Sam felt like a fool.

"Please, Art. Ah need to see ma fam'ly. Ah canna do this now." Sam's head throbbed.

"OK. One second. The waste disposal system is really important. The toilets deliver waste into a tank here." He pointed to a map of the shelter. "Right next to the growing fields. We're set to turn shit into Shinola." He grinned at Sam. Sam didn't get the joke.

"Art, please. Ah gotta go."

Arthur didn't stop. "Human shit is full of bugs. People don't even know they've got parasites and then, wham, you use the waste for fertilizer, the bugs pass into the soil and the plants. We have to worm everyone as soon as they get over being deloused. And, oh, Maddy has really stirred people up about that. You'd swear the itches were the village's best friends the way she talks.

"Let's see. The incinerator. This incinerator uses a flash principle. Flash! Whatever you put in it is burned to *nothing*. Not just ashes. Nothing. It will burn all the trash." He lowered his voice. "It will also burn bodies. We don't have room for a cemetery. The incinerator burns bodies in seconds."

"Ah canna hear more." Sam dashed toward the door.

"Wait, Sam! I've got copies of the manuals for you. Oh. I forgot. You can't read. Well, have Emily read them to you." Arthur ran around the room pulling out stacks of documents, and shoved them at Sam.

Sam staggered into the hallway, arms full of papers and files, feeling as if he'd run a race and lost.

14

Sam stood in front of his wives' room, pushing on the bell. "It's Sam. Let me in," he shouted into the intercom. No answer. "Ah know yer in there. Open 'er." He wished he'd gotten the door's combination from Arthur. "Open 'er! Ah'm yer *headman!*"

The door opened slowly. Mollie stuck her wide face out. "Whadya want?" Her face was blotched and swollen. Her appearance gave Sam a start. A rage was coming. They needed to lock her up, and soon.

"Ah want to see how ye are. Ah ain't had a chance to come by since ah been sick."

"Ye been sick, a'right. Stoofin' that witch. Foockin' her day an' night. Not a thought for us, not to see if we had anythin' to eat. Not a thought but"—she held her hands out in front like she had a dick and rammed her hips back and forth—"That's what ye care for, Sam Baahuhd. Ye've been ma husband all ma life. Ah know ye."

"That is na true. Ah never foocked her." Jeers from inside greeted his statement. "An' ah saw that ye had food." Arthur actually had had food and water delivered to their door, but they didn't know that. Arthur had left bedding and other necessities as well.

"Hah! Ma brother Lester brang us food. Him and Ronny brang it and blankets and everythin'. Laid 'em outside the door. We'd be daid without them. Ye stinkin' foock gin . . ."

Sally shoved herself into the doorway. He was surprised to see her so angry. "Ah known ye were a wastrel, Sam, foockin' every one ye could get. But a witch? Ye know she's a witch, don't cha?"

"Em'ly isn't a witch. Nothin' witchy 'bout her at all."

That brought Fannie to the front, gray hair flying. "Yer a bad man, Sam Baahuhd. Ah thought ah were lucky when ye took me an' ma kiddies after ma dear Danny died las' year. But yer a wastrel and a hoochman and a cunnie-head as well. Now ah got ma three precious babes and the cockson ye put in me to raise. An' ye leave us a' the end o' the world! Get outta here! Ne'er come back." Spittle flew from her lips and her wrinkled cheeks shook. She opened her mouth as though to bite, showing wide gaps between her brown teeth.

Sam took a step back. "Where's Winnie? Ah want to see Winnie."

"She can come out if she wants."

"Winnie—'re you OK?"

"Ah'm a'right, Sam Baahuhd. No thanks to ye." The hostility in Winnie's voice shocked him. "Ye've left us to make our own way best we can. Get outta here. Ye'll just make 'er worse."

Sam reeled at that. Mollie put her hands on his chest and shoved him backward. He staggered, dropping the papers and books Arthur had given him.

"Get out! Get to yer witch and don't come here no more. Ma brother Lester will see to us, Sam Baahuhd. Yer no' our husband no more." Mollie slammed the door.

Sam scrambled around on the hall floor, picking up the papers. He couldn't believe it. He let them talk to him that way. The Voice was gone. All of it, gone. He had no way of controlling his own wives, much less the village. And Winnie! She felt the same as the others. He staggered up the hall in the direction of his room.

Through the peephole in the door, Mollie watched Sam disappear. She would kill him and the witch. She opened the door, intending to run after him with her knife.

A folded paper on the floor stopped her. She opened it up and stared at it, attempting to make sense of its markings. Lines and letters and symbols. Arrows. A circle with lines through it. This was a devilish thing.

"C'mon," she said to Sally and Fannie. "We gotta talk to Maddy Ewaneth. She'll know what this is. Winnie, ye mind the kiddies." She glared at Winnie, who cowered. Her face was covered with bruises and her uniform was torn.

A crowd gathered around Maddy's perch in the main hall. The old lady reveled in the attention, holding the paper at arm's length and studying it, then bringing it close to her nose and peering at it intently.

"Oh, is witchery. Bad witchery. See this here?" She pointed to a circle with a cross through it. "It's here and here and here. An' lookit these lines, goin' from one place to the other. Connectin' things."

Maddy suddenly realized what the drawing portrayed. "It's the *shelter*! It's where we are. See—here's the fields. An' look, there's a great . . . cookin' pot here, a big trough next to 'em. Comes from here . . ." She gasped. A simplified icon showing a toilet appeared in one corner, with dotted lines connecting other toilets throughout the shelter.

"It's the new kinda shitters! She's witched the shitters!"

The villagers recoiled in fear, and then leaned close to hear Maddy's terrible pronouncement.

"Ah. Them shitters is the devil's work. Ah knew they ain't nachrul. They're dangerous an' evil. They're gonna suck us into this big cooker." She pointed at the large round circle near the fields. "An' she'll *cook* us there."

"What should we do, Maddy?"

"Don' use 'em. They'll kill ya."

"Where should we go if we don't use 'em? Ah thought them shitters was kinda nice," Lester said.

"That's how the devil works, Les. Cuddle up to ye, and then—" She clapped her hands. They jumped. "He gets ya. Yer in hell fire, burnin'.

"Ye shud go out in the fields, Les. That's nachrul. Shittin' in the dirt. The fields is the only dirt we got now."

The group nodded silently.

"Maddy, what should we do with the witch?" Sally asked. "She's witched Art'ur, too. Sam come out of his room with the paper an' lots more. We watched in the peephole. Ah know it's from her."

"Oh, she's a bad'un. Witchin' that nice boy, Art." Maddy thought. "Well, y' know, only one thing to do with a witch." She looked around.

"What, Maddy?"

"Burn 'em. Witch will only die from fire. We need to catch her and burn her."

"Ah'll burn 'er," Mollie said. "Ah'll burn her good." She swung her head from side to side like a bull's, looking for the witch. The others jumped back. The only thing that scared them more than a witch was Mollie Baahuhd on a rage.

15

Sam dragged himself to his room. The lines around his mouth felt as if they'd been gouged out of stone. His feet would hardly move.

When he got inside, he could see that Emily had been working. The place was cleaner and more organized. The pile of clothes was half as high, and little stacks of folded things sat along the wall. She had a bunch of silver stuff on the table.

"Oh, hello! Look at this, Sam. This is an eighteenth-century footed compote." She held up a silver bowl with little legs. "It's got the maker's mark on the bottom. I don't know . . ." She really looked at him. "Sam, what's wrong?"

"Ah went to see ma wives."

"Your wives?" He forgot he hadn't told her about them.

"Well, they're not ma wives any more. Jeremy called off our marriages on account of us being cousins."

"You were married to your cousins?"

"It's the way of the village, Em'ly. Almost the whole village is cousins."

"But you're divorced now?"

"Yeah. *Really* divorced." He told her what had happened, though not what they had said about his amorous activities or drinking. Or what they were saying about the two of them. "Ah been married to them mos' of my life an' they wouldna let me in. Ah jus' wanted to know how they was. See if ah could help."

"Do you have kids?" She acted as if he'd punched her in the belly.

"Yeah. Ah got fourteen livin'. A bunch more died."

"You have fourteen children." Emily's mouth tightened. "OK. I shouldn't be surprised. You're old enough to have been married and had kids." She thought for an instant. "You're divorced. They wouldn't let you in. What about visitation rights? Can't you demand to see your children?"

"Nah. In the village, if people split, the kids stay with the ma. If she gets another man, the kids become his."

"So you lost your kids, too?"

"Yeah."

"You should just go down there and apologize. You can offer them some of this stuff." She indicated the mass of furnishings in the room. "You can't use all this."

"Nah, Em'ly. This is my stuff. Ah'll not give it away. An' that's not it. They've shunned me. Ah'm not part of 'em any more. They're linin' up with Lester an' Ronny. They're lookin' for a war."

"A war?"

"'Tis the way of the village, Em. Feuds an' war. Ah can't stop it. Ah've lost ma Voice, ah've lost the Power . . .'"

"What are those?"

He had to explain them to her. "They've been gone since the day everything blew up." He hadn't told her about the end of the world either. So he did. That stopped the conversation.

"When did I fall and hit my head?"

He had to explain the two of them being in the sick bay and Jeremy and the underground shelter. He lied about them detoxing, instead saying stuff had fallen on them. Sam hadn't talked so much in his life.

"Why can't I remember any of this, Sam? It's all a blank. I just remember you and the field and me with a gun."

"Ah don't know, Em'ly. An' ah don't know why my Voice and Power only work with you."

"What? You mean you can make me do anything you want? I don't believe it."

"Em'ly, put that thing down and come over here to me. Pet my head."

She got up and stood next to him, stroking his head and blinking. "I don't know how you did that."

"Ah've been able to do that since ah was a babe. Ah used to heal sick birds and such. An' make the other kids do what ah wanted." He felt so weary. "Ah won't use 'em on you, Em'ly. Ah just needed 'em to heal you. Ah won' make you do a thing. It's jus' that ah can't use 'em on the village, an' ah need to. They're a scrappy bunch of brawlers. Fightin' comes easier than gettin' along. Ah'm afraid of what's comin'."

"We need to go out there more, you and me and Arthur, and make them listen to reason."

"No! Em'ly, ah forbid you to go into the hall." He used the Voice for that one. "You will not go there. You will not go anywhere unless ah'm with you."

"You used the Voice on me. You said you wouldn't."

"Yeah, ah did. They say yer a witch, Em'ly. They'll kill you. They will burn you to death. Ah can't let that happen."

"I'm not a witch. Witches don't exist."

"Ah know that, but they believe in 'em in the village. Witches and hants and spells and hell an' damnation. Curses. They might as well be true for how people act. That's why ah need the Voice an' Power back."

"Arthur thinks it's from trauma?"

"Yeah, an' ah think he's right."

"So, we have to get you untraumatized. Meanwhile, what's all this?" She pointed to the folders jammed with manuals and plans.

"The systems of this place. Ah'm supposed to study 'em." He waved at the pile. "Only one problem. Ah can't read."

"You can't read?"

"None of us can read. The lady never sent out a teacher so we could have a school. We asked her time and again, but she never did."

"She lived with all this priceless stuff and couldn't send you a teacher? She could have sold that silver bowl and paid for a teacher for ten years. That's horrible."

"Well, mayhap it wasn't all her fault. Mayhap as not so many teachers wanted to live in the Hamptons." He smiled crookedly. "Might have been a bit hard on their health, y' know. Hirin' was likely a problem."

He'd never talked to a woman like that, or a man either. No one was interested in what life was like for him, or how he felt about it.

"Maybe ah felt like ah didn't deserve more, ugly thing that ah am. We was all so low compared to the lady and them that came to the big house. They was kings and important people.

"The village was diff'rent. No one talked like we're doin'. In the day there was lots to do. Ah worked in the fields, ah worked with the horses, took care of the cattle and sheep. Got the crops planted and tended. Harvested. Paid the lady her share.

"But, at night, all there was was sittin' by the well with the other fellas, passin' a bottle. Always the hooch. An' mushrooms an' weed. Ah didn't do them, though ah did like a drop. We'd get to talkin'. Ah told stories at the bonfires. They loved the bonfires. So did ah.

"But that was it. Weren't no books—nobody could read anyway. No telly. No movies. No shoppin'. We could go fishin' and huntin'. Ah liked to ride . . .

"Oh, an' there was one other thing to do." He blushed. Sam didn't know when he'd blushed before.

"Your four wives?"

"Yeah. Like that." He didn't want to tell her about the rest of them in the village. What he did hadn't seemed excessive when he was doing it, but what Arthur had said and what his wives had said about him made him think maybe it was.

"Nobody talked like you and me're talkin'. Nobody asked me what ah felt. Didn't matter what ah felt, the world went on the same. Ah kep' workin' like a mule and seein' Mrs. E got her share." His chest started heaving. He didn't know why. "Nobody talked about why things were that way, or how they could be different."

She studied him. "That's really sad. You're so smart, and you never got a chance to use most of it."

He shook his head. "Well, ah don't know that ah'm so smart." He felt his cheeks flame. "Ah really wanted to see New York City once. But that's gone. About the rest, well, ah'm here." He looked around the room. "Beats fire an' hell."

She laughed. "Would you like some dinner, Sam?" She cleared off the table and set it with some of Mrs. E's fancy silver. Even though they were eating army grub out of plastic trays, it seemed nice.

After dinner, they sat on a sofa she'd unearthed and he talked more about the village. He told her about the river and the forest and his favorite horse, Oned. She listened so intently, it made him feel as if he had something to say. He found himself laughing. She laughed, too.

And then she reached out and laid her hand on his forearm. He felt a jolt all over his body. He didn't dare move.

That night, she didn't have to be careful about what her gown revealed. She'd found a jacket-thing made of the same soft material as her nightdress. She wrapped it around herself and tied it with a length of the same cloth. He couldn't see anything except her soft curves and how luscious she was. She got into bed on her side, not jammed all the way to her edge of the bed, but not on his side either.

He shucked his clothes off the way he had the night before, not making such a big deal out of it, but not hiding himself either. She could have watched him, or not.

Not was the case. She turned away from him on her side and pulled the blankets up. "Goodnight, Sam," she said.

"Goodnight, Em'ly," he replied. This was OK with him. He wasn't what his wives had said, and Arthur, too, and what sounded like the rest of the village thought. He wasn't a grot-headed cunnie-hound.

Sam curled up with his back to her. Soon her soft breathing said she was asleep. Such sweet sounds. Some of his wives had roared like the guns the general's men brought out. Could have torn up the countryside with the noise. She breathed quietly, like a lady. A little gurgle or snort every once in a while to let him know she was human.

He shifted around and waited for sleep to come. It didn't. He wanted to hold her. He wanted much more than that. But he wasn't what they said. She would have to come to him and beg before he'd touch her. He'd show everyone what he was made of.

Sam lay in the dark, stiff, wondering if his balls would turn blue.

16

"Sam! Sam! Get out here! Maddy Ewaneth died last night. We've got to get out there!" Arthur's voice brayed from the intercom.

Sam pried his eyes open and struggled out of the few minutes of sleep he'd managed to snag. He jumped up and almost fell. His legs were rubbery from exhaustion. He pulled on his pants and grabbed his shirt, heading for the door.

"What happened, Art?" he said, standing in the doorway, swaying.

"Jesus, Sam"—Arthur's face screwed up—"what have you been doing?" His mouth tightened. "I guess I don't have to ask."

"No, Art, it's not like that." He managed to project a fairly high level of indignation. "Not like that at all. Couldna sleep is all." Sam's knees buckled. His face felt chalky and brittle. If he'd slept, it must have been just before Arthur woke him up.

Sam noticed that Arthur was suited up in his commando outfit with a belt bristling with weapons. He also carried a medical kit.

"This is very bad timing, Sam. They're ready to riot. They think Emily killed Maddy."

"What?" Sam went back into his room and got the one useful object Emily had found in her cleaning. His sledgehammer.

"Looks to me like a coronary," Arthur said to Sam when they were out in the hall where Maddy had died. He'd listened to the old lady's heart, but it was obvious to everyone that she was gone. "Because of the pattern of broken blood vessels on her face and the blue coloration of her skin."

The entire village stood around them, Lester and Ronny out front.

"It was her heart," Sam announced. The assembly snarled.

"Weren't her heart," Ronny said. "She were fine yesterday. 'Twas the witch. Maddy tol' us about the witch, and the wicked thing killed our dear Maddy."

"What?" Arthur said. "That's ridiculous."

Ronny looked patronizing. "Sorruh to tell ye, Art'ur, ye bein' a good fella all these years. Ye're witched, too."

"What?" Arthur said again.

"Yeah. Ye an' poor Sam need to know what's been done to ye. Mollie found the signs. Show 'em, Les."

Lester brought out a soiled and rumpled sheet of paper and showed it to Sam. "Mollie found this in the hall after ye tried to bust into her room yesterday. Witchin' signs, all of it. From the devil hisself. Maddy saw it right away."

"Give me that." Arthur grabbed it. "This is the engineer's schematic for the waste disposal system. It's part of the plans used to construct the place."

"Nah. Ye have to know how to read 'er. See this circle with the cross in it? That's the devil's own brand."

"That's a conventional symbol used to indicate an electrical outlet." Arthur pointed to the icon of a toilet. "This is a toilet. They're linked together by the sewer system, emptying into this holding tank where the sewage is purified, and then used as fertilizer. What's the problem?"

Lester and Ronny looked a bit confused. "Maddy said that sign meant the devil had hexed the crappers."

"What?" Arthur choked. Sam was glad Arthur was so upset because it kept the attention of the people off him. His eyes felt hollow and he kept swaying on his feet. He knew what they'd think.

"Maddy said the crappers were hexed; we'd better not use them."

"What? Where have you been going?"

"Well, we all been goin' out to the field. We got it all roped off."

"You're shitting in the fields? You ignorant, stupid, superstitious . . ." Arthur launched into a fit of cussing that caused the people of the village to step back. Then their eyes opened and their mouths hung loose. When he was finished, they looked at him with admiration.

"You *contaminated* the fields. That's where your *food* will come from, you idiots." Arthur launched in again. "You thought the best sanitation system in the world was the work of the *devil*? And you shit in your own breadbasket? You are the stupidest, most hard-headed idiots—" He pulled himself up short.

"You know what else? *Witches don't exist.* Emily is *not* a witch. The closest thing to a witch down here is that old lady." He pointed at Maddy's body. "She thought the sign for an electrical outlet was from the devil. That's stupid. If you knew how to read, you could read the labels and know what this is." He waved the sheet of paper. "You fucking—" Art stopped himself, yanking himself erect and standing stiffly with his jaw clenched.

"OK. Reading lessons start tomorrow. I will see that every one of you can read in six months or I will crack your skulls open. Now you're gonna clean the shit up. You personally, Ronny Naahuhd, will clean up every turd. Now." Arthur's hand went to the long stick on his belt. "Get the shovels."

17

"Sam, come to my room." Arthur grabbed Sam's arm when the funeral was over. "I need to talk."

The room was pristine and spare as always. Arthur stood in the middle, running his hands through his hair. "They're using the fields as toilets. Tearing up plants. They believe in *witches*.

"This shelter was supposed to be for geniuses who would build a better world. Mrs. E spent billions of dollars on it, not to mention the federal government and the general. And who's in here? Total illiterates."

Sam scowled.

"Oh, I'm sorry, Sam. I don't consider you like that. I know they're your people. I just can't stand it.

"I didn't have to be here, do you know that? The people from Eliana's planet wanted me. I could have beamed up with them and lived in the golden world, eating ambrosia and watching Ellie dance with Jer and the others. I didn't go. I love the earth and wanted to create a new world. I knew you couldn't do it without me. So I came down here. For *you*, as much as anything."

He changed the subject abruptly. "You're in love with her, aren't you? You spent last night fucking her. That's why you look so awful. And now you're in love with her."

"Ain't none of yer business what Em'ly an' ah do." Sam took offense. "An' ah wasn't foocking her."

"OK. If you say so. But while you romance a mass murderer, I have to manhandle a gang of sociopaths. That killer in Emily is going to come out, Sam. I've been reading up on amnesia. Her memory could come back at any time. All she needs is a trigger and—pow!—she'll be mowing them down again. I'm afraid for you, and for all of us."

"She won't hurt anybody. Ah won't let her. Ah won't let anythin' happen to ye or this place. Ah promise."

"Sam, I want you to promise that you'll neutralize her if she gets out of control. That means *kill* her. Remember what she is."

"Ah'll remember. She ain't gonna get away from me, but ah will kill her if she does. Are ye happy, Art?"

"Uh. Yeah."

When he came into their room, she was sitting at the table. She got up and walked toward him. She was the most beautiful girl he'd seen. Emily was wearing Mrs. E's clothes: a wide skirt just to her knees and a sweater that was almost tight on her. Must have been so tight on the lady that it pretty near strangled her, to fit Emily like that.

"Hi, Sam," she said, smiling. Her voice could melt him. She wore bright red shoes with heels so high and pointy, you could have used them for nails. They clicked on the floor when she walked and made her legs look longer. He couldn't take his eyes off her.

"None of her clothes fit, except for this outfit." Emily sounded a bit awed. "Was she really that big, Sam?"

"She was that big, a'right." Sam ran his hand over his jaw. "Pretty much knock a man's eyes out."

"Oh."

He saw her kind of flinch when he said that, but didn't think more of it. She had the table set and put their food out. She asked him what had happened that day. He told her about Maddy and the people shitting in the fields and how upset Arthur had been. He didn't tell her anything Arthur had said about her. But the talking didn't catch on the way it had the night before.

"Lass, ah've got to get to bed. Ah didn't sleep much last night."

He was asleep before his clothes hit the floor.

The room was dark, illuminated a little by automatic lights. He was on his side with his knees drawn up. Something touched him. He sat up fast, ready to swing.

"It's me, Sam. I'm sorry. I didn't mean to wake you up." She was lying close to him, on her side, facing him. She had touched his shoulder. Her knees brushed his. "I was just a little lonely. Go back to sleep."

He couldn't. The thin fabric of her gown didn't cover her knees. Was she wearing it? He was rigid in an instant. What was he going to do? He'd given up the hooch; he could give up this, too. He didn't want to be known as a cunnie-loving fool. Her knees were definitely bare.

Struggling, he finally said, "What do you want, lass?"

"Um, I'm sorry. I'll leave you alone." She started wiggling back to her side of the bed.

He grabbed her, hand landing on her hip. Definitely no gown. "Tell me what ye want."

"I'm sorry. I'm not built like Mrs. Edgarton. I understand why you don't want me. I won't bother you again."

"Wait. Why'd ye touch me, lass?"

"I just . . . I . . ."

"Lass, ah told ye that ah would na bother ye while ye were here. But if ye get close to me, or touch me, ah canna promise that."

She moved up next to him. Her lips brushed his chest.

"Oh, lass." He reached over and stroked her.

"I'm not good at it, Sam."

"Don't worry, lass. Ah am."

He lay next to her, belly to belly, slowly sweeping her flank with his hand. He felt drunk, but not like with the hooch. Maybe with the lady's bubbly wine. But more like he was floating in the river and everything was moving past him, the trees and clouds and the light. Every time he touched her, the river grew stronger. It rushed in his ears. She was in it with him.

"What's happening, Sam? Do you feel it?"

"Yes, lass." He began to hum, the way he did when he was healing. The river surrounded them, sweeping through them. It was time.

He ran his hand down her side, then between her legs. He spread her lips. "Put yer leg over mine, Em'ly."

Then he moved forward until he was inside her, pushed all the way in. "Do ye feel that, lass? Do ye feel something in there?"

She squirmed. He put his hand on the small of her back, pressing her to him. "Do you feel that? Do you feel me?"

"Yes." She was breathless.

A groan escaped him. He was feeling something, too. She was slick and tight and quick as an eel. She felt so good all around him. He kept rocking softly, pushing into her, pressing on her back. Then she felt too good.

"Ah'm sorry. Ah'm going to be fast. Ah'll make it up to ye."

It started in his feet, roared up into his ass and out his dick like it usually did. But this one kept going. Waves of pleasure rolled up his back and burst out of the top of his head. They kept coming. He clutched her and jerked, groaning. Seemed like a long time until the flood subsided. He kept jerking for a while.

"Sam, are you all right?"

"Yes, lass."

"Your face looked like you were in pain."

"Not pain, lass." He laughed. His laughter kept coming, too. "Are ye OK, Em'ly?"

"I'm OK." Her voice said she wasn't OK the way he wanted her to be.

He pulled her close. "Let me rest a moment, and ah'll make ye feel good."

Sweat beaded on his face and slicked his body. The sheets were wet with it. Sam raised himself drunkenly. She was lying on her belly next to him. He touched her. She was still, sleeping. He laughed and flopped on his back. He could barely move. He'd never had such a night, not with all the women he'd known. Never. She excited him so much, he worried his heart would stall.

She was like a cat, fast and nimble. And smart. She learned what he liked so fast. He'd made her happy. Happier than she knew she could be. He thought about her and something came out of his heart. A force like when he was healing, but more. For her. He wanted to lie with her forever. He wanted them to have children. He wanted to have everything with her.

The lights turned up to indicate dawn. Jeremy had programmed the place like that, to seem natural. When Sam's eyes opened, he saw her looking at him.

"Come over here, girl." He grabbed her to him, kissing her. She wiggled against him the way she did. It made him crazy. Her lips sought his neck where it met the shoulder. She sucked and bit. It tickled.

"Sam, is it always like this for you?" she whispered breathlessly. She was as sweaty as he was.

"Never in ma life. Ye give me shivers. Oh, lass. Put those red shoes on and let me see ye walk around naked."

She did and he watched her, speechless. Breathless. He felt something for her he couldn't name.

His lips hurt from kissing and his chest felt like it was going to break open. The feelings for her kept erupting like the geyser out in the forest. All he could think about was her.

He wanted to say it. Tried mouthing the words: Em'ly, ah love ye. But he couldn't go that far. Women were a tricky business. Better be sure of her.

"I love you, Sam. I'll love you forever. You saved me. Out in the field and when I was in the hospital. And here"—she patted the bed—"that was so wonderful."

He dropped his face into his hand.

18

"Ah already *know* ma letters." Sam could hear Ronny Nahyuhn braying before he reached the reading class. It was in the middle of the hall where Jeremy had broadcast that first morning. The picture-showing wall was lit up. Arthur stood next to a stand with a bunch of papers and a portable computer. The rest of the people sat on the tiered cement floor.

A B C D E F G H I J K L M N O P Q R S T U V W X Y Z ran across the top of the screen.

"Ah know *all* ma letters." Ronny Nahyuhn smirked. "The one there on the lef' side is the *pointy* one. The one next to it lookin' like a couple of tits squeezed tight is the *tittie* one." Sam's brother-in-law Lester guffawed, along with all his and Ronny's buddies. They formed a knot in the assembled villagers, as far as they could get from the screen. "An' the next one that's sorta round is the *sorta round* one."

Everyone in the village laughed. Soon they'd leave.

"Ye want some more uh ma med'cine, Ronny?" Sam said quietly, his voice amplified by ricocheting off the hard walls. "Ah got more to give ye."

"Ah, no Sam. Ah's jus' havin' a little fun before school." Ronny ducked his head and almost bowed.

"Ah don't want no med'cine, Sammy," said Lester, standing straight and regarding Sam with a calculating look. "Ah jus' want to say my letters. Let's see, next is the one with three legs stickin' out. That's called *three legs stickin' out.*"

People laughed, but not as hard as before. The rowdies' attention was fixed on Sam, and he understood why. Normally he'd defuse this with the Voice. If he had to use violence, something was wrong with his Voice, and his Power, too, most likely. They watched him like bird-hawks. They'd realized something was wrong with him.

"'Nuff o' that," Sam barked. "Art'ur, start teachin'." He turned to Arthur, hoping they'd drop it.

"OK," Arthur said. "The alphabet is on the screen. All twenty-six letters, upper and lower case. The lower case is below the bigger letters on the screen . . ." Art was off and talking.

Ronny, Lester, and the rest were silent. Sam had bested them without violence, but he had a terrible feeling they knew his Power had deserted him. It was a matter of time until they provoked a war.

Meanwhile, Art droned on, pointing at the symbols on the screen. Sam didn't know why there were two sets of letters or why there had to be so many of them. He had a bad feeling about this class, in every way.

"Words are made of letters." Arthur spoke in a monotone. "They are the building blocks of reading. I know you've seen writing and may recognize some of the letters, but I doubt you've ever seen the whole alphabet in order like this, with both cases. There's also a distinction between vowels and consonants, but we'll get to that later."

Sam had to force himself to keep his attention in the room. Only Ronny and Lester, giggling like kids, kept him from leaving. He didn't trust them even when he was in the same room.

Arthur droned on. "The top line is in upper case. That's used for important writing like this." He typed into a small computer on his desk and letters appeared on the screen: WARNING. "Does anyone know what that means?" Everyone was silent, so Arthur asked Sam.

"It means, 'Look out; danger,'" Sam said. "It was all over the big house where Jeremy 'lectrified it. And on the fences around where they were makin' the underground."

"That's right. The word means to look out, something dangerous is there. When you see all upper case, you really should pay attention to what's written. Another use of the upper case is for the first letter of names of people or places like . . ." He typed: Sam Baahuhd and the United States of America. "Do you know what those say? Anyone? Sam?"

Sam was on the spot. He was the headman. He thought "Sam" was his first name and that maybe the second word was his last name. He guessed. "The first part is ma name. Ah don't know the second."

"That's right, Sam. The first part says 'Sam Baahuhd.' The second part is the country we live in: the United States of America. See how the capital letter is used to begin the word. We'll get into that later."

Art looked like he hated doing what he was doing as much as everyone hated being there. But Sam was determined that they would live by the Commands, and they required everyone learn to read within six months.

"OK. Every letter has a sound associated with it." Arthur kept going like one of those big earthmoving machines that tore out the dirt in the meadow and didn't mind what it ran over. "If you know the letters of a word and the sounds that go with them, you can sound out a word without being able to read it.

"The letters sound like this." An arrow appeared on the screen by the letter farthest to the left. "This is A, the first letter of the alphabet. The upper and lower cases sound the same. 'A' sounds like this: ahhhhh." He made this stupid sound. "You make the sound. Come on, Sam."

Sam dutifully went "ahhh," feeling idiotic.

"OK. Everyone now," Arthur said. Sam looked around. Everyone blushed as though they felt the same way he did.

"Great," Art chirped. "Actually, A can sound a whole bunch of ways, like ah, uh, ä, aaah. We'll get to that later."

Arthur made them "sound out" all the letters. It was humiliating. Arthur led them, dauntless: "A-Ahh. B-Buh. Cuh, Cha, Ci . . . L–Luh. Luuu. Luuuu."

"When're we gonna get to oooh! oooh! oooh!" Ronny made a sound like a woman coming. "Oooh! Y' gimme a good one, Ronny!"

"Hey! Shut yer face an' listen." Sam stood and yelled Ronny down. "All o' ye. Shut 'em." They did, with hungry looks in their eyes.

Arthur remained serious. "In addition to learning the letters one at a time and putting them together, you can also learn to read by recognizing whole words. For instance, everyone knows what this is." He pushed a button and a picture showed up on the wall. "What is it?"

"A cow."

"That's what this says." The letters c-o-w appeared below the image. "Cow. Keep looking at those letters. See if you can pick them out here." He showed another image that had more words on them. "Do you see c-o-w?"

"Yeah, it's there," said one of the kids, pointing.

"Right, so when you see those letters on a page, you'll know it means cow. You've learned to read your first word."

"Why do we need to learn words for things we'll ne'er see again?" Lester whined. "We'll ne'er see a cow, nor a horse. Or nuthin'."

"Well, Lester, we learned cow because it's short," Arthur said with a scowl on his face. "I figured you could handle something short. Let's do another exercise. To learn most efficiently, you need to let your hands and eyes get into the act.

"Have any of you tried writing before? I've got tablets and pencils for you." He had them draw the letters in cow one by one and then put them together. "That's good. You just wrote your first word."

Sam realized how many words there were. Learning to read would take forever. And what was all that "we'll get to that later" Art kept talking about? The rest of the village seemed to realize the same thing.

"Ah canna come here t'morrow, Art," Ronny said, with Lester and his pals behind him. "Ah gotta . . ."

"Ye gotta be here," Sam said. "An' quit the bull. Ye gotta learn to read. Ye will read." Feeling a bit desperate, he turned to Arthur.

"Is there a way to do this faster, Art?"

"Working in small groups and doing lots of homework. I've got workbooks for you to take home."

Arthur gave them their workbooks. "Please do the first exercise for tomorrow." Sam wanted to groan. He glanced through the book.

"Art, ah can't see the letters," he whispered.

"Oh, shit. I forgot about *eyesight*. How many can't see the letters in the workbook? Or they're blurry?"

Sam raised his hand, which encouraged others to do the same.

"I'll have to test your vision." Arthur sighed and pushed a button on his computer. A chart showed up on the screen. "OK. This is an E. Can you see how the legs stick out, Sam? Here, they're going up. Here they're pointing left. I'll point to an E on this chart and you tell me which way it's pointing."

Sam looked at a chart and told Arthur the E's directions. He got down a couple of rows. "Ah don't know, Art. Could be any whichway."

"You need glasses. Probably bifocals." Art looked disturbed. "Everyone stay here. I'll be right back."

Arthur came back from the VIP corridor a short time later carrying a big box. "Jeremy scoured the thrift shops in New York and got all these glasses. I can't really test your vision, but you can go through this box and try them on. If you can see better, they're yours."

Sam ended up with two pairs, one that had a line across the middle that let him see better near and far, and the other just for close-up things. He felt totally stupid and certain he'd never learn to read.

Sam headed back to his room, wearing the glasses with the line across them. He dreaded going back the next day. He opened the door and walked in, then stopped dead. To his left was the cement wall. All the tall pieces of furniture were lined up to make a wall on his right. Their backs faced him.

"Come in!" Emily called. "We've been working all day. Rupert and his boys helped me move the big stuff. I hope you like it!" Her grin practically split her face. She took his arm and pulled him along the hallway.

"I put the armoires side by side, facing in. You'll see why. Don't look back until I tell you." She pranced, leading him along. At the end of the passage was an area with a sofa and big chairs and tables and lamps. One of the rugs that had different colors swirling like a painting was underneath everything.

Beyond that was a fancy wood table with chairs where they could eat. The table was big enough for a family. One of the ornate ceiling lights that had metal branches and glass things hanging off them hung over the table. The glass pieces made light fly around the room. Another rug was under the table. He looked around, his jaw slack.

They could live there just as if they were the lady and her friends.

"I'm going to ask Arthur to work on the electrical for the chandelier. I think we can hook it up so it works. Now turn around."

He gasped. The bed was pushed back against the far wall. A metal framework rose high over it, with creamy curtains hanging to the floor. The big plumes sat in clumps on each corner and over the middle. Something like a painting made of cloth covered the bed. Beautiful rugs covered the floor. The tall pieces of furniture made a wall along the right side.

"Those are eighteenth-century French armoires. I lined them up so we could have some privacy in bed. We have our own little nest." She'd put lamps and tables next to the bed, and some big upholstered chairs on one side. The mirrors on the armoires' doors reflected light onto the bed.

"Do you like the walls?" Dark red velvet fabric covered the room's cement walls. "They're the draperies from Mrs. Edgarton's bedroom. Nice, huh?" The walls covered with the luxurious draped velvet were the only surfaces in the underground that weren't cement. A painting of the meadow by the village hung over the curtains on one wall. A portrait of a stallion hung next to the bed. It wasn't Oned, but it was close enough.

"Do you like it, Sam?"

He couldn't speak. "It's like the big house."

"Yes. That's what I was going for."

"Ah get to live in the big house."

"Yes."

"Oh, Em'ly." He sat heavily on one of the chairs. "They never let me in the big house. Now ah'm livin' in it."

"Are you happy?"

"Yeah, girl. Come over here and let me hold you."

"Those glasses look great on you, Sam. Very distinguished."

He thanked her as well as he could that night, discovering something unexpected about their new room. With the lights on a bit, the mirrors on the armoires reflected them in bed. He saw himself moving on top of her and almost lost control. He hadn't counted on that.

Sam lay in bed, blinking back the feelings that wanted to leak out his eyes. The world had ended and everything had blown up, yet he was happier than he'd ever been. He was in love with the smartest, most beautiful woman anywhere. And she loved him back, he knew that.

He could talk to her about anything. She had made this beautiful room for them. She understood how he had felt about being locked out of the big house and how important the room was to him. She liked how he looked in his glasses. She even said she'd help him learn to read.

He wondered if she'd marry him. It was kind of stupid to think about, since if she married anyone, it would likely be him. But would she say yes if he asked her? He wanted that.

19

"Sam, I found something today. It was sewn into the lining of one of Mrs. Edgarton's fur coats." He had just come in from another terrible reading lesson with Arthur. Emily held out a small, clear cylinder. "It's for data storage. It's got your name on it."

He took it, feeling his throat tighten. Jeremy had said that his mother had left a private good-bye message for him. He held the thing in his fist, frozen for a moment.

"Do you want me to get it set up on the laptop for you?"

He nodded. "It's from the lady."

"Do you want me to leave while you watch it?"

He nodded again.

"Just press here to start it." Emily left the room.

"Don't go out in the big hall," he called after her, uncertain whether she'd heard him. He didn't go after her; the call of whatever was on the cylinder was too strong.

The screen flickered and the lady came on. She was wearing a brilliant blue gown, low cut, but not as low as she wore sometimes. She had rings on her fingers and a sparkling blue necklace around her neck. Her refined face and black hair were perfect. She was as beautiful as ever, almost.

"Sam, I wanted to say good-bye to you." Her eyes darted to the right, just once. He knew by that and the tension in her body that someone was watching her. She couldn't be frank. The camera panned in closer. She looked like she had a bruise under one of her eyes, covered with makeup. Smiling, she turned her head. A fine row of something ran down her jaw. Stitches? She raised her hand to fix her hair. Four dark streaks ran across her forearm like fingers where someone had grabbed her.

She was being frank. She was a prisoner. The general beat her. He felt sick.

"I want to thank you for continuing to care for the village, and for Jeremy, if he's there with you. I appreciate it so much. I know you'll take care of everything forever."

Tears came to her eyes. She left them there, keeping her tone jovial.

"I wish so many things had been different. Remember the fun we had? Remember when we were thirteen?" She smiled. "I think of that day all the time. Every day. I wish things could have been different, but they couldn't be. Not in our worlds. Maybe in worlds to come, but not in my world, or in yours.

"Let's think of that, my old friend: the worlds to come. Perhaps the estate and the village can come together. Perhaps our descendants will have a chance."

Her lips compressed and she looked to the right again, quickly, and then smiled into the camera. "You've meant more to me than you know. Part of me has lived in a fantasy about what might have happened between us. But it's time to give up fantasies, my friend, as we face earth's end. Do what you must to live a good life, Sam. If you find someone special, love her the way you would have loved me. As for me, I need to accept what I've created and live with it as best I can. Heaven help us both, my darling.

"I've given you *everything* in my rooms; enjoy it."

The screen went dark and the lady was gone.

"Em'ly, could you come in here?" He was so shaken, he didn't mind if she heard the message. "Will ye watch this with me? Ah want to look closer at some of it."

"Oh, she's so beautiful," Emily breathed as Veronica Edgarton's form appeared on the screen again.

"Stop 'er right there. Can ye make the picture bigger?"

The lady did have a blue-black bruise under her eye that makeup couldn't hide. Those were stitches on her jaw and the bruises on her arm showed the imprint of the general's hand.

Sam's throat felt as if they'd poured some of the cement for the underground down it. His eyes burned and his chest was rigid. "He's beatin' her. Ah can't b'lieve anyone would do that."

Emily studied him. "You love her, don't you?"

"Eh?" He was surprised by the words. He'd never talked about how he felt about the lady. He snorted, then admitted, "All my life. She come up to the estate with her fam'ly. Treated us like a bunch of mangy dogs she kept in the shed. 'Cept for me. Always was a spark between us. But that weren't enough." Sam felt pain building behind his eyes. "Dammit," he said, rubbing his eyes with the back of his hand.

"What happened when you were thirteen, Sam? If you don't mind." Emily sat next to him while he wiped and snuffled.

"'Scuse me. Ah'm actin' like a woman."

"I'm a woman, Sam. There's nothing wrong with crying."

She looked at him like that was true. His chest began to heave up and down. He couldn't understand why. He felt as if he might start sobbing.

"When we was thirteen . . ." He'd never spoken of it to anyone. "We used to go ridin' together. We rode by the river one day." And then it was as if he were back there. He described how the river drifted by and the wind made the leaves rustle. They had got off their horses. She had put her hand on the front of his pants, stroking him for an instant. Then she jumped away, climbed on her horse and took off. She didn't come near him again, unless someone else was there.

"Ah didn't know nothin' then, but ah did know just from that touch that she knew everything about makin' a man feel good. Ah never forgot it. It was a big hole in me, eatin' at me. Gnawin'. Ah couldn't stop thinkin' of her, even when ah was married. Even when ah was with another woman. That touch never left me.

"Not 'til ah met *you*." He couldn't meet her eyes. "Ah think maybe all of it, the hooch and ma runnin' an' rippin' an' all the cunnies—oh, scuse me Em'ly. All o' it was because she ran from me an' ah was tryin' to plug a hole somehow. Ma life stopped on that river, in a way."

Emily listened with a serious expression on her face. "But she loved you, too, Sam. She said she thought of that day every day. Her life stopped, too."

"Not as much as mine. Weren't nothin' for me in the village, Em'ly. Just work and drinkin' by the well. Just chasin' what ah could get, which was all of 'em, Em'ly. Ah've had ever' one of the women in the village, all but my own daughters and their daughters." He studied her carefully, half hoping he'd driven her off. The happiness he'd felt with her was hard to take. He expected it to end up bad at any time.

"You've done what we do in bed with every woman in the village?" The whites of her eyes showed all around. "You mean every woman out there knows . . . all about you? What you look like?"

Now she'd leave him.

"Nah. Not like what we do. Never like that. Ah was like an animal, an' so was they. Don' think it was like us.

"Ah'm used to bein' alone, Em'ly. Never really joinin' up with anyone. That's what the lady did to me—left me alone no matter who ah was with. Ah loved her and she loved me, but it was never a real love.

"She's never given me anything like you have, Em'ly. She never helped me with a damned thing. She'd never fix this room like this. She'd never love me like you do, and touch me."

"She said that you needed to let go of your fantasies about each other. Can you do that?"

"She's gone, Em'ly. Seein' her again stirred me up. But ah ain't thought of her since ah touched you. An' what she said was right: nothin' could ever happen between her and me in the old world. That's dead. What we got is the new world, an' that's you an' me."

She was silent.

"Em'ly, don't leave me because of what ah said about them others. Ah got some bad things in ma past, the hooch and women. Ah'm prob'ly not as much as ye think ah am. Maybe ye'll find out ah'm even less when ye know me. But ah love ye, Em'ly. Ah've never told anyone that, even the lady or ma wives.

"Y'er the one ah love. Y'er real; y'er here. Y'er not so far above me that ah'll never reach ye. An' ye don't make me feel like ah'm low. Ye help me, an' ah'll help ye. That's what ah want, Em'ly, a frien' that ah love."

"You want a partner," she said.

"Yeah. Livin' together an' helpin' each other. Bein' friends, an' bein' together in bed. Bein' equal."

"I want that, too, Sam. That's what I've always wanted. You say you have some dark things in your life. At least you can remember them. I probably have things in my past that I don't know about. Why don't we forgive each other? What's real is what we've got."

"All right. Let's." He cleared his throat. "Would ye be ma wife? Ah'll be the best man ah can be for ye and take care of ye all ma life." Sam's chest froze again. He hadn't known her long. And he hadn't used the Voice to make her love him.

"Yes, Sam. I'll marry you. When?" She beamed like the sun over the bay when Ellie's people had come to take Jeremy and the rest away on the last morning of the world.

20

A rt married them the next morning in his room, Sam in his elite guard uniform and Emily in a long white dress of Mrs. E's she'd pulled in to fit her.

Arthur's mouth pinched tight. Sam knew he wanted to voice dire warnings about his lack of wisdom in marrying Emily. Sam didn't want to hear them.

"Seems like there should be a cake or something. Or a toast." Emily looked teary. "I've never been married before."

Sam remembered the days and nights of feasting that accompanied his other weddings. "Ah'll make it up to ye, lass. Ah'll give ye a party we'll all remember." If he could ever convince the village that she wasn't a witch, and when he felt it was safe to let her out in the main hall.

"Oh, I forgot something." Arthur took off out his door. When he came back, he produced a stunning sapphire ring surrounded by diamonds. "This was in the sick bay. I forgot to give it to you. You were wearing this when Sam found you."

"What a beautiful ring," she said, looking at it as though she'd never seen it before.

"Ah can put 'er on ye, at least," Sam said, slipping it on her ring finger. It flashed, lighting up the room.

"Oh, Sam, it's beautiful. Thank you. I always dreamed of the man I loved giving me something like this."

When Arthur's eyes met Sam's, they said, "See, I told you so." She didn't recognize her own ring. And then she spoke of it familiarly. What else had she forgotten? When would she remember?

He was even more discouraged after that day's reading class than before. Arthur had gone on and on. Sam dragged into their room, almost unaware he'd gotten married that morning.

"What's the matter, Sam?" Emily said, bright as a spring morning.

"Reading. Ah'll ne'er learn to do 'er."

"Let me help you. Is that your workbook?" She took it and led him to the table. "OK, what this means is . . ." And he could understand it. When Emily explained letters and words, reading seemed like something he could do.

They quit after an hour. "That's enough for one day, Sam." She knit her brows. He could tell she wanted to ask him something.

"Sam, I need to work out. I'm getting fat." Her brown eyes bored into his. She looked pained.

If there was any fat on her, he hadn't found it. "Art'ur works out. He could take ye to the gym," he replied.

"I can go by myself."

"Nah. Some of the punks hang out there. An' there was that talk about you bein' a witch. Ah'd rather Art went with ye to start."

"OK. I'll go with him the next time he goes. Can I help teach the reading class tomorrow?"

Sam didn't want her out of their room. "Ye got anythin' to do here?"

"Well, I could sew. Arthur found a bunch of sewing machines. I tried one on an exercise suit and found out that I can really sew. I don't remember where I learned." She shrugged at the mystery.

"I could remake Mrs. Edgarton's clothes so they fit. I could make clothes for you."

"Why don't ye do that t'morrow?" He called Arthur on the intercom. "Art, ye doin' anythin' now? Em'ly would like to go to the gym."

"She shouldn't go alone," Arthur's voice said from the speaker.

"Ah know she shouldn't go alone. That's why ah'm askin' ye to take 'er."

"Sam, you've got to control her." Arthur looked almost hysterical. He'd called an emergency meeting after his trip to the gym with Emily. "She doesn't understand the first thing about the village. She's going to get herself killed."

"Tell me what happened, Art." Sam had already heard a half-dozen versions of Emily's exercise session.

"She came out of your room in gym clothes from the hippest New York workout joint. Skintight leopard-print leotard, tights, leg warmers. A headband. And Mrs. E's best running shoes. Do you know what those suits look like?"

"Nah."

"Like she was wearing paint. You could see every inch of her. She was down the hall to the gym before I could stop her. One of the kids was going in when she got there, so she slipped in."

Sam inhaled sharply. Women in the village wore layers of long, full skirts and blouses with sleeves to their wrists. They never wore pants or shorts. "They look like peasants in an eighteenth-century painting," one of the lady's guests had once remarked. Whatever that was, it wasn't like they were wearing paint.

"Some of the teenagers were in there. Your four youngest kids from Mollie—everyone but Rupert. Fannie's three boys. Plus Ronny Nahyuhn's and Lester's kids. She walked in and they froze."

Sam inhaled. Not a good bunch. Mollie's younger boys had the peevish bad temper that pointed to their mother's disease. All Fannie's kids from her first marriage were troublemakers. The whole bunch of them felt that being his sons gave them permission to do whatever they wanted. And any kid sired by Lester or Ronny was a foul business.

"One of them was trying to lift weights. She went marching up to them, friendly as can be, and told the one lifting weights that he was doing it wrong and was going to get hurt. Which was true."

Sam's eyebrows went up. A woman never approached a man in the village, never spoke first, and certainly never told him he was wrong.

"And, of course, she wasn't wearing a long skirt and a million petticoats and practically a burnoose, like women wear in the village. She told the kid he should be wearing a weight-lifting belt, and asked me where they were. She got one and then buckled it around his waist! Then she showed him how to lift, touching his shoulders and back while she explained how he should keep his back straight and his head up so he wouldn't get hurt. She touched his lower back.

"In New York City, no one would bat an eye."

But in the village, a woman would never touch a man in public, especially below the waist. Sam wiped his face with his hand. "Then what?"

"She did what she went in there to do—run. The solar treadmill works great, by the way. First, she laid towels out all around the treadmill, and then she turned it on and warmed up. I went over to do damage control and showed the kids some things about lifting. I connected with them. We were going along fine. I was showing them how to do bench presses, when, all of a sudden, we heard heavy breathing and looked at the treadmill.

"Emily's the best runner I have ever seen. She was just booking along, running at I don't know what speed. You could hear her feet pounding the treadmill and she was breathing like a freight train. Sweat was flying all over, which is why she put the towels down. And her workout suit was sopping wet. You know what that means, don't you?"

"Nah."

"It was almost see-through. I walked over and said maybe it was time to quit. She said, 'I've got ten minutes left.' I would have had to drag her off the thing, so I let her run. She upped the speed and just hauled. She'd leave me in the dust.

"When she was finished, I said, 'Why don't we leave?' and grabbed her arm. She pulled away and she said, 'I'm just warmed up. I want to put on the gloves.' We've got a nice boxing layout there. So she put on some light gloves and started on the speed bag. You know what that is, don't you? It's a small punching bag that hangs from an armature. It's for developing speed and coordination.

"She was punching away, bumpety, bumpety, bumpety. The bag was moving faster than I could see. The kids' mouths fell open. They were totally silent, watching. You couldn't tell if they were more impressed or outraged. All the time, bumpety, bumpety, bumpety. I was ready to grab her by the hair and haul her out, but seeing her punch made me think about that."

"How did it end?"

"She quit, wiped herself off, waved to the boys, and we left."

"Did she do anythin' wrong?"

"No. It's just that she's a better athlete than any of those kids could ever be. And she looked hot."

Sam had heard that she had worked out naked, fondled one of the boys while he was lifting weights, and picked a fight with Arthur. Also that she was a witch with supernatural powers. No one could box as fast as she did. Had to be magic.

"We have a problem, Sam. She said she wants to work out every day."

21

"Come and dance with me, Sam," Emily ran to him and grabbed his hand when he opened the door. "It's our wedding night. Let's dance!" He had intended to talk to her about what had happened at the gym, but she was so excited, he put it off. Music like they played at the parties at the big house was blaring and she was dancing around.

"I found the sound system in one of the cabinets. Isn't this recording great? It's the hottest band, Ripped." She wore a short white dress of some shiny, soft material he hadn't seen before. The front fell down loosely, half exposing her titties, while the skirt was wide, and swirled as she danced. "Isn't this dress beautiful? It's silk. I just finished taking a few tucks so it fits me."

It did fit her, where it touched. When she twirled, it spun out straight, showing her legs. She mesmerized him.

"Come on, Sam. Dance with me." She grabbed his hands and began jumping around. He could do a stomp, which is what they did at the hog slaughters and on feast days, but he didn't know how to do whatever she was doing. "I'll show you." She held one of his hands and put the other on her waist. She began pulling him around and rocking from side to side. He got the hang of it a little.

His hand felt glued to the silk on her waist. He wanted to stroke that dress all over her. The music changed tempo, and she danced up close. She shimmied all the way up his body, touching him from here to there. He couldn't breathe. She spun out and her dress flew all the way up. She wasn't wearing anything underneath it. He could see everything from her dark patch right down her legs to the high-heeled shoes on her feet.

"Come over here, girl." He pulled her over to a chair. Sam undid his pants as fast as he could. "Come here, Em'ly. Sit on me."

The rest of the night was like that, rocking with her, tasting her, touching her. Feeling the explosion that shot up his back. Hearing her mewling and crying as she shook.

Sam lay back in the bed, listening to her breathe as she slept. He was caught. He couldn't refuse her anything. Couldn't reprimand her. Certainly couldn't punish her. She held him in the grip of soft flesh and silk dresses. And love. He was in love. Ah'm an' old fool, he thought. An' ah do think with my dick. He dropped off to sleep.

"Da! Da!" A voice from the intercom awakened him. Sam sat up sleepily.

"Who is it?"

"It's me, Ewan." That was his younger son with Winnie.

"Can't it wait 'til tomorrow, son?"

"No, Da. It's Ma. They're gonna use her as a whoor! Ye gotta help." Sam was pulling on his clothes. "Who?"

"Ronny and all 'o them. They's in our room. Come fast!"

Sam grabbed his sledgehammer and shot out of the room. He ran down the hall, Ewan next to him. The door to his family's room was wide open, bright light flooding the hallway. Raucous voices spilled out. "Get 'er. Don' let 'er get away! She's a fast un!" A dozen voices cried out, all familiar.

Sam stepped into the doorway and stopped. Winnie was at the back of the room. Her shirt was torn open and they'd gotten her pants off. He saw blood between her legs. One eye was swollen shut and her face battered blue and black and red. She was struggling as hard as she could, but it wasn't doing any good. Ronny Nahyuhn's older sons held her arms while Ronny moved in between her legs.

"Get away from my ma!" Sam's son Jude was the only one defending her, and he was but fourteen. Ronny punched him and he fell, scrambling to get back on his feet and help his mother.

"Stop!" Sam bellowed. "What do ye think yer doin'? That's ma wife!"

"Not anymore, Sammy boy." Ronny turned around, sneering. "The Great Tek called off all our marriages. Ah ain't married to my own Carly no more. Gotta do somethin' with ma urges. Ah don't have a little bitch like you."

Sam stepped forward, seeing what he was up against as he got farther into the room. Thirty or more men were in the room, plus Sam's former wives and all their kids, except for Sally and hers. More than forty people. His wives were as good at brawling as the men. Ronny and Lester were making their play, declaring war.

Lester stepped in. "Art'ur tol' us we could'n have no more kids today at readin' class. 'Gotta be careful about the population of the shelter.' So what're we s'posed to do? Play wi' ourself?" The men in the room exploded with laughter.

They were jiggered on weed. Sam could see Lester's hands shaking and hear it in the craziness of their voices. Someone must have brought some into the underground. They were probably growing it in the fields. Weed was the worst of the drugs that had plagued the village. People on weed acted like those with the disease. Before it rotted their brains entirely, it made them into monsters.

"Nah. Y' don't need this un anymore," Lester went on, indicating Winnie. "She's bleedin' like a pig—got her monthlies. She'll give us a week or more before she can make a brat. We're gonna use her hard."

"No." Sam hefted the sledgehammer. He had neither the Voice nor the Power. Strong as he was, he was no match for that many. "Ye'll na touch her." He hovered just inside the room, trying to gauge how far in he could go before they rushed him. He realized he would die that night, stomped to death.

"What abou' yer Voice, Sammy? Cat got yer tongue? Why don't ye use yer Power and blast us away?" Ronny hollered. "We been noticin' ye use that hammer 'stead of yer Power. Summat wrong wi' you?"

The room fell silent. Sam could feel them tense to spring. A black shadow moved past him and stopped a few feet from Ronny Nahyuhn.

"If you want to hurt a woman, why don't you try one who can hurt you back?" It was Emily, speaking in a low, taut voice Sam had never heard. A tight hood fit over her head and the rest of her was covered in black. The fabric was so black, she seemed to disappear. Weapons hung all over her belt, more even than on Arthur's suit.

"Ah, ye called yer cunnie in to fight for ye, Sammy. Good idea. Ye can be the woman ah always knew ye were." Ronny turned to face her. "Wanna a good poke, missy? Tired of that ol' man?"

"Leave her alone and get out of here." Emily's voice was steely, very different from the dancing girl's. "That's your warning."

"Oh, ho! She's givin' a warning."

Emily pulled something off her belt and held it in front of her. It looked like the handle of a sword, but with no blade. She squeezed the handle. A blue light rose five feet into the air, shimmering. The villagers stepped back.

"Whatcha bring, a toy, missy?" Ronny stepped toward her and she moved the blade in a slow arc. The top of Ronny's body fell first, then his legs. Blood spurted and then washed the floor. She swung the blade in the other direction. His sons, right behind him, fell the same way.

"It's not a toy," Emily said. And then she attacked.

Lester stepped in when he saw Ronny fall. She decapitated him, and then turned on his sons.

"That's ma brother!" screamed Mollie. "Ye killed ma brother!" The disease took her and she charged like a screaming banshee, arms flailing, mouth open to bite. Emily stabbed her with the laser sword and then drew it out of her body, cutting out a quarter of her corpse.

The remaining people screamed and tried to get out the door. Emily stepped in front of them and herded them to the back of the room, where she began the slaughter. People tried to run around her to escape, but she was too fast. They screamed and turned on each other, creating a scrambling, howling pile three or four deep. She dove in. Blood plumed and made fountains of metallic red. The stench of opened guts made him choke.

The blade flashed and people fell. Sam had never seen anything like her for ferocity. She went after the villagers, no holding back, nothing spared, no mercy. But she picked her targets. No swinging wildly. She took out specific people, leaning over the groveling, shrieking human heap to pick out this one, that one, and that one over there. Skewering them with the light stick as if they were pigs.

Sam stood by helplessly, unable to join in the slaughter of his people and unable to move so he could stop it.

Finally he cried, "Em'ly, stop. That's enough. Winnie's safe."

She didn't stop.

"Em'ly, please stop. No more." The coppery smell of blood filled Sam's nostrils and bit in his mouth. She was like a dervish, moving faster than his eye could follow. "Em'ly. Stop. Please." She paid no attention.

"SOLDIER, STAND DOWN." Arthur burst into the room, suited up like Emily. "STAND DOWN."

Emily stopped the sword in midflight, retracted the blade, and holstered it. She swung to face Art and stood at attention, her feet parted and her hands behind her back. "YES, SIR."

"Lieutenant, hand me your weapons belt." Arthur stood eye to eye with her.

Emily took off her belt and handed it to him. Arthur slung it over his shoulder, checking the handle of the laser sword to make sure it was disarmed.

"Go to that corner and stand there. DO NOT MOVE."

"Yes, sir." Emily did as she was told.

"Everyone. Stay where you are or I will kill you myself."

Sam was surprised to hear the words from Arthur's mouth. Arthur closed and locked the door, trapping them inside with the survivors.

"Let's clean it up." Arthur surveyed the wreckage, beckoning Sam to join him. The blood-soaked survivors clumped in the far corner, clinging to each other and wailing. Winnie and her boys were in the back of the room.

"Sam, you go check Winnie," Arthur said.

Sam made his way over to her. "Winnie, are you all right? Did they hurt you?"

"They done nothin' but hurt me since ye left. But they didn't do what yer thinkin'."

"Jude, Ewan, take your ma to ma room. Ye can sleep there. Ah'll get this place straightened out and join ye. The combination to the door looks like this." Sam drew the pattern of the buttons on his hand. "Got it?"

He walked around the room with Arthur. Blood, arms, legs, opened torsos. Heads with arteries hanging out of severed necks. Bodies were everywhere, mostly in the corner where Emily had driven everyone. The room had been filthy even before the carnage. The stench of sewage poured from the bathroom. Arthur and Sam peeked in. Shit was piled up in the corners and slopped all over the toilets. The sink was clogged with it. Sam's family had never stopped heeding Maddy Ewaneth's warning about plumbing fixtures. Their few pieces of furniture from the big house were ripped and stained. Filthy mattresses lay on the floor.

"How could it get this bad so fast?" Arthur said.

Sam shook his head. "The disease. An' maybe ma boys were doin' weed."

"Sam, we can't have people who aren't trustworthy down here." Arthur leaned over and spoke softly. "We have to separate the survivors into those you trust and those you don't. I'm going to present them to you one by one. Say yes if you trust the person, no if you don't. Take the first word that comes to your mind. Yes or no."

Arthur got the survivors in a line. There were no wounded; they were either dead or unharmed. He presented them to Sam one by one.

"Sam, yes or no?"

"No. Yes. Yes. No. No."

"If you got a yes, go stand over by the door. You can join your families in a few minutes." Arthur had the blue sword out and armed before Sam could object. He executed the three men Sam had indicated he didn't trust in a style as surgical as Emily's.

"All right, you can go." Arthur opened the door. The survivors bolted, sobbing.

"That's a bit hard, Art," Sam finally said. "All ah said was ah didn't trust them."

"They'd be the next Ronny and Lester, Sam. That's the village." Arthur left the room to close and lock the steel doors on each end of the VIP corridor.

When Arthur returned, Sam said, "Now let's see who's dead." The two men began the grisly task of identifying the bodies. "She got Ronny, Lester, their oldest kids, Mollie an' all her kids but Rupert. Fannie and her three kids. She got Sally's an' my boy, Jim Bobby." Sam could barely speak. His wives and children had wanted to kill him.

The list went on. Emily had killed twenty-eight people, including two of Sam's former wives and their children. Of Mollie's kids, only Rupert was still alive. He hadn't been there. Sam thanked God his favorite hadn't been part of this.

"Thing is, she got the bad guys," Arthur remarked. "These are the troublemakers and punks. She did us a service, in a way. But, Sam, this is exactly what I told you could happen. She's a killer. You saw it. I can put her in a holding cell that she'll never get out of. Or I can give her an injection that will take care of the problem forever. Let me lock her up, at least."

Sam stood shaking. He had watched his family and all those others hacked to pieces. He'd seen Emily attack ruthlessly and mercilessly. But he'd also seen Arthur do the same.

"No. Ah'll take her to ma room. She's ma wife."

What had happened to his dancing girl?

22

"Em'ly, let's head back to our room. It's late." She was right where Arthur had told her to wait, except that she'd slid down to the floor. Sam looked around the killing room one more time. Blood, shit, filth.

"Em, do you want me to help you out of your suit?" They were back in their room. The commando suit was bloody, though not as bloody as you might expect. Most of the gore had been left on the floor or the people, dead and alive. He turned the lights in their room on low. The white silk dress was lying on the carpet.

"I want to keep my suit on."

"We're going to bed. Don't you want a gown?"

"No."

Somehow, he managed to go to sleep. Winnie and the boys were sleeping on the floor on the other side of the bed. In the middle of the night, he felt something moving in the room and sat up.

She was standing at the end of the bed, prancing on her toes, so full of energy that he thought she might explode. Her hands made fists and she punched rapid-fire. Her feet went up and down, up and down, like a boxer's.

"Sam," she cried. "Is she all right? Is she all right?"

He got out of bed to hug her, but she wouldn't let him close.

"Is she all right? Did they hurt her?" She was wailing now, loudly, moving her feet as if she wanted to take off.

"She's all right, Em. Ye saved her."

"Is she all right, Sam? Oh, Sam. You can't lock girls up and hurt them. That's not right."

"No, it's not right, Em. Let's go to sleep now."

"It's not right to hurt girls, Sam. Is she all right?"

"Winnie, stand up and tell her you're all right."

Winnie stood up. He could see the boys peeking over the bed. "Ah'm all right, Em'ly. Thank ye for what ye did."

"You're really all right? Oh, Sam." She collapsed into his arms. "Oh, Sam. I thought they were going to hurt her. I thought they were going to *kill* you." She buried her face in his chest, sobbing.

He picked her up and put her in bed. "That's all right, Em'ly. Let me hold you." He had to use all his Power, but he got her calmed down and asleep.

"Ah'm sorry, Winnie, but you see how it is." The next morning he tried to heal her ruined face, with no luck.

"So ye have lost yer Power," she said. "They were sayin' that."

"Ever since ah been down here, except for with her." He nodded toward Emily, sleeping heavily. "Ah can heal her. Art'ur thinks maybe ah'll get the Voice an' the Power back. Ah dunno. Ye'll have to go to Art for bandages and such. He'll give you an' the boys a new room."

"The question is, where did she get the suit and the weapons?" Arthur said. "That suit is the top of the line for the Russian army. The general's private guard has them; that's all. You can't stab through it, shoot through it, burn it, or blow it up. And it's as close to absolute black as exists. It's almost invisible. And the laser sword. Nobody even knows what those are, they're so advanced. Where did it come from?"

Sam had the same questions, but he wanted to ask Emily privately. Arthur kept saying he had a nice room to lock her up in. Or the shot. But Sam would never allow him to kill her. Never lock her up. It would destroy her. He knew he'd been talking to Pearl the night before: the child who'd been locked in the pink room and taught to be a killer.

She sat silently in their room with the lights down low. The sparkling girl who'd danced with him was gone. The commando suit lay over the sofa. She wore jeans and a shirt; her body was covered from head to toe.

"Em, where did you get that suit?"

She looked at him dully. "It was in the armoire. It has a false back. There's another one."

"Show me."

She took him to one of the armoires. "It's here." She showed him a very clever hinged door in the back, almost invisible. "The other one would fit you. And there's a belt, too."

Hanging on a peg was a weapons belt just like the one she'd worn. He could see the hilt of the laser sword.

"Em. When did you find these?"

"A couple of days ago."

"Why didn't you tell me about them?"

"I don't know." Her blankness bothered him as much as what she was saying.

"Have you found any other things in the room?"

She nodded and proceeded to pull out a small arsenal of unfamiliar but deadly-looking devices. "These are the latest weapons. They don't cause sparks. You can use them safely down here."

"How do you know about them?"

She shrugged, looking straight ahead. "I just know."

"Why didn't you tell me about these?"

"I think this is what Mrs. Edgarton was saying that she left for you. Weapons so you could protect yourself."

"Is there anythin' else you want to tell me?"

She nodded. "The closet has a door in the back. I don't know where it goes."

Sam knew all about the door. It went to the computer labs and the cache of deadly weapons the general had forced Jeremy to store, the most hazardous and vital part of the underground. The door was as concealed as Jeremy could make it.

Sam stifled his alarm. She *was* as dangerous as Arthur had said. She'd lied to him. Should he let Arthur lock her up?

Everything in his soul said no. No jail, no lethal shot. He had to heal her, really. He needed to get to the little girl in the pink room and Valerie Zanner, both.

Sam was dizzy. He hadn't been underground two weeks and could barely recognize his life as his own. On the good side, he was learning to read. Maybe on the good side, he had just spoken to Emily in words that could have come straight form the big house. He was turning into what Jeremy wanted. Left Sam feeling a little hollow, like he'd lost part of himself.

On the bad side, he had lost his Voice and Power. He'd fallen in love with and married a beautiful woman. A beauty who turned out to have a killer inside her. And who had slaughtered a third of the people in the village and deceived him about deadly weapons.

What was next?

23

A rt sat at his computer, typing away.

> This is Arthur Romero. I just cremated 31 people who had been hacked to pieces, and then argued with a Neanderthal about what to do with a mass murderer. We haven't been here two weeks, and I'm fucking exhausted and up to my elbows in blood.
>
> I think I got through to Sam. Emily must be neutralized.

He sat back in his chair, feeling the tension in his face. His body drooped with exhaustion. He'd showered, standing under the water for seven minutes, using up a week's allotment scrubbing himself, but he still felt filthy.

Art went back to typing.

> I should title this "Dear Diary." It's writing therapy. Who am I supposed to talk to down here? Sam? The villagers? "Em'ly"?

He chuckled.

> I'm going to log on like this from time to time.
> My mission includes keeping records of our "experi-
> ment." I'm supposed to write a report and upload it
> to a satellite for some analyst to study in the sweet
> by-and-by. As though anyone is out there.
> What works and what doesn't?
> The life-support systems that Jeremy designed
> work. That's about all.

Art thought for a moment, reviewing his time underground.

> On second thought, there's another area of
> improvement. Sam's spoken English is a little better.
> He's learning to read. Must be the lessons plus inter-
> acting with Emily and me. There are a couple others
> who look like they'll be able to read. Maybe.
> Nothing else works, though . . .

He felt himself reeling, remembering Emily moving like an arrow
in the black suit. She'd used the laser sword as if she had been born
holding it. Precise. Lethal. Exquisite. The best technique he'd ever seen.

He wiped his face with his hand, trying to clear away the image.
But the slim figure still moved in his mind's eye. He felt himself
stirring. What am I, getting a hard-on for a murderer? A murderer
married to my boss? Tell the truth, Romero, he thought. Get it out.
No one will see this.

> Watching her work out in the gym was a total
> turn-on, but watching her kill was a thing of glory.
> I'm not Arthur Romero, Jeremy's driver, the nice
> boy from the city.

I'm Captain Art Romero. I was on the front for three years. I've killed more people than Emily has. Only difference is I didn't torture mine first. And I didn't see most of them die. I used missiles. Some was hand-to-hand. It was war. That's what you do.

I like killing.

But I do it when I'm ordered to, not when I feel like it. I'm in control; she's not.

He sat up straight.

The highest levels of the revolutionary command gave me my mission. I will carry it out. I will not let Emily ruin it. I will not cause conflict with Sam.

She has to be eliminated.

Then I'll stop thinking about her.

Arthur selected all his text, and hit delete.

24

The sun was behind her, carving beams of light in the heavy mist. He held up his hand, trying to see her better, but could make out only the outline of her head and body as she walked toward him. Just her outline and the light glinting off the barrel of her gun. They were in a forlorn place with no landmarks but the sun and brilliant fog.

"What do you want?" Her voice was hard.

"Ah wanna talk to ye." Speaking the village brogue with her in that place came naturally.

"I only killed the bad ones." She approached him as she had the first time, holding the pistol in both hands. She looked the way she had when he had first seen her, covered with muck and filth from the river. Shivering in her thin black suit.

"That ye did, lass. An' ah thank ye, though twill be hell to pay for it. Ah come to make ye an' offer."

She kept the gun on him, circling him. She was much more focused and dangerous than she had been at their first encounter.

"Ah hope ye see fit to take it."

"What offer?" The gun was inches from his chest.

"Yer name is Valerie, isn't it?" She nodded, sneering. "Ah thought so. Valerie, what do ye want, lass? More 'n anything." Sam had never done a healing this way, but it was the only way he could think of to get close to the murderous Valerie Zanner.

"Shut up. Why are you really here?" She slipped around behind him. He could feel the gun's barrel pressing on a kidney.

"Ah'm here to make a deal, Valerie. Y' know we're livin' underground. Ye know we're probably the last people on the earth. We got to have peace. No violence, no killin', no torture. Jus' peace."

She snorted. "You'll never get that."

"We gotta try. So ah come to make a deal. What do you want, Valerie? More than anythin'?"

She was in front of him, looking up at him. She looked so much like Emily, and so little. Hatred suffused her features. Her body was stiff with it. The way she moved was quicker and harsher than Emily's way. Everything about her said she was deadly. Her hard eyes focused on him.

"The president of the United States sent me out here to the Hamptons. He knew what was going to happen. He sent me out here to die."

"Ah know, lass."

"No one gives a shit about me. I killed for them. I killed so many people I can't count." A snort of a laugh escaped her. "I thought I was doing good." She forced herself even more erect. "I knew I was going to die that morning. I knew the atomic weapons would go off.

"But I didn't die. I found you. You saved me, even though you knew what I was."

"What happened then, lass?"

"We watched the explosions on a screen. You and Arthur and I held each other and screamed."

"And then what happened?"

"You got sick, and then I got sick."

"And then?"

"You saved me again." The gun was wavering. "Oh, my back hurts."

"Does it, lass? Let me touch it."

"Keep the fuck away from me." The gun was right in his face. "You came here to kill me. You're going to break my neck. Or Arthur will give me his *shot*. Or you'll lock me up. I'll kill both of us before that happens. I'll kill everyone down there."

"Ye can't want to die so much, Valerie. Ye wouldna have saved Winnie if all you wanted was death."

She flinched when he said Winnie. "Is she all right?"

"Yeah. She's fine."

"Oh, good." She wavered, then hardened. "Why are you here?"

"Ah came to make a deal. Ah don't want to kill you and ah don't want to lock you up. Ah want you to stay inside Em'ly like you've been. Ah don't want you to hurt anyone, or kill them. Stay in the background, and ah'll do whatever you want."

A sneer covered her face. "Anything? How do you know what '*ah*' want?"

"Oh, ye'd be surprised what ah know."

She chuckled, a nasty sound. "Well, you'll know more when I'm done with you." She looked him up and down, appraising him. "And '*ah*' will know a lot about you, Sam Baahuhd. You'll do whatever I want?" Her smile was a sneer.

"Yeah. Jus' call me an' ah'll come to you. Ah'll do what ye say." He dropped his shoulders and relaxed, willing her to accept.

Holding the gun to his head, she stalked around him again. "All right. You got your deal. I'll stay in the background. I've already killed everyone worth killing. I'll call you when I want you."

"Where—" Sam started, but she'd disappeared. He found himself lying next to Emily in their bed. Sam's eyes narrowed.

He'd seen them like Valerie and Emily, a couple of people in one body. Some of them had escaped from the torture camps the feds had set up. Closest one was near the town of Jamayuh, but there were other camps around, too. Some of the prisoners got out and made it to the village. All the scars on their bodies said they'd been beat to hell. Sometimes he thought the feds had turned 'em loose. They'd got all they could from 'em. Why keep feeding a burnt-out shell? Would've been nicer just to shoot them.

Escaped or turned loose, the newcomers drifted into the village and asked to stay. If you couldn't see any scars, you'd think they were as normal as anyone. Until somethin' scared them or riled 'em up. Then they'd be screamin' and actin' like kids, or raging. Different voices than anyone had ever heard would come out of them. Or they acted like one person one minute, another person the next. They'd be screaming and clawing, scared near to death of things no one could see.

He couldn't deal with 'em. Hadn't tried to heal them. He sent them west with the next trader. That was the best he could do.

And here he was, one of 'em in his bed. What Arthur had said about Emily's life sounded like she had grown up in a torture camp. Her whole life was torture. Easy for her to turn into one of them.

He loved Emily. Beyond that, she was the only woman in the underground he could claim for a wife.

When he woke up, he had his arms around her. He brushed her hair with his hand. She raised her head and looked at him.

The expression in her eyes was just a little bit sharper than before, a little bit more aggressive. He stroked her again and that hardness receded. The Emily he loved lay in his arms.

"Good morning, lass," he said, kissing her. "It's going to be all right. We'll all live together."

25

He and some of his boys found the weed Lester and them had been chewing that terrible night. Sure enough, Ronny and Lester had a whole farm going. Enough to fry the brains of everyone in the underground. Sam cleaned it out and Arthur incinerated it.

"Ah been easy on ye 'til now," Sam told the villagers. "If ah find any more weed, ah will kill whoever's behind it."

After that, one thing after another got handled. He and Emily reached an agreement on what she'd wear to the gym. She spent hours there every day, working out and teaching classes. She invited him to see what they were doing.

"Come in, Sam," she said, throwing the gym door open. Emily wore a short skirt and a little jacket over her leotard—mildly scandalous, but no longer over the line.

Kids filled the gym. Teenagers. None of the adults wanted to be in the same room with her. Boys *and* girls wore Russian army uniforms with cutoff legs and arms. "This is just for in here, Sam. They have to be comfortable to work out and able to move to work out.

"The first thing we do is warm up." The exercise machines had been moved away from the wall in order to create a small track around the outside.

"First we walk, then we jog."

The kids demonstrated by walking around the track in pairs. They loved her, he could tell, hanging on her words and copying everything she did. These were the brave youngsters not scared off by what they'd heard about her killing people, and those who didn't think she was a witch.

She ran him through the whole routine, ending at a wooden bench with a heavy metal stand at one end, bearing a long barbell. "This is a bench," Em said. "You do this with it. It's called bench-pressing." After putting heavier weights on each end of the rod, Emily lay down on the bench and grabbed the bar above her. "Spotters!" Two of the bigger boys moved, one to each end. "Never do anything without spotters. I'm not warmed up, so this is a demo only."

She lifted the barbell off the stand, held it above herself with straight arms, and then slowly lowered it to her chest, finally returning it to the stand. "Add some more weight," she said. They repeated the process until Sam reckoned she was lifting more than her weight. Emily wiped the sweat off her face with a towel, then looked at him expectantly. All the kids had the same look on their faces.

"You want *me* to do that?" he said, surprised.

"There has been some discussion of how much you could lift, Sam. But don't feel pressured. You're not warmed up or trained."

They couldn't have motivated him more with a gun to his head. Everyone in the underground would know how he'd done—or *if* he'd done it at all—the instant the kids left the room.

"Ah'll try 'er," he said, taking off his shirt. Couldn't stand sweating on a clean shirt. The kids' eyes widened when they saw his torso. They stepped back. Sam chuckled. "Ye shoulda seen me when ah was a young buck," he said. "Then ah was a sight."

After giving him more instructions than he could remember, Emily had him lie on the bench. She corrected everything about his position. "We'll increase the weights as you lift them. *Don't* try your hardest. You're not ready."

It was very much like handling bales of hay. They used to play with them in the old days. "Here, Ru, catch this." He'd throw a hundred-pound bale to Ru with one hand and another to Del with the other. They'd also tossed clay bricks for hours. He and Ru and a couple of the others could build an adobe fence five-feet high and two hundred feet long in a day. Or lift bales of hay into the loft, hauling on a pulley for twelve hours straight. Bench-pressing wasn't any harder.

They kept adding weights and he kept lifting them. He grinned and said, "You want me to lift this ten times?" He wasn't grinning by the end. Sweat covered him and his muscles shook. "Put more on," he grunted.

"No. That's it." Emily cut the exhibition. "Three hundred and eighty pounds! Why did I let you keep going?" She fussed at him all the way home, but he knew the kids would have something to report to their parents. Sam Baahuhd could still take any of them.

The pain in his muscles the next day wasn't so bad. He could get out of bed, if he went slowly. He stumbled around while Emily clucked over him. "I should have stopped you, Sam. You were showing off." And she had been letting him, he knew.

"I'll be OK. Go see Winnie."

Em and Winnie were turning into best friends, giggling like girls. Em did up Winnie's hair so she looked like she was from New York City. And she shared the lady's clothes with her, showing Winnie how to make them fit.

Winnie would have been a beauty, but for her face. The beating Lester and Ronny had given her had spoiled her looks. If he'd been able to heal her, Sam could have fixed the damage. Arthur knew how to bandage and stitch, but he didn't know how to set bones. They'd broken her nose, and smashed her cheek and jaw. Knocked out a couple of teeth. It made Sam sick to see what they had done to her. He was glad that she and Emily had hit it off. At least Winnie had a friend.

"I'm here," he called, walking in the door to their room at the end of the day. This was the best time. Emily jumped him, plastering herself against him.

"I'm glad you're home. Come here."

She had him down on the bed before he could object, straddling him and laughing. "Look! Do you like it! I found it today." She pulled back so he could see what she was wearing. It was a dress that looked like it was made of three handkerchiefs and a button. "It's an Aldo D'Giovanni! Almost the latest collection. Don't you love it?"

He did love it. Especially the button.

26

"Going! Going! Gone! A home run by Sam Baahuhd of the village Sledgehammers!" Arthur made the call as Sam jogged around the bases. "Ewan! Jude! Go out in the fields and find the ball. But don't mess up the plants.

"Sam, we've got to stop playing baseball in the hall," Arthur said. "You hit too many into the fields. And I'm worried about breaking the light fixtures."

Sam bent over and put his hands on his knees, catching his breath. "If you say so, Art. But baseball sure is fun." The new games Art had introduced had transformed life underground.

"I've got a new idea: we'll play basketball. You guys are certainly tall enough for it. The ball won't go out of the hall. We'll get some hoops set up. We can play tomorrow."

Sam walked back to his team. They gave him the high five Jeremy had shown him and a chorus of encouragement: "Hey, slugger Sam!" "Sam the man!" "Go Sam!"

"Ye sure are a hitter, Sam. Best hitter of all."

"Are ye goin' to the movie t'night, Sam? It's a western."

"Aye, sure ah will," he replied. Movies were another new feature of life underground. So was his speaking regular English when he was around Arthur and Emily, and slipping back into the old ways without thinking when he was with his own people.

Sam could hardly stop smiling these days. They'd been underground three months. The knot of whispering, plotting instigators was gone—permanently. Dead. The cooperative spirit of the villagers had never shone brighter. They seemed to have grasped the fact that they were all down there together and had better make the best of it.

The life-support systems Jeremy had created to last two thousand years were doing exactly what they were supposed to; everyone had air, water, and food. Arthur had taught him how to maintain them. He didn't know exactly how the mechanics worked, but he knew which buttons to push if there was a problem. That would hold them for a while if Arthur got sick.

The crops were coming in healthy and strong, bristling green, and alive with beans. Jeremy had gotten the crops and orchard started before he left, and everything was flourishing the way he'd planned. The solar provided them with plenty of light.

Sam liked going out to the fields and being with the plants. It was the closest he could get to his old life. They were picking the soybeans a few at a time, learning to like their taste. A big harvest was coming up soon.

Something else really good that he hadn't expected happened. He was leaving the hall when his second wife—in the old days—walked up to him. Sally said, "Sam, could ah have a word?"

He nodded, remembering the way she'd screamed at him when he'd stood in his ex-wives' doorway in their early days in the shelter, and what she'd said. He hadn't spoken to her since. They had been married when he was seventeen years old and she was fifteen. They'd had eight children. Now she avoided him.

"Ah want to say ah'm sorry for what ah said when ye come to the door in those first days. Ah was so scart and stirred up, ah blamed everythin' on ye. Mollie an' Fannie was part o' it. They was poundin' on ye fierce all the time, sayin' stuff that ah won' repeat. But ah said some bad things and ah want to say ah'm sorry."

Sam blinked, feelings coming up fast. He put his hand on her shoulder and squeezed it. They had been married for almost twenty-four years. Their oldest boy would have been almost twenty-three, but he'd been killed in the epidemic of spots, along with their Belle. "Ah'm glad to hear that, Sally. We been a lot to each other. Ah din' mean to hurt ye."

"Ah'm not taken back sayin' what a rooster ye was, because ye were, but ah know yer a good man in spite of it. Just not meant to be with one woman." Sam tried to protest, but she cut him off. "We'll see how the Commands work out for ye, Sammy me boy. Ah'm not yer wife anymore. What ye an' yer new wife do is not ma business."

Tears came to Sally's eyes. "Ah had a hard time talkin' to' ye, Sammy, because o' her. She killed our Jim Bobby, Sam. Killed our boy dead." Moisture gathered above her lower lids, but anger showed on her face. "She better be good to ye an' everyone else to make up for what she did." Rivulets of tears rolled down Sally's lined cheeks. She was still a good-looking woman, busty and round, with gray-streaked hair. Sally was thirty nine, two years younger than he was.

"Our Jim Bobby was a bad'un, Sam. Ah gotta say that. Got into the weed so young. Ah'm sorried by him bein' in that room, lyin' in wait to kill you—his own father—as much as ah am by loosin' him." Sam swept her into his arms and held her tight. She dropped her face to his chest. "Oh, Sammy, everythin' changed so fast. First ah'm yer wife, the headman's wife an' *somethin'* in the village. Now ah'm nothing, just a' old lady."

"Sally, ye'll always be somethin' to me. A good friend. Someone ah trust. D'ye and the kids have enough room? D'ye have furniture an' beds?" They had five children still living. The boys, Sam Rupert and Chad, both almost twenty. And the girls, Meg, Millie, and Sadie, teenagers.

"Ah could use a room for the boys. They're big an' full o' shit and nonsense." Sally and Sam smiled. "An we could use some beds and stuff."

"Ah'll see that Art'ur gets ye what ye need." He gazed into her eyes, feeling sad.

"Now don't get mopey on me, Sam. We're alive. We got food. Ah'll take care of the kids an' see 'em grown right. And ah'm takin' care of the baby."

Sam didn't know what she was talking about.

"Billie Sam. Yer baby with Fannie, only three months old when we come down here. Your woman didn't kill him, just Fannie and her other three. An' they was troublemakers, sure an' simple. Fannie was the worst."

Sam had forgotten one of his children. "Oh, Sally. Thank ye," he gasped.

"Don' worry, Sam, ah ain't gonna let a babe starve, even if he's a son of a she-devil. He's yours, too." She laughed heartily. "Ah can see ye fergot the lil' shit. It's OK. Ah didn't."

"Oh, Sally, if ye need anything, anything at all, come to me. Ye got ma help an' ma heart."

"Well, ah may do that, Sam. Ye never know." The wrinkles on her round face made her seem even softer and warmer than she'd been when she was young. "An if ye need somethin', ye ask me." She wasn't referring to sex, either, he could tell. She smiled at his expression. "Ah know ye mean to keep yer Commands, but if ye need help on anythin', come to me."

They hugged each other quite a while, enough for people in the hall to notice. "We better leave off, Sally."

"Oh, ah know how you are, Sam Baahuhd. Ah won't tempt ye away from yer terrifyin' lady. Ah was just takin' a nip."

"Sally, if ye meet someone . . ."

"Ah've been wife to ye, Sam Baahuhd. That's enough for one lifetime."

When they parted, they were laughing. Their years together had been good. He'd make sure Sally was well taken care of.

27

Sam strode down the VIP corridor heading for the fields, swinging his arms and smiling. Five months had passed and life in the underground felt bearable, even normal.

"Foul ball!" shouted Jude. Ewan had swung and tipped the ball, which shot into the air, bounced off the ceiling, rebounded to the other side of the corridor, and hit Sam's knee. Ewan and Jude were playing baseball in the corridor outside the room Arthur had set up for them and their mother.

"Hey, you two! Stop 'er right now. If ye canna play baseball in the hall, ye canna play 'er in the corridor!"

At the sound of his voice, the boys stopped as though they had been cast in stone. They turned to him.

"Yes, Da. What would ye like us to do?"

He'd never seen teenagers respond like that. "Drop down and do ten push-ups like Em'ly showed you."

They did it instantly. "Now shake hands." Immediate compliance.

His Voice had come back! What about his Power?

"Kids, is your ma at home?" They nodded.

"Winnie, it's Sam. Could ye open the door?" She did and peeked out. Sam could see in the room. It was bare, except for mats where they slept. "Ye don't have nothin', Winnie. Why didn't ye tell me? Ah got extra tucked away. Talk to Em'ly about it. She'll fix ye up.

"Do ye mind if ah touch your face for a bit?" He put his hands on Winnie's face, gently molding her nose, pulling the indented cheekbone out, and smoothing her jawline. Sam wiped away the scars and then placed the palm of his hand on the side of her mouth, humming for a few seconds. "OK. Ah think ah got 'er. What do you think, boys?"

"Ma! Da fixed yer face!"

"Yer beautiful, Ma!"

"Do ye have a looking glass, Winnie? Ye might want to take a peek." Sam was overjoyed.

Winnie ran her tongue over her teeth. "Lord ha' mercy! Ma teeth're back!"

"Ah got the Voice and the Power back. Ah'm the man ah used to be!" Sam crowed.

"Nah, Sam. Y're a better man than ye used to be," Winnie corrected.

"Em, do ye want to go out in the hall?" he asked that night. "Ah got ma Power back an' can protect ye." His Power really didn't matter that much, since everyone in the village was aware of what she could do by herself. She was an object of terror and hatred. But he wanted the village to accept her, and his Power could ensure that.

"Yes, Sam! I'm so bored I could die. I'd like to start teaching reading. And go to the fields. Everything!"

So he brought her out the next day.

"How do, everybody! This is ma wife, Em'ly. Ah'd like to introduce her to ye. An' one other thing. Ye's to fergit anythin' bad ye mighta heard about her. She's nice as pie." Sam stood in the main hall, holding Emily's hand. The people clapped and cheered with no hint of animosity over what she'd done, or even remembrance of it.

"Good t' know ya, lass! Welcome to the village! Good wishes, Em'ly."

His Voice worked. Would it be strong enough to suppress memories of a massacre—permanently?

28

Mist rose from the ground and around the edges of the big flat area where Sam stood. Everything was white and bright and empty. The glare made his eyes pucker up. He felt as if he were in the meadow by the big house back in the old days, though little in the scene indicated that. Dead tree branches stuck out of the fog in a ring around the pasture, the only reminder that life had once existed there.

Sam walked toward the center. When he had made the deal with Valerie, he had told her he would come when she called him. He'd awakened next to Emily, knowing Valerie was calling. He didn't know how to get to her, but he closed his eyes. The next thing he knew, he was in this white world, and naked.

He turned around, trying to spot her in the fog.

She was not twenty feet away, her pistol held in both her hands and pointed at him. She looked the way she had the first time he'd seen her. She was wearing a short black skirt and jacket, covered with muck and filth, stinking from having been in the river. Soft white flesh showed in the opening of her jacket. She wasn't wearing anything under it.

"Ye don't need the gun, lass. Ah'll take care o' ye." He stood still, shoulders down, relaxed. This seemed like a replay of what happened before the atomics went off. He'd talked her down and brought her into the shelter.

"Shut up, you imbecile." Her lips curled. Bright red lipstick framed white teeth. "Get over here." She jerked her head. "*Now*, asshole." He didn't move.

She switched the gun into one hand, holding it parallel with the ground like a real shooter. She yanked up her skirt with the free hand and shoved her hips forward. "I want you on your knees. Now!"

He recoiled, revolted. When he didn't move, she unleashed a stream of profanity. Red lips spitting out words. Her eyes flashing. She seemed to be searching for the most insulting thing she could say. "You don't even know how to *read*, do you? Stupid!"

Sam lunged toward her. The pistol flared. She nailed him three times in the chest. He felt the bullets' impact and saw his blood explode all over her. He fell backward, feeling himself dissolve into the white.

She was on top of him. He never saw the knife; it was just a flash in her hand.

The blade entered the meat of his shoulder above his collarbone, stabbing all the way through. She yanked the knife out and raised it again. Blood spurted from the hole. She'd hit an artery.

He grabbed her wrist, crushing it. She dropped the knife. Her breath came fast, lips drawing back from her teeth, trying to bite.

His other hand shot out, seizing her throat. He tightened his grip. She fought, throwing her body from side to side, eyes flashing in desperation. He'd cut off her air.

"Stop," he said in the Voice. "Get off an' help me. Help me now." Blood spurted from his neck and chest. He was blown wide open. Why wasn't he dead? No need asking; he would be soon enough if he didn't stop the bleeding.

"Gimme yer jacket. Press it here. Press." She shoved the jacket into the wound on his shoulder, stanching the flow. His chest kept gushing.

His face stiffened and his mouth curved in anguish. "Oh, Gawd a' mighty, ye hurt me." His hand was covered with blood up to the wrist. His chest was a gaping hole. He could see his heart beating. "Power, come to me now. Ah need ya."

Sam hummed, healing himself. He worked as hard as he ever had.

The blood flow slowed. Became a trickle. Stopped.

"Lie over there," he ordered her. "Don' move. Don' say a foocking thing." He sat up, breathing hard. She rolled over as directed and glared at him, crazy eyes flashing. The blood and violence had excited her. He examined himself. His shoulder was fine. Didn't hurt. And the cavern blown in his chest was healed.

"Ye better be glad ah can heal maself, ye stinking cunnie. Did ye think ye'd kill me like them ye tortured an' murdered for the feds? Don' work that way in the village, lass."

He stood up and looked down on her. She struggled, but couldn't move. He laughed.

"Ye look like ye got a sack full o' cats an' dogs inside yer skin, biddie. Fightin' each other with no room to move. Ye can't fight the Voice. Not *my* Voice. An' ye can't beat ma Power. Ye made a mistake with me, ye filthy shinny."

Fury arose in him. His hands made fists. He wanted to use them. "Ye wanted to kill me? Yer life would take a turn for the worse if ah was daid. Know what would happen?" He shoved his face into hers.

"Art'ur would come for ye. He don't like ye much, an' ah can't say ah don't agree with him." Sam made a gesture like depressing a syringe. "He's got a shot that would kill you faster than that." He snapped his fingers. "That's what he wanted to do with ye in the beginning. An' ah'm na sure he weren't right.

"But think of it, cunnie. What if ye got past Art'ur, an' Rupert got ye? He'd be the headman with me daid. Know what he'd do?"

Sam squatted and spit his words at her. "Ye ain't no one's cousin. The Commands don't apply to you. Rupert would throw you out in the hall. Ye know what that would mean?" He could barely restrain himself from slugging her, but his words seemed to be doing the trick well enough.

"Art'ur counted out all of us, right an' proper. There's twenty-nine men in the hall. All twenty-nine of them strong, rum bulls would foock ye until you didn't have skin between yer legs. They'd breed ye, year after year, an' ye'd have nuthin' to say about 'er."

Her eyes were wide with terror now.

"So be glad ye didn't kill me. Ah'm what's keeping you from bein' a pincushion." He wanted to slap her so badly. Slap her silly. Slap her black and blue.

"Ah'm not gonn' use my hands on you. But, if you try to hurt me again, ah will break your neck."

He stood up, practically leaping to his feet. "Ma kind feelin's for Emily irregardless, ah will tear ye to bits if ye try to hurt me again." His temper got away from him and he screamed, pacing in front of her. Her wide eyes said she got his message.

"An' never, *ever* say ah'm stupid. None that has lived as long as me and fought as hard is stupid.

"AH WILL NOT HAVE ANY *BITCH* from *NEW YORK CITY*"—he wagged his head from side to side as he screamed the words—"COMIN' TO *MA* HOME AN' TELLIN' *ME* OR ANY O' *MINE* THAT WE'RE STUPID. The Egertons done enough o' that.

"So lie there, cunnie, an' think about what ah said. Yer here because ah like the other one of ye. That is all that's keepin' you alive. Lie there an' go to sleep."

He lay down, then rolled over on his side, his back to her. Not touching her, not saying anything. He couldn't sleep. She'd shot him point-blank. Why he wasn't he dead? What was this place? Was it some magic place where she could kill again and again?

Sam didn't pay any attention to her. Nor did he pay her any mind when he heard her weep.

He woke up in his bed next to Emily. She was sitting up, clutching her gown to her chest, white and scared silly.

"What's wrong, lass?"

"Oh, Sam, I had the worst nightmare I've ever had."

"What was it about?"

"I can't remember."

29

"I don't feel very well, Sam," Emily said. "I have horrible dreams, and, during the day, I feel like something terrible is going to happen. I can't do my plans for the reading lessons."

He gave her a hug. "Don' worry, darlin', ye'll feel better soon." That night, as a matter of fact. He had wanted to teach Valerie a lesson, so he had ignored her shrieks for two days. She would lie in the white world unable to move until he felt like setting her free.

She had screamed night and day. He could hear her in his mind, hollering her lungs out. The cries went from rage to panic and terror, down to whimpering. He liked the progression. He wanted to break her, and it sounded as if he had.

He'd never tried to heal one of those people who were two-in-one, never wanted to. But he needed to now.

Was it just Valerie and Emily, or were there more? He'd seen a little girl he thought was Shira once, and he'd heard a child he knew was from the pink room. Were these children killers, too? One thing the bunch of them needed to learn was that they couldn't push him around. He'd been teaching Valerie that the last two days.

He waited until Emily was asleep, and then closed his eyes and thought about being in the white world where Valerie waited.

The mist was higher this time, up to the middle of his calves instead of hovering around his feet. The place stank like shit, but he'd expected that. He'd left her for two days. Screaming the way she had been, she undoubtedly had lost control.

Where was she? He walked toward the middle of the meadow, or whatever it was. Nothing was there but white fog. The place was silent. Not even any whimpering. Sam began to suspect something had gone wrong. He had wanted to break her, not destroy her.

"Valerie? You here?" He walked around. She definitely wasn't where she'd been. The mist was heavier on one side, as if there were a pond or a lake hidden there. Heavy vapors rose from it.

A lump stuck out of the fog. He hurried toward it. It was a red-streaked shoulder.

She looked dead. Drawn up and dried out, flesh pulled in so he could practically see her teeth through her cheeks. Worse than that were the marks all over her. Red lines sliced along her skin, pairs of lines, with circles carved in between. One eye was swollen shut and her face was marked and bloody.

He bent down and touched her. She didn't respond. "Oh, Valerie, ah'm sorry." He didn't know what had gotten her. The place had seemed safe before. He rubbed her upper arm lightly, healing the sores as well as he could. He couldn't heal dead people and she was pretty close to that. "Ah didn't mean for this to happen, Valerie."

Her throat fluttered. She opened sunken eyes and stared at him without emotion. "Monsters," she whispered, her voice a barely audible rasp.

"What?" He leaned closer to her. A big hunting knife appeared out of nowhere and floated over her body, circling at a leisurely pace. Nothing was holding it up; it just floated there. A pistol hovered a little farther away, a black one, fancier than any he'd seen. Something the feds would have. The pistol disappeared, and a rifle began circling over her feet.

"What is that, Valerie?" he said.

"Nothing. They won't hurt . . ." Something rose out of the mist, a delicate feeler, homing in on her. "No! No!" She screamed with her ruined throat, and then she gasped with hoarse cries.

The tentacle, like a mottled green snake without a head, wrapped itself around her leg three times, almost faster than Sam could see. It began to drag her toward the lake. She shrieked, but she couldn't move to fight it.

Sam grabbed the big knife floating above her and hacked the snake off where it cleared the vapor. The rest of it remained coiled around her leg, pulsing. Blood dripped where it touched her flesh. "Oh, it hurts! It hurts!"

Grabbing one end, he unwrapped the tentacle, throwing it away. It disappeared into the mist, but not before he had seen its underside. It had little round mouths down the middle and cutting edges on each side. She'd been attacked by that thing for two days.

"Valerie, ye can move now," he said in the Voice, removing his control of her. But she didn't move, just dragged in ragged breaths. She didn't try to lift a hand or look at him. Or talk.

"Don't let him get me," she said eventually.

"Who?"

"He lives in the lake."

Sam now could see dozens of flexible limbs rising out of the lagoon, making its surface boil. "What is it?"

"It's him." Her mouth fell open. She crossed her arms over her chest, trying to shield herself. "Don't let him get me, please. Please." Her tone almost crushed him. It was the pleading of a child who knew help would never come, a child with no rights and no expectation of kindness. "Please. Kill me."

And then she was begging him to kill her, over and over. "Kill me. Please kill me."

Sam picked her up and ran.

They were in his bathroom. He held her in his arms and she hung limply, still begging him to kill her. "I'm no good. Kill me. Please. I want to die. Break my neck." Her dull eyes said she didn't believe she deserved even that much mercy.

"Ah'm gonna take ye in the shower, Valerie, an' clean ye' off." He stripped her of her filthy skirt and stepped into the enclosure, not knowing how he'd be able to bathe her in the one minute of water the appliance would deliver.

But the water kept flowing. He wiped it out of his eyes. This was some magic place, not a real place. It had to be something like that misty pasture. What reality did she live in?

He got her cleaned and went to work on her wounds. He could heal her now, and he did. When her skin was soft and clear, he dried her off.

"Valerie, what would ye like to do now? Would ye like to go to sleep in ma bed?"

She looked at him, uncomprehending.

"Ye can, if ye want."

She gave the tiniest gesture of assent. He carried her into his room, half expecting to see Emily sprawled in the bed.

It was empty.

He put Valerie down and lay down next to her. She curled up facing him, not touching him. He reached out and stroked her shoulder.

"How is it for ye, Valerie?" He'd been trying to figure out what had happened. "D' ye have to fight the monster all the time?"

She nodded.

"Ye have to have weapons an' ye have to be rough."

Another nod.

"Because if ye aren't, he'll get ye."

"Yes!" She gasped, curling into a tighter ball.

"When ah made ye lie still, he could come. Ye couldn't fight him, so he hurt ye."

She nodded.

"Valerie, is it like that for ye, with a man? Ye have to fight him or he'll hurt ye?"

Her chin dropped a tiny bit. Her eyes looked huge. She nodded.

"Have ye ever been with a man when it was nice, Valerie? When you were gentle and he made you feel the way ye always wanted t' feel?"

She shook her head. "No. Don't tell anyone."

"Or what will happen?"

She couldn't speak.

"If a man sees ye soft, he'll do what your father did to ye."

She held her lips together, and didn't cry out. He put an arm around her shoulders. She went rigid.

"Ye have to be tough and mean, or ye'll get hurt. That's why ye were that way with me."

He felt rather than heard her say yes.

"Ah'm not going to touch ye, Valerie. Not now, maybe never." He brushed the top of her head with his lips. "Let's just sleep now."

"I remember you," she said, lying next to Sam in the dark. "I was in a field. I had a gun. I was going to shoot you. I would have, but you talked me out of it. You took the gun, and then I was in your arms. That was the most wonderful thing that ever happened to me."

They were talking in the middle of the night. She had awakened abruptly and started talking. "I can remember lots of things. You picked me up and carried me into the house, and then down the stairs.

"Then I was here, in our room. I took a shower. The end of the world showed up on the screen. And then I got very sick." She spoke quickly, as though she might forget.

"I woke up in a hospital. I was so scared. I was tied down. And then you came. You got in bed with me and held me. Do you remember that?"

"Aye, lass. Ah remember." She could remember everything Emily couldn't. "Can ye remember before the meadow? Can ye remember when ye were little?"

She nodded, averting her eyes. "Yes. I remember everything. What happened to me and what I did. My sister, Pearl. All of it."

"Ye remember what Em'ly can't?"

"I make sure she doesn't remember. That's my job."

"Ye keep her from rememberin'?"

"Yes. I protect her." Valerie's expression softened the tiniest bit, as though she could see Emily dancing in her mind's eye. "She's happy because of me." Her jaw tightened. "I keep them from knowing. I don't let any of them get hurt."

"Ye did what ye did for the feds to protect Em'ly? An' in th' army?" Sam heard the "them," but sensed that he'd better not mention it.

"I had to do what I did so we could live. I've killed so many people to keep us safe." She stated at him, her eyes too intense, too focused. "And I did it because I like to kill. I'm sick." She didn't blink. "You should kill me."

"Ah will kill ye if ah need to, Valerie. If ye try to hurt me or anyone again, ah'll kill ye."

"I didn't want to hurt you."

"Why did ye shoot me?"

"Because it's what I do." He started to object. "And because I knew where we were isn't real."

"Ye couldn't kill me there?"

"I didn't think so. But I didn't think the monsters were there, either. I didn't mean to hurt you. I thought we would..." She shrugged significantly.

"Tha's how ye start off?" She nodded. He jerked back, exhaling hard. "Not any more, girl. But le' me see if ah'm gettin' what ye're sayin'. Ye did wha' ye did before ye came here to protect Em'ly."

"Yes. I make sure she's safe."

Sam nodded, trying to absorb the implications of what she was saying. "An' ye shot me because ye wanted me?"

She looked down and didn't move.

"Well, whatever y' were doin', ye hurt me bad, an' that's true. Tha' will ne'er happen again. Ye seem to have one bad thing after another floatin' around ye. Like those guns and the knife."

"They come when I'm in the white place, but not when I'm out."

"Ye've been there before?"

"Yes, but not when I couldn't move. Usually it's nice. I go there when . . . she's with you."

"Em'ly."

"Yes. When you're alone."

"Ye know what we do?"

He could feel her skin heat up as she blushed. "I know what you're doing. But I'm not there."

"That's OK with ye?"

"I want her to be happy."

"Well, ye've given me a lot to think on, lass."

"Sam. There's something else."

"What lass?"

"I love you. I've loved you since I first saw you. You saved me. You brought me down here and kept Arthur from killing me. I've never loved anyone the way I love you.

"I'll protect you from *anything*." He could hear the breath going in and out of her hard, and almost see her sharp teeth in the dark. "I'd die for you, Sam. And anyone—*anyone*—who tries to hurt you is *dead*." She grabbed his arm, fingers digging in. "I'll *kill* them. *Anyone* who comes near you."

He exhaled hard. She was like a coiled up panther in his bed.

30

"How're ye feelin' today, lass?" He didn't really need to ask. Emily sat at the computer, printing out things for her reading class, practically chirping. If he and Valerie had anything in common, it was wanting to see Emily happy. She was. The reading lessons she'd given him privately were so much more fun than Arthur's terrible classes that he'd made her teacher for the whole village. Today was her first day. Arthur was delighted, and so was she.

When Emily had given him lessons, she had made cards with pictures on them and, whatever the picture was, spelled out below it. She called them "flash cards."

"What is this, Sam?" she'd ask, pointing to a picture.

"A dog."

"These letters say 'dog.' Remember the shapes of the letters."

He could remember what a whole word looked like, instead of sounding out letters and thinking about upper and lower case and what vowels and consonants might be.

She'd show him a bunch of cards, and then turn them over. Just the word was on the back. He'd had to read the words and tell her what they were. He could do it, easily. She added more cards every day and made them harder. She made cards about things he needed to know. The names of the controls for the underground's systems. Where dials should be if everything was fine. He was reading and learning, faster than he thought possible.

"What're ye doin' for today, lass?"

"You'll see."

She stood in front of the village, wearing a skirt just above her knees. It wasn't tight, but it wasn't loose either. She had a silk blouse on and shoes with low heels. Sam thought her dress was just short of shocking, but she told him that that was what teachers wore. Sam decided he'd stick close in case she caused a riot. She started talking as if she had taught all her life.

"You know me; I'm Emily Baahuhd. I'll be teaching you to read from now on. How would you like to be reading by the end of today's class?"

The villagers nodded enthusiastically. Sam smiled. Their mood was a combination of relief that Arthur was no longer teaching and an anxious desire to please her. Despite what he'd done with his Voice, everyone still had a feeling she was responsible for some terrible thing. And no one could ignore that almost a third of the village's population was missing.

"What's your name?" She walked up to one of Rupert's sons.

"Ah'm Harley. Harley Baahuhd." He looked away from her, embarrassed by her visible knees and the fact that she was talking to him without being addressed first.

"OK." She had some little squares of paper and a thick black pen. She wrote on the paper, then handed it to Harley. "That's your name. Harley Baahuhd. Keep looking at the letters. You can trace them with your finger, or, better, go over there, get a tablet and pen, and copy them." She went on to the next person and the next.

People got restless after a while. "Shh!" she said. "Keep tracing your names. We're going to do something with this. And, if you don't like this, remember that Arthur can always come back. He doesn't have to work on the computers."

The hall was again silent as people copied their names.

"OK. Now form into groups of five. This many." She held up her hand. "Make a circle. You know what your own name looks like. Now hand your name tag to the person to your left. That's right, all around the circle. That's his name, or her name. Look at the person and the writing on the card. Say, 'You're Winnie Baahuhd,' or whoever is next to you. Look at the person's name tag and trace the letters."

She had them work like that until the whole group could recognize the names of everyone else. "See. You're reading. You can read your name and everyone in your group's name. Do you want to try a larger group, or call it quits?"

They looked around, uncertain. "How big a group?" someone asked.

"I thought we could do groups of ten, but all new people."

Sam could feel them balking.

And so could Emily. "Let's do something else. These name tags are sticky on the back. Peel off the back"—she demonstrated with her own—"and stick the tag here." She stuck the tag to her blouse. "Wear your tag all the time. When you're walking around, look at other people's tags. You can take your tablets and copy the letters.

"Tomorrow, I'll have a prize for the person who can read the most tags and match them to the right person. OK? No big deal if you don't get it right away. This is just a game."

Sam hugged her when they got out of sight in the VIP corridor. "Perfect, lass. Got 'em thinkin', but it's not too hard." He slapped his name tag on his chest and headed back into the hall.

"Where are you going, Sam?"

"Ah'm gonna learn as many names as ah can. Ah wanna earn that prize."

"Great! Tomorrow we're going to start learning proper English, too."

The days fell into a rhythm. Sam was learning so much and the people were so happy, that Emily could have been just a very smart, beautiful woman he loved. He'd almost forgotten about the "them" that Valerie had mentioned. She'd been so quiet, she might have disappeared. Six months had passed and everything was turning out right.

31

Valerie was wearing her black suit, neat and clean this time. She had a white blouse under the suit. Her hair seemed shinier and cut sharper than before. She paced, chewing on the sides of her fingers, shooting fast glances out of the corners of her eyes. A hunting knife almost a foot long floated lazily behind her. A pistol made a leisurely circuit around her. He stepped inside its circle.

He wore the canvas pants and rough shirt he'd worn in the village, but they were clean and didn't have bugs. After the black uniform he'd been wearing, his old clothes felt stranger than the whiteness and the mist, yet comfortable.

"Ye wanted me, Valerie?"

"Yes." She turned her back on him.

"Ah'm here."

She turned toward him, then away. "I'm sorry. I shouldn't have said what I did."

He thought she was talking about telling him to get on his knees. "Ye shouldna have shot me, neither."

"No. I meant the last time we talked. I shouldn't have told you I loved you."

Sam's brows knit. "What?"

"I didn't mean it. Don't pay any attention to what I said."

"Ye called me here to tell me that?"

"Yes." The sides of her fingers were bleeding where she'd bitten them. "Forget what I said."

He studied her, considering. "Lass, have ye ever told anyone that ye loved them?"

She averted her head. "My sisters," she whispered.

"And?"

"My father . . ." Her voice dropped lower. "He made me say it. I didn't want to." She turned and walked away, heading into the mist.

He ran after her. The knife and pistol that had been moving so dreamily now spun toward him. More guns appeared, all aimed at him.

"Stop!" she said. "Stay away from me."

"Talk to me, lass. Yer bothered."

She tossed her head. "Yes, I'm bothered. I don't need anyone. I don't need you." She walked away again.

"Ye called me here to tell me ye don't need me."

"Yes." Flashing eyes.

"Valerie, stop." He used the Voice. "Turn to me." She turned to face him.

"What do ye want, lass? Do ye want me to hold ye?"

Her chest trembled as she pulled in a breath. Her nod was barely perceptible.

"Ah'll tell ye what we'll do. Ah'm tired. Ah want to lie down. We'll lie together, not doin' nothin', just restin'. Don' mean nothin' anyway, not that we like each other. Where do ye sleep, lass?"

She took him to an area defined by mist. "Here. It's quiet here. There's a bed."

He lay down. She lay next to him, stiffly. A few shots of the Voice, and she cuddled next to him, head on his shoulder.

"See, this is nice." He stroked her hair. She didn't object. "Yer hair is soft. Shines pretty. Now, go to sleep."

She did, and he commenced to heal her.

He visited her like that six or seven times. She'd lie on his shoulder and go to sleep. He'd go inside her mind and pull out the snarls and try to get them straight. He went through her whole life as though it were his.

She guarded herself, even in the deep places he visited. He got no hint of the "them" she'd mentioned. Not even a glimpse of Emily. Valerie could have been just one person, except he knew she wasn't.

Her life had been pretty much the way Arthur had outlined, but living it through her mind and feeling it in his body were much worse than he had imagined. He felt sick after their sessions and had to heal himself.

Every time he came back, she was a little brighter, a little happier. Smiling more. And she was more embarrassed.

He knew everything about her. Everything about her and the man who had adopted her. What had happened in the army. How many men she'd been with and when and why. Many, many men. More than he wanted to know about. She'd done everything a woman could with a man and had gotten very little pleasure from it.

Emily had been right when they had first got together. She had said she didn't feel anything, and she didn't come.

The reason was curled up on his shoulder. Did Valerie think she had to do all that? Or always say yes? She had been as aggressive and hard with her men as she was the rest of the time. Did she do it to show off or was that all she could do?

Even with what he was finding out about her, she was a little softer every time he visited her. She let him stroke her shoulder or hold her hand. Everything about her changed as she healed, including her clothes and the way she looked. She'd meet his eyes. She was coming around.

"Hello," she said softly, looking down, when he arrived this time. They were alone in the meadow. The floating guns and knives had thinned out during the course of his visits, and then disappeared. A warm breeze ruffled the mist. She wore a pretty summer dress such as the lady might have worn. It had a wide lace collar and was printed with little flowers. It opened in front, crossing over and closing with two buttons. She looked strum pretty. More than that. Kind of like a fawn. New and shy.

"Hello, lass. Ye wanted to see me?" He wore his canvas britches and clothes from the old village. He felt like himself.

"Yes."

"What was it?"

She was silent, her lips closed tightly.

"Ah can't know what it is unless ye tell me."

She fidgeted and seemed to stop breathing.

"Tell me, lass."

"A long time ago, you asked me if a man had ever made me feel the way I'd always wanted to feel." He nodded. "I was wondering if . . . you could make me feel like that sometime. Not tonight . . ."

"Ah can do that."

"But not tonight."

It took two more visits.

"Ye want me to love ye?" He was surprised the way his gut jumped toward her.

She nodded. "Yes. But you have to stop if I want to."

"Ah can do that."

She led him to her bed and stood awkwardly.

"Ye need to shed yer clothes, lass. 'Tis the way it's done. Go ahead. Ah won't look." He turned away from her and shucked off his own clothes.

"OK." She was lying on her back, arms crossed over her chest and her knees pulled up. Her eyes looked like brown coals, burning him. Her skin glowed against the mist. He was surprised the way he reacted to her fair skin. Kind of a jolt inside. It was as if she weren't Emily. He hadn't expected that.

"Now, lass, the way we'll do this is, ye lie on yer side. Ah'll lie behind ye and pet ye. Can ye do that?" The question didn't mean much; he asked her in the Voice. She didn't have any choice. The minute he touched her, he knew this wasn't going to end until he got what he wanted. She thrilled him.

"OK. Ah'm gonna pet ye." He cupped her body with his and fit his face into the curve of her shoulder. "Just like this." He stroked her, his hand moving softly from her shoulder, down her upper arm and forearm, ending at her hand. "Like this . . ." The strokes remained soft and light, and he murmured the words of the village. "That's a nice lass. A strum fair an' fine darlin.'" All in the Voice. She would have been gone in a minute if he hadn't used it.

His hand made a longer sweep, moving from her arm to the point of her hip and down her thigh. "Jus' like that, lass." She was relaxing. He could feel her muscles letting go, and her mind unwinding. He felt dizzy and a little drunk. She was taking him with her into bliss. He kept his strokes long and light. His hand dipped to her belly, caressing its full length.

"My ears are ringing." She'd started breathing longer and harder. "I feel dizzy. What is it?"

"It's jus' us, girl. We're lovin' each other. All's fine, chitlin.'" And he kept on stroking, his own thoughts slowing down. She was intoxicating him. His hand kept moving.

"That feels so good." She moved her body against him, and then jerked away when she felt him stiff against her back.

"Don' mean nuthin', darlin'. It's jus' there. Ah don't have to do nuthin' with it."

She barely moved, almost paralyzed by the pleasure. He'd known that's what would happen. Every woman he'd been with had reacted the same way. But he hadn't reckoned on her effect on him. He was already in love with Emily. He loved everything about her.

The feel of her skin, her smell. The way she moved. The way she rubbed on him.

Valerie was almost the same to touch. She seemed a bit thinner. Harder. More electric. He raised his hand to her chest. Her titties were . . . no, her breasts. Emily had told him that's what they should be called. Her breasts seemed harder than Emily's, tense like the rest of Valerie. He fondled them, feeling the firm mounds.

He bent over her, chest rising and falling.

"Darlin', it's time. Lie over on your back."

She did, looking at him with eyes so wide he was surprised they didn't pop out. Her legs were stretched flat and her hands were crossed on her belly. He looked at her carefully, riveted. She was beautiful. Like Emily, but not exactly. Naming the difference was hard, but she wasn't Emily.

His hand moved up her belly and around her breasts. The ends stood up hard and long. He pulled them a little and rolled them between his fingers. "Yer a beauty, lass." He started stroking her again. Her head lolled to the side and her legs parted.

"Oh, Sam." She seemed pained as much as anything, and scared. "Sam."

"It's all right, lass." A harder jolt of the Voice. He leaned over her and began kissing her. First her mouth, and then her breasts, getting to know them and how they reacted to his touch. Her back arched and she made a little cry.

He kissed down her belly, positioning himself between her legs. When he reached the lower end of her body, he lingered there, parting her, and then nuzzling and kissing. Taking his time. As long as she needed. She moaned and threw her head back, but didn't turn over. She was stuck, frozen in her past.

Sam put his finger inside her, found her spot and rubbed it, putting the Power behind it.

Her hips flew up and then began jolting. Her whole body convulsed, and kept convulsing. He used the Power to keep her going. She thrashed, hands grasping his head.

"Oh, Sam. Oh, oh." Then she was moaning. And crying. Whimpering when he let her stop. He didn't let her stop until she ran out of juice.

The rest was easy. He just did what he wanted.

"Well, do y' feel the way ye always wanted?" he said to her, soaked with their sweat, lying in the bed of mist. Time had stretched, or collapsed. He had mounted her again and again, not able to get enough. They'd rolled and kissed and cried out. She excited him so that he felt like a young man. "Did ah make ye feel the way ye want?"

"Oh, yes, Sam. I love you." She kissed him and kissed him again, frantically.

"Don't worry, lass. Ah'm na goin' anywhere. Ah'll be right here with ye." He didn't say he loved her. He didn't say that to many of them. Only Emily, really.

"I didn't know what it could be like." Valerie was teary and shaken. "I didn't know. Oh, Sam, I love you so much." She got up on her knees next to him and put her hands on him, trying to start things again.

"Lass, what're ye doin'? Ah'm an auld man. Ah'm not up for . . ."

But he was.

She went to work on him with her hands, her mouth. All of herself. Sam hadn't liked it when he had found out how many men she'd been with. But they had taught her tricks, tricks she was using on him. Her hands kept moving.

"Oh, sweet Jesus," he cried. "What are ye doin' to me?" Sweat burst from him. He trembled. He moaned like a lass. She kept doing those things. Things she'd learned in New York City. He'd always wanted to know city ways.

"Oh, lass." Then his speech was unintelligible.

"Do you feel like you've always wanted to, Sam? Did I make you feel good?" She lay on her side next to him, studying his face.

"Oh, lass. Ah feel mor'n that. Oh, what ye did to me." He picked up her hand and kissed her fingers. "Ah love ye, Valerie." The words slipped out like a belch; he couldn't stop them.

"Ah've loved ye since that first moment in the meadow when ye came up to me with a gun. Beat to hell, stinkin', about to die, an' ye still wanted to fight. Ah've loved ye since then." He crushed her to him. "Yer the kind for me, lass. All ma life ah thought ah loved the lady. But ah don't. Ah need ye."

She pulled away and looked at him. "Really? But I shot you."

"Yeah. An ye did what ye just did to me, too. Ye can do 'er whenever ye want. Now let's sleep."

She was passed out, sleeping on her stomach, when he left. "Ah've gotta do somethin' with Art in the mornin', lass," he whispered to her still form. "Ah'll be back soon, ah promise."

He was in his bed with Emily. Couldn't see the clock. He snuggled down, seeking oblivion.

Emily sat up the minute he hit the bed. "Sam! Thank God you're awake. You wouldn't believe the dreams I've been having. Oh, baby, I want you so much." She leapt at him, shoving him down in the bed. Shoving her tongue into his mouth. He tried to protest, but she started rubbing on him the way she did. Damned if he wasn't ready again.

"Oh, Sam . . ." They rolled the rest of the night. Emily was never one to be satisfied with just one time. And neither was he.

When blackness claimed him, he no longer had any thought of what he had to do the next day.

"Sam! Sam!" A voice came from the speaker on the wall. The doorbell's shrill tone had awakened him, then Arthur's voice brought him the rest of the way. "Sam! Are you in there? We have a meeting in the hall in ten minutes."

"Uh. Ah'll be right there. Jus' a minute. Ah'll come to yer room."

Sam staggered out of bed. Turning the light up a bit, he saw

Emily out cold on the bed. He pulled on his clothes and headed out the door.

Strangely, his legs didn't seem to work. The knees kept buckling, and he slumped against the wall. Also, he felt like laughing. A smile split his face and he couldn't make it go away. He felt so good. Fortunately, he met no one on his way to Arthur's room.

He had two wives. His laughter echoed down the corridor. And he was keeping the Commands! Smiling and chuckling, Sam weaved along. Two wives were no problem. He'd had four. Two would be easy.

He was in front of Arthur's room. Sam rang the bell. "It's me, Art. Ah'm ready." What meeting in the hall? What were they working on? He couldn't remember at all.

Arthur opened the door and Sam fell into his room. Art stared at him.

"What the hell have you been doing?" Arthur's nose wrinkled as Sam's aroma hit him. "Jesus Christ! You fucked your brains out all night!"

Sam's brows rose and the silly grin covered his face. "Yeah. Ah sure did."

"Get out of here, Sam. For Christ's sake. You can't go out in the hall like that. Go home and sleep it off."

"What's the meetin' about?"

"Don't worry. You couldn't understand it now anyway. Go home. I'll deal with it. Get out!" Art shoved him back into the hall, shaking his head.

32

A rthur typed into his computer:

Dear Diary,

Sam came to my room this morning reeking of pussy and come. Her pussy. She has a sharp smell, like a cat's. Different from any woman I've known. Got me going so my hands were shaking. And him. He smells like a bull. Like fifty men.

What am I supposed to do? I'm going crazy here. I hate it. Surrounded by idiots. And the two of them fucking night and day.

I want her. It's getting worse.

I had women whenever I wanted in New York. Anywhere in the world. But the village?

I never went near village women. They were filthy and infected and crawling with parasites. But that was then. Maybe now is different.

I can't make a play for Emily. I will not alienate Sam. I will not do that.

OK, Romero. From your gut. What do you really think of Sam? Take the first thing that comes. No editing.

Arthur sat back, the air going out of him when he realized the truth.

"If I was a woman, I'd be in love with Sam Baahuhd," he whispered. "He's everything a man should be." Arthur had seen him shot by marauders at the old estate. In agony, but tough and commanding as ever, running the attack. So brave he made heroes look weak. Sam was a warrior's warrior.

Arthur had seen how well he ran the estate. And he'd seen Sam passed-out drunk in that terrible last year, but that wasn't Sam. And now, down here, married to Emily and learning to read, he'd finally come into his own.

"If he'd had half a chance, he would have been the president of the United States. Everything would have turned out different. None of this shit would have happened," Arthur thought.

"What do you want, Romero?" he whispered, really a shadow of a whisper. "I want him to like me. I want to be his friend."

Arthur erased the screen and ran from the room. Was he in love with Sam? Or just Emily? God, he had to do something before he went crazy.

33

Sam heard the laughter of women when he opened the door to their room. He stood in the hallway formed by the backs of the armoires and listened. It sounded like it was coming from the closet.

"It's perfect! That's the one, Winnie," Emily's voice said.

"But it dinna fit . . .," Winnie answered.

"Don't worry. I'll fix it. Let me measure you."

"Em'ly, Winnie, ah'm here," he called. They giggled, caught in some mischief.

"No. Don't come in. You can't see us."

Sam smiled at that. If they were trying on the lady's clothes and were half naked, it didn't matter. He'd been married to both of them. Did they think there was something he hadn't seen?

"It's a surprise," Winnie said, the laughter leaving her voice. "Ye have to wait."

"Wait for what?" Sam was puzzled, both about having to wait and the coldness in Winnie's voice. Thinking of it, he realized now that she'd acted as if she were mad at him all the time they'd been down there, except for when he fixed her face.

"We've been invited to a party. The invitation is on the computer. Read it," Emily replied.

He went to the desk and picked up a piece of paper in the printer's catch box. He held it gingerly, as if it might bite him. He'd been taking reading lessons for almost ten months, but could he read something Art had sent? Sam tried to remember everything Emily had taught. Pick out whole words first. Try to get the sense of what the message is saying. Sound out words you don't know. Ask for help. He sighed.

He could read Arthur's name, and his own. He read Winnie's name. He knew the words "dinner," "tomorrow," "7 o'clock," and "do not tell."

"Is he invitin' us to dinner tomorrow? An' we're not s'posed to tell?"

"Yes."

The invitation irritated Sam, because it was longer than the words he'd figured out, and he wanted to know everything Art had said.

"Put the voice utility on the computer on," Emily called from the closet. "It's not cheating if you match it with the words."

The computer said the words and they were highlighted on the screen as it did so.

> *Captain Arthur Romero requests the pleasure of the company of Mr. and Mrs. Sam Baahuhd, for dinner tomorrow evening at 7 o'clock. Formal dress is optional.*
>
> **(Note that those invited are Ms. Winnie Baahuhd and Mr. and Mrs. Baahuhd. Please do not tell anyone else about the party.)**

"Why does he say it like that?" Sam asked.

"It's a formal invitation. That's how you write one."

Sam studied it, having the computer say the words again.

"Would you message him that I'd like to put it off for two weeks?

I want to go really formal and I need time to sew," Emily asked, as though it were nothing for him to send a message by computer.

His breath caught. Did she think he knew everything? He did know the words "two weeks" and "sew."

He cheated and used the voice recognition in reverse. That wasn't really cheating; learning to use the voice on the computer was difficult enough. Sam typed the message and sent it. The answer came back immediately.

"Two weeks? What's Emily going to do, weave the cloth?" was Arthur's reply. Sam read it by starting with the words he knew, and using the computer's voice to prompt him for the rest.

"Tell him he'll have to wait and see," Emily directed. Sam dutifully sent the new message to Arthur's room. The women came out of the closet wearing their everyday clothes and smiling.

"Sam, I want to make this really special. Can I use some of Mrs. Edgarton's clothes?" Emily asked.

"Aye. Ye always can."

"Not like the usual. I want to take things apart and make them fit Winnie and me. And I want to make something for you to wear. Can we borrow some of her jewels, too?"

"Yeah an' sure. Do ah get to wear a ball gown?"

"Yes."

Emily had pulled out the mirrored door of the last armoire in the row so he could stand in the middle of the room and see himself, scalp to toes. And that's what he saw. He'd taken a shower and she wouldn't let him put clothes on.

He was an ugly brute. Face beat to hell, broken nose zigzagging all over his face. Shot three times by marauders with scars to prove it. Gray-haired and old.

Emily held something out to him. "Put these on first." They were black. Some kind of short pants. "They're boxer shorts. I know the people of the village don't wear underwear, but I thought you might like to try them for tonight."

He took the garment, feeling it between his thumb and forefinger. "What is it?"

"Silk. The general must have liked silk a lot. He's got dozens of pairs of them. You can button them up to fit."

"Ah don't want to . . ."

"The pants to the suit I made you are much thinner fabric than you're used to. And they're fitted. You'll want the extra coverage."

Would you be able to see through the pants she'd made, like you could some of the lady's dresses? He put on the shorts, trying not to touch the silk. Disturbingly, it lay across his buttocks like a whisper.

"OK. Now the shirt." She had a big hanger stuck on the back of a chair. Something was hanging on it, black like the shirt Emily was putting on him. She pulled it up one arm.

"Wait a minute. Ah can put on ma own shirt."

Nonetheless, she pulled the shirt around his back and helped him with the other arm. Standing in front of him, she drew the shirtfront forward from his neck, working down to his waist. Emily carefully buttoned the garment. "There," she said, tugging on the cuffs. She stepped back and nodded, then went to get the suit.

He looked at himself in the mirror. The shirt wasn't tight—he could move easily—but it followed the contours of his body. He ran his hand down his chest. It was silk like the shorts, but heavier. Its collar didn't bend over like a regular shirt's collar. It stuck up an inch or so, the edges curving in front. The collar had a shinier edging on it. The buttons were black with an eagle design in the middle.

"This is the hardest sewing I've ever done." Emily held out the suit's pants so he could step into them. "You're six inches taller than the general, bigger in the shoulders and chest, and smaller in the waist. I had to use two suits to make this. Don't even ask me how I pieced everything together."

He took the pants and put them on, one foot after the other, pulling them up. She tucked in the bottom of the shirt and did the buttons and zipper.

"Let me look." She examined the front closure, and then looked down at the leg. "It looks good. I was afraid it would look like 'loving hands at home.' I hate anything I do to look homemade." She ran her hand down the front of the pants and then squatted and adjusted the cuffs. "I had to take the bottoms of the legs of one pair of pants and piece them to the top of the other pair to get the length."

He looked at himself in the mirror. When they'd gone underground, Arthur had shaved Sam's hair and beard, part of getting rid of the bugs. He'd kept it shaved for a while. But then Emily had begun her redecorating and remodeling, including him in the project.

His hair was an inch or so on top, but short and tapered around the sides. She'd put something on it when he got out of the shower that made it stiffer. It stood up a bit. He'd grown a beard, but, instead of letting it bush, Emily trimmed it tight along his jaw, with some growing on his chin and up and around his mouth. His neck and cheeks were shaved. "You look intellectual, Sam," she had said.

"OK, here's the jacket." She helped him slip on one arm and then the other. She tugged the back down and smoothed the front, pulling the sleeves taut, buttoning four buttons. Like the shirt, the jacket had a collar that stood up all around. It had braid around it, and the same braid went along on the shoulder seams and around the bottoms of the sleeves. Emily looked at him critically.

"What do you think?"

He looked at himself in the mirror, then got his glasses and looked again. His hair was gray on the sides and his beard showed a little more white than his head. But, cut the way it was, he looked good, not old. He looked like one of the men who might have come to the estate with the lady. A city man. Someone who meant something. The glasses made him look even more important.

His brows drew together and he frowned slightly, wondering at the tall stranger in the mirror. He'd always been big. He'd always been broad in the shoulder and chest, but he didn't look so broad as he did now. The jacket did something to him.

Sam ran his hand down the suit's smooth front. He'd had the start of a gut back in the village. His belly was flat now. No hooch and better food, he guessed, and Emily making him exercise. His shoulders tapered down to a trim waist. His hips weren't skinny like some men's; they matched the rest of him. And his thighs were massive. The suit's pants wrapped around them, showing their substantial girth, but they were roomy enough to allow him to move.

"One more thing." She disappeared into the closet. "The only thing I couldn't fix was shoes. Your feet are bigger than the general's. I did this." She pulled out an old pair of his boots, which she had dyed black and polished.

He looked at them. "Ye did this?"

"Yes. Do you like them?"

He sat on the bed and put the boots on. The suit pants fell over them, smooth as cream.

Then he stood up to really look at himself. A tall man with glasses. Sharp hair and beard. Fine clothes. He ran his hand over the suit's soft fabric.

"It's the best wool. There's plenty more. I can make you more suits. I can make you all sorts of things. What's the matter? Don't you like it?"

He couldn't talk. He kept staring at himself, mouth open a bit, a little frown on his face. He couldn't make a sound. She walked up behind him, eyes on the apparition in the mirror.

"You're beautiful," she said.

"Nah." He shook his head. "Ye made me so." He looked like a New York man. Someone who'd traveled and had a big job. A man who had been to school, and college even. He looked like someone who mattered.

"Sam, you've always been beautiful. The first time I saw you, you took my breath away."

He turned to her and smiled. "So much ye wanted to shoot me?"

"I'm sorry about that." She squirmed. "I still thought you were beautiful."

He turned toward her, opening his arms.

"No, Sam. We have a dinner date. Winnie and I have to get dressed." The doorbell rang. "That's her now. You'll have to scoot."

"Where should I go?"

"Anywhere you won't get dirty. We're supposed to be at Arthur's room by seven. That's forty-five minutes."

He walked out into the corridor, feeling dizzy and awestruck. He was a beautiful man. It didn't seem possible, but it was true. He wasn't Sam of the village, reeking of hooch and crawling with bugs. He was a new man. He could read and write and send messages on computers. He was learning how to run the systems of the underground.

He headed toward the main hall without thinking. The cavernous space seemed unreal that night. He was as good as anyone. And he had these beautiful clothes that his Emily had made.

Warmth rose in his chest, as though the sky was exploding in there. He was in love with her. With her, with both of them. Valerie had faded into the background as if she didn't exist, but Sam knew she was there.

The hall was dimmed. The villagers would have eaten their rations: soybeans and some of the army grub. They would be sitting in groups, families and bunches of friends, wishing they could smoke and have a nip while waiting for the movie to begin. They had movies every night at seven. Jeremy had supplied them with a thousand years' worth of films.

Sam wandered out of the corridor slowly. The light from the hall cast his shadow in front of him. It was the elongated shadow of a lithe man. A substantial man who could go anywhere in the world. A warrior.

The first group of people was on his right. He walked quietly up to them, boots almost noiseless.

"Oh! Sam. Ye gave me a start!" old Manny said. "Quite a start." The six people around him, his wife and kids, and some of their kids, stared at Sam, mouths opening. "Well, ye look right fine, Sam. Ye must be doin' . . ."

Sam bowed at the waist. "I'm bound for a dinner party in a while. How are you this fine evening?" His best regular English came out effortlessly.

"Ah. We're good. Uh, good. All of us."

"Well, I'll be making the rounds. Enjoy the movie." And he moved on, slowly, not wondering what they were plotting, not expecting complaints or jibes. And they gave none. He felt like the lady making the rounds of the village with her accountants. Now his people greeted him with respect, when they greeted him. Most were silent, nodding.

He went around to each group. They gaped at him and his clothes. His bearing. The way he spoke, quietly, with assurance and authority. In regular English. No Voice, no Power.

Sam looked at his watch. It had been the general's watch and was solid gold, band and all. It was 6:50, time to go meet Arthur. He knew how to tell time now.

"Well, I'll be taking your leave," he said to the last group. It was Cooty Gill's family; Cooty was the barrel maker back in the village. An enchanting child of about four pulled away from her family, then batted her eyelashes at him.

"Well, who are you?" he said. He bent and held out his hand to the blond angel.

"Ah'm Janelle," she said. "Ah'm four years old. Who are ye?"

Her father was aghast. "Now, sir, don't take offense at her. She's a bit spoilt, is all."

He laughed. "Don't worry about it, Cooty. She sounds like a liberated woman. Are you liberated, Janelle?"

"Yeah." She stared at him boldly.

"Don' take offense, sir. She don't mean nothin' by it, sir."

The village called him "sir" and treated him like a king.

34

The instant Sam stepped back into the VIP corridor, the solid steel door that separated it from the main hall slid out of the wall and closed behind him. Arthur must have been watching on the monitor. Sam headed down the hall to Arthur's room.

"Come with me." Arthur was waiting by his room. Another steel door—really a wall—beyond Art's room had been rolled shut. It was the first time Sam had seen the corridor shut down. Made his heart jump a little.

"What's happening, Art?" he asked.

"I had to close everything down to make sure only the invited guests saw where we're going." Arthur led Sam to one of the unused entrances along the corridor. Typically, no one took any notice of the doors; they were just locked entries to rooms that had been intended for the scientists who'd never arrived. Art punched in a code and beckoned Sam inside.

They walked down another corridor, lit with pretty lights like torches on the walls.

"Jeremy built all sorts of things into the shelter. I'll show them to you, little by little." Sam stiffened at that. He was the headman. He needed to know everything, and now.

"This club was intended to keep the scientists from getting any crazier than they were." He opened another door along the hall. "Come on in."

Sam walked into a room like none he'd ever seen. Pinpoints of light highlighted the room's furnishings but left intimate shadows everywhere else. A mirrored ball spun lazily from the ceiling, casting sparkles throughout the darkness. A curved bar ran along one side and cabaret tables and leather-upholstered booths ran down the other walls. The room's center was a smooth wooden floor. Viewing screens hung in a bank from the ceiling, and a pool table and smaller game tables were way in the back. Jazz music from a big band such as had accompanied Jeremy's famous father, Chaz Edgarton, played softly.

"This isn't the sort of thing you find in most bomb shelters," Arthur quipped. "Jeremy figured that a hundred geniuses would want extraordinary quarters. Not to mention, need stimulation. This is a pub, sports bar, dance club, and gourmet restaurant. VIPs only. I thought we might as well use it. Let me make you an espresso and then I'll get the ladies."

Arthur was dressed for a party, too, but his clothes made Sam nervous. He had on black pants tighter than Sam's that clearly showed the outlines of Arthur's hips and legs. His shirt was white. Silk. Sam recognized the fabric by its soft shimmer. The shirt was opened almost to his waist. A streak of Arthur's smooth brown skin flashed in the opening. Sam could see the muscles of Art's chest and belly. The commando worked out every day and his body was even fitter than when they had come underground. Arthur's hair was slicked back with shiny stuff and he seemed to sparkle. A woman would be attracted to him, no doubt. Arthur was aroused; Sam could feel it.

"I'll go get the ladies," Art said and marched out of the room, the big gold ring on his hand drawing the light. He also had a gold chain glittering around his neck. Sam leaned against the bar, sipping a bitter drink. Who was this Arthur he'd never seen? What else existed down here that Arthur hadn't told him about?

Winnie swept into the room like one of the hot air balloons the lady had brought out to the estate once. Majestic and awe-inspiring. Her dress was a pale blue with a little green in it, matching Winnie's eyes, and went all the way to the floor, with layers and layers of fabric you could see through.

Her face was painted with the lady's face paints. Emily had done up her hair so it was piled on top of her head and fell down in curls all around. She wore a crown—a tiara, Emily had told him—of greenish blue stones. A necklace and earrings of the same gems flashed at her neck and ears. Rings sparkled on her fingers. Winnie could have been one of the guests at the big house.

His mouth fell open when she turned toward Arthur. The front of the dress was open to the waist. It stayed closed, mostly, but her skin glowed in the opening when she moved. You couldn't see anything exactly, but, still, you could see everything. The beautiful dress was the kind the lady had preferred, one that would drive a man to his knees.

Winnie was the sort of fleshy woman Sam had favored before he met Emily. She wasn't fat, but she had round hips and a soft, pillowy belly and her full breasts had filled his hands. The dress made the most of her body. In former days, he would have grabbed her and taken her home to bed just seeing her like that. Now he wanted to chide her for wearing that dress in front of Arthur and him.

He might have, but then Emily burst into the room and it was as though the ball of mirrors in the ceiling spun faster and all the lights turned to shine on her.

He saw her smile first, and then the way she walked, prancing as his stallion, Oned, had in the old days. Her hair was cut even sharper than usual, shining as if it had been varnished, but swinging as she moved. Her dress caused his heart to break rhythm and his breath to pause.

It was black, with little shiny circles all over it that reflected the light. Its front, held up by strings that looked as if they might break, was so low it barely covered her nipples. The dress was all one piece, top flowing into the skirt and all as tight as her skin. The skirt stopped way short of her knees. Below her waist, hundreds of beaded threads fell. When she moved, they swayed and threw out light. A rope of diamonds wrapped her neck, and clusters of them grabbed her ears. Her fingers sparkled. Her lips and fingertips glowed red. Her flashing white teeth were almost blinding. He grabbed the edge of the bar.

She wore see-through black stockings with lines up the back. Her shoes were so high and their heels so pointed, they could have been used as weapons. He didn't know how she walked in them. Those heels snapped like branches in a freeze when they hit the floor, popping a fancy tune as she marched toward him.

"Well, what do you think?" Emily grinned, spinning in front of him. "Was it worth waiting two weeks?"

"Ma God." That was all he could say. Not even the lady was as breathtaking as Emily. Or as close to naked. "Uh. Ah . . ." He was going to demand she go home and change, but she wheeled up to him and stroked his chest.

"It's just for tonight, Sam. Let's pretend we're in New York. Let's have a party."

He was shaking, but he didn't say anything. He'd wanted to go to the clubs of New York since he could remember. Now he had the fanciest woman of all. Yes, let's pretend for tonight, his heart whispered.

"Welcome to Arthur's magical cabaret." Arthur joined them by the bar after securing the steel door. "This is the special treat I invited you to. We've been here ten-and-a-half months and we're still alive. I thought we should celebrate."

"Look at this place," said Emily, craning her neck. "It looks like something from the city. This could be Rumba, or even the Flamingo."

"Jeremy got the Flamingo's designer to do the plans," Arthur said. "He told him his mother was going to open a new club. She did, too. This is it." Art was lit up brighter than Sam had ever seen him. "I cooked dinner for you, the best of Casa Romero. I figured it's time to kick back and have a good time."

Sam was taken aback by the existence of the club. "Why did ye not tell me of this place?"

"The shelter has many secrets, Sam. You know the most important of them. Some secrets have to stay 'need to know.'"

"*Ah* need to know, Art'ur. Ah'm the headman. An' ye will tell me, verra soon." Things were quiet now, but what if a new generation of punks arose? What if more of the devil weed cropped up? What if the underground ended up at war and they needed places to hide? Arthur *would* tell him everything. Sam gave the other man a hard look.

Arthur didn't notice. "It's hard to do haute cuisine with powdered ingredients, believe me." Art was talking to Winnie and Emily. Sam noticed how he was so tense, he seemed to bounce as he stepped. He looked ready to pounce. Sam followed his eyes. They rested on Winnie.

"Please be seated. I'll bring your aperitifs." He led them to a booth set with more silver and glasses than Sam had ever seen. Then Arthur glided smoothly through doors in the back of the room, returning with a tray laden with four stemmed glasses full of pink liquid and a pitcher of the same stuff.

"Oh, my God, Arthur! You even got umbrellas!" Emily took a glass and sipped through a straw. The drinks did have tiny paper umbrellas on them. Sam tried not to look surprised.

"Yep. Nonalcoholic strawberry daiquiris. Some people would say that's a sin. I would say it's a sin, but we're following the Commands. Drink up. There's lots more."

"Chopped salad. I copied this from Baxter's, my favorite restaurant in Manhattan." Arthur slipped in and out of the kitchen, bringing them food. He walked with a swagger, his commando's body taut and his smile brilliant.

Sam had a bad feeling about Arthur. In the beginning, he had wondered if Art were really a friend. He'd decided he was. But he'd never seen this smooth, cocky man. A man who liked women very much. Who opened his shirt so far and kept secrets from his headman. What else was he up to? Where did he get this food? Did he eat like this all the time while they ate slop? Who gave him the orders to withhold information from his headman? Who did Arthur really work for? Why was he there? Sam scowled.

"*Arroz con pollo*—Spanish chicken with rice, the way my mom made it." Arthur set down a platter with a flourish. "This is Latino-mutt cooking—my family is a combination of Puerto Rican, Mexican American, and South American mix-it-up. We've been in the US for centuries, but everyone always asks me where I'm from. *I'm Arturo Romero from NYC.*" He said the words with an accent. Spanish, Sam guessed.

Art brought out a half-dozen other dishes. "A Latino feast!"

They ate. "Nah. Ah canna eat more, Art," Sam said, wiping his mouth with his napkin. The food was delicious, but his questions about Arthur were leaving a bad taste. He looked at the other man with hard eyes. What was he hiding? Arthur didn't seem to notice. He went into the kitchen, emerging with a round platter.

"Here's the pièce de résistance: my mom's flan. It was a real bitch to get the caramel candied without a flame or making any smoke. The whole dinner was a bitch, actually." Sam had never seen Arthur so talkative.

"I didn't know you could cook," Emily said.

"Oh, yeah. I'm a mama's boy. I followed my mom around the kitchen when I was a kid. I love to cook. Not that I get to very much here. When I said I did this with powdered foods, I lied. We have a couple of freezers of frozen foods for special occasions."

Sam burst out, "Ha' ye been eatin' like this all the time, Art, while we ate grub?"

"Oh, *no*, Sam. I wanted a special night. I've been eating just like you. I thought you'd be pleased." He seemed genuinely hurt.

"Ah am. Is summat a surprise is all. Yer good food." And your tight pants. Sam sat back, smiling, while wondering what other surprises Arthur held. Or treachery.

An awkward moment passed and Arthur asked, "Who wants cappuccino? It's a coffee drink."

"Oh, I do," Emily responded. "But decaf. Do you have that?"

"I've got whatever you want, Emily." His mouth curved into a tiny smile and he cocked his head at her.

Sam's eyes opened. Was Arthur flirting with Emily?

"How did you end up down here, Arthur?" Emily asked, sipping her cappuccino.

"Nowhere else to go," he said flippantly, and then got serious. "They recruited me. I graduated from the academy." He shrugged significantly and held up his finger with the big gold ring. Sam realized that the academy must be a very important school. "I was on the front for three years." He looked at Emily. Sam thought Art was going to ask her something about her being on the front, too, but backed away from it.

"I mostly shot missiles at people I couldn't see, using computers. I was good at it. They sent me back to school to get an MA in computer science. I studied urban guerrilla warfare. A few other things. I was posted around and saw what was going on in the country. Nothing like what the government said. So I got political."

Sam glanced at Winnie, then studied her face. Her eyes never moved from Arthur.

"One of the generals approached me about Jeremy and the shelter. And the revolution. All top secret, even from the majority of the military. I ended up doing security for Jeremy and working on this place."

That was the most Sam had heard Arthur say. He realized he knew almost nothing about him, other than the fact that he was a commando and had been with Jeremy all those years. And he knew computers.

"I volunteered to come down here. I didn't have any relations or dependents. Of course, no one does now . . . They tested me like crazy before sending me down here. I'm perfect material for the underground."

"You aren't married, Arthur?" Emily asked.

"I was married. My wife left me." That was a revelation. Sam couldn't imagine the serious Arthur he'd known, married. "She got tired of waiting for a husband who was gone 90 percent of the time and was exhausted the 10 percent of the time he was home. She took off with our neighbor." He shrugged.

"I'm sorry, Arthur."

"Nothing to be sorry about. Do you guys want to dance?"

Music surrounded them. Colored lights joined the reflections of the mirrored ball, flashing around the club. Mist drifted down from the ceiling. The room immediately became exciting and mysterious. Sam was taken by the change. The wildest harvest stomp hadn't moved him so. Of course, at a stomp he'd have drunk half a barrel of ale and would be falling on his face by now.

"Want to dance, Ms. Emily?" Arthur slunk up to Emily and asked her to dance. She took his hand and they glided to the center of the floor. The music changed into something lively.

"Oh, Arthur! It's from the Golden Age! The Beatles!" They jiggled and shimmied around the floor, arms flailing. When she moved her hips, the little beaded strings on her skirt stuck out straight and flashed. She moved her hips a lot. Every once in a while, Arthur would grab her and twirl her under his arm, flinging her out. Pulling her back in. Strutting around. The little strings flew, sparkling.

This went on until Sam was about to pop Arthur. All the time the mist was falling, lights were moving, and the music played on, changing rhythms, singers, and bands. It became pounding and insistent.

Arthur stopped and pulled Emily over by Sam and Winnie. "Well, you've seen how New Yorkers do it. How did you dance in the village?" Arthur knew perfectly well how they danced, having watched half-a-dozen stomps during his years at the estate guarding Jeremy, Sam thought.

"We don't do anythin' like ye, but Winnie and ah can move our feet." Sam pulled her out. The music was pounding as hard and fast as the drums around the fire. He and Winnie bent their knees and faced each other, leaning forward and stomping. They stomped to the right, to the left, around each other and came to a halt, still moving their feet. Sam whistled and Winnie whistled back. He yodeled and she yodeled. They locked arms and moved in a circle, not paying attention to Arthur or Emily. Winnie seemed stiff, as though she didn't want to dance with him. That was as strange as the way Art was acting. Had he done something to offend Winnie?

Sam looked up as Arthur streaked onto the floor, doing some kind of a dance to the primitive drums. He moved like a snake, barely picking his feet up, but inching forward. He waved arms so that they looked like they didn't have bones. He tossed himself onto the floor, and then pushed himself up so he was standing on his hands. He walked forward on his hands. Lowered himself down to the floor, rolled onto his chest, his belly, back to his feet. Threw himself down again, flipped onto his back. Spun around on that. The music went wild, and so did Arthur.

Now Art lay on his stomach, pushed himself up on both arms, body rigid as a board, and moved himself up and down a few times. Then he did it on one hand, then the other. Jumped onto his feet, did a handstand again, dropped down so his head was on the floor, spun on that. And then he flipped back up and began moving in that boneless way, arms, legs, body, head.

"Oh, Arthur! You're breakin'. My God, you're the best break-dancer I've ever seen." Emily was jumping up and down clapping. "Do it some more."

So Arthur did, balancing and flipping and spinning. He pushed himself up on his hands, swung his legs out to the side and forward, lifting a hand so he could rotate his legs where his arm had been, lifting the other hand to let his legs pass, throwing his legs in a circle, again and again and again. He ended with a backflip and walked off the stage as if he'd done nothing.

"I can't *believe* you can dance like that!" Emily squealed.

Sam really was going to pop the little jerk, except that he had made such a good dinner. Plus Sam could see how hard that dance was. Arthur's muscles bulged and sweat dampened his shirt.

He looked at Winnie. Winnie gazed at Arthur in adoration.

"Let me wipe myself off a little," Arthur said, heading for the kitchen, sweat dripping off his face. The music slowed and the lights dimmed. The twinkling ball barely seemed be moving.

"Dance with me, Sam," Emily said, holding up her arms. "I've saved all the slow dances for you."

He put his arms around her the way she'd shown him they'd danced in the city, and she snuggled up just as if they were alone in their room, her head nestling into his chest. He felt the little fish scale things her dress was made of and he felt her under the dress.

"Let's go home, Em'ly." His voice was hoarse.

"No, I want to dance." She snuggled even closer.

Arthur came out of the kitchen and sidled up to Winnie, looking like a panther on the prowl. Sam saw the hunger on his face.

"Would you like to dance with me, Winnie?" They practically ignited when they touched.

He pulled her close. It took her a while to snuggle up like Emily was doing, but Winnie did take the bait. She was a little taller than Arthur, but looked like she fit fine.

As he and Emily finally left, Sam turned back to see Arthur and Winnie plastered to each other as if they were trying to be one person. They were barely moving and Arthur had his lips on Winnie's neck.

So that was what the evening was about. Arthur wanted Winnie. This was how a New York man courted a woman. Art didn't need to do all this though; Sam would have given her to him if he'd asked.

Sam stumbled over his feet as he remembered. Those days were over. Winnie wasn't his to give.

35

When they got into their room, Sam snatched Emily up in his arms. He could feel the scratchy texture of the sparkling dress on his hands and measured the heft of her as he walked. He sat her on the end of the bed.

"Take off your clothes." His voice came out deeper than he expected. Sam stepped back so he could watch. She smiled at him, head tilted to one side, and stood up. Holding his gaze, she dropped the string that held up one side of her outfit. The sparking dress sagged. When she pushed the string that held the other side over her shoulder, the dress's front fell down to her waist. It gathered there, gleaming in the dim light.

He stiffened, unable to look away. Her round breasts bobbed just a bit, like a young girl's. The brown buttons on the ends riveted him. She had no fat anywhere. She was perfect, like a statue. Her eyes never left his.

She picked up the dress and put it aside. When she turned, he could see the length of her legs and ivory curve of her belly. He was a bit surprised. Emily had told him that people from the city wore underwear, but all she had on under her dress was a lace thing with straps that held up her stockings. That and the high-heeled shoes.

Tilting her head to the other side, she said, "Do you want me like this or naked?"

"Take 'em off." Blood rushed to his face. His nostrils stiffened as his breath went in and out.

She stripped slowly, flaunting herself. First undoing the stockings from their straps, peeling them off. Dropping them to the side. Removing the lace belt.

"Is this how you want me, Sam?" She stood before him. A flash of white skin, nipples, curves. The darkness between her legs. Her mocking grin, white teeth and red lips, that varnish-bright hair.

"Get up there on the bed." He motioned with his hand. She crawled toward the headboard on all fours, buttocks shifting like pale peaches. She lay back on the pillows, arms crossed above her head, feet together, knees parted a bit.

"Is this how you want me, Sam?" Mocking full on now, challenging him.

She was beautiful, her curves smooth and inviting. Her breasts flattened when she laid down, their brown knobs standing erect. As many times as he'd seen her, she took his breath away. But he didn't go to her.

Sam turned and went into the closet. He turned the dial on the safe inside and opened it. Using his hands as scoops, he removed most of the contents.

She looked puzzled when he returned. "What are you doing, Sam?"

He laid all of it on her belly and held up a piece. "What's this stone called?"

"They're emeralds. Emeralds and diamonds in a necklace."

He circled the collar around her breast.

"And this one?"

"Sapphires." That went around the other breast.

"And this one?"

"It's topaz." Around her neck. "Amethyst." Another necklace around her neck.

"A tiara of aquamarines." He settled it carefully on her head.

"Opal . . . amber . . . garnets . . . pearls . . . rubies and diamonds." He laid rows of necklaces on her chest and wrapped strands of pearls down her arms. "Jade . . . lapis and gold." The rings he put on her fingers, bracelets on her wrists. "Peridot . . . coral." The brooches he laid down her torso. Other pieces he arranged low on her belly. He carefully nestled a diamond ring with a stone as big as a quail's egg on her curly mound.

"What's all this?" She sounded bewildered.

"It's the lady's jewelry. There's more, too. Ah didn't show ye all of it before."

He gazed at Emily, lying before him studded with precious stones and gold. Her tiniest movement caused the gems to catch the light. She was a shining angel. His angel. His jewel. Sam's ribs heaved, barely able to contain what he felt.

"It's for ye," he said. "Ah'm givin' it all to ye."

And then he loved her.

36

Moisture saturated her blond eyelashes. She was looking down, so her eyes appeared to be closed. "Ah'm sorry, Art'ur." The tears fell, making glistening tracks on her cheeks. They had just made love and the same thing had happened. Or hadn't happened.

He stroked Winnie's hair, white blond and finer than any other he'd ever touched. So like threads of silk. She had the sheets pulled up around her breasts. Her shoulders shook. "It's OK, Winnie. It will work out." He whispered, "Were you able to before?"

They'd been sleeping together since his dinner party, three weeks before. He'd set up a private room for them next to the one she shared with her boys. Taking that blue chiffon dress off her the first night had been one of the highlights of his life. Her body. The lushness of it. She was so fair and soft, with those pink-tipped breasts that overflowed his hands. Her white hair and the paleness down there.

"I'm sorry, Winnie. It's been a long time." He was so fast the first few times, he'd had to apologize. Any kid in his neighborhood back home would have come in his pants seeing her naked. He loved the way his brown skin looked next to her whiteness. He loved her. That was the surprise. When he was with her, Emily fled from his thoughts. He wanted Winnie. The exotic village orchid.

It had taken him awhile to realize she hadn't come. Ever. Not once.

He'd said something to her about it and she'd recoiled as if he'd struck her. "Ah'm sorry, Art'ur. Ah'll do better. Ah'll try."

How could she *try* to do something like that? So he tried to do better. His tongue was sore and so was his mouth. His dick felt shredded. He couldn't do it any better, and still nothing. He was worried. She looked at him with scared eyes. They kept trying.

"Will ye leave me, Art, because ah can't do 'er?" she whispered.

He took his time answering. "It's better for me if I know you're coming, too. If you don't, I feel like I'm using you."

"It's OK if ye use me, Art'ur. Ah don't mind."

"I mind, Winnie. I feel like I'm failing you." She started to get up and he pulled her back. "Let's just hold each other for a while, and talk. Don't worry about anything.

"Did you ever . . .?" he asked her.

"Yeah. Ah did. A long time ago. An' with Sam."

"Always with Sam?"

"He has the Power, Art'ur. No one can resist."

Arthur exhaled. Sam had had to use the Power to get her to let loose? What was *he* going to do? "Did you ever do it without the Power?"

She nodded. "At first, lots of times. When ah was twelve an' we wed, yeah."

"You got married when you were *twelve* years old?"

"My da said it were the chance of a life—Sam was the most powerful headman anywhere. Ah'd not get a better offer. So ah took 'er. Sam was nineteen. Ah was his third wife."

"And it was good at first?"

"At first, not so much. Ah was scared. But Sam made it fine."

Arthur bet he did. "When did it change, Winnie?"

"After . . . Ah did a bad thing once." The tears kept tipping over her lower lids, drenching her face. Splattering on the sheets.

"What, Winnie?" He stroked her and held her close, kissing her hair and drying her eyes with the sheet.

She pulled away from him and gazed into his eyes. "When ah was sixteen, there was a boy, Jamie. He was beautiful, but ordinary like me. Ah liked him because of that, and 'cause he didn't love anyone but me. We . . ." She shrugged her shoulders.

"You were lovers?" A nod. "Were you OK with him?" Another nod. She covered her face with her hands. "Winnie, what happened, sweetheart?"

"Sam sent him west and sent me to Orly Watchman."

Sam slipped about five hundred notches in Arthur's eyes. "That old guy with no teeth?"

She nodded her head and told him the rest of it.

"Oh, Winnie." That and everything else she'd said staggered him. How could they fix this?

"Did you ever talk to Sam about this? Does he know what he did to you?"

"He knows. He sent me to do it."

"Not that, Winnie. Does he know how he hurt you? And what happened as a result?"

"Nah. Why should he care?"

"He should care because you're a human being. He should care because he damaged you. If you talked to him about what he did, things might change. We might change."

She wasn't crying, but she held the sheet to her chest, looking at him hard. "No one talks to Sam Baahuhd about what he done wrong. No one."

"I will. Do you want me to do it?"

"No." She was turning a corner; he could see it. Her eyes hardened and her jaw clenched. Winnie was angry. "It was wrong to do what he done, wasn't it, Art? Wi' Jamie and all the rest."

"Yes, it was Winnie. Very wrong."

"Ah want to talk to him, but ah don't want him to hurt me."

"I can arrange that." He told her how. "I'll be right outside, listening. If things get out of control, I'll come in."

Arthur was angry, too. His heart pounded. Feelings were coming up inside him, strong feelings. He wanted to kill Sam.

"Winnie, I love you." The words surprised him, but they were true. Her silvery whiteness wiped away any thought of Emily. He wanted Winnie. He wanted Winnie to unfold in ecstasy around him. He wanted her to be his wife. And he wanted to punch the shit out of Sam.

"When should we do it?" he said.

"Now, Art'ur." She got out of bed and put on her clothes.

37

"Sam? Sam? Are ye OK?" He heard old Ned's voice somewhere. Ned was one of the older men of the village, gnarled and grizzled from years in the fields. At the sound of Ned's voice, Sam shook his head and brought himself back to where he was. Which was at the end of the growing fields, listening to Ned explain his idea for improvements to the irrigation system.

"Yeah, Ned. I heard you. I think it's a good idea, except I'd run the new line back over there, then put a branch out here. You'd get more irrigation from less pipe. We have the pipe, right?" Regular English flowed off his tongue now, almost as if it had been there first.

Ned's jaw slackened. "Yeah. Yer right. That's the way to do 'er. Ah have to give 'er to ye, Sam. Ye got the bes' eye for the crops an' sure."

"Thanks, Ned. It's my job. You and the boys start on the trench. I'm going to take inventory of the pipe and fittings. This new line should handle that spot where it always dries out." He paused. "Oh, yes. Is everyone ready for the one-year celebration? Only a month to go."

"Oh, yez, Sam." Ned's face flashed his approval of the headman. "We're doin' fair an' fine, down here, sir. Ne'er thought it would be so."

"We're doing fine with other things, too, Ned. A bunch of you can read a little now. And speak regular English."

Ned's leathery face registered a blush. "Well, sir, ah'm . . . *I'm* trying as hard as I can. It's a new thing, is all."

"You'll get the hang of it, Ned." Sam patted his shoulder and headed across the hall toward the storage bay to check the supply of irrigation pipe. That silly grin spread over his face again, this time prompted by the image of Emily wearing nothing but jewels.

He looked at the sleeve of his new shirt. In the three weeks since the dinner party, Emily had made him a new shirt every couple of days. This was called a "rugby shirt." It had wide stripes and a white collar. She had to use two shirts to make one to fit him, so it had more stripes in more colors than it was supposed to, according to Emily. He didn't care. He'd never seen a rugby shirt in his life. He liked it very much; the soft knit fabric was smooth and flexible.

This was being in love. He'd never known it. The laughter inside, the need for her. Night and day. He was an old man; he shouldn't be able to do what he did every night, but he did it. When he wasn't with her, he was thinking about her.

All his life, Sam had thought he loved the lady, Veronica Edgarton. But love wasn't waiting around all year for her to appear, only to have her ride off with some other man on a horse he had saddled.

Love was rolling with Emily. Love showed in the proud way she watched him put on the clothes she made him. Love was the pleasure in her eyes as he mastered new words or read to her. Or booted up the computer and started typing with no help.

He wanted to be nice to everyone because of Emily. The people noticed it. He could feel their eyes on him as he crossed the hall, and see their smiles. They still called him "sir," as he showed up in new finery. He'd changed. Now he was the man he was meant to be.

"Sam," Winnie said from close behind him. He jumped and turned quickly. She had come from the VIP corridor, looking like a she-badger ready to defend her cubs. "I need a word with you."

"Sure," he said. "Talk away."

"Not here. In private."

She spun and headed up the corridor toward Arthur's room, walking faster than Sam. She seemed angry at him, the way she had at Art's party. He didn't understand why.

He knew that Winnie and Arthur had been keeping company since the dinner party. But Winnie went around mean and pinch-faced. Arthur seemed worried. He didn't have a grin all over him like Sam. Something was wrong. He thought it was Arthur.

"Sammy." He heard a woman's voice by his elbow. It was Leah Elberts, Larry's wife, carrying a basket of soybeans.

"Uh . . . hello, Leah. I didn't notice you."

"Well, ye were following her who ye allus fancied." Her voice was husky. "I saw you walking, Sam," Leah continued, making a try at regular English. "I just thought, being as you an' me always was good friends, that maybe sometime you'd like to keep a little company with one who knows you from the old days."

Sam turned toward her. "That's over, Leah. I live by the Commands. We all live by the Commands. 'One man, one wife. Fidelity.' That's how I live. Don't you keep the Commands? I ordered you to."

She smiled, a tilted little smile that told him no one in the village took the Commands seriously, or spoke proper English out of his hearing. "Oh, yeah, Sam. What was I thinkin'? The Commands, o' course." She turned to walk away. "But if ye ever want a bit wi' meat on it"—she swung her hip toward him—"ah'm here."

38

Arthur stood in the hallway outside his room, shifting from foot to foot and looking nervous. "Hi, Sam," he said when Sam arrived. Winnie stood next to him, flushed from walking fast. "Winnie needs to talk to you about some things. I thought you could talk in my office. I'll wait outside."

"What's the matter, Winnie?" Sam said when they got in the office. He motioned her to a chair, but she ignored him.

"Ah need to talk to ye of things that happened." She made no pretense of speaking proper English.

"Go on."

"Was ah not yer wife, yer third wife, but yer dear wife, just the same?"

"Yes. Y' know you were." His grip on his new language grew shakier with each exchange.

"An', as such, ye shoulda taken care of me, an' kep' me safe? An' loved me?"

Winnie was rigid, her face pale and her mouth tight. Her brows knit over her eyes. Sarcasm dripped from her words.

"Yes, Winnie. Ah did. Ah loved ye when we were wed, an' ah took care of ye." He slipped back further into the old speech. Whatever this was, Winnie had been stewing about it for a long time.

She threw her head back, snorting in derision. "Ahh. It was tender love an' care ye gave me. It was that that made ye give me to Fred Odenell when ah was fourteen years old. Ye wanted his wife, and he would not give her unless he got somethin' in return." Her nostrils flared and her hands clenched at her sides.

"Ah went, because ah was a good village wife. An' all the same, ah was but a girl, yer wife for jus' two years. Ye had me to wife when ah was twelve years ol', Sam. Ah hadn't been bleedin' for half a year." Her eyes filled and he thought she might weep, but she didn't. She turned on him.

"Ah went, because ah was your wife and should obey ye in all things. *But ah did not like it.* Later, after what happened with Jamie an' me, an' ye sent me to Orly Watchman, ah thought it was 'cause o' Jamie. But it wasn't. Ye kept on givin' me after ah was punished good an' fair. Ye gave me to Jimmy Lock, and Harlan Beanell, and Fred again, and also Billy and Mark and the others. *And ah did not like it.* And ah did not like having to go to the pile-ons because ye wanted to trade me. Ah knew that ah was pretty and no one wanted your other wives. BUT AH HATED IT AN' AH HATED YE!" she screamed, veins in her throat distending.

"They did bad things to me and they said bad things. Ah cannot forget." The tears spilled over. Sam wanted to hold her but she would have none of it.

"Ah went because ah was a good wife, your favorite, the 'sweetest lass in the village.' Ah did it because ah was *stupid.*

"And when the end came and we were down here, ye put me and Jude and Ewan in that room, with *them.* Ye knew they'd kill us if they could. When the 'splosions came, ye left us, so ye could be with *her,* and with Art'ur. We screamed, and poor Ewan was so frighted, he pissed himself. They gave us no food until we fought for it." Now tears coursed down her cheeks, and she didn't stop them.

"If ah was your favorite, why did ye do that to me in the village? And why did you leave me to face the 'splosions alone? Ye could have had her, if ye'd wanted. When did the fact that ye were married ever stop ye from taking any woman?"

She stood, fists clenched, feet parted, screaming at him. "When they were gonna use me as a whoor, *she* saved me, not ye." Winnie waved in the direction of his room. "*She* saved me. Yer Em'ly that ye love so now."

Chuckling bitterly, Winnie said, "Ah better have a talk wi' Em'ly. Tell her ye like a bit of fresh meat now and again. She might have to spread her legs to buy what ye want once the new o' her wears off."

Temper flaring, Sam stepped forward. "No, ye'll not tell her nothin'." His face flushed when he thought of Emily knowing what he'd done.

"Won't ah, then? Art'ur is just outside with the intercom on, listenin' if ye try to do me harm." She struck her chest. "It's *my* turn now, Mr. Headman. Winnie gets to talk an' ye listen.

"So now, ah'm tossed out for the fine new one. Ah can bear that. But what ah cannot bear is the *stench* of ye that sticks to me. Ah canna do nothin' with Arthur because o' what ye done to me. Ah don't feel nothin' an' ah don't turn over *ever* an' ah'm gonna *lose* him because o' it. Ye *ruined* me, ye puffed-up ass!" She pulled away and began shouting at him in earnest.

"We are done, Sam Bahuuhd! Ah *divorce* thee! Ah *divorce* thee! Ah *divorce* thee!" She slashed her hands horizontally, cutting their ties.

Then she was out the door. He'd thought they already were divorced, but, when she said the words, it was final. And her choice. He felt stung. A village woman had never divorced a man before.

Sam could hear Arthur in the next room through the intercom. "Are you OK, Winnie?"

"Take me to the club. Ah want ye *now*," she said to Arthur. Sam heard them moving off.

Sam turned to leave the office, eyes on the floor, sad and dazed. Emily stood in front of him, arms crossed in front of her.

"Did you hear all that?" he said.

"I need to talk to you, right now. Let's go to our room." The fury on her face told him she had heard everything.

39

"You traded her to other men so you could have sex with their wives?" Emily was on him before his back cleared Art's door. Her lips drew back from her teeth.

"Aye, ah did. But it's how the village . . ."

"The village! I'm so sick of hearing how the village did things. Don't you have any morals?" She shook her head and stomped around. "She was the prettiest one, so you could trade for her. *Jesus*!" He managed to steer her to their room as they walked, trying to keep her from alerting the whole underground to what had happened.

"I'm leaving." The instant they entered the room, she dashed inside and grabbed a sweater, then ran back to the intercom on their wall. "Arthur! Arthur! Can you get me a room of my own? Arthur?" Art didn't answer. "Well. He's *busy*." She turned on Sam with more venom. "You traded Winnie—your favorite wife—to other men so you could get some *fresh meat*?"

"Ah tol' ye that ah'd had all of them, Em'ly."

"You didn't tell me that you'd traded Winnie to get them!"

"Ah didn't trade her for *all* of them." Sam ducked his head. It had seemed all right at the time.

"And they did 'bad things' to her and said 'bad things' to her? Sam, you've been her husband since she was twelve! You're a *father* figure to her. Jesus Christ! I thought you were such a nice guy.

"I'm sleeping in the closet." She disappeared behind its door. He heard the lock turn. And then unlock. The door flew open.

"If you *ever* try to pull a move like that on me, I will kill you. Don't think you can *ever* . . ." She retreated, slamming and locking the closet door again.

He wanted to say loud enough so she could hear him, "It was the hooch. Ah did that when ah was drunk," but he knew what she'd say. Whose fault was it that he was drunk? And he hadn't always been drunk. Sometimes he had just wanted some woman. Or women. Yes, he'd made Winnie participate in the pile-ons, but that was harvest; anything was OK then.

He didn't realize he had *hurt* Winnie. He'd told her to go, and she went. She came back the next day, and the woman he'd been with went back to her husband. It was all friendlylike.

But it hadn't been, he remembered. Winnie had been silent for days afterward and wouldn't look at him. Then he'd forget that the next time some wench swung her rump at him, and he'd send Winnie somewhere else. She did as she was told and never said anything. If she was less enthusiastic with him later or had trouble with her side of it, he hadn't noticed.

What he had done had made trouble for her with Arthur. *She* was the one with the problem, not Arthur. The realization struck him like a bolt. She was spoiled somehow, not the fresh thing she had been with him in the beginning. Fresh and hot as a young filly. She hadn't been that way for years.

Sam groaned. He lay in the bed and tried to sleep. He couldn't. It was almost dawn when he fell into a piddly half-sleep, jerking awake, and then drifting back to some boggy place. When morning came, he clawed out of bed, feeling as if he'd slept on the bottom of the river. Sand clogged his eyes and he felt like rocks had dug into his back. He'd ended up on that sandy bank many a time after a slaughter feast. But now he wasn't happily hung over.

The closet door flew open and Emily leapt out, spitting words as if she'd been doing it all night. "You know, I thought I'd finally met a nice guy. What a crock of shit. *Nice* guy! They don't exist.

"I'm going to ask Arthur for a room of my own." She headed for the door. "I'm going to teach my reading class, then I'll move my stuff."

He gathered himself together and pushed the intercom button.

"Art'ur. It's Sam. Can ye send Winnie over here? Ah'd like to talk to her." Silence.

Finally Arthur spoke. "I don't think that's a good idea, Sam. Let me ask her what she wants to do." The speaker went dead for a moment. "She said she'll talk to you, but not in your room. She'll talk to you in the club. She wants me there, too."

"Nah. Ah canna do 'er. Ah'm not gon' hurt her, Art'ur. Ye ken that."

"I'll talk to her some more."

They met in the nightclub, with Arthur standing outside the door, listening on the intercom.

"You wanted to talk to me?" She spoke regular English, but slowly.

"Aye." He gazed into her eyes, and she looked back with an intensity that made him look away. "Ah thought about what ye said, Winnie.

"Ah did wrong, an' ah hurt ye." Tears that wouldn't come out stung behind his eyes. "An it were Em'ly that saved ye, not me. But ah tell thee, Winnie, 'twas not from not wantin' to help ye."

She scoffed, "Oh, 'tis true, Sam. You couldn't stop them. Your Voice was plain gone, and your Power, too."

"Aye, 'tis true. They were gone from the minute ah stepped into the underground. Ye know that."

She looked at him, scornful. "You got them back. You fixed my face."

"Ah did get ma Power back, but not till many days later."

He dropped to his knees. "Will ye forgive me?" He held out his forearms, hands up. "Ye divorced me, an ah accept the blame for it. But will ye forgive me, too? Ah don't want a blood feud. Ah don't want to be out of our boys' lives."

He looked at her as intently as he ever had. He saw how pretty she was. Nay, beautiful. "Say sumthin', Winnie, please."

She seemed both shocked and contemptuous. "I never thought to see you on your knees, Sam Baahuhd. Maybe you can learn. I don't know that I want to be your friend, or even see you, though I know I will in this place." She stood proudly, with her head up. "Our boys love you and want you to be their da.

"I accept your apology. I forgive you as much as I can today. Maybe I will forgive it all later." She spoke with deliberate, correct English. Her green-blue eyes fell on him without a quiver.

"Will ye take your revenge on me? Will ye cut me, Winnie?" he whispered.

"Aye. That I will do."

He pulled his big knife out of its sheath and gave it to her, handle first. He kept the blade honed on both sides and sharp enough to cut the end of a hair in quarters. He pulled his new rugby shirt off and wadded it in a ball. "Cut as ye wish, Winnie," he said, turning sharply to the right as he threw it on a table.

The blade was already in motion. He barely felt it at first, the knife was so keen. The gash started out just a graze on his right side, then ran all the way across his chest, cutting deeper into the muscle on the left side where his torso had turned with the throw. The blade hung up under his left arm, then bounced back into his ribs. Winnie had to yank the knife out.

"I have taken my revenge on you, Sam Baahuhd. We will have no blood feud." She set his knife in front of him and walked toward the door.

Sam held his left arm tight to his side, holding it down with his right hand. He looked at his hand in disbelief. Blood spurted between his fingers to the rhythm of his heart, drenching his side, and pooling on the floor. He couldn't stop the bleeding, not with all his Power.

"Help me!" he cried.

Winnie turned around. "Ma Gawd, Sam, what happened?"

Sam slumped, and then fell on his side. Humming filled his ears. His vision lost focus and faded into a red film.

40

Sam clawed his way to the surface of a black sea. When he reached it, everything shifted so that up became down. Somersaulting blindly, he couldn't tell which way he was moving, where he was, or where he was going. He knew he was fighting for his life. Reaching the top would save him. If he could find it.

Others were there, fleetingly. They appeared like mirages, shimmering at a distance. Arthur, Winnie. Emily. No, it was Valerie. She came back again and again, holding on to him. Keeping him in this world.

"Don't die, Sam. I couldn't stand it if you died. Don't die."

Heaving blackness claimed him, but her hands clutched at him. She kept him fighting.

"Sam, stay. Don't leave me."

Daylight came as a surprise. He blinked his eyes. The white walls of the hospital rose around him. White walls, white floors and ceiling. White lights filling squares above him. He had a tube stuck in his arm, the way he had the first time he had awakened there.

"Sam, are you alive?" Arthur's voice was near him.

He moistened his lips. "Ah think so, Art. What happened?"

"Winnie took her right of revenge. She cut the artery in your left arm and side, the one that comes straight from your heart. And stabbed you in your chest. She got another artery. You're lucky you didn't die." He stood by Sam's bed, adjusting a bag of something red feeding into his arm.

"I've put four pints of synthetic blood in you. The only reason you're alive is your Power." Art looked into Sam's eyes. "Winnie didn't mean to cut you like that, Sam. You turned to throw your shirt when she made the cut. It was an accident."

Sam cracked a tiny smile. "Ah don't know, Art. She looked mad enough to kill me."

"It was an accident. You can talk to her yourself."

"Ah think ah will." The harsh tone of his voice surprised him.

"I didn't know what she was going to do. I knew what she wanted to talk to you about. She couldn't . . . *function* with me because of it. But I wouldn't have let either of you go in that room if I had thought she would cut you—or you would let her."

"Nah. Ah expect ye wouldna. That woulda been wrong. She would call a blood feud an' made war down here. She's taken my blood for hurtin' her, an' ah'm forgiven."

"She took blood all right. That club's floor will never be the same." Arthur shook his head sadly. "I'll never understand the village, Sam."

"Oh, ah expect ye do. Didn' ah hear ye tellin' one of the general's men we was like apes, but smarter? 'They're a primitive tribe that jus' happens to look human'? Ah felt *fine* when ah heard that, Art. Like ye said what ye really thought, for once." His anger surprised him. He used the village tongue without a thought.

"You weren't supposed to hear that. I said that years ago, before I really knew you."

"Well, ah did hear it. An', yeah, we have our customs. But we're not apes." His eyes bored into Arthur's face. "We're gonna have that walk-around where ye tell me the secrets of the underground." Sam peered harder. "What're ye keepin' from me? Yer worryin' on somethin', ah can see it. An' where's Em'ly?"

Arthur heaved a huge sigh. "I sent her away so I could talk to you. She was with you every moment you were out, Sam. For almost two days, she sat right next to you until we knew you'd live.

"I tried to tell her about the village's customs. About how the right of revenge—cutting someone who did you wrong—kept blood feuds from starting and saved lives in the long run. I told her that it was an accident. She could see how upset Winnie was."

Arthur was hemming and hawing, keeping something back. Sam wanted to joke and say, "Did she kill someone?" But the look on Art's face said she might have.

"What did she do?"

Arthur pulled a chair over. "It was bad, Sam."

"Tell me what happened." A thousand possibilities roared through Sam's mind.

"Like I said, she was with you all the time you were out, didn't even change her bloody clothes. When you were out of the woods, she told me she wanted a meeting with Winnie and the boys and me.

"I was pissed at Winnie myself. I thought Emily wanted to clear the air. And, knowing her, I was glad the boys and I would be there to break anything up." Arthur ran his hand through his hair.

"We were in my room. Emily walked in, still all bloody." Art shook his head. "I'm having trouble describing how *scary* she was. She didn't yell. She wasn't decked out with weapons, but she was a fucking murder machine.

"She looked at Winnie as if she was a bug that needed squashing. She jabbed a finger at her and said, 'If my husband dies, I will *gut* you. I will cut off your head and kick it around the hall.'

"Then she turned to the boys, pointing at Ewan the same way. 'Then I'll do the same thing to you.' She poked her finger at Jude as if it were a death ray. 'And then I'll come for you.'

"I butted in and said, 'Wait a minute.' She turned on me.

"'You knew what she was going to do, didn't you, Arthur? After she killed Sam, you would be the headman.'

"I said that was crazy. Emily exploded. She called me every name that exists.

"Then she said, 'If anyone or anything hurts my husband again, or if he dies, I will show you a *blood feud* like no one has ever seen before. I will kill everyone in this place, starting with you.' She pointed at me and I stepped back. But I wasn't going to let her run me around.

"I said, 'You can't kill me. No one else can run the underground.'

"She gave me this *look* and said, 'I can run every system down here, better than you. Do you think I've been sitting in my room all day, being the good housewife? You gave Sam the schematics to everything. They're on our desk. Jeremy set up our computer to teach Sam how to run the shelter. *Anyone* could learn how to run this place from it.

"'You ought to check your passwords, *Arturo*. They might have been changed.'

"I said, 'You can't be serious.'

"She said, 'I'm serious. I would have played nice if that *bitch*'—another jab at Winnie—'hadn't tried to kill Sam. Now, it's war. The meeting's over.' Before she left, she leveled a few more rounds. '*Bitch*'—she pointed at Winnie—'tell those whores out on the floor that, if they put their hands on my husband, I will cut them off. If they keep looking at him the way they do, I will have their *eyes.*'"

Sam couldn't say a word.

"Winnie hasn't left her room since; the boys either. I checked my passwords. They've been changed and I can't change them back. Emily is running the underground."

The air went out of Sam. Valerie was running the place, not Em. He'd not thought of this.

"She can kill all of us any time she wants to."

Sam nodded. He'd promised Art that he'd break her neck if she got out of control again. And she was verra out of control.

"All right, Arthur. Ah'll do it."

"Get the new passwords before you kill her, Sam."

41

Sam sat in their room, sick at heart. Sick in the rest of his body, too. He had a bright red scar across his chest, freshly healed. Where Winnie had stuck him under the arm and on his chest looked as if a butcher had hacked out a hunk of meat. Pain shot from the area if he moved. If that was the best healing his Power could manage, he'd hate to see what would happen if he really got hurt. Or maybe he had really been hurt. Walking from the hospital to his room had felt as if he'd run all the way to Jamayuh on a hot day.

He had the Book open on his lap. He needed guidance. Emily kept out of sight and Valerie had disappeared. He could have called out the boys to search the shelter, but none would come out, they were so frightened of her. He sighed. Valerie must be in the white world. As soon as he'd rested a bit and figured out the right of it, he'd go there and kill her.

As he remembered, Jer the Tek had given them clear commands on how to treat bad people. Valerie was bad. Threatening to kill everyone, and meaning it, was bad. Breaking into the computer and changing the passwords was bad.

He scratched his chin. Or was it? The computer was in plain sight, not hidden or locked up. Anyone could have done what she did. Was it bad to take advantage of something that was there?

No, but the sneaky way she'd done it and what she'd threatened to do with what she learned was bad.

He leafed through the Book. Its radiant words sent beams of light throughout the room. He could read it now, in addition to marveling at its beauty. What did Jeremy say about bad people?

The first thing he noticed was that Jer had given him, Sam Baahuhd, unlimited power over the village and the underground. That was Command Two: "If I'm in the shelter, I'll enforce the Commands. If I'm not—and this is command number two—Sam will enforce them."

After reading the whole Book, Sam realized that Jeremy hadn't said anything about how to handle bad people.

The angel Eliana was the one who had said how bad people should be handled.

Sam traced the words with his finger, saying them softly.

"How should we handle bad people, Ellie? How do they do it in your world?"

"No bad people, Jeremy."

"There aren't any bad people in your world?"

"No. All good. All nice."

"Well, here, they're not always nice. There are evil people here. How should we handle them?"

"Love them. No let do bad things and love them."

That was the key. How was he to love Valerie until she stopped wanting to kill people?

But this was not the real point. Sam knew that the Book with its Commands wasn't a real holy book, like the one the snake men waved around, preaching doom and pestilence. The Bible was a real holy book that should be given true credence. But before they came underground, no one, including the snake men, could read, so no one had known what the Bible really said.

Now he could read, but, unfortunately, Sam had not been able to make himself read the Bible or any of the other holy texts Jeremy had left for them. For some reason, when he sat down to begin, something requiring his attention always came up. When he read a word or two, the begetting and begatting got in his way. The language in the Bible was not the same as that on Emily's flash cards. Somewhere in that mess of words that comprised the Bible, he'd heard that a real list of what you were and weren't supposed to do existed, but he'd never found it.

The Commands were a bunch of half-baked ideas a messed up sixteen-year-old boy yelled in a fit of something. Rage at his mom or because the earth was coming to an end. Sam had known Jeremy all his life, mostly as a weird kid who walked around the estate muttering to himself. Jeremy had been very heated when he shouted the Commands. He had intended that they keep the Commands, and made keeping them his condition for letting anyone into the shelter. Sam agreed to them because of that, and also because he felt that a man needed something to hold on to when the whole world was being destroyed.

But the Commands weren't the word of God. God was bigger and truer than Jeremy's ravings.

Sam believed in God because he didn't see any reason for the world to have lasted as long as it did without some very powerful force keeping it together. He figured the nuclear holocaust happened because God had got fed up, or maybe blinked for an instant and let people do what they had always wanted to do. Every human thing he'd ever seen, be it from New York City or the surrounding villages, was the product of greed, viciousness, or just plain hate.

An occasional bright spot stuck up, like his stallion, Oned, and the forest and the river, but life on earth was mostly people spending their time trying to con each other. He certainly had lived that way. Every year, he had juggled the count of the crops so that the

Edgartons had thought they had grown less than the real yield. He had sold the excess and pocketed the difference. He was no better than the rest.

Good and evil were complicated. Good was easy to see: things got better and people got happier. Evil was easy to see, too, with one con after another happening all around him. But pure evil like the horned devil the snake men preached? Only when the lady started bringing the general and his men out to the estate had Sam learned that true evil existed. Well, the feds' camps dotting the countryside had showed him evil, too. And the look on Mollie's face when the disease had her. The destruction of the world with the atomics was just another step.

But they had survived. Sam attributed that to God. Certainly, Jeremy and all the others who had built the shelter had played a part in their survival, but Sam didn't think they could have put all the pieces together without God.

The work parties had fought over how to read the plans and who got to run things. He knew how much stuff the contractors had stolen from the site, until he put an end to that and put it in his own warehouses. No way the underground could have gotten built without something huge running the show.

Also, God had spoken to him. Right before the world exploded and he found Valerie, God spoke to him. Sam had been standing there in the field, weeping like a sissy girl about being able to manage the underground shelter and about everything he loved being destroyed.

God had talked to him in loud, very normal English, and had told him He would protect him, answer his prayers, and be with him all the time. He'd also told him to look out for Valerie, sneaking up on him with a big black pistol. Sam was sure God had kept her from plugging him.

God had been silent ever since. Though it was true things had gone pretty well. Except for Winnie knifing him and Valerie threatening to kill everyone and kick Winnie's and Jude's and Ewan's heads around the hall, plus her murdering a third of the villagers, things had been peaceful.

The systems Jeremy had designed, worked. They had food and water and air. Valerie conveniently had eliminated the worst of the troublemakers. Plus he'd fallen in love with and married her and Emily, a couple of women more exciting than he could have imagined.

So maybe God was keeping His end of the bargain.

But what to do now? He didn't want to execute Valerie; that would kill Emily, too. But he'd promised Arthur he would kill her if she got out of control and he kept his promises.

Sam was moved to get on his knees and pray, but wasn't sure he'd be able to get up again. Given the state of his wound and his aching knees, he decided to give it a go where he was. He even spoke regular English.

"God, if I could trouble you for a little advice? We've been doing fine down here. Much obliged; I'm real grateful. But I've just got this situation." He laid out what had happened.

"Should I kill Valerie?"

Silence.

42

Sleet slashed Sam's face. Shards of fine ice blown by vicious gusts ripped the white world. He couldn't see anything, except for a darkening of the already dark skies over the monster's lagoon. Shrieking wind filled his ears. He leaned into it, shirt plastered to his body.

"Valerie, where are ye?" he yelled.

A hunting knife ripped past his head. A pistol appeared, and then more weapons, all screaming toward him at full speed. They hadn't been around for ages, and, when they had been, they'd floated along lazily. Something was wrong.

"Valerie!" He shouted her name over and over. Nothing, except guns and grenades and knives. They missed him, but passed close enough to keep him lively. "Valerie, are ye here?"

"Valerie!" Sam didn't know how long he could stay out here. The squalls beat against his barely healed wounds. His eyes searched the maelstrom, hoping to see her.

She appeared as a shadow in the storm. As she got closer, he could see she was wearing a shirt covered with blood. It must have been the shirt she had worn when he'd been in the sick bay. She looked white and shrunken. Red gashes and circles from the monster's arms were all over her. She packed a pistol in each hand.

"You're dead," she said, stopping fifteen or twenty feet from him, peering at him with distrust. "I went back in the hospital after I set Winnie straight. Arthur came in and told me to leave. I knew you had died. He didn't want me to see."

"Ah didn't die, lass. Ah'm here."

"No! You're a trick. He said you were dead. It's all my fault."

"Who's he? Why is it your fault?"

She jerked her head toward the pond where the monster lived. "My father told me you were dead. I didn't protect you. I let Winnie do it. It's my fault." She began to dash past him.

"Ah'm alive." He grabbed her arm as she passed. "Touch me."

"No." She pulled away. "You can't fool me. You're dead. I have to die." Without warning, she raised a pistol to her temple and squeezed the trigger.

Sam was faster and knocked the gun away. It discharged into the air. He wrestled the revolvers from her. Using his uninjured arm, he pulled her close and tight.

"Give me my guns," she cried. "I should die."

"Lass, lass. That's not true." He held her to him with his good arm, grasping the firearms in the free hand. "But we have to talk about some things. Is your room quieter than this? And warmer?"

"No. It's all been like this since you died." She looked poorer than he'd ever seen her. Caved in. Beaten. Some of the monster's marks on her flesh were fresh and others were scabbed and full of pus. He pulled her closer, huddling against the storm. It didn't help much.

She touched him and felt his warmth. "You're *not* dead."

The effort of restraining her caused a thin line of blood to seep through his shirt under his arm. She shrieked when she saw it. "You're bleeding!"

"Shh. Ah'm OK. We need to leave. We'll go back to our room."

"The only way I can leave here is dead. He told me." Sunken eyes, dull skin. She put her hands over her ears, shuddering.

"What's the matter, lass?"

"My father is talking."

"What is he saying?"

"He says that, if you die, there's nothing for me but this place." She turned to him. "He says you *will* die and leave me here." She appeared to listen to something and then smiled faintly.

"You came here to kill me, didn't you?"

"Maybe, Valerie. But not until we've talked."

It was like a switch flipped inside her. She threw her head back and screamed. He dropped the pistols and grabbed her. He could barely hold her, even using both arms. The sleet formed eddies around them and she kept screaming, "No! No!" Then broken sobs.

"Why're ye screamin', Valerie?" he said.

"I can't live without you." Rivulets of tears ran down her cheeks. She kept screaming and struggling, saying she couldn't live without him. Then, after a while, a silly grin came to her face.

"I was going to kill myself because I thought you were dead." She raised a hand to her brow, shielding herself from him. "But you're not dead. You came here to kill *me*. You don't want me. I can't believe how funny that is." She bent over laughing.

"*I* want to live because you're alive, and you want to kill me." Her laughter tipped into hysterics. She struggled in his arms, laughing and sobbing. "He's right. I don't deserve to live. My mother should have had an abortion . . ."

Sam gasped. "No, lass. Not that."

"He says that I never should have been born."

A mottled green tentacle poked up out of the frozen ground, searching for her leg. Sam aimed a pistol and shot it off.

"Let's get out of here, lass." Sam held her and willed them away.

They were sitting in their room, tight against each other on the luxurious sofa. Valerie wore her thin bloody blouse; her wounds were painful to see.

"I shouldn't be here. I'm dirty." She struggled to get off the sofa. He held her there.

"Ye belong here same as me, Valerie. We need to talk about what ye said to Art'ur and them when ah was sick. Tell me what happened."

She told him exactly what Arthur had told him. Sam listened carefully. She didn't lie or try to make herself look better. After screaming at Winnie and the others, she went back to the hospital to be with him. When Arthur told her to leave so he could talk to Sam, she thought it was because he was dead.

Sam realized something. "Ye thought ah was dead, and ye went into the white world."

She nodded.

"Ye *didn't* kill Art'ur or Winnie or the boys like ye said."

"No. All I could think of was that I couldn't live without you."

She'd tried to kill *herself*, not anyone else. Sam sucked in a breath. "D' ye think ye'd have killed them if ye'd thought of it?"

She was silent a long time. "I don't know. I think I knew that Winnie didn't do it on purpose. If she had killed you on purpose, I would have killed her.

"I need to get something." She struggled to her feet and went to the desk. She picked up a pad and pen and sat down next to him. She began writing. "These are the new passwords for the shelter's systems. You should have them before you kill me." Ripping off the sheet, she handed it to him. Her eyes said she expected him to kill her, and that she wouldn't fight it.

"Why didn't ye tell me that ye were learning the underground's systems?"

"It's how I am. I was taught to spy and sneak. And steal."

"To kill?"

"Yes." Gaunt face, sunken cheeks. "I'm very tired. Would you please kill me?"

He studied her. She wasn't evil. She was hurt. She would prob-ably kill herself if he died, and not anyone else. She understood that what had happened was an accident. She would have killed Winnie if Winnie had murdered him, but that was within the village's code. If someone murdered another woman's husband, the wife could take her revenge by killing the killer. That was the code of the Hamptons. Kill who kills yours. Simple, instant justice.

Was Valerie evil? She had scared Winnie and the boys and Arthur, but was that a crime? He'd cussed out many of his people when they'd done something wrong. Made them piss themselves, he scared them so. And they sure as hell had stopped doing whatever they had been doing that got him so mad.

Was what Valerie had done so bad? Art expected him to kill her for it, but that didn't feel right. What should he do with her?

Sam heard the angel Eliana's chirpy voice, sounding as though she were there. "Love them. No let do bad things and love them."

That seemed like something God would say. It seemed more in keeping with what he thought was in the Bible. Sam thought that God, as the force that kept the whole universe together, must at least *like* what He was holding tight. Otherwise, why not let go and let everything go to . . . hell? Did hell exist? He didn't know, but he knew that the world would be up troll's creek if something didn't make things turn out right.

God *had* to like everything that existed if he kept it going. Maybe He loved it.

Something deep inside him opened. A feeling of warmth. And sadness, looking at Valerie's pitiful state. He loved her and wanted her to be happy, to want to live.

Was that how God felt? Yes, Sam realized, and much more. A glow flooded up inside him.

He should love bad people the way God loved him. The fullness rose to where it threatened to pour out. His prayer was being answered right then. God loved him and everything else. He turned to Valerie in wonder, mouth a little open, staring.

"Are you going to kill me now?" she said.

"No, lass. Ah want to talk to ye." She looked different. Tiny. Young. "How old were ye when he got ye, lass?"

"Nine."

"An' he started trainin' ye to be the way ye are, to kill and such, right then?"

She froze. "Yes. And other things." She told him the other things. Sam listened, and the ache in his heart grew so large, it filled the underground.

"Since ye were nine, he's been sayin' stuff like that to ye." Just a little girl. Taken from her parents when she was six, adopted by a monster at nine. She'd never had a chance. His mind's eye opened and he could see her as a little girl, dressed in a pink dress with ruffles, such as he had seen the lady wear when they were small. A pink dress, a laughing little girl, clapping her hands as her family ringed around her. They were laughing because it was her birthday. He saw balloons and a cake.

Valerie had never had anything like that.

"Ye said back there, in the white world, that he talks to ye all the time. Is he talkin' to ye now?"

"No, because you're here. It's when I'm alone."

"Do ye pay attention to him when he talks?"

"Yes, because I have to. He's my boss. What he says is true."

Sam leaned toward her, holding her shoulders and looking into her eyes. "From now on, *ah'm* your boss. Ye do what ah say. The monster can't tell ye anything. Ah'm your boss."

"But what if you leave?"

"Yer gonna stay with me from now on. Next to me. Forever if we need to. Ah'm your boss. Ah tell ye what to do."

She nodded.

"Ye never go back to the white world. Ye stay with me, inside of Emily. If ye want to come out, ye ask me. Ye know how to take orders like a soldier. Ah'm your general. Only me."

"You aren't going to kill me?"

"No. Ah will never do that. And ye will never . . ." What? Kill anyone? He'd want her to avenge his death if someone killed him. He'd want her to defend herself. "Ye will follow my orders."

She looked much brighter.

"Now ah'm going to heal your cuts and all. And then ye're going to show me how to run this place. Ah want ye to teach me all the underground's systems on the computer. An' no more sneakin' or lyin' to me. Ye understand?"

While she was teaching him, he'd figure out a way to make her want to live after he died.

43

Heeeelloooo, boys and girls! This is Captain Art Romero reporting from the Good Ship Underground.

Arthur wobbled at his computer, looking as if he'd fall off the chair.

What's the newwwws of the day?

He giggled.

Captain Art is in love! I'm drunk out of my mind. I'm a babbling idiot.

He lolled in the seat, unable to sit straight.

I've seen Sam like this when he's spent the night banging his brains out. But I never thought yours truly
...

She's a wet dream. Seeing her lying in bed with that blond hair all around. Her huge breasts with those pink, and, I'm telling you, *pink* tips. Her white skin. You can't believe how soft it is. The place where her legs open. Most of the guys I know would have heart attacks being where I am.

And it turns out, after she got over that shit that Sam did to her, little Winnie is really hot stuff. New York City gals ain't got nothin' on the village's best.

He shook his hand as if he'd touched something hot.

I spend all the time that I'm not working inside of her or getting ready to get in her. Or resting from just having been . . .

I can't believe what I feel for her. I didn't feel this way about my wife. No one else either. Not the fanciest chick in Manhattan.

He dropped his head as though he were whispering, and kept typing.

I want to get married. I want to have kids. I can't believe it. I want to be a dad . . .

She's smart, too. She likes my teaching better than Emily's and so do the boys. Of course, I can't blame her. Emily threatening to decapitate her and the boys pretty much totalled that relationship.

Winnie is very smart. If she'd been born anywhere but the village, she would have really been something.

But then I wouldn't have her.

He gazed into space.

She's funny, too. She tells me all sorts of stories about the village that I didn't know.

She also told me that she and Sam had had four children, not two. Two girls were killed by the "spots."

His expression sobered.

But that means we can only have two kids; then she'll have had six, which is the most a woman should have.

Only two kids. I couldn't imagine having any kids a year ago.

She's getting married in the blue dress she wore that night in the club. She looks amazing in it. She's the most beautiful woman in the world and I'll love her forever.

So that's the news.

Captain Art, signing off.

He deleted it all.

"Someday, I'm going to have to really write up a report. But not today," he said. He shut the computer down and walked out of his office.

The best thing about being in love with Winnie is that I never think about Emily, he told himself.

44

"We're celebrating a great thing!" Sam raised a glass of apple juice. He stood in the middle of the picture-viewing wall, all sixty-four occupants of the underground arrayed before him. "We have been down here one year today! We're alive!" He neglected to mention the thirty-one people Emily and Arthur had killed. "We're healthy! And we got the harvest in!"

He threw his head back and unleashed a powerful ululating sound, which all the villagers echoed, clapping and whistling.

"Remember a year ago when we were so scared? Didn't think we'd live the night?" He looked out at the people, still wearing their black Russian uniforms, but cheerier now, decorated with strips of colorful fabric and fur. Emily had convinced him to let her give a few of the lady's dresses and a fur coat to the people. The village women had adorned the uniforms with scraps so that each was unique.

"Here we are, settled in to stay!" Everyone raised glasses of juice, liberated from Arthur's hidden stock. Which wasn't hidden from Sam anymore. If Arthur was a little disgruntled by what Sam had had to do to get him to cough up his secrets, good. Art had revealed hidden passages and hiding places, whole rooms, caches of almost everything—and the amazing fact that the underground had two additional floors. The hall and corridor had two unoccupied floors above them. "For legroom, when people get stir crazy," Art had said. Sam kept to himself everything Art had revealed.

"We've got a good place to live." He looked around, seeking agreement. Since he posed the statement in the Voice, the people concurred immediately. "We've got fields that can feed us so we don't have to eat army slop anymore. We've got an orchard better than the one in the village. And we've got a feast right now!"

They cheered and gathered around a huge soup kettle. Sam had ordered one of the sheep slaughtered for the occasion, and the only way to share one sheep sixty-four ways was to make a soup out of it. But they also had turnips and sweet potatoes, beets, greens, and regular potatoes in the soup, and all sorts of greens for salad. Plus soybeans, which everyone was coming to hate.

"Eat up, everyone! We've got dancing and movies tonight. Just like a stomp!" Sam downed his apple juice, hoping the people wouldn't notice there was no hooch and a pile-on wasn't scheduled. "It's the new way, and it's a good way." They cheered wildly; he used the Voice to ensure they did. "Everyone's peaceful and getting along. Most of us can read a little. Some more. Some of us speak regular English; some are still workin' on it. But we'll get there! Look at me, I can talk just like the lady!" Sam grinned.

They gathered around him with their bowls, faces alight. Soon they were slurping down soup.

"I've got to say something else. Rupert, come up here." Rupert looked startled, but he put down his bowl and joined his father. Sam put his arm around him, smiling broadly. Sam had spent much of the year loving and healing Emily and Valerie. And loving them more, and again. He'd been absorbed by the woman, or women, in his life. Then he'd gotten knifed by Winnie and had had to rest up. He hadn't put his attention on the growing fields or the operation of the underground the way he should have. Rupert had covered for him. He'd done a great job and gotten little credit. Sam would fix that.

"I want to tell everyone how proud I am of my firstborn son, Rupert Baahuhd." Beaming, Sam clutched Rupert close. "He's been as good a son and a man as he could be. Ye"—Sam lapsed into the village dialect when speaking to Rupert—"know that he's yer headman when ah'm gone. Ah just wanted to tell ye that it's ma wish an' from the bottom o' ma heart. Rupert is the next headman!" Sam grabbed Rupert's hand and raised it above their heads.

"Rupert!" "Rupert!" Voices rose in cheers and ululation. Whistles rang out. Everyone approved of Sam's choice, though it was not really a choice since it had been spelled out in the Commands, which a few could read by now.

Sam turned to Rupert and kissed him on each cheek, then hugged him tight. The people kept cheering, glad the succession had been sealed.

"Now, everyone, we have a treat. Arthur found a bunch of instruments." Sam had forced him to disgorge them from one of his caches. "I know how much you like your music. Now we can play up a storm. You know that we of the village can play with the best." Arthur passed out guitars, a mandolin, a stand-up bass, a cello. Followed by cymbals, drums, a saxophone, and several brass instruments.

"If you know how to play these, go ahead. Just put what you can't play in a pile here. Arthur says he's got electric guitars and things, too. We'll try them another time."

Sam watched Arthur handing out instruments. Sam stopped him when he got to a couple of shiny pieces.

"Wait, Art. I'm taking those." He took the saxophone and the clarinet. Jeremy had played a clarinet and Chaz Edgarton had played the sax. Sam wanted them because of the memories they held. And maybe he could learn to play them. Or one of his unborn sons could.

"You just go on and dance and have fun. We have to have a meeting," Sam said.

Arthur, Rupert, Emily, and Winnie detached from the crowd and headed for the VIP corridor.

Sam waved his hand and then followed.

45

"When Sam called this meeting a couple of weeks ago, he said he wanted to form what we'd call a 'think tank' in the army—a group of high-level people he could bounce ideas off." Arthur looked at Sam before going on.

"Yeah. I wanted those I could trust to know about the workings of this place so they could back me up if anything went bad. And I want to know what you think about some things." Sam signaled Arthur to continue.

"So, here we are, the executive committee for our little society, except that we aren't executives," Arthur explained. "Sam's the boss. He makes the decisions." He shot Sam a look that said, I'll do what you want, but I don't have to like it. Sam smiled happily at Art's expression. "We're the *gofers*."

"We are na gophers," Rupert said.

"Not animal gophers, Ru. *People* that 'go for' and do the work that Sam sets out," Arthur explained.

"Ah don't see why he needs anybody but me. Ah'm his son. Ah'm the next headman."

"That's right, Rupert, but even you and Sam can't do everything.

We'll do the stuff that you can't do. And give Sam a sounding board."
Seeing Rupert's puzzled look, Arthur added, "People he can talk to
about problems."

Rupert's eyes narrowed. His shoulders tensed. He opened his
mouth, but, ultimately, didn't object.

"OK. Back to business. This is a pretty exciting occasion. As Sam
said, we've been down here one year today and we're still alive. A lot of
it is due to us, and a lot is due to Jeremy's engineering. Let's have a toast
to Jeremy!" They toasted with mineral water. Arthur had broken out
a pizza from the frozen trove and microwaved it. It tasted like rubber.

"So far, all the life-support systems have worked exactly as
planned or better. We're getting along as a society—and we've had
two marriages: Sam and Emily and Winnie and me." He beamed.
"I think we can feel good about what we've achieved. Good, but not
complacent."

Sam saw that Arthur had a stack of papers next to him. He also
knew what some of them were, from having seen the lady's father
bring his fancy horse trainer to the farm to discuss breeding race-
horses. They were pedigrees, family trees.

"I need to bring up something that's been on the back burner
while we attended to staying alive. Specifically, our responsibility
to future generations. Jeremy and I—and a team of scientists—ana-
lyzed these documents for the villagers. We were going to use them
to determine who got into the underground. As it is, everyone did.

"I've deliberately not brought this up until now because we
needed time to settle in *and* I knew what a loaded issue what I've
got to say would be."

"Loaded with wha'?" Rupert said, looking lost.

"I meant that it's hard to think about, Rupert. But we can't put
it off forever." Art pulled out a computer printout. "What I've got
here are the ancestral lineages for everyone in the village. Jeremy
and I collected the data last year. Do you remember, Sam?"

Sam nodded. They'd asked everyone about their relations back
to their great-great-great-grandparents, which everyone in the

village knew and was happy to discuss. Kinfolk were very important to the villagers and everyone in the Hamptons. They knew more about who was related to whom and how than anyone but royalty, Sam thought.

"We fed these documents into a computer and came out with this report." He patted the printout. "What this says is that, basically, the whole village is a variant of Sam. He represents the gene pool for the village in its most concentrated and perfected form. What that means for future generations is obvious." Arthur looked around the table.

"What d' ye mean?" Rupert said.

"Basically, Sam should not have children with anyone from the village. And the people of the village should not have children with each other. They've intermarried too much already. It's amazing that the type of genetic disorders we see aren't worse."

"But that's how we get the Power and the Voice, Arthur. From strong lines," Sam tossed in.

"Strong is good, in some cases. But what we're looking at down here is the same population intermarrying *forever*, essentially. The problems are going to get worse, exponentially."

"What is that?" Rupert's mouth opened a bit and he looked from Arthur to the others.

"Much worse, fast, until the people down here will be exhibiting mutations and genetic breakdowns. You'll have . . ."

"I think we know what we'll have, Arthur. You can see people with problems in the hall," Emily said.

"Expect much worse than that."

Sam scowled, reverting back to the village brogue in indignation. "Yer talkin' abou' ma people. Yer sayin' they shouldna have kids. How dare ye."

"I have to dare, Sam. It's that important. People are going to be down here for a long, long time. The radiation indices don't show any drop at all. The worst case is what we've got. That means people can't just have kids with anyone they want. That has to be planned, and, for as long as we're alive, by us. We're the leaders.

"We have to say, 'You can have a kid with this person and no other,' even if the people aren't married or are married to other people. It has to be like that, or we'll get mental and physical disabilities all over the place."

"Ah know that kind o' chart," Sam said. "The lady's father used 'em to say which horse went with another. Dinna ye think that a horse is different than a man? Ye can't tell a man to go to that woman and have a baby. Ye can't tell a woman to go with a man she dinna fancy because a chart says she should." Sam had seen this coming when they did the charts, but it still outraged him.

"That's exactly what I'm saying, Sam. For the good of the future generations, it may be necessary for people to put the good of the people to come *ahead* of their own preferences."

"Ye mean foock a lass like a stud dog would do a brood bitch?" Rupert said, mouth opening in delight like a thrilled child's.

"Yes. We're talking about the survival of a whole society. It's got to be more than hearts and flowers and 'I'm in love with Joey.' A whole new ethic will have to apply. We'll have to determine who can have kids and with whom. We must do that—and see that it sticks."

"Do you believe that, Arthur?" said Emily. "Sam and I are married. I'm not going to have a baby with anyone else just because you say so."

"In your case, Emily, that's fine. You and Sam are a genetic outcross. You come from completely different genetic stock. You can have a bunch of babies and it will be fine—up to a point. Say you and Sam don't practice birth control and you have twelve kids. That's a pretty big impact on the next generation. Twelve out of, say, one hundred people, will have the same genes. Since the villagers are already closely related, your kids will create another genetic problem in the generation after. If the villagers have babies with your babies, it will increase the concentration of Sam's genes so that another unhealthy situation occurs."

"It's again' the Commands," Sam sputtered. They were all he could think of to stop the discussion.

"The Commands. There's an interesting topic. I know that you believe in the Commands, Sam, but they're basically a bunch of ideas that Jeremy threw out as he was planning on skipping the planet. I don't know how much attention should be paid to them."

"The Commands are the Commands," Sam reiterated. "Ah follow them. Everyone here will follow them. 'One husband, one wife. Fidelity. No affairs.' Those are the Commands."

"We'll have to think of it as different from having an affair. It will have to be doing one's duty to the future of the underground."

"Don't tell me I'm supposed to have a baby with someone beside Sam. Forget it, Arthur!" Emily barked.

Arthur took a deep breath. "OK. Well, let's look at who definitely shouldn't have children." He held up a printout. "Basically, almost everyone in the village shouldn't, except for Sam and Winnie. Winnie's Sam's first cousin, but she's not from the village. Three-fourths of her genetic material is from a different base. For the rest, the data on IQ, aptitude, and achievement are very clear. Ditto tendencies to addiction and alcoholism as well as social aberration. The village shouldn't reproduce at all."

Sam half stood. "What? These're ma people."

"We're talking about planning for the future. We don't need very many more people. Just enough to replace those who die. The age distribution of the population shows that about twenty should die in the next five to ten years. That's all we need to produce."

"I can't believe we're talking about this, Arthur. It's so cold."

"We need to get cold, Emily. We don't have the luxury of being sentimental."

"What about all the people who have gotten pregnant down here already?" she barked. "The villagers are obviously having sex. What do you do about that? Can we expect twenty babies next year?"

Arthur smiled. "No. There will be no babies next year, unless someone at this table is pregnant. The minute the bombs stopped going off, I inoculated the population against most diseases. I also implanted a birth control chip in all the women of childbearing age—excluding Emily and Winnie and a few others who had genetic patterns divergent from the norm. The chip will prevent them from bearing children for about forty years, their reproductive span."

"You did *what*? Did you tell them?" Emily's eyes bulged.

"No. And I think it best that we don't. We could have twenty or thirty kids a year, forever. We'd breed ourselves into starvation."

Emily sat blinking while Sam stewed. What Arthur said was true. He knew enough from breeding animals to know the village was doomed if everyone had all the kids they wanted. Sam had controlled the number of children his wives had, so they'd had a very small total compared with what four healthy women could have borne. The village could only support so many even when they'd been aboveground. Every year he had sent groups of young people off to neighboring villages, or to the wild lands to the west, to form new villages.

But to take away a woman's ability to bear children without her having any say? "'Y' did that, Art, without tellin' me? Ah'm the headman, Art, not ye. Ye seem to be cuttin' me an' Jeremy's Commands short. *Ah* am the headman."

"Yes, you are, Sam. But I have a different mission and it overrides yours. My mission is to make sure the population that comes out of the underground when all this is over is fit to fight the general's men. I'm the military portion of this operation. I will make sure that the underground is healthy—as long as I'm alive."

"Ye're telling me that yer mission is more important than mine?"

"Yes." Arthur's hand crept to his belt, seeking a weapon, but he was unarmed. "You can rough me up all you want, but my mission takes into account the well-being of the entire population of the underground, not individual happiness or desires. And it comes from the highest levels of the military, which would have been running the country had the revolution succeeded."

"Are ye *crazy*, man?" Sam was aghast. "Ah'm the headman of the village. Ah'm named in the Commands. Ye were there when Jeremy gave me control of the underground, and my son after me." He glared at Arthur.

Arthur sighed. "My mission comes from the highest level of the military. That's my authority. It supersedes everything Jeremy said. But we can make it work. People can have their relationships and marriages."

Sam sensed something. "What aren't ye telling us, Art? What's the rest?"

"Nothing worse than what I've already said. Except for one thing. Me. I'm a complete outcross to all of you. I was selected to come here because of that, among other reasons. I've got no genetic or other diseases, and I come from a line of people who live forever. I've got a very high IQ and achievement scores. I was sent here to start a new line of people."

"Well, swell, Art. Have a blast." Emily spit out. Sam could see her seething.

"Yeah, well that's sort of it. I can pair up with pretty much anyone I want, from a genetic standpoint. However, the statistical analysis says that almost no one in the village should reproduce.

"The three women who were taken captive and made into wives are an exception. These women are not related to the village stock." Arthur picked up a paper. "Minnie Whersher, Donna Reebecker, and Suzie Willstatt. I've seen them in the hall. What do you know about them?"

Sam burst into laughter. "All three're ugly as a cow's butt and jus' as smart. Ah wouldna go stickin anythin' into them, Art'ur. No tellin' what ye'll pull out."

"Diseased?"

"More 'en ah can heal."

"I've got antibiotics that can kill anything. I'll heal them. There's one pairing that Jeremy and I didn't consider, because the possibility didn't exist when we were talking. There are two people down here who aren't related in any way. A total outcross. They have no genetic diseases and are bright as hell. The offspring of that pairing would be a gift to all the future generations." He looked straight at Emily.

"Are you crazy, Arthur? I won't have a baby with you!"

Sam caught on to what Arthur had been saying an instant later than Em had. "Ye will not have a child wi' ma wife!"

Rupert had been looking from face to face, obviously lost. At this, he looked up, highly animated. "*Ah'll* have a babe wi' her. *Ah'll* make a good babe."

Sam stood up. "NO ONE WILL HAVE A BABE With MA WIFE BUT ME!" He used the Voice as powerfully as he could.

Rupert flushed red, then got up and left the room. Sam glared after him. He'd seen Rupert staring at Emily. He should have known what it had meant.

"Well, OK. It's just an idea," Arthur said. "But, logically and genetically, Emily and I are the best mix. Even better than Emily and Sam. The underground could use as many of our babies as it could get. They would swamp the influence of Sam's genes."

"NO ONE'S SWAMPIN' MA GENES!" Sam bellowed. They were silent for a while.

"Well, that's all for today." Arthur gathered up his papers. "Happy anniversary, everyone!"

Sam glared across the table as Art put his papers in a folder. An ashen-faced Winnie sat at Arthur's right. She'd sat silently during the meeting, which Sam would have expected. She was a village woman, however recently liberated. Her rigid posture and expression of horror told him that Arthur hadn't shared his vision for the future generations with her. Or his plans for Emily. Or anything about his perfect genes.

"Hey, Art, don' ye think ye should tell yer wife wha' yer thinkin'? She seems a mite stoofed." The old village word for shocked didn't express how stunned Winnie looked.

She dashed out of the room.

"Wait, Win . . ." Arthur ran after her. The room was silent again.

"Could I just say one thing?" Emily spoke softly and looked at Sam. "I've been trying to find a good time to tell you, Sam. I'm pregnant." She beamed.

"Oh, ma darlin'." Sam wrapped his arms around her. He'd known since he started the baby within her months before. He was just waiting for her to tell him.

"I'm so happy, Sam. I think I'm about three months along." She bounced up and down in his arms.

Sam kissed her and smiled broadly. He'd figured out a way to make her want to live after he died. A sweet, smiling baby would make her happy. And they'd have as many children as they wanted, Arthur be damned.

PART II

THE MIDDLE YEARS—
FROM YEAR EIGHT TO YEAR
THIRTEEN UNDERGROUND

46

"Arthur! Sam's having a heart attack! Help us!" Emily screamed into the intercom.

"It's nothin', Art. Jus' somethin' ah ate." Sam pushed her aside and yelled into the microphone. But he lost his balance and fell into the wall, hitting his head. He slid down to a sitting position, blood dripping down his forehead. He clutched his chest. Fear gripped him.

Seconds later, Art appeared at their door with a gurney, and with Jude and Ewan, Sam's kids with Winnie. All of them looked horrified.

"I'm OK. It's something ah ate. Ah just tripped," Sam protested, until a pain cut him off. He bent over and put his hand over his heart, grimacing.

"You're going to the sick bay, Sam," Arthur said. "If it's hurting that much, it's not 'something you ate.'"

Art did the same things he'd done eight years earlier when he had detoxed Sam. He clamped the thing on the end of Sam's finger, wrapped the cloth around his arm and tightened it up. On his chest, he put stickies hooked to a machine that made wavy lines. Arthur looked into his eyes and listened to his heart. Took his blood and piss. Sometime in there, he bandaged Sam's head. The only new thing Arthur did was move a big metal box in front of him.

"OK. Sit up straight, Sam." Sam sat as straight as he could in the hospital bed. "Put your hands up on the handles and don't move." The box made a noise and Art said, "Chest X-ray. I'll develop it and look at the rest of the results. I'll be back."

His son Shane stood next to the gurney, peering at Sam through the bed's metal rails. "Da, are you all right?"

"Yeah, Shane, ah'm fine. Fair an' fine." Most of the time Sam spoke regular English, but he lapsed into the dialect when he was worried. And he was worried about Shane and Emily and their other two kids. Emily had Eli on her hip. At three years old, she could still carry him. Shane was seven and Joshua was five.

"You're not going to die, are you, Da?" Shane asked. Joshua's pinched face was visible behind Shane's. Their brown eyes were so big, it was clear they expected him to die on the spot.

"Nah. Ah just ate somethin' bad is all. An' that's what Art's gonna say when he comes back from lookin' at ma piss."

The boys' giggles lifted Sam's spirits.

Sam knew he was going to die soon, but it wouldn't be like this. They had been underground eight years. He was forty-nine years old. Not a single man on either side of his family had made it to forty-nine. Their hearts had gotten them, every one.

His da had died at forty-three. When Sam had hit forty-three, he was sure it was his last year. But he didn't die. With every passing year, he grew more convinced his days were numbered. When his heart took him, it would be fast and final. No gurney. None of Arthur's tests. No coming back.

That's how his da had died, from fit as a bull and doing the work of two men, to lying in the field dead as a stove. That's how he would go.

Sam didn't mind dying, but who would take care of Emily and the boys? And the underground? He worried about it constantly.

Arthur came out of the depths of the sick bay. "Everything's fine, Sam. You've got the heart of a twenty-year-old. It must have been something you ate. Or stress. Stress can affect your heart. Are you under stress?"

Emily almost collapsed with relief, but got hold of herself. She was carrying Eli, and she'd never drop any of her children. "Oh, that's so wonderful. That's great." She beamed at Arthur and at Sam.

"The only thing I'd say is that you could do more aerobic exercise," Art added solemnly.

Emily looked smug. "I told you, Sam."

"Ah get plenty of exercise in the fields. Ah'm strong."

"Absolutely, Sam. You're very strong. But aerobic exercise makes your heart work harder so it pushes blood and oxygen around your body. It's good for your heart. May prolong your life."

"How do ah do it?"

"Em, get him suited up and we'll meet at the gym tomorrow at one." Arthur flashed him a smile. "I'm glad you're OK, Sam. I'd better get back to Winnie. The baby's teething and driving her crazy."

Sam waved at him. "That's how 'tis to be a da, Art."

"What are we gonna do now, Da?" Shane asked when they were back in their room.

"Well, since I scared everyone, how about if we make some popcorn and read?" Sam always spoke regular English with his kids by Emily. It seemed somehow that it might matter with them. As if they might have a higher calling than being stuck in a hole forever.

"The book about Oned, Da?"

"That one, or the harder one your ma just finished. It's about the zoo."

"What's a zoo, Da?" Since he had started talking, Shane had pretty much talked nonstop. About everything. Sam had never seen a person more interested in the world.

"Darned if ah know, Shane. Ah've never been to a zoo maself." Sam smiled, teasing.

"Do it more, Da. Talk like the village!" Shane's eyes glistened.

"Ah, ye lil' gobster. Ah'll wreck yer English sure if'n ah do. Ye'll talk like m'rauders an' the bes' people won' have nothin' to do wi' ye."

"Who are the best people, Da?"

"Ah don' know, Shane, bu' they must be aroun' here some-wheres or Jeremy the Tek wouldna tol' us to talk proper."

The kids looked puzzled. "There aren't any best people, Da. It's just us down here."

"Yeah, ah been thinkin' abou' that, Shane. Ah'll let ye know when ah have the answer. Now let's speak properly."

"Read us the one about the zoo, Da," Shane begged. His little brother Joshua crowded up on the sofa behind him. Eli toddled over waving a mixing spoon.

"You know that I don't read to you anymore. You read."

When Shane had turned four, Emily had begun making books using photos she found in the files and adding text to them. Then she had loaded them onto the reader. They were very simple to start, but she'd added more difficult text as Shane's reading had progressed.

The first book had been a surprise to Sam. It was about Sam's stallion, Oned. Turning on the reader and seeing the stallion's image had brought him up short. Em had found photos of Oned, and some moving pictures, and put them together so the kids would know what a horse looked like and would be able to see their father riding.

"Let's read *Oned* first," Shane said, balancing the reader on his lap, then turning it on and opening at the start. Sam's mouth still went dry whenever he saw the horse. To think that the boys would never see a horse. Or a dog. Or a lake.

Three years ago, when Shane had pointed at a word and read the letters, Sam had been shocked. "H O R S E. That spells 'horse,' Da," Shane had said. "This says 'ran.' And this is R I V E R. What's a river, Da?"

He'd called Emily over. "Do that again, Shane." The boy could read the entire book. "He learned by himself, just with me reading to him. He's only four years old!"

"I'll make some more books, Sam. You can keep teaching him."

Shane learned the one on dogs in one day. Then farm animals. Wild animals. Farm equipment. He learned to spell the names of everyone in the underground.

Shane astonished Sam. Arthur had said that Emily came from genius roots, that she was very smart herself and maybe could have done as much as her parents if she'd had the chance. He'd talked about the effect of genetics, which Sam had always thought of as simply breeding, and how important strong genes were if the underground was to survive.

"Da! Da! Let's read about the zoo." Shane pushed him, bringing him back from his reverie. "And where's the popcorn?"

"I've got it," Emily said. "And some lemonade. Don't get it all over the sofa." She smiled at him. "Are you OK, Sam?"

"Fair an' fine, Em. Don't worry." He had never been happier. It was such a shame he would die soon.

They went through the zoo book. "Why does a rhinoceros look like that, Da? Why does it have a horn? Have you seen a rhinoceros? Let's do the *Wild Animals of North America* book." Shane was still going, but Sam was flagging and Josh and Eli were asleep.

"How about if I teach you something new?"

"What, Da?"

"It's a game Art was showing me the other day. Gave me a set to practice on. I'll get it." Sam set up a chessboard on the coffee table. "It's a real hard game. I've got a book that explains it. And there's a video.

"This is how I think it goes, Shane. You're supposed to capture the other person's king. But you can't just grab it; you have to follow rules." Sam explained everything he could remember from Art's introduction. "You move this like this." Sam moved a piece.

Shane was transfixed by the shapes of the pieces and how they sat on the board. "How do you learn this game, Da? I want to play it."

"Shane, it's time for bed," Emily called.

"Another day is over, Shane. A fair an' fine day."

He was often up in the middle of the night, thinking about the usual things. His death. Emily. The underground. The boys. His boys with Emily were different from any of his other children. Not just smarter, but smaller and more finely made, with bright brown eyes and brown hair. They were beautiful. Sam loved them more than he'd ever thought possible.

Shane, Joshua, and Eli. They had named the first one Shane because Emily thought it was the most beautiful name in the world. Joshua and Eli were named for her brothers who had died in the camps.

"I want to give our boys the lives my brothers never had," she had said. Emily's past never did come back to her; she had no idea who she had been and what she had done. Sam had made up a story about her life, about how happy her family had been until they got picked up, which he made out to be not much before he had run into her in the field. Sam showed her the photos Art had found of her parents and brothers. She'd printed out the pictures and put them on the walls. She looked at them over and over, eyes brimming.

Having the kids hadn't fixed Emily's sadness. He'd thought they'd give her a reason to want to live after he died. She did love the children, fiercely. But she had dark times, too, when the evil of the swamp dragged on her. He could almost see tentacles coming up through the cement and fine carpets of their room. He had healed her as best he could, but the darkness was always lurking, nipping at her.

47

"Do I *have* to wear this?" Sam complained. Emily had suited him up for his exercise date with Arthur. He had pants with almost no leg to them, made of bright yellow slippery material, and with white lines around the bottoms. The shirt had no sleeves and its arms were cut almost to his waist on the sides. The neck was just as low. Bright yellow and white, like the pants. Em had found some shoes big enough for him. They had rubber soles. Running shoes, she called them.

"I don't know why I have to wear this." He grabbed at the front of the shirt, trying to pull the neck up.

"Sam, that's the general's own workout suit. That's what you wear to go to the gym." She eyed him, then went to a drawer and got a stretchy thing, mostly straps. "Here. You're supposed to wear this, too."

"What is it?"

"You put it on under your shorts." She demonstrated with her hands. "So your balls don't fall out."

Sam gasped, then put it on. "Like this?"

"Yes. We'd better get going. Arthur hates people to be late."

Sam snuck out the door, sure the entire population of the underground would be there. They weren't. All he had to do was make it to the end of the VIP corridor and into the gym. He was tiptoeing along, almost there, Emily close behind him.

"Sam! Sam! There's a waterline broke in the fields. We gotta stop 'er. She'll run us dry." Walden Ort came running up the corridor with two of the boys behind him. Seeing Sam, he skidded to a stop. "Oh." His mouth hung open. He looked Sam up and down.

"These are the general's workout clothes, Wally. I was going to the gym to do aerobic exercise with Arthur." Sam stood proudly, acting as though he wasn't in the slightest bit embarrassed.

"Oh. Ah just thought ye come out wi' out yer clothes."

"No, this is how the Russian army dresses to exercise, except better than most of them."

"We gotta stop the leak, Sam, an' right now." Wally looked Sam up and down again. "Ah expect the general never walked though the underground like that."

"No one has, Wally. Let's handle that break. Em, tell Arthur we have to make it later. Let him know what's happening."

He walked into the main hall, conscious that village men wore long pants and shirts with long sleeves even when cows were falling over from the heat. Men might roll up their sleeves on such a day, but they would never wear indecent bright yellow shorts. But he had to stop the water break. "Tell them to turn off the main. That's by the reservoir tank. Get it shut down."

Arthur came into the hall wearing a bright red version of Sam's outfit. The villagers stepped back. None of them went to the gym. They hadn't seen Art dressed this way either. Sam shouted, "Art, get on the computer and see what you can do to shut down the water. I'll go out in the field. We can work out later."

Arthur sprinted back into the corridor.

Wally followed Art with his eyes, studying him carefully. "Ye fellas work out like that often?"

"No, this is the first time."

"That's good." Wally looked relieved.

Sam shot across the hall. The underground looked so much different from the way it had when they had first got there. The big room, once so depressing, now screamed with color, ever since Sam had commissioned Winnie to paint scenes all over the walls. Winnie was such a good artist that, if she painted a cookie on a plate, he'd want to eat it.

Winnie had created huge paintings of the old village. You could walk around a corner and—wham!—there was main street or the barns, big as life. Around another corner, you'd see horses and cattle. Another wall showed everyone doing the planting, then harvesting. The big house stood up there, with its gray stone turrets, and so did the converted stables where Sam and his family had lived. Winnie had started to paint Sam's horse, Oned, but he thought he'd start crying if he had to look at the horse every day, so he made her stop.

The brilliant paintings weren't the only change in the underground. People's clothes also flashed like rainbows.

At that time of day, women filled the hall, doing their mending and gossiping, the way they had in the old days. The men had their own doings and kept separate, which was how things always had been.

The women again wore long skirts, as was proper. Right away, the ladies had transformed their Russian army uniforms. It took a couple of pairs of pants to make a decent long skirt, but they had plenty of uniforms.

The women's heads pulled together as he passed, appraising Sam's lanky form. "Looks sorta like a bumblebee, don't he?" Blanche observed. Her outfit was trimmed with shocking pink. The women formed a dazzling cluster of color in their fanciful outfits. Magenta. Green. Blue. Gold and silver braid. Lace. Fur. Sam had let Emily give the women in the hall more of Mrs. E's clothes and decorations. They had sewn fancy trim all over the black uniforms, competing for the wildest effect.

"That's a *big* bumblebee," Millie replied. The others laughed.

"He's got a long stinger," said Jane. They collapsed into laughter. "Ah'm surprised it don't fall out in those togs."

More laughter. "Ah wish it would. Ah'd like to see a little more."

"C'mon, Millie, all o' us has seen *much* more of him. Don' be greedy." Laughter swept the hall.

Sam charged across the open space, heading for the fields. Right now, all the color of paintings and clothing was a blur, and Sam never heard the women's words either.

It was a filthy, difficult job, but they got it done. Art used the computer to shut off the flow from the reservoir, and they backed it up by shutting the line down manually outside the field. They didn't have to do much to get to the broken pipe. The water had created a geyser that had blown the dirt away.

They did have to make the hole bigger so they could work three feet down, where the pipe was. They dug out a four-foot hole all around it.

Sam climbed into the hole and cut the pipe above and below the broken elbow joint, then took the piece to the equipment bay. There was another one that fit. Bless Jeremy's hoarding little heart. They had plenty of everything.

He fitted the new elbow joint with sleeves and glued it to the pipe's cut ends. "We have to wait a couple of hours for the glue to set up, but I think we got 'er."

He looked around. The field was a muddy disaster. The break had created a glut of water in the immediate area while depriving other parts of the field. "We've got to move this mud around to water the other plants."

They formed a shovel brigade to get the water to the dry areas.

It worked. The spliced pipe held, water flowed, and the emergency was over.

Sam stood tall as he faced the journey back across the hall. He was covered with mud, his arms were like living bogs. His legs matched. The yellow outfit could have been pulled out of a swamp.

The whole village was assembled when he headed back to the corridor. "How do, Sam. Run into a briar patch?" They tittered but didn't break into laugher. That would come later.

Arthur was at the end of the corridor, still clad in red. "Let's hit the gym, Sam. We've got time."

"I'm filthy."

"You'll be worse in a little while."

"I'm going for my aerobic exercise," Sam announced to the onlookers, and sauntered into the gym.

48

Sam found himself running on a treadmill, wishing he were back in the muddy hole.

"A couple of minutes more, Sam," Arthur said, watching lines bouncing up and down on a screen. "I'm measuring your heart rate."

When Sam could barely stagger, Arthur began his own work-out, running full tilt on the moving belt. Leaning against one of the machines and drying his hair with a towel, Sam watched Art. Wearing those clothes made sense if you were going to sweat that much. He intended to put his suit in the incinerator and never come back to the gym.

While watching Art, the phantoms that kept him up at night paraded before him again . . . his death . . . keeping Emily from killing herself. To keep his demons away, Sam focused on Arthur. The red suit showed him off.

His body was sculptured and brown. He had more muscles than he'd had when he came underground, and he'd started with a commando's body. His white teeth shone like lamps against his brown skin. His dark eyes sparkled. He was a good-looking man. He must be attractive to women.

Sam got an idea that shocked him. If Emily had a man to love her, she would have something to live for when he died. The boys would have a father. Sam again entertained a thought that had been on his mind a great deal: Shane should be the headman when he died. He was brilliant and would make an excellent headman. Unfortunately, he was only seven years old.

But, if Emily were married to Arthur, he could run the underground and raise Shane until he was old enough to take over. Arthur would be strong enough to handle Rupert's reaction to being pushed aside. Or Art and Emily could do it. That was the solution. He needed to get Emily and Arthur together. Winnie could be a second wife or something. They'd work it out.

After his speech at the end of their first-year meeting, Arthur had come around every year to speak to Emily and Sam about their "responsibility to the future generations." Arthur had shown them studies that said a woman should have a maximum of six babies, and they should come every two years at the closest.

Two years had passed since Emily had had Eli. Sam knew he should allow what Arthur wanted, for the future generations. And to solve his own problem.

Arthur came around and made his pitch again a few days later. "It's not like I want to have an affair with Emily," Arthur said. "It's for the future generations. We really need the outcross. I can measure ovulation so well, it might just take a time or two."

"Can't you do it artificially?" Emily asked.

"No. We don't have any way of doing that."

"Oh, come on. You must. You have every kind of equipment in the sick bay. It's a hospital," she retorted.

"We have everything but the AI kits—artificial insemination—and anything to do with them. They didn't get here." Arthur's mouth tightened.

"Where are they?"

"In France, with all the gynecological equipment. And the gynecologist. Or, more accurately, what's left of them is in France."

"Why didn't they use someone local?"

"Because of Jeremy and the French girl." Art heaved a sigh and then shook his head. "You don't know what it was like trying to get this place provisioned. It was an international effort. And it had to do with the project." He ran his hand through his hair.

"The project?" Emily asked.

"Yes. They had found a girl outside Paris as smart as Jeremy. A certifiable genius. She and the gynecologist and half a planeload of equipment was supposed to arrive the day after everything blew up."

"If they had Jeremy and the girl, why did they need artificial insemination kits?"

"For the same reason you're asking me about them. Jeremy didn't want to have sex with someone he didn't love. And neither did she. The gynecologist was a specialist."

Art looked around as though he thought someone was eavesdropping. "OK. I might as well tell you all of it. This was genetic engineering. Down here, they wanted to breed a race of people as smart as Jeremy and the girl. They would be the rootstock for the new civilization. The gynecologist was an MD and a scientist, pretty much a genius himself.

"There's something in experimental science called 'regression toward the mean.' That means that, if the two smartest people in the world had kids, their kids wouldn't be geniuses, too. They'd be closer to normal IQ—average. Outliers regress to the mean.

"The French doctor had found a way of preventing that. He was a geneticist; he'd figured out how to select the really smart sperm and eggs and combine them. With his techniques, Jeremy and the girl's offspring would get smarter, generation after generation." Art flushed. "They would make a super race. But it was very complicated. That's why he needed all the equipment and it had to be his. So all the AI-related stuff was in France. With the girl and the doctor.

"It wasn't supposed to be this way. There was supposed to be a medical team." Arthur sighed again. "The only thing we can do is . . . the regular way."

Sam leaned over the table and said, "If it's for the future generations, we should do it."

"No, Sam!" Emily's eyes widened. She shook her head and opened her mouth to object.

But he used the Voice on her. "It only will take a time or two. We owe it to the future generations." If she fell in love with Art, Sam could stop worrying about what would happen after he died.

49

The first time she came back after being with Arthur, Emily ran into their room holding her hands to her mouth. She headed straight to the bathroom and threw up, then curled up on the bed, shaking.

"Did he hurt you, lass?" he'd said, stroking her shoulder. He'd kill Arthur if he had.

"No. It made me sick. I never want to have to do that again, Sam. Never."

But Arthur's test said she hadn't ovulated yet. Sam convinced her to go back the next night. And he told Arthur to make it nice for her.

"Cook a dinner in the club, Art. Play some music."

When she came back that time, she looked dreamy and sleepy, the way she did when they'd been together. She'd turned over for Arthur. Many times. Sam knew she had; he could feel it when it happened.

He tore out of their room, fists clenched. Sam headed straight for the room where Winnie and Arthur and their two kids lived. He stood in front of the door, hands knotted at his sides. His lips pulled back from his teeth and his jaw clenched. Should he ring the bell? Should he call Arthur out?

What would Sam accuse him of? Doing what he'd told him to do? He'd hoped for this, but, now that it had happened, it wasn't what he wanted at all. He stood in the hallway, furious and fuming, until it seemed stupid to stand there any longer. No one was around. Maybe Art wasn't even inside. Maybe he was sleeping it off in some unknown cubby.

Thinking about Arthur passed out from fucking Emily made Sam want to smash his fists into the concrete walls. Or better, Arthur's face. Sam no longer cared if Arthur could run the underground until Shane grew up. He wished he'd never let this horrible thing begin.

"Hey! It looks like we got lucky!" Art said to him a week later. They hadn't spoken since that hideous night. "The test says she's pregnant!" His smile lit up the computer lab. "The countdown begins. You guys should take it easy for about six weeks, then you can go at it until the last month. You'll have to quit then, and for about six weeks after the birth."

Sam couldn't move. He stood there, letting this swiving foock gin tell him when he could have sex with his wife. He turned and walked out of the lab.

But Sam's outrage was overshadowed by something very strange happening in the hall. Minnie Whersher was starting to bulge. She was ugly as a sow and stank so much that none of the men would go with her, including Sam back in the old days. She didn't have a husband, no need to say. Yet, there she was, sticking out as if she had a sail flying in front of her. And her smell was gone. She wouldn't say who made the baby.

"Sam, ah don't know who done it. Weren't none of us," said Willis Cone, leading a delegation of men. "None of our women got a babe since we been here." He blushed at talking to the headman about their intimate lives, which they weren't even supposed to be having, according to the Commands. "Ah know Jeremy said we weren't married no more, but your papers said some of us were still wed, on account of not being cousins. Those wives ain't caught, an' no one knows why. 'Cept maybe those shots Art gave us all. But that don't do that, do it?"

Sam was caught short. Should he tell them that Arthur, Jeremy, and whoever else had set up the rules had deemed them too dumb to have babes? Should he tell them that Arthur was just doing his duty to the future generations with Minnie because she wasn't related to any of them? Sam sat speechless in the hall's dining area, the men around him. Fortunately, Willis went on.

"Em'ly and ye, an' Art an' Winnie, 're the only ones that have had babes, 'cept for those who came into this place with 'em inside their bellies. People're sayin' it's a curse."

"May be somethin' about comin' down here, or bein' from the outside," Sam said, reverting to the village dialect without thinking. "Art's not from the village, an' neither is Em'ly. Mayhap that's it. Somethin' down here." He nodded gravely.

"Then why is Minnie out to here?" Willis held his hand out in front of his belly. "Why her?"

"Well, she's not from the village either; she's an outsider. One of the marauder women. Maybe that's it." He lied bald-faced.

"Well, that could be it." Willis scratched his chin. "Sure is a puzzle."

"Yeah, ah'll think about it and see what ah can figure out." Sam clapped Willis on the shoulder and waved to the others. "Ah gotta go now." He had to get away from his lies. The villagers were so mild since Valerie had killed the bad ones that meetings were a snap. Lester or Ronny would never have accepted what he'd said without fighting him.

He stalked out to the fields and started pulling weeds, then hoeing frantically. Arthur was doing his duty with more than Emily. Sam had been forced to lie about it to uphold the Commands.

But what about the Commands and Arthur's orders from the military? Some of the Commands were impossible to carry out and Arthur's orders gutted his authority as headman.

Jeremy's face came to him. The Great Tek. The man Sam once had thought of as a god. The one who'd foisted the Commands on them forever. He was so used to accepting what Jeremy and the lady said, he had accepted the Commands without objection.

Sam's eyes narrowed. It wasn't the first time he'd hated Jeremy, but it was the most intense. He burned, his hoe tossing clumps of dirt in short arcs. He had followed the Commands, except for having two wives, but nobody could tell that.

But why should his people follow the Commands in all things? Their wives couldn't have babies. Why couldn't they lie with each other?

Sam could see banning the pile-ons they used to have at harvest, or any time he called one. Men would go from one woman to another, or they'd all pile on, men and women alike. Sam had been with women who'd had a dozen men before him. With all the hooch, everything blurred into thrusting asses and wiggling cunnies.

That seemed wrong to him now. But, given what Art had done to the women, what was the harm in telling all of them to resume their marriages?

When the doubts came, they came in a rush. Why did they have to speak regular English? So they'd be the people Jeremy and his friends from New York City wanted them to be? What was wrong with their dialect, other than outsiders couldn't understand it? He could read and write regular English just fine, and speak the village brogue or proper English whenever he wanted. Most of his people had had a terrible time with making the change, though. Most of them hadn't made it.

They were supposed to speak regular English so people would take them seriously when they got out. The people with him in the underground would never get out. Probably their kids wouldn't either. The map showed they were the only people in the world. What difference did it make what they sounded like?

Sam's jaw clenched. He'd accepted the Commands because he accepted that Jeremy was better than he was, just as he had taken orders from the big house all his life. He was a slave obeying his master. And that's what accepting his master's language was about, too.

He hoed so fast he could barely see the blade. What should he do about Arthur? He'd gotten Emily and Minnie with babes. For the good of the future generations, good an' sure. Sam paused and hawked a glob of spittle over the fields. Foocking, poxy cunnie, Sam swore silently and viciously. Devil's wart. Judas. Orders or no, the gobber was out of bounds.

Donna Reebecker and Suzie Willstatt began to stick out next. Like Millie, they wouldn't say who put the babies in them.

One, two, three; the mystery was solved. Three brown babies popped out of their mothers. The thoughts of everyone in the underground turned to Arthur when they saw the babies' brown eyes, black hair, and darker skin. Art was the only one who could have sired those children. And, after they turned to Arthur, the people began to focus on him.

"It' ain't fair, Sam. We aren't s'posed to lie with our own wives, an' Art'ur makes three babes without a word." Willis Cone led the second meeting as he had the first. "What about the Commands? They say 'one man, one woman, fidelity'. Ain't that so?"

Sam was forced to nod. "Aye. They do."

"Art'ur has a wife, a good un, Winnie. He's got two beaut'ful babes from her. How can he do wha' he's doin'? And how come we cannot do the same? With our wives, I mean?"

Sam was caught. How could he uphold Arthur doing what he did with strangers, while couples whose marriages had been tossed aside by Jeremy were forbidden it? How could he tell them what

Arthur had done to all their women? The nice boy Arthur they loved?

"Ah'll tell ye what, Willis, an ye all. Ah live by the Commands. But ah canna see everythin' that happens down here. If a thing happens that ah don't know about, ah'll not look for 'er." He sighed enormously, setting things right and throwing off principles he'd sworn to uphold. "Ah'll talk to Minnie an' Donna an' Suzie an see if he took 'em by force. If he did, he'll pay for 'er."

The group relaxed, realizing what Sam meant. Most of them had already been doing what Sam had just permitted, but now it was official. They could lie with their wives with Sam's blessing, as long as he didn't know about it.

"An' somethin' else. Ye all been tryin' to talk regular English. Ah know that; ah heard ye practicin' an' workin' on 'er. Ah know how hard it is, an' how ye slip back easy. Ah can speak proper English, but, even after all these years, ah feel like ah got someone else's tongue in my head when ah do.

"Well, if ye work on yer writin' an' readin' in the English of the big house and say, 'How do you do, Sam?' to me once 'n a while, that's OK with me. Yer workin' on learnin' an' that's all a person can do. Now ah got to go talk to Minnie and the others."

Sam's jaw clenched as he walked toward the area where the women clustered. If Arthur had taken them by force, he would call him out. Either way, he'd fucked them without his permission. Sam was the headman. Arthur needed to learn that.

He dragged his feet across the hall, feeling that he'd just gutted Jeremy's Commands.

But had he? He had been given the power to do *anything* necessary to keep the peace and make the underground work. Even the mild souls who inhabited it now would rebel if Arthur could plant his seed wherever he wanted while they lay in want. Lord help him if they figured out what Arthur had done to their women.

But he'd deal with that, too. He had permission to do whatever he needed to do. Jeremy had thought of that in terms of killing people. Sam thought in terms of making their lives bearable. He always had.

Fuck Jeremy. Fuck his Commands. Fuck the big house. And fuck the lady. *He* was the headman. He would no longer speak proper English or insist that anyone else did. He'd enforce the Commands only when they made sense.

50

When the first brown baby came out of Emily, Sam gaped. There it was, black hair growing down its back, dark eyes wide and alert. Its eyes fastened on Sam's, locking on them as if Sam were its real father. The thing looked like a fucking monkey. It made him sick.

Arthur was there; he took care of all the mothers having babies, but especially this one. Arthur had beamed as Emily put the baby to her breast.

"Oh, he's so cute," Emily said. "Look at him." She and Arthur snuggled together and cooed, tears of happiness falling from their eyes.

They named the monkey Carlos, because of Arthur's Spanish roots.

Sam had tolerated the pregnancy. He had tolerated Arthur's presence in their room. Arthur touching her and giving her medical tests. Arthur everywhere, and Emily happy about it.

"Oh, I can feel him kick," she had squealed months before, sitting on their sofa with Art one evening. "Put your hand here." She had directed Arthur's hand to her belly. "Do you feel it?" She was bright-eyed, brimming with joy. Had she been that happy with their kids?

"Oh, yes. I can feel it. *Him*. He tested as a boy." Art had turned to Sam. "The big day's getting close, isn't it?"

He had tolerated it all and smiled at the good deed they were doing for the future generations.

The birth made him snap.

When that abomination came out of Emily, Sam turned and ran. He slammed through the sick bay door and headed for the fields, anywhere away from the hideous travesty.

"Is it comin'?" Willis said cheerfully when Sam stalked past. Everyone knew Emily was in labor. "Number four's the best!"

Sam ran to the far end of the fields, stopping when he hit the cement wall. He leaned against the wall, shivering in horror. He was trapped in this tomb with nowhere to go.

When the village saw Emily's brown baby, you could have heard a mouse fart.

When the marauder women had given birth, everyone had turned to Sam for reassurance. He had accepted the infants, so they did, too.

The villagers again looked to Sam when Emily and Arthur brought Carlos into the hall, but, this time, Sam walked away, scowling. He didn't give his blessing to the baby, but he also didn't beat Arthur or kill him for it. The villagers shifted from foot to foot, silent.

They had accepted Arthur's prowling. After talking to the marauder women, Sam had told the village men that Arthur not only hadn't forced them, they'd invited his attentions and wanted him back. Plus, he'd cured their infections, which Sam hadn't been able to do.

But when they saw Emily's babe, it was a different story. Sam was the headman. They looked at the baby and then at Arthur. The people were silent. And then they turned away.

Emily became known as "the whoor."

Sam could feel his power eroding like sand on a riverbank. He'd allowed Arthur to take his wife. He let him get away with it and now he was doing nothing about them and their baby. Who was the most powerful man in the underground?

For the next two years, Arthur practically lived at their rooms, "bonding" with his son. Sam didn't understand why Arthur didn't spend more "quality time" with his own family.

When they had started having children, Sam and Emily had opened the door in their closet that went into the next room. That became the kids' room. They had been wild for each other. Wouldn't do for the little ones to live in the same room with them, given what they did at night.

They didn't need that privacy anymore; they had scarcely touched each other since Emily had become pregnant with Arthur's child, but the adjoining room was a great place for Arthur's baby. Sam wouldn't allow Emily to bring him into their room.

"He's not mine. Keep him out of here." Sam was surprised how good being hateful felt. He didn't allow Arthur to bring the baby into their room during his visits either.

Arthur acted hurt. "It's for the future generations, Sam. The baby will be healthier if he has two parents loving him. It would be better if you got involved, too." When he saw that Sam would never do that, Art said quickly, "My visits would be allowed by any definition of parents' rights in any legal system."

The bastard could out talk him.

"Ah don't care. He doesn' come in here." Sam stood in the doorway between the closet and the kids' room. Shane, Joshua, and Eli stood like stairsteps, tallest to smallest, looking a little afraid, their wide brown eyes taking in everything.

"You don't want your kids to hear this, do you?" Arthur's head jutted from side to side self-righteously.

"Boys, get in here." Sam pulled his children into his room. "Ye got an hour, Arthur." He closed the door in the closet and shut Arthur and Emily out.

When two years had rolled around after the birth of the first abomination, Arthur's calculations said Emily was ripe for another. She had said yes right away.

"It's for the future generations, Sam, that's all," the couple had assured him.

Arthur and Emily had two little ones, a boy and a girl. Both brown as crap. Carlos and Juanita Romero. Were those names for village kids? Arthur's children lived with Sam and Emily and their three sons, as was the custom. Children stayed with their mother.

Arthur's children stayed in the kids' room. Sam didn't let them out unless Emily or Arthur took them to play.

"No, ye canna come in," Sam roared. Arthur had arrived one night when the children were already in bed and he and Emily were turning in.

"Look, Sam, I just wanted to say good-night and read them a story. They're starting to . . ."

"Get the foock outta here before ah punch yer stinkin' face in," Sam screamed. "Don' come back without an invite. From *me*!"

"Sam, don't take it personally. It's just good parenting."

That slimy bastard. He didn't come back, not to their door. He went straight to the kids' room. Sam made Emily keep the closet door and their door open if she went in there with him. Arthur said he was just bonding with his kids.

But he was bonding with Emily every chance he got, too. Did they think Sam was stupid? You can't slip around a concrete tomb and not be noticed. Laughing together. Sharing jokes. Pulling away from each other quickly when anyone approached.

They didn't know how good Sam was with the equipment in the underground. He handled the intercom as well as Arthur. He could track anyone anywhere.

Why had he turned it on that night? They were in the night-club. The music played sweetly. Sam could imagine the lights and the mist coming down. He heard them talking and laughing.

"Oh, Art. That is so funny! I used to go to the Penguin, too. That was my favorite club. Did you ever go to . . ."

"Hush, Emily. You've got something in your hair. Let me . . ." Silence. "Oh, now it's on your mouth."

He turned the intercom off when all he could hear was breathing.

That marked the first time Sam grabbed the sledgehammer and shovel, and ran into the hall. The people still awake scattered. The underground was built to last thousands of years; its columns and supports could have held up a skyscraper. Sam slammed his hammer into the cement uprights of the growing field until his shoulders ached and he couldn't breathe. Then he picked up a shovel and began to dig.

When old Ned found him asleep on a pile of dirt in the morning, he said, "What are ye doin', Sammy? Diggin' yer way out?"

"Yeah, Ned. That's what ah'm doin'. Diggin' out. Ah'm a digger." He used old dialect most of the time now.

All he needed to do to end it was say, "I divorce you," three times in public. It would be over.

He couldn't do it.

He had the Voice and he had the Power. He could have blown them apart. Made Emily tell him she loved him with every breath. Made her hate Arthur's guts. Made her never leave their room. He could have killed Arthur with a thought.

He didn't do any of it.

51

"They'd think ah was crazy if they could see me, Valerie." A naked Sam lay next to Valerie in the healing place. They didn't go to the treacherous white meadow anymore. They'd created a new place, sunny and warm, that smelled like his meadow from the old days. He could hear Oned prancing in the background, as though he would come into sight any minute. Birdsong charmed him. Valerie rested her head on his chest.

"Ah'm a crazy old man," he said, "makin' love to a woman who doesn't exist in a place no one can see."

Valerie Zanner had saved him. She'd kept him sane all the years Emily ran wild. She was clean and bright. She wore a pretty dress and looked happy. If she brought a gun, she kept it holstered. She looked and acted more and more like Emily. Valerie had stayed in the background of Emily's mind all that time, never coming out to cause trouble, unless you counted her chasing down a playground bully once or twice. She was a ferocious mother. Not to her own kids, but terrifying to any who threatened hers.

"I do exist, Sam. I'm part of Emily. But I exist by myself, too. With you, I'm real."

"So am ah cheatin' on Em'ly with Em'ly?" he said.

"Yes. I'm part of Emily. I am Emily."

The second time Emily came back from being with Arthur, she had wanted to cuddle and kiss. Make herself believe that everything, their whole world, hadn't collapsed. He had turned away from her. Sam didn't know why. He'd been with women coming straight from other men. That's what the pile-ons were about in the village. But he turned his back to her and went to sleep.

He turned from her in every way. When Arthur said it was safe—his baby was developed enough—he told them they could start up again.

Except he couldn't. He had looked down at himself, shrunken and immobile. That had never happened before. More than that, she made him sick. "Get away from me," he'd barked, backing off. "Ah don't want ye."

As the years went by, he ignored her unless he had a need, and then he satisfied himself exactly as he wanted, with no thought for her.

Only Valerie knew the truth. He was torn in pieces. His heart had been pulled out and shredded.

"It will be all right, Sam. She'll come back to you. It will be all right." On nights when the sledgehammer didn't help, when he couldn't dig enough, Valerie came to him and held him. "Don't worry, my love. It will turn out."

"Why, Valerie? How do you know?"

"Because I am Emily. She'll come back to you."

"How do you know?"

"I know. But do you want her back now, Sam? Say the word, and I'll have her back here in five minutes." Valerie had on her ferocious look.

She could compel Emily to return, just as he could. But what difference would it make? He wanted her to come back because she loved him.

He wanted things to be the way they had been at the start.

52

Sam looked around for someone to talk to. Arthur had been a good friend; he could have talked to him, once. Now he was dead as far as Sam was concerned.

He didn't talk to Rupert. Ru would say, "Ye should beat her and kill him. Kill them brown bastards. Yer the headman." He knew something else Rupert might say: "Divorce her and give her to *me*. Ah'll fix 'er." Whenever Emily was around, Ru stared at her as if his eyes were stitched to her face.

One desperate night, Sam went to Winnie. He leaned against her doorjamb, close to tears.

She looked at him coolly. "Ye can come in, Sam Baahuhd, this once." The two of them made no pretense of using anything but the village brogue.

"How d' ye stand it, Winnie?"

"Ah was married to ye, Sam Baahuhd. Ah was your third wife, out of four. Ah had to share you with three others—and every other woman you fancied. An' now ah'm Art'ur's second wife. Naught has changed." Her bitterness filled the room.

"But you divorced me. You were the only woman to divorce a man."

"Who said ah won't divorce Art'ur?" She laughed, a witch's bark. "Ye made a mistake, Sam Baahuhd. Ye didn't know about Art'ur when ye sent her to him. Ye shoulda asked me."

"Know what, Winnie?"

More of that acid laugher. "About him as a man." She smiled enigmatically, saying nothing more.

Sam's eyes bugged out. What had he done? Every woman he'd been with had told him he was the best they'd had. He'd sent Emily to someone better? He tried to ask her what she meant, but the words wouldn't form. Winnie was speaking again.

Reeling, he could barely make out her words. "But, Sam Baahuhd, who else is down here? Do you fancy sitting by yourself forever? Have ye seen them out in the hall? Droolin' morons, they are. A husband that ain't here an' is in love with another is better than them. Ah've got the boys ye an' ah made and ma childr'n with Art. Mayhap Art'ur will remember us and come to his senses. Ah'll keep company with ye, Sam. Ah'll sit with ye in the evening, nothing more. Mayhap they'll look up an' see us. Mayhap it'll make them jealous."

But that was no good. Winnie wasn't the rose she once had been. Sitting with her was like bathing in tannery waste. Plus, the tactic didn't work. Emily didn't notice, being too busy slithering around.

And lying. "I'm going to go out to the fields and pick some herbs, Sam . . . I need to do some research for my class at the library. It will take a while . . . I need to be alone. The kids are driving me crazy. Can you watch them, or should I take them to Sally? . . . I'm starting a flower garden next to Winnie's. I'll be back in a couple of hours."

Sensing her lies was so easy. When she came back from wherever she'd been, she looked too bright and interested in what he had to say. Too involved with the kids' projects or her classes. Too good a mother, always attentive and kind.

Why didn't he stop the insanity of pretending things were OK?

Why couldn't he make a decision? Solace finally came from a direction he hadn't expected.

"Ye look like a squirrel been dead three weeks, Sam. D' ye need a one t' talk to?"

He had run into Sally out by the orchard. The trees were green and leafy and producing well. He tried to smile, but his chin tipped down and then he was blinking his eyes hard, fighting down what he felt.

"Ah thought so, Sammy. Ah could allus tell when ye were ailin'. What is it, darlin'?"

His shoulders began to shake at that endearment. Sally had been his second wife and a good friend. Not his passion, but a warmhearted, good woman. "Sally, ah've made such a mess."

"Ah'd say ye have. The whole un'erground is awash with it."

He looked at her sharply, but her direct eyes simmered him down.

"Tell me what's really goin' on, Sam. Ah won' tell anybody, swear."

He knew that was true. So he told her all about the future generations and genetic diversity and Arthur and Emily having perfect genes. And him telling her to go to Art because he thought he was going to die.

"Well, ye ain't daid yet. An' yer talkin' about breedin', like with horses or pigs?"

"Yeah."

"It's a good idea, Sam, but we ain't horses or pigs. Won't work the same way."

"Ah know that, but ah started this rum thing, an' now they're in love."

"Of course they're in love. Go stickin' that thing up there, ye fall in love."

Sam could feel himself blushing.

"Oh, don't pretend t' be a virgin with me, Sammy boy. Ah was married to ye most o' my life. Ye an' ah both know how 'tis. Question is, what're ye gonna do about it? Cause ye need to. The place is boilin' with folks not knowin' what to think.

"Ye gotta divorce her or kill him. Either one will do."

Sam looked glum.

"An' what keeps ye from doin' it?" she asked. He looked more depressed. "Ah, ah see. You like her more than anyone, that's it. Ye like doin' it with her and rubbin' on her an' all the rest. Ye can't find another like 'er.

"Lemme tell ye, Sammy, right an' true. We're all the same where your thinkin'." He looked even worse. Sally laughed.

"Well, that might na be true for you. Ye certainly looked hard enough for the perfect cunnie when we were together. If ye found 'er, ye'd better hold on. How about killin' him?" she asked with pert interest.

"Ah don't know enough about the computers yet, Sally, or ah'd have slit his throat years past. He hides stuff, so ah won't know it all. Smart bugger."

"So yer stuck between the tar patch and the briarwood, Sammy. Ye'll have to hold on until somethin' busts loose. An', in the meantime, d' ye want me to watch yer kids when she asks me?"

He knew Emily had asked Sally to babysit for her during her excursions. "Yeah. Ah do. Ye're the best ma ah know. Ah'd feel better with ye watchin' 'em when ah gotta work an Emily's . . ."

"Ah'll take them kids every day if ye want. Lemme know."

He put his arms around her, pulling her tight. She struggled loose.

"What's the matter, Sally? No one's out here to see."

"Ah know, Sam. Ah don't want loose for that." She adjusted her garments. "It's like ah said. Ye stick thay thing up there an' ye fall in love. Ah never fell outta love for ye. Don' wanna shake up that which ain't gonna be soothed."

Sam laughed and then blushed.

"Oh, ah can still make ye blush. Ye were the best man ah ever had, Sam Baahuhd, an' if that lil' hussy is too dim to know what she's got, others down here might show her." She squeezed his hand. "Ah'll take ma leave. If ye need to talk, find me. Ah'll *talk* to ye." She winked.

Sam smiled as she walked away. Sally'd said he was the best man she'd ever had. That was the nicest thing he'd heard in years.

53

"Ah don't care if ye already washed it twice today," Sam bellowed. "If ah say do 'er again, ye do 'er again. All o' ye, every one, ah want the whole hall clean. If ye don't do 'er the way ah want, ye'll clean the pissers next!"

He made damn sure everyone had a job to do and did it all day. Tending the crops, harvesting, cleaning the place. Cooking in those square ovens that never made anything brown. Doing dishes. He knew better than to allow the village to be idle.

Or himself. He pushed past all limits of body or mind. Digging trenches, checking all the equipment. Verifying the programming of the systems. Handling most of the fields and orchard himself. He tore around like a tornado, packing his sledgehammer and scowling. The people were afraid of him, and Sam didn't care.

"Quiet, ye mobsters! Turn 'er down. Ye're killin' ma ears."

The village kids had started bands and played in front of the screen every night. Rock 'n' roll, they called it. The kids and the grown folks, too, had discovered the joys of electric guitars and amplifiers.

Life went on. Time passed. People did what they did.

Sally watched the kids when Emily made her mysterious disappearances and he had to work.

"They look just like ye, Sam. Ah never could resist yer babies," Sally said.

Emily had kept up her reading classes. Quite a few could read now, so she was having them read and discuss books. Em also taught public speaking, as a way for people to learn proper English, if they wanted to.

Emily looked just the same as she ever had, better maybe. Beautiful, slim, radiant. She worked out as hard, often with Arthur. Sam had never seen a woman who'd had five children who looked as good as Emily.

Art looked great, too. Went to the gym every day. Kept the computers and programs going. Once Sam had trusted Art almost as much as Emily. Sam smiled. He *did* trust Arthur as much as Emily now. He wanted to kill both of them.

"OK, kids, we've got teams of five. Billy, don't let him get past you like that. Goal! Two points." Arthur's cheery voice rang in the hall all day long as he played one game or another. While the adult villagers held Arthur in suspicion and contempt, to the young people he was a rebellious, dangerously alluring hero. He came up with all sorts of games. Indoor track. Basketball. Field hockey. And he brought more musical instruments and ever more rock 'n' roll. The teenagers loved him.

They'd been in the underground close to thirteen years. The village kids who had been tots or babies or inside their mothers' bellies when they had entered the underground now ranged from thirteen up. The only little kids were the ones he and Em had had, Winnie's babies with Arthur, and the brown children who kept appearing.

The marauder women were bulging again, and they weren't the only ones. Arthur's program for the future generations was in full swing. Winnie didn't seem to mind and neither did Emily.

The villagers attributed their lack of babies to evil spells. Or to Emily being a witch, something he'd overheard but had never been said to his face.

Sam stalked around the hall like vengeance. The people thought of him the way they had the feds who had terrorized the village. He wasn't the Sam you could tell your problems to, the good headman. They respected him only because they were afraid of him.

He scoured the place almost every day, looking for weed and mushrooms. Tore up the fields looking for a still. He took Jude and Ewan, his kids with Winnie, with him. They were in their midtwenties. Rupert also helped them. He was strum skilled with plants.

Sam kept an eye on Rupert, too. During the day, Ru was a great help. He was almost as strong as Sam and knew more about farming than anyone but him. "What do you think, son?" he'd say, talking about planting more or less of a particular crop. Ru would tell him what he thought. It was always exactly what Sam thought.

"Ru, yer a good son," Sam told him. He'd put his arm around Ru's shoulder when they walked around the fields. His son smiled, basking in his father's attention. It was like the old days in the village, before Rupert had been overshadowed by his and Em's band of young superstars. Rupert's earnest desire to please shone.

The night was different. Every night, Ru sat in the hall with a bunch of men, their voices rough and harsh. Raucous laughter punctuated the racket. They sounded as if they were drinking. The first time Sam had heard them, he went over. His son waved a canteen, grinning foolishly.

"What's going on, Ru?" Sam had asked.

Ru answered without ruffling a hair. "We're tellin' tales o' the ol' vil', Da. Havin' a fair an' fine time. 'Member when ye killed the bear?"

That made Sam smile. He had killed it, but not before it had run straight through the village and people ran screaming. "Yes, ah remember."

"We're tellin' tales to keep up our spirits an' such."

"That's good, Rupert. We need our spirits up. Mind if ah have a taste?" He indicated Ru's canteen.

"Sure, Da." It was nothing but water. Sam looked carefully at the men. No shaking hands to indicate weed. No dilated pupils. What was in the canteen was harmless. "Well, I'll let you have your fun."

"Sure, Da." Rupert waved as Sam walked back to the corridor. The voices and laughter started again.

Was he crazy? Did he suspect everyone because of Emily and Arthur? He had no reason to suspect Ru just because he was having a good time. Or because of his few other failings.

Rupert could barely read. He did only the simplest math and couldn't do the easiest things on a computer. And he couldn't speak regular English at all. Rupert's voice had deepened and coarsened. He rolled when walked, loping from side to side.

He sat with his buddies every night, laughing and making rough jokes. Rupert didn't show any signs of his mother's disease. No one had developed it this late in life—Ru was thirty-six. But that didn't mean he *couldn't* develop it.

54

The worst part was that he hadn't died. If he had died the way he was supposed to while Emily was pregnant with Carlos, everything would have been fine. But he kept living. Almost five years had passed since he'd pushed Arthur and Emily together. Sam was fifty-three. He should really die now. But he didn't.

"Da." Shane's dark eyes looked at him over the chessboard. "Are you thinking again?"

"Yeah, Shane. Just thinkin'. We can play, but you'll beat me. Why don't you play with your brother?"

"I'll play both of you. And Eli, too." Shane was eleven, Josh was nine, and Eli was seven. "Hey, guys! Let's play chess!"

Shane got more boards while the kids trooped out of the closet, yawning.

"We'll play you, but you win too much."

"Give me a handicap. I'll give you three of my rooks."

They started to play, four chessboards in a row. Shane moved from one to another, enthralled. His eyes sparkled. "You're getting good, Josh," he said to his younger brother.

Sam wasn't getting better. Shane beat him quickly. "How do you do it, Shane? You're so fast."

"I just think ahead, Da. See if you move here, then I know you're going to move like this on your next turn." He moved the pieces around to illustrate what he was saying. "I'll do this, so you'll think I'm going to move here. But I'll move here. Check. And you'll do this. Checkmate. It's easy."

"How many different possible games do you think of, Shane?"

"Five or six, and I work out seven moves ahead."

"I do five, but I'm only nine," Josh said. "He won't be able to beat me much longer."

"I'm good, too," said Eli. "I'm going to beat you all."

Sam sat back, astonished. They were brilliant. Smarter than adults.

He saw a movement out of the corner of his eye. Carlos had grown into a little kid while Juanita had become a toddler. They'd sneak from their room into the closet and sit silently in the door, watching Sam interact with his children. Watching the family eat together. Sam would see four brown eyes looking at him with longing.

"Get back," he'd growl. They'd jump back. He had nothing to do with the brown bastards. He didn't touch them and seldom spoke to them. He waved them off, while playing with his own children. "Get back in there, ye shits. Ye don't belong out here." They retreated.

His sons regarded him with solemn faces. Eli was brave enough to pipe up with, "I don't understand, Da. They're really nice. And they play chess, too."

Sam got up and walked out of the room. Shane ran after him.

"Da, are you mad at us? We love you. Don't you love us?"

Sam pulled him close. " I love ye. I'm just a mean ol' bear now, Shane."

"Will you always play chess with me?"

"I will always play chess with you, Shane, even if you've got me beat before we sit down. I will always play with you. I will always love you. You're my Shane." The boy hugged him and Sam hugged him back.

"Da? Where's Ma?" Shane asked hesitantly.

"I don't know where your mother is, Shane." Sam dodged back into their room and picked up his sledgehammer.

55

When he finally caught them at it, he'd been heading to work in the orchard. He'd walked around the corner and there they were, in a little alcove out by the fields. Kids went out there and rolled around. Arthur was sitting on the edge of the raised planter. Sam could see Arthur's brown length and her, skirt pulled up, one leg thrown over his, ready to straddle him.

"Well," he said. He thought he would have started screaming and beat Arthur to death, but he didn't. He just stood there and said, "Well."

She whipped her leg back and her skirt down, staring at him openmouthed. Arthur struggled to stand up, trying to look tough while pulling his pants up from around his ankles.

"Look, Sam. We love each other. You must know . . ."

"Shut up, Art'ur. Shut yer damn trap."

He turned to her. "Get yer stuff out of ma room. Yers and the kids. Ah'll be back there in an hour, and ah don't want to see a thing of yers or yer kids in the place. Ah don't want to know ye exist. Ah'm done with ye. Those childr'n are not mine."

"You're divorcing me? You're throwing the kids out?" Horror covered Emily's face. It made him strum happy.

He didn't answer her, just walked away.

When he got back to their room, everything of hers and the kids was gone. All the clothes she'd fixed for herself and the children, the pictures she'd hung of her family. He went in the children's room.

She'd left all the furniture. For a stabbing moment, he wondered what they'd sleep on, Em and the five kids. Where they'd put their clothes. Then he remembered her leg, thrown over Arthur. Fuck her. Fuck her and her filthy bastards.

Sam dashed to the safe in the closet and opened it. All the jewelry was there, including her sapphire ring. He had told her the gems were hers, but she'd left them. His jeweled girl was gone.

56

Sam paced around his room. He'd lived alone for six months. Emily had been alone, too. She'd had the decency not to move in with Arthur and scandalize everyone any more than she already had. Art stayed with Winnie and his kids while Em lived in a room that Arthur had set up for her and the five children.

Art and Emily slunk around like a couple of wild cats in a barn. Sam had seen cats make themselves invisible, hiding in places only they could see. At least the two of them didn't flaunt themselves in the hall. Everyone knew, of course. Gossip about them had replaced gossip about everything else.

Sam's tension ratcheted up. He was as tuned in to Emily as ever. In a couple of weeks, Emily would be fertile. She and Art would conceive Arthur's baby number three. When she gave birth, Emily would have had her six babies and her childbearing would be over, according to Art's rules.

He needed to work. Had to dig. Had to move. Couldn't be in that room, permeated with misery. The kids being gone left a hole in his heart that nothing could fill. He hadn't spoken to them since he had kicked them out. They kept away from him when they saw him outside. Emily had explained the village ways. He no longer acknowledged them as his children. If she and Arthur wed, they would become Arthur's. But he had to divorce her first. He couldn't do it.

Sam walked out his door and into the hall. He was halfway across when Shane accosted him.

"Da! We can play chess." He held out the box containing the chessmen and board. "It's been months and months. Ma said you didn't want to see me anymore, but I knew you would miss me like I miss you." His face radiated hope.

"Yer not ma son," he said, using the brogue. He used it exclusively now. "Ye know that. Yer yer ma's an' ye got nothin' to do with me. Yer not mine." He pulled away from the boy, turning to go back to his room.

"I *am* your son." Shane's eyes swam with tears. "You're my da."

"No more. Ye went with yer ma. Yer not my boy, and neither are the others. Ye belong to her and Art'ur."

"You're my da!" Shane shrieked. Every head in the hall turned, and then swiveled away. People pretended not to hear, but listened hard.

"YOU ARE MY DA!"

"Na' any more, lad. Now don't be talkin' to me. Ah've nuthin' to do wi' ye."

"NO!" Shane screamed. "NO!"

The anguish in his voice made Sam's heart quail. But he wouldn't go back. He'd thrown Emily out; he'd severed his ties with her and her children. They were no longer his.

"Accordin' to the village ways, childr'n go with the ma. The da has nothin' to do with them after they're split."

"You and Winnie are divorced. You talk to Jude and Ewan. You eat dinner with them and play ball and read with them. You're their da." The boy shifted from foot to foot, struggling to stay in control.

"That's diff'rent."

"What's different about it?"

Sam had forgotten how smart Shane was, and how persistent.

"It's diff'rent . . ." Sam flared. "It's diff'rent because ah say it is. That's all ye have to know."

"It's because of Arthur, isn't it? He doesn't live with us. He's not our da. He could *never* be our da." Shane's fingers were white where he clutched the chess set. "I hate him! I'm going to kill him!"

Sam hustled faster. He didn't want to entertain the villagers any more than they already had. "Ye're not ma son. Ye're hers. If she's livin' with Art'ur or not don't matter. She's not with me."

"I'm your son no matter what. You *love* me. I'm your *Shane*."

Sam started jogging, trying to get away, but Shane dogged him. He speared Sam with words. "The little kids cry for you, do you know that? They cry all the time."

Sam punched the code into the lock on his door.

"This isn't our fault! We didn't do *anything*." Shane dropped the chess set and grabbed at his father's arm. "I love you, Da! You're my da!"

Sam jerked his arm away, raising it reflexively to backhand the boy. Shane cowered. Sam pulled his hand to his chest. He had been that close to striking his son. What craziness was this? How could this be happening?

"That's the way things are, boy. Sooner ye get used to it, the better." He slipped into his room and locked the door. The intercom was on. He stood inside, shaking and stunned. Not knowing what to do. He could hear Shane just as if he were standing next to him.

A thud and a clatter of pieces falling said that Shane had thrown the chess set against his door. "I hate *you*," he screamed. "I'm *done* with you. I'm *not* your boy anymore. I HATE YOU!" Then he was weeping.

"Shane, what's going on?" a woman's voice said. Sam's eyebrows went up. It was Emily. "I heard yelling. Why are you at your . . . at Sam's door? You know you're not supposed to . . ."

"I HATE YOU! THIS IS ALL YOUR FAULT," Shane screamed. "YOU'RE A WHORE AND A SLUT AND A BITCH LIKE EVERY-ONE SAYS."

Emily was silent, as stunned as Sam was, he expected.

"If you hadn't *fucked* Arthur, none of this would have happened. You ruined our family. Da *hates* me because of you. He won't talk to me. He won't . . ." Shane's tears overtook his anger.

"He doesn't hate you, Shane." Emily tried to be reasonable. "It's difficult. It's a transition . . ."

"It's not difficult. You wanted Arthur more than Da, so he kicked us out. That's *easy*." Sam could hear Shane's harsh breathing. "You don't care what you did to us."

"That's not true, Shane. It's been very hard for me, too. I love you . . ."

"YOU DON'T LOVE ANYONE BUT YOURSELF! YOU ARE A WHORE!" Sam heard some shuffling, as if they were pushing against each other.

"I *hate* you. I hate you so much, you don't even know how much I hate you," Shane shouted. "I will *never* live with you again. I will *never* talk to you again."

Sam could hear Shane's feet slamming into the floor, moving up the corridor to their room. He adjusted the intercom so he could hear.

"Shane, please," Emily said.

"Don't touch me," Shane shouted. "Don't think you can make it nice. It's ruined. I hate you. I will *never* forgive you."

They must have been outside the room Emily shared with the kids. Sam reset the speaker so he could hear inside. He heard thumping and movement in the room.

"Let go of me, Ma. I'm leaving."

"Shane. You can't go. You can't."

"I've got my stuff. I'm going."

"Where will you sleep? Let me call Arthur to get you a room."

"FUCK ARTHUR! FUCK *YOU*." The door slammed. Sam heard Shane make his way up the corridor toward the hall. Fights happened in the hall, and thefts. Sam was sure some kind of drug was being used there. What would happen to Shane?

Sam staggered across his room and landed at the table. He sat, cradling his head in his hands. How had this happened? How had everything fallen apart? He wouldn't talk to his boy, his Shane. The child who meant more to him than all the other children in the universe. Did the village ways matter so much?

Sam sat at the table, unmoving. He'd found peace sitting there, sometimes. Felt a presence that filled him. Not now. Darkness more desolate than the bitterest night settled on him.

His wife had betrayed him. His only male friend had betrayed him. He'd thrown out his children. His beautiful children. He'd told Shane he wasn't his. And now Shane had left his mother because of it—to go where?

No one could hear his sobs. Sound couldn't penetrate the concrete walls. Neither could light or air. Or love. She had left him for Arthur.

After a while, the only sounds were his breathing and the splat of tears on the tabletop. No light came. No healing presence. Nothing but despair. Nothing could fix the ruin around him. He spiraled downward until he could fall no lower.

A familiar voice came through the intercom. "Sam. It's me, Sally. Le' me in."

The room was dark. He shambled toward the door and the lights turned up at his movement.

"Oh, Sam," Sally said, taking in how he looked. "It's as bad as that. Come o'er here." She led him to the sofa and sat him down, then got a wet rag and wiped his face as if he were a babe. He didn't object. She sat next to him, patting his knee. The eyes in her lined face were kind.

"Did ye hear, Sally?"

"The whole underground heard, Sam. Shane was na exactly quiet." Sam shrunk further. "Ah've got him, Sam. Ah come to tell ye that."

Sam looked up.

"He was walkin' past ma room, draggin' his kit, headin' for the hall. Ah stepped out an' said, 'Good, Shane. Ye knew where to come,' an' ah pulled him inside. Ah'll keep him until all this gets sorted out. He's in ma room now, with his half brother Billie Sam, yer boy with Fannie. They're of the same age. Damned if ah'll let one of my kids end up in the hall." Sally's jaw clenched. "Ah'll not lose another child."

Sam's ribs started pumping and he dropped his face into his hand.

Sally cleaned him up again after the tears stopped.

"Ah tol' Shane he wasn' mine." His ribs started moving again.

"Oh, ye did, is right. Bein' the perfect village man." Her expression turned a bit harder. "Them days is over, Sam. Ye *gotta* think of them babies and look to 'em. Ah don't know how much she can do right now."

He stared at her. "There's summat a matter with Emily?"

"She looks just a tad better 'n you, but puttin' a smile on it and some face paint. She's heard everything they're sayin' about her an' took it in. Yer a sad pair."

Sam's mood dove deeper at the mention of Emily. His face went into his hands again.

"Oh, Sally. Can ah talk to ye of a thing?"

"That's why ah'm here, Sam, to listen to ye. Ah figured ye could use it."

"What bothers me the most is . . ." He could no longer speak.

Finally he began again. "The worst thing of all is . . . Oh, Sally. Ah loved her. Ah love her still . . ."

"Sam, ma dear, jus' tell me what it is." Sally patted his knee.

He looked into her round, kind eyes. "She said she loved me. She kissed me, an' touched me. For years . . . Was it all a lie? She's lied so much. Did she love me, or was it an auld man's dream?"

"She loved you, Sam, and ah think she loves you still."

"But how can she go with Art'ur? How can she . . . ?"

"Ah think she loves him, too." Sam groaned. "All this 'having babies for the future generations' stirred up what oughtened be stirred up. Ah think right now, she loves both o' you."

All the air went out of Sam. "Ah gotta wait until she makes up her mind?"

"Yeah, if ye want to keep her."

Anger came up again. "Ah am the headman. Ah don't have to wait for nobody."

"'Cept when ye do. Ah want to tell ye some things, Sam. Ye might be a bit surprised. How long were we married?"

"A long time."

"Twenty-four years. Ah learned the math of it. How do you think ah felt about you all that time?"

Sam was mystified. "Ah dunno. Like ma wife."

"Ah loved you the way you love Emily. When ah was with you, the sun was up there in the heavens and the trees an' everythin' was smilin'. When you touched me—every time, all twenty-four years—ah was a bride again. Did ye know that?"

Sam's jaw went slack. "Nah."

"Ah shared ye with two other wives, three at the end. Ah could hear you through the walls when ye were with one o' them. Ah hated Mollie and Winnie as much as you hate Art'ur, but ah had to be a good wife and be nice to them.

"When Winnie come, ah wanted to kill her. Ah knew ye loved her more than me. Ah stood outside her door many a night, sharpenin' ma knife. She don't know how close she came to bein' headless." Her face was grave and dead serious.

"Really?"

"Oh, yeah. An' that didn't count all the others. Everyone with a skirt all over the village, 'ceptin' yer own daughters, o' course, an' theirs. Ye did have some scruples. In ev'ry house in the village, a woman or two or three couldn't sleep at night because they felt about you like you feel about Em'ly.

"An' not jus' the village Sam. Ye liked to rut about. Women

all over the Hamptons that had ye once were pinin' and sufferin', awake all night. So it's kind o' fittin', don't ye think?"

Sam couldn't speak. "Ah did all o' that?"

"Course ye did. What did ye think ye were doing, goin' up all them skirts with that pole of yours? Couldn' get enough, never. Yer lucky ye didn' start a war."

"Ye felt about me the way ah feel about Em'ly?" Sam couldn't fathom it.

"More 'an that, maybe. But ye didn't know, did ye, ye simpleton? Ye didn't know a lot that happened under yer nose. Ye knew that a village man could have whatever he could catch. But did ye know that when the rooster's out of the house, the hens may stray? That's village, too." Sally skewered him with her eyes.

"What're ye sayin', Sally?" Sam didn't know if he could take any more revelations.

"Ah'm sayin' as when you took off to some other village for a week or so, or when ye moved in two houses down when it suited you, we sometimes soothed ourself on another pecker. Ye understand?"

"All of you?"

"Yes, Sam. All of us. That's village, too. Any man leaves his wife, she can do what she pleases. An' no one's gonna tell on her, man or woman."

"You did that?"

"Yes, Sam. Not too many times, but ah did. Ah never would have moved from your side if ye'd been true to me. Or even true to us."

"Didn' ah make ye happy?"

"Ye made me happier than all the happiness in heaven. But ye didn't know how much ah loved you, an' ye didn't feel the same way about me." She laughed. "Oh, Sam, ah didn't come here to hurt ye. Ah come to make ye feel better."

"Ah really can't say ye have, Sally. When do ye get to that?"

She patted his knee again. "Ah wanted ye to see that ye ain't the only one this happened to. It ain't uncommon. An' ye sowed enough seeds, Sam. Don't ye think it's time for a reapin'?"

She held out her arms and he collapsed into them.

"What do ah do?"

"First o' all, ye need to get those kids back. Ye need to let 'em know ye love 'em. And ye need to make up to Shane."

"Ah almost struck him, Sally. Ah could have hurt him."

"Oh, you hurt him, deeper 'n a slap. You hurt him bad, Sam. Ah don't know if it can be fixed now. He's like you, Sam. He can get angry and stay that way. An' get vengeful. Ah hope he don't do anythin' foolish.

"That's what else ah come to talk about, Sam. There's weed in the hall." He sat up, chalk-faced. "Ah've not seen it, mind you, but ah can tell by how folks act. It's a new kind that don't do the same things. No jiggling hands and wide-open eyes. Not the ragin', now anyway."

"Who's got it?"

"Them that sit in the hall. Ah don't want Shane in that hall, Sam. Ah don't want him ruined or dead. We lost one son to the weed. That's enough."

"We'll keep 'em safe, Sally. Lord help any as try to turn him wrong."

57

Aside from speaking however he pleased and giving his people the same liberty and a bit more, Sam had kept the Commands. He'd been true to his wife, stretching that definition in a way the most silver-tongued lawyer would admire. But he'd been faithful.

He had allowed himself a few games, however, hoping to hurt Emily into coming back. Or just hoping to hurt her.

Everyone knew he was a few words away from a divorce. That knowledge could have given him magnetic powers from the way the women acted.

The older women threw themselves at him, the barren ones whose ability to have babies Arthur had taken. But the younger girls—those who had been babes, toddlers, or not even born when they went underground, and so had never been plugged with Arthur's device—dogged his footsteps like flies attracted by the stench of his decaying marriage. Every one of them hoped to become the headman's wife and bear him a bunch of kids.

Janelle led the pack. He remembered her as a golden angel when she was four. Now she was sixteen years old, still golden, and as developed as a grown woman.

He only let Janelle and the girls catch him when Emily was likely to see. She was still teaching the few who would come to her. He knew when and where she taught and planned a surprise for her as often as he could.

Sam hit the jackpot that afternoon. The girls clustered around him as he sat on a bench in the hall. Big girls with broad hips, and breasts made for a man's hands.

Janelle perched on his lap, rubbing her butt across his crotch and stroking his chest. He was so hard he thought he'd let loose right there. They'd made him do it before. Not that he'd let them know. The others whispered in his ears and stroked every part of him they could reach.

His face reddened and his breathing lengthened. Something took over inside him. Why not? Why not do it? He reached up under Janelle's skirts and slipped his fingers inside her. She leaned back against his chest and spread her legs, settling in for the ride.

Emily came out of the corridor and crossed the hall. Her dark eyes flashed and her eyebrows flew up as she saw him and where his hand was. Sam smiled brightly. She looked away and walked faster.

When Emily was gone, Sam pulled his fingers out, gave Janelle a lingering kiss, and said, "Not now, pretty."

The fact that that night Emily would go to Arthur and conceive her last child made the look on her face more delicious. Sam sniffed his fingers.

58

Sam sat at the table in their room with the Book spread in front of him. Its letters flashed and shimmered, casting brilliant rays around the room. He had other lamps burning, and the big one overhead with the lights like candles. The crystals beneath it made prisms and rainbows. He didn't turn the big one on very often—some of its bulbs had burned out and they didn't have replacements. But, tonight, he needed it.

He rifled through the Book, though he'd read it so often, he knew it by heart. Jeremy had been very clear on the point in question: "That's a command—one spouse per man or wife. Fidelity. Period."

He had other books out, too. The Bible sat on the table, opened to the list of rules he had finally found. He agreed with them heartily and followed them more than the Commands. The Bible was clear on his problem. The issue hinged on the seventh commandment, but a couple of others were involved, too. He had the Koran and Buddhist and Hindu books out. He leafed through them, hoping some words of wisdom would catch his eye and help. Sometimes that happened.

But not tonight. Tonight, he needed a full-fledged visitation. A burning bush or something. But God never talked to him that way.

"Ye know what's going on, God. Can't Ye help me?" he whispered. To show how serious he was, Sam went over to the bed. He got down on his knees, hard for a man almost fifty-four. Propping his elbows up on the bed and interlacing his fingers, Sam bowed his head and said, "Well, things are OK, God. Many thanks for all Ye've given us."

Then he stopped. That was bullshit. His God didn't tolerate bullshit. "Ah thought Ye were going to be with me and keep me safe. Ye know what's happening. Ah don't know how much longer ah can stand it. Ah'm fallin' to pieces. Ah know how bad ah've been now an' what ah deserve. Sally told me. But help me. Ah need Ye. Ah don' know if ah can make 'er through the night."

He searched around the room, looking for a sign. Nothing. No answer. Sam went to the kitchen and made himself a cup of tea, then sat sipping it, waiting. Maybe God would send him a delayed message. The room was so quiet now since the kids were gone. And her. Sometimes he thought he'd go crazy from the silence.

He'd never thought it would end like this.

The answer did come.

A soundless voice whispered two words: "Keep going."

Sam moved over to the computer desk and logged on, checking the readings of the life-support monitors as he did habitually. All fine.

He looked at himself in the armoire's mirrored door. When he'd thrown her out, he had wanted to let his beard grow out shaggy and wild. Never wash. Put on a gut. But he hadn't. His hair was almost white, but a few darker hairs were still mixed in around the sides. He hadn't lost much of it. His beard was white and trimmed tightly along his jaw.

He'd looked at his body in the bathroom mirror. He was thinner than he'd been when they went underground. Everyone was.

All those soybeans and not much meat. All his muscles stood out more. Digging kept him as fit as Arthur with his gym. He looked good. The way the women looked at him told him that.

Sam studied his face. Lined, but the lines stacked up nicely. He didn't look like a turkey under the chin. He stood straight, shoulders back, and spine erect, wearing a Russian uniform. All the clothes she'd made for him hung in the closet, but he couldn't bear to put them on. He wore Russian black every day.

"Keep going." What did that mean? He was heading for a divorce with Emily. Was God saying he should get it over with? Or did it mean that something bigger than him was operating and he should let it work things out?

Sam didn't care. He had plans for the evening.

59

Sam slipped into the main hall carrying his pick, shovel, and sledgehammer. The hall was empty; everyone had gone to bed. Emily and Arthur would have finished whatever delicious meal Arthur had cooked up. They'd be dancing. In a little while, they'd be . . .

By then, he intended to be deep into a work-induced trance. He scanned the hall carefully. The clumps of men talking loud and gambling had cleared out. Everyone had gone to bed early. The village knew Arthur would breed Emily that night. Every one of them had some of the Voice or the Power. A little bit. It bound them together as if they had one brain.

They also knew Sam would take comfort in a pick and hammer, slamming the hammer into the pillars until they chipped and cracked. None of them wanted to get in his way. They were as afraid of his temper as they had been of the raging Mollie years before.

He headed out to the fields, dimly lit at night. He could see where he was going, but not too far into the distance. He'd discovered a new spot to dig. Sam dropped the tools and took off his shirt, throwing it aside. He hefted the pick over his shoulder and slammed it into the soft dirt. His arms and shoulders reverberated from the impact. He did it again, and again, until sweat covered him.

Tossing the pick, he picked up the shovel. He had been right; the dirt was soft. It went all the way down to the center of the earth. Maybe he could dig out the other side. Sam dug, jabbing the shovel into the ground, leaning back on the handle to tilt up the dirt, then shoveling it out. The pile beside his new hole grew. He planned to dig the entire night, digging out. Digging under. Digging for a solution. He dug all the time.

"Sam." He jumped at the unexpected voice.

"What are you doing here, Janelle?"

"Ah thought you might like some company tonight."

"You thought wrong."

"When ah was sitting on your lap this afternoon, it seemed like y' liked me. Ah thought ye'd be glad to see me," she said in a whispery voice.

"Ah was just having fun. Ah didn't mean anything by it."

"Ah thought ye'd like some company, it being *tonight* and all." He stiffened. "Ye're a beautiful man, Sam. Someone should take care o' ye."

He started digging again.

"Ah can make ye feel good." She stepped out of the shadows. Janelle was naked. Long blond hair fell down her shoulders. Her pink-tipped breasts swung subtly. Her patch looked like curly corn silk. Something inside him lurched toward her.

Sam stood taller and pulled away.

"Ah can make ye forget, Sam. Forget all about what she's doing tonight. Ah can make ye forget about what she's doing *right now*. Where she's got her mouth, and her hands . . ."

He should have yelled at her to make her shut up, but he couldn't. The whole underground knew what was going on. She was saying what everyone knew.

"They'll be doing it all night, Sam, over and over. Ah know ye can feel it. Ye've got the Power more than anyone." Her lips were slightly parted and her eyes drilled into him. She rubbed her hand down the front of her body. "Ah can make ye forget those brown babies. Forget all about everything. Ah'm like ye, Sam. Ah'm from the village. Ah'm not a foreigner."

"Clear out, Janelle." He used the Voice. He was shaking. "Get out."

"Ah'll be waiting," she whispered before drifting away. "Ah'll wait for ye forever. Ah've saved myself for ye." She disappeared into the shadows. He could hear her putting on her clothes and walking away. She hadn't saved herself for anyone. Half the underground had had her. She was a ruthless, ambitious little cunnie, as trustworthy as . . . *Arthur.*

Sam felt cold now, despite his sweat. She *would* wait. They all would wait. And, one day, he'd be weak and take one of them. Then he'd have to make a choice because he kept the Commands. He would be faithful to one wife. He should have divorced Emily long ago. Any headman he knew would have divorced her and killed her lover. Maybe killed both of them. But he couldn't do it. He loved her, and she loved Arthur. He wouldn't hurt her by killing him.

He ran away from the fields as though Janelle and her pack were on his heels.

Sam dropped the tools inside his room and leaned back against the closed door, breathing hard. He hadn't intended to be in his room that night. The place felt so empty.

Emily had probably already gone to Arthur. They never did live together, keeping the pretext of decency in that one way. She and the kids had a room. Arthur lived with Winnie and their kids. They kept the fiction of their happy families alive, barely.

Sam knew how she had looked when she had gone. He'd seen her: one of those tight short skirts, a blouse open down to here, high heels. Clipping along the concrete like a mare in heat, waving her hind end as if it were on fire.

He shoved himself away from the door, finally making a choice. He would divorce her. Right now. All he had to do was say it three times. He turned to the intercom. Where were they tonight? The nightclub? One of the secret rooms Art hadn't shown Sam?

Sam decided to broadcast their divorce to the entire underground. Let everyone know he'd had enough. He raised his hand to start flipping switches when he heard the door open. It was locked. Who could get in?

"Sam? Are you here?" It was Emily, still dressed in tottering high heels and a skirt that barely covered her ass.

"I'm here. What do ye want?"

She walked up to him, slippery like the little cat she was. Smiling. "Well. Tonight's my night to make a baby. Would you like to make a baby with me?"

He reared back, staring at her. "Sure, ah'll make a babe with ye." Sam yanked up her skirt and cursed when he saw she had nothing on underneath. He grabbed her and threw her on the bed, undoing his pants as fast as he could. He had no trouble getting hard that night. He plowed into her, holding her hands over her head. "Ah'll make a babe with ye, whoor. Do ye like that, whoor?"

She took it for a while, then started to struggle. "Sam, you're hurting me. Stop."

He pulled out and stood quaking. "AH CANNOT STAND IT WHEN YE GO TO HIM. AH CANNOT STAND IT. AH WILL NOT HAVE IT." He wanted to backhand her.

"I know. I never will do it again. It's over. I just told him that. I'm sorry, Sam. Really sorry. Will you have me back?"

"Will ah have ye back? Just like that? After all these years? Why do ye want me now?"

She stammered, looking as if she might cry. "It was Janelle. I saw her sitting in your lap this afternoon. I saw where your hand was. And all those other little girls behind her, wanting you. I got so jealous that I wanted to kill her, and you. And all of them. Then I realized how you must have felt for years and years. I don't know why it didn't hit me before, but I realized how I'd hurt you. I don't care about the future generations. I've done my share. I care about you."

Sam inhaled sharply. "And ah'm s'posed t' jest take ye back t' ma bed, cunnie? Like nothin' had happened atall?"

"Yes. That's what I hoped."

He laughed. "It's been five years, cunnie."

"Don't call me that."

"Ah'll call ye whatever ah want."

"Oh, Sam. Please let me come back. I'm so sorry. I was wrong."

"Yeah, lass. Verra wrong. Tell me, why did ye do it? Or, ah should say, why'd ye keep on doin' it, past any need for any but for yerself? Ah thought ah took good care of ye. Ah thought ye were happy. That ah made ye happy. Why did ye do 'er?"

Tears spilled out of her eyes. "I don't know, Sam. I *was* happy. You made me happy in bed and everywhere." She wiped her eyes with the backs of her hands, shaking her head. "I don't know how it happened. It started because you told me to go and because what Arthur said about the future generations is true. It's just some-how . . . he touched me and everything changed. It wasn't like it was supposed to be, just something to do for genetics and those to come. He touched me inside—and he really touched me. I was wide open and . . . and I was . . . you know."

"Ah know. Ah felt ye comin'. Ah felt every one. Ah knew every time." His cheeks pulled back so his face was rigid. Disgust filled him like a bitter poison. Who was this lying stranger? Did he want her back?

"It just grew. We didn't mean it like that. First he touched me. I came. I couldn't stop it. I didn't want to stop it. And then we were in love, and having an affair. Trying to hide it from you and everyone. Pretending no one knew. I don't know how it happened. It just did.

"And then the babies came. We do love them, Sam, both of us. That's the way things are. People make love and have babies and love each other.

"But it was wrong. All of it. I never should have gone with him. I should have said, no, never, kill me first. But it seemed so logical, and there was Arthur with his statistics and Jeremy up on the screen talking about what good genes Arthur had.

"I'm sorry. If you don't want me back, I'll go." She rolled off the bed and stood up. "Even if it ends, I want you to know that I'm sorry." She doubled over and started to cry, covering her face with her hands. "Oh, I'll go. I'm sorry. I was stupid to think we could get back together."

She was scrambling toward the door when he stopped her. "Are ye goin' back to him, lass?"

"No, Sam. That's done. I have to figure out what to do with my life. I can't . . ." She looked lost, and then slapped herself across the face as hard as she could. The sound resounded. "I don't deserve . . ." She slapped herself again, leaving a red handprint to mark the sound. He grabbed her wrist.

"No, lass. If ah'll not beat ye, neither will ye. Come to me." He enfolded her in his arms, humming. She felt so sweet. He never could resist her. "Hold me, lass. It's been a long time."

"Ah do want a baby, lass. Shall we make one tonight? It's been a long time, Em'ly. A very long time."

He took her all night. He was rough, but she didn't complain. He took her over and over. Beating the stench of Arthur Romero out of her. Beating the lies out of her. Beating out years of pain.

The room was black when a sound awoke him, a roaring, screaming noise. A repetitive noise that couldn't be stopped. He sat up, heart beating, ribs plunging in and out. His chest rose and fell convulsively.

"Oh . . . Oh . . ." *He* was making the noise. "Oh. Oh, ma God. Oh, help me!"

"I'll help you, Sam." She put her arms around him.

"Oh, God. Oh." He turned to her. "Ye broke ma heart, Em'ly. Ye broke ma heart." He clutched his chest. "Oh, ma God. Ye killed me. Ah'll ne'er be the same."

60

As Emily's belly swelled, Sam got more and more nervous. Had she stopped at Arthur's for a fond farewell before coming to his room? Would this be another brown baby, or his? He picked up his sledgehammer and walked toward the door.

"Ah'll be back in a while," he said.

People shrunk away when they saw him. The underground felt the way the earth had the night before it blew up. As if it were heading over a cliff and couldn't turn around. Janelle and her friends packed after him, smiling like it was a matter of time until they had him.

His hammer had marked most of the pillars and walls of the underground. The chips and scrapes measured Sam's time in the shelter better than a calendar. It was the only thing he could do to defuse his anger. Sam swung the hammer until he couldn't raise it.

Nothing had changed after she moved back in. He felt awkward being in the room with her. They didn't talk, except stiffly. The bulge in her belly drove him wild. He'd see her sticking out and want to punch her. But he'd never hit a woman. He'd jump up and grab his tools, face contorted, and rush out of the room.

"Foocking sow. She's na but a cunnie bollocks." Sam swore all the way to the fields, screaming at anyone who looked at him. "What're ye lookin' at? Put yer eyes somewheres else." He'd dig until he fell on his face. But he didn't hit her or the children.

The kids kept their eyes on him and didn't get rowdy in the room. Shane didn't come home. He stayed with Sally. Emily walked bent over, apologizing to him every five minutes. They shared a bed but little else.

He and Sally took care of Emily when she had the baby. Arthur was the usual midwife, but Sam wouldn't speak to him, and certainly wouldn't let him attend his wife. The baby came easily, slipping into the world as though birth was a lark.

Sam held his hands out to catch her, trembling. The tension that had been in him for nine months was released when he saw her. Red hair, a few shades lighter than his own. Green eyes, wide open, looking around the world as though it already belonged to her. Sam belonged to her the moment he touched her. He lifted their daughter and put her in Emily's arms. She cried. Were they tears of delight or relief?

They named her Samantha. Called her Mandy instead of Sammi because there were so many Sams. She was his sweet angel baby. Every time he touched her, Sam's heart swelled. She was a miracle. A delight. She slept through the night right away. With two adults, five kids, and a baby packed in two rooms, that was important. Mandy didn't fuss. Didn't have colic. She seemed to love him as much as he loved her.

Even though the baby was obviously his, nothing changed. Emily walked around with her face drawn. They scarcely spoke. He felt for the first time that perhaps the situation was hopeless. Perhaps he didn't have the skill to mend their marriage. Perhaps he didn't want to.

Mandy turned six weeks old, though it felt as if no time had passed since she was born. Sam finished feeding her. Emily had expressed breast milk into a bottle so he could give her lunch while she and Sally took the other kids on a picnic at the far end of the fields. He burped Mandy and put her in her cradle. He smiled as he watched her sleep. At least one thing was right.

"Da?" Carlos, the older of Arthur's kids, had crept into the main room with him. He was five and the girl was three. Carlos had banged his knee playing and it was too sore for him to walk to the picnic. Sam was surprised to hear the boy call him Da. He knew that Arthur's children called him Da among themselves, but had never heard one of them address him that way.

"Yeah." Sam felt his gut constrict talking to the boy. He'd seldom had anything to do with Arthur's brats, though they'd lived in one of his rooms all their lives, except for that six months when he and Emily were split.

"When I grow up, will I be big like you?" The boy had wide brown eyes and looked at Sam with utter seriousness. Sam noticed something for the first time: Carlos looked like Emily. Same eyes, nose, head shape. He had her neat, precise way of moving. His body was put together like hers.

"You'll be very big when you grow up—" Damned if he would call him Carlos. "Would you like a new name? A village name?"

"What name?"

Sam thought. "How about Randy? For Randy Estreth. He was the headman of a village up north. A good friend of mine. That's a good name for a little boy."

"Randy?" The child glowed. "Randy Baahuhd, like you?"

"Yes. Randy Baahuhd. Would you like that?" Sam felt the cosmos open up around him as he spoke. He was moving through something huge.

"Yes, Da. Do we get to stay here forever?"

"What do you mean, Randy?"

"We won't have to move away again? We were so lonely when we lived in that other room. We missed you. Juanie cried."

Something made Sam's eyes sting. "You missed me?"

"Yeah, Da. Really bad. Can we stay here?'

"Yeah. You can stay here no matter what."

"Da, why didn't Shane come back? Doesn't he like us anymore?"

The breath went out of Sam. The little one was saying what no one else talked about.

"He likes you, Randy, and the other kids. He doesn't like me or your ma."

"But he'll come back one day?" Those bright brown eyes and the sweet face.

"I hope so, Randy. I miss him."

Randy smiled, but a cloud flitted across his face. He lowered his voice. "Da, why does Ma cry?"

"She cries? I never see her cry."

"She cries when you're not here. Sometimes she goes in there and closes the door." He indicated the bathroom. "She cries all the time. When we were in the other room, she cried all day."

"She must be sad."

"But we're back with you. Why should she be sad? Aren't you happy? We're *home* again."

That rocked Sam back on his heels. Even a child could tell things weren't right. And home was their room, where he was.

"Can things be like before, when she was happy?"

As far as Sam was concerned, things hadn't been OK since Emily went with Arthur. "When was she happy?"

"When I was a baby and we lived here with you." He looked at Sam with such hunger that he pulled away.

"You remember that?"

"I remember you, Da. And so does Juanie. We remember you all the time." Longing burned in his eyes. "I wish you were my da."

"Don't you like Arthur?"

"Yes, but he's not you."

"Would you like to be my boy?" Sam had treated those kids terribly. He was stunned that they loved him. Guilt rose inside him.

"Yes, Da!"

"I think I can do something to make things how they were.

Would you like that?"

"Yeah, Da. Really, really." He nodded his head vigorously, wide brown eyes solemn.

"OK. I will then. Come to me and I'll tell you a story." Sam helped the child up into his lap. Sam had never held him before, never really acknowledged him. Now the boy was shaking like a whipped dog needing affection more than anything, but expecting the opposite.

"Da." Randy looked down as though afraid to speak.

"Yes, son." The boy jerked at the word.

"Can Juanie and I come out of the closet?"

Sam's throat seized up. What had he done to these children? "Yes. You can come out whenever you want. And eat with us. Everything."

Randy's brows knit. He looked bewildered. "Did we change, Da?"

"What do you mean?"

"You kept us in the closet because we're bad. Did we change?"

"You never were bad, Randy. I was bad. I was very bad." Pressure built up behind Sam's eyes. His vision blurred.

"Are we still 'brown bastard whoorsons' if we're your kids?"

"Who called you that?"

"Everyone." He waved toward the hall. "They call us that unless Ma is there. And they call her 'the whoor.' What's that, Da?"

Sam crushed the child to him. "No one will call you that again, Randy. I'll take care of that. Who calls you that the most?"

"Everyone. They say Juanie and me are a waste of air."

"Oh, son." Sam rocked the boy, holding him tight. "Don't worry. I'll make everything right." Randy clutched him frantically.

"We can stay here for sure?"

Sam was so filled with remorse he could hardly speak. "You'll be with me as long as I live. Things will be different now, Randy." He ruffled his hair. "Would you like me to tell you a story?" The boy nodded vigorously.

"I'm going to tell you a story about my friend the headman Randy Estreth and the pissing contest."

61

Sam thought about what he'd have to do to really heal things between him and Emily. Talking to Randy had made up his mind: He wanted his children, all six of them. He wanted Shane back. He wanted their family to be happier than they ever had been. He wanted Emily back and he wanted them to be the way they were before Arthur came into their lives. That would take some doing.

"OK, kids. Be good with Sally. See you tomorrow."

"Ah'll keep them good, Sam." Sally kissed his cheek as she hustled the brood out the door. "Ye have a good night."

He and Emily were alone in their room.

"Ah've wanted to talk to ye, Emily," he said. She burst out before he could say anything more.

"I'm sorry, Sam. I wanted everything to be the same when I came back, but nothing is. I've wrecked everything. It's all my fault." She began to weep. "I thought I could come back and things would go back the way they used to be. But they haven't.

"I was so lonely when I was pregnant with Mandy. I know you thought the baby was Arthur's. You'll never trust me again. Everything is ruined and it's my fault." Her face was tight, blotched and white, and streaked with tears.

Emily tumbled to the floor at his feet, trembling and dropping her forehead to his boots. "Oh, please, forgive me. Please, please, forgive me. Make it the way it was. I'll do anything you want. I'm so sorry. I was wrong. I lied to you. I did everything wrong. Please forgive me."

Sam was astonished and delighted. This was the kind of abject apology even the most old-style headman would accept.

"It's all right, Emily. Ah think we can fix it. Would you like to try?"

They lay on their bed, belly to belly. He'd used the Power to get Emily to calm down. Just a little, just enough to do that. He stroked her side.

"Remember the first time, Em'ly? We were like this. Remember? That's a good lass. Let me touch you. You're such a lovely thing." He stroked her, humming softly. "Do you want it to be the way it was, lass?" She nodded. "Good. Ah do, too.

"Let me love you, girl." He ran his hand down her flank and then between her legs. "Such a good girl, Emily. Put your leg over mine. Just like that." She did and he pushed himself inside her. "Remember—this is the way we did it the first time.

"Do you feel me, Em? Do you feel that? Ah feel you." He groaned, keeping himself in check. This time called for all the control he had. "Ah can feel you all around me. You fit just fine." He hummed a bit and then rocked forward. She arched back. He put his hand on the small of her back.

"It's time, Em'ly." Sam rocked slowly in measured movements. "Let go of it, darlin'. Give yourself to me."

She flailed and pulsed while he held her. "Good." He rocked some more. "It's easy, Em'ly. So easy. Let it go . . ."

He kept at her until she scratched and bit. He took her past mewing and sobbing. He kept her opening and opening until she lay there, unable to move, wide as the starry sky. Flowing.

"Keep going, Emily. Ah want more from you."

When there wasn't any more of her, Sam asked, "Who do you love, Emily?"

"You, Sam. Just you."

"Who do you belong to?"

"I belong to you."

"Good, because ah belong to you." He gave himself to her, feeling the golden light course up his spine and out of him. Jerking and flailing as he grasped her.

"Ah love you and you love me. We belong to each other forever." He said that in the Voice. He held her, the Power shooting through him, filling them.

62

Sam called Arthur on the intercom. "Meet me in the gym."
Arthur knew what was up when he got there. His hands
were bandaged like a fighter's and he had on boxing shoes.

"Look, Sam. Can't we be reasonable about this? We're adults."

Sam maneuvered him into the middle of the room. He'd already
laid out the fight in his mind and knew where Art would fall. He
stood with his hands at his sides, shoulders down, watching his
adversary.

"It wasn't what either of us intended, Sam. It just happened. I'm
sorry."

Art danced around using skills they'd taught him at the academy and in training. Play fighting. Sam dodged his punches, taking
his time. Staying just out of reach.

"Come on, Sam, let's get it over with," Arthur challenged.

A little smile lit Sam's mouth. He lunged forward, giving Art
a target. When Art punched, Sam wasn't there. Sam's fist rammed
Arthur's belly. He doubled over, winded. He managed to back
away, his fighter's shoes working hard for a fast retreat. Sam followed him, but didn't take him down. Not yet.

"Ye foocked ma wife for five years, ye filthy whoorson. Ye foocked ma wife an' thought ye'd get away from *me*? Yer stupid as well as dead."

Fear flashed in Arthur's eyes. Fear that said he'd never thought Sam would kill him. He was forty-five years old to Sam's fifty-four, a trained fighter and a superbly conditioned athlete. But he couldn't speak, could barely stay out of Sam's reach.

Sam dropped him exactly where he'd planned, an open spot with plenty of room. A red haze of blood lust and hatred claimed him. He was aware of the repetitive movement of his shoulders and arms. The pain in his own hands as they connected with Art's face. Blood exploding. Its copper tang on his tongue. Sounds of bones breaking.

He could feel the movement of his boot-clad feet, his leg swinging in an arch and connecting. Arthur's body moving like a deadweight. Kicking again and again, hitting mush instead of bones. A shivering hulk lay on the floor. His leg kept moving.

He heard something. A voice. He didn't stop swinging. The thuds. His legs were bloody to the knees. He felt nothing but hatred. The voice was louder. Something touched his shoulder. He whirled.

"Oh, please, Sam. Ye'll kill him. Don't kill Art'ur." It was Winnie. "Please stop, Sam. Ye may have killed him already."

He turned back to what he'd been doing and saw a bloody lump, shaped like a human, almost. Arms and legs at strange angles. Blood all over. Face unrecognizable.

Winnie ran to Arthur and bent over him. She surveyed the damage and wailed. "Art'ur, Art'ur!" She held him to her bosom. "Oh, Art'ur." She turned to Sam. "Look what ye've done to him! Look! Did he d'serve that? To look like that?"

Sam was silent.

"Heal him, Sam. The ribs is through his lungs. He's bleedin' inside."

Sam healed him, enough so that he didn't die. The rest, Arthur Romero would have to fix on his own.

Setting things right with Arthur made Sam feel as if he had been given a new life. The sun burst out of the clouds and created a fresh world. He and Em and the kids could live happily forever.

As he felt this rising new existence, the fear that he was going to die soon left him. Why couldn't he live on and on? The people from the city did. Why couldn't he be like someone from New York? There was no reason he couldn't.

Somehow, Sam felt he was going to live a long, long time.

63

"When Emily and me got married, I told her I'd give her a party. She's had to wait thirteen years, but this is it!" Sam stood up as they began the feast, voice booming over the crowd. They ate in the dining area at the end of the hall. His family was front and center.

"Eat up!" Sam had unearthed more of the hidden food stores and slaughtered a lamb to make a hearty soup. Sally had made a cake, and he'd provided a real treat—microwaved popcorn. They drank lemonade made from the orchard's lemons.

When all had eaten their fill, Sam rose again and got everyone's attention. "You know my wife and kids. Emily, take a bow." She stood up and bobbed her head quickly. "And the kids are Shane and Joshua, Eli, Randy, Joanie. And little Mandy. All of them are my kids, Baahuhds to the bone."

He looked around the crowd. Everyone smiled and nodded to Emily and his children. He made no distinction between Arthur's brown kids and his other children, and neither did they. No one referred to Emily as a whore.

And no one would, as long as he held the Power.

"They tell me the kids have put together a show, so let's go over in front of the screen and give them a big hand." Sam acted as emcee. The teenagers, who'd spent their free time trying to copy the recordings of the most popular bands of Jeremy Edgarton's day, had set up a talent show. Sam smiled indulgently, hoping it would be brief.

Skinny kids who'd grown up in the underground crowded to the front. They had formed trios and quartets, all playing rock 'n' roll. Or stomp music, as they would have called it in the old village days. They'd discovered the electric guitars and amplifiers and had all the plates on the tables shaking with the sound.

The kids ranged from thirteen up. There weren't any kids younger than that, except for his children with Emily, and Arthur and Winnie's. And the brown babies. What Arthur had said was true: none of the village women had had babies. Whatever he had done to them worked. But this young batch playing instruments? Had Arthur taken care of them?

Rupert sat at the table next to his da's during dinner. He was close to his father's inner circle, but shoved down the line. His wife, Jennie, was way over on the other side with her friends. She didn't cotton to Em'ly an' didn't like bein' near her.

Rupert didn't care. He didn't like to be near ol' Jen himself. Her monthlies had quit and she'd been a she-bear since. Plus getting skinny like all of 'em had, her tits hung down and shook when she moved. Some of her teeth were gone. He didn't want anything to do with his wife.

But over there, sitting next to his da, was a woman he thought about all the time. Em'ly had had six kids and looked just the same. Hadn't gone to fat or thin. No missing teeth. A set of tits he wanted to lay hands on and an ass he'd dreamed of since he saw it that first time, slung over his da's shoulder. But Em'ly was Da's woman. His wife.

Rupert got up and helped himself to another bowl of soup, a couple of ears of corn, and a big hunk of cake. He was always hungry down here. Tonight he would take what he wanted. He snatched a peek at his da with his new kids. The brown ones stuck in his craw. They got to sit with his da and they weren't even totally human. "Joanie" and "Randy." Those weren't their names. Their names were Shit and Shit. His da liked the monkeys better than him.

When the bands started, Ru settled down a little. He loved the music the kids played all the time. Rock 'n' roll, they said it was. Stomp music, he called it. A smile ran across his face as he listened, moving his head and tapping his foot. This was like the old village.

Janelle was the final act, and Sam felt as though someone had dropped a rattlesnake in the middle of the stage. She was wearing an outfit that looked like she'd copied it from Emily. A tight skirt above her knees. A blouse cut so low it looked as if her breasts might fall out. Big breasts like a grown woman's. Long pale hair, and a guitar. She hiked a hip up on a stool and began to play. The stage lights made her glow gold and silver.

The teenage boys' eyes followed her. They barely breathed.

Sam felt a tightening of his gut as he listened. Janelle's soft, breathy voice was whispering a ballad she might have written.

> *Ye said ye loved me, but ye lied.*
> *Ye said ye loved me; ah cried and cried . . .*

She didn't look at Sam when she sang, but her friends shot him nasty looks. He hadn't spoken to her since that night by the fields. Avoided her as hard as he could. Now she had his attention. Who knows what stories she'd told?

> *If ah'd known what ye were, ah'd have run away;*
> *Ye're a no-good lover, that's all ah can say . . .*
> *Now all ah can do is cry an' cry,*
> *an' hope for the day ah finally die.*

She really could pick that guitar, and kept wailing, verse after verse. He wanted to shut her up, but he looked around and saw the people listening to her, breathless. He realized Janelle was the queen of the underground, the hall part of it anyway. The people loved her. Grown men gaped at her.

He'd better make sure Arthur plugged her as soon as he could get up off a bed. Her and all the young ones. They'd have babies popping up everywhere. Janelle bowed, and he thought those tits *would* fall out. She finally left.

When Janelle got up to sing, Rupert couldn't move. She was wearin' clothes such as *she* might wear, like what they wore in the city. A skirt that showed her legs up above her knee. And a shirt that almost didn't have a front. The lights fell on her, shining on titties bigger than any woman's. Janelle had jiggly mounds on her chest that made Em'ly's look like a little girl's. Her hair shined silver and gold, like a village woman's should. Face was as pretty as the angels the snake men talked about, and Janelle's voice was so sweet, it made his eyes sting. He rubbed them with the back of his hand, hoping no one saw.

She was singing about what his da had done to her, Rupert knew. The stories were that his da had taken her, but not brought her back to his room as his second wife. He'd turned his back on the village girl to lie in bed with the whoor.

Rupert caught himself. He was not to call Em'ly a whoor, or think of her that way, even though she had two babies with Arthur and clearly deserved to be called that.

Janelle left the stage and he felt his chest openin' toward her, his heart about to walk out and follow her. He watched her move to the rear of the room, every head swiveling with his. Time seemed to stop for a moment.

When he turned around, Da's new brats were walkin' up to the front like they owned the place. Rupert scowled.

Unexpectedly, Shane walked out into the empty space holding a saxophone. He had sat with the family during dinner, but that's all. He now looked at Sam, sneering, anger pouring off him so Sam could almost see it. His lips tightened. Oh, God. What had he done? His other kids came streaming out holding instruments. Sam hadn't noticed them disappear.

"We cooked up a little surprise for everyone. We've been practicing the last year, but the last six months mostly. We've had a lot of time by *ourselves* recently." Shane gave the "by ourselves" a nasty bite. He was lean and tall and very good-looking. His dark hair had grown out a bit. He wore it greased up like the kids in the hall. Shane sneered as he looked around. He fancied himself a tough guy.

Sam scanned the crowd. The girls looked at Shane the way the men and boys had looked at Janelle. Sam ran his hand over his face. Shane was only twelve. What problems lay ahead?

"To learn to play, we used the tapes and lessons Jeremy left. Chaz Edgarton played a saxophone. That's what this is." Shane held the instrument out.

Joshua had a clarinet, Jeremy Edgarton's instrument. Eli had a flute. They stairstepped down from Shane's twelve years to Joanie's three. Five-year-old Randy had cymbals and Joanie held a string with a little metal triangle hanging from it. They'd obviously worked hard preparing for this performance.

Shane stood in the middle of the kids. He was tall for his age, closing in on six feet. They were beautiful children, neatly formed like their mother, with Sam's features showing up here and there.

Shane held the saxophone as if he'd been playing it all his life, standing with one foot forward and his hip cocked. Joshua joined in, weaving his clarinet's sound in and out of his brother's notes. It reminded Sam of something . . .

The last night before the earth blew up! Jeremy had played with recordings of his famous father's music. Chaz Edgarton had been the most famous musician of his day, playing a sax as though God had handed it to him personally.

As the music rolled on, Sam's eyebrows went up, and then his jaw and face dropped. He stared spellbound as his son toyed with his soul. Shane's notes rose and circled and fell, like love being born. Sam felt himself lifted. And charmed. The notes were a shower of starshine.

It was as though Chaz Edgarton stood before them. The way Shane stood reminded him of Chaz when he had played for the village. When he and the lady came to visit the estate, Chaz never had talked down to the villagers or forgotten them. He came out and played for them, jamming for hours. He also could be counted upon to slug down his share of hooch. Sam usually had to carry him back to the big house.

A light went on in the projection booth. Images of Chaz Edgarton playing at a club appeared on the screen behind the kids. The club was smoke and magic. Fancy people leaned on tables puffing cigars and drinking, sparkling like the music. Tall, elegant ladies in shiny dresses danced to Chaz's melodies with men in black tails.

Shane played along with Chaz and the film. He wasn't as good. Couldn't form the notes as perfectly or make the changes so smoothly that no one could tell a change had been made. But he was brilliant just the same. Joshua stood next to him, blowing on the clarinet. He wasn't as good as Jeremy had been, but Jeremy hadn't learned to play from a video machine. Then they stopped so Eli could do a solo on his flute.

The little boy stood tall and straight, his fingers moving along the instrument, producing the notes perfectly. At the end, Randy slammed the cymbals together. Shane took up again, making a final burst of music that ricocheted off the cement around them, transforming it into a container for enchantment rather than their prison. When he stopped playing, he turned to Joanie. She hit that little triangle just once and it rang bright and true, the perfect final note.

"Shane! Shane!" The villagers leapt to their feet, whistling and ululating and clapping. The other children might not have been there. Sam stood, ready to hug his son, but Shane turned and walked into a mob of kids on the other side of the stage. Sam's ribs began jerking in and out. He didn't understand what they were doing, pumping like that. He couldn't speak. Feelings rose over his head like the notes Shane had played. Sam knew he had ruined everything. Shane had turned his back on him.

"Oh, my children. Ma babes." He grabbed the others and held tight, kissing and hugging them. "My babes." The children grabbed him back. The crowd surged forward, lifting Shane over their heads. He never returned to his family's table.

When his da's brats came up to play, Rupert froze. They carried instruments like Jeremy and Chaz Edgarton had played, not the guitars and such the village kids played. When Shane started to play, horror bathed Rupert. A film of sweat burst out on his forehead. He would steal his da for sure.

He had to admit that the little shit was good. They all were. The music rose and fell. "Jazz is the coolest thing in the world, Ru," Chaz Edgarton had told him. Chaz was cool. Ru had loved Chaz more than any man he knew, except for his da. And now the brats were playing his music.

He could see his da's face from the side and was glad he couldn't see any more. His mouth was open a little. He looked the way he used to watching the sunset sometimes, like nothing was more beautiful.

"Shane!" "Shane!" "Shane!" everyone cried when they stopped playing. His da leapt up and hugged the kids, spreading his arms wide. He kissed them on each cheek. He kissed the brown brats the same as the others. She got up and did the same thing. The bunch of them shone brighter than Janelle's hair. Everyone crowded around, yelling and whistling. His da stood there with tears in his eyes, he was so proud of *them*.

Ru's eyes burned now. He wanted to start swinging, but he couldn't do that. That would make it worse.

Seeing Shane walk away made Rupert happy. He and Da were fighting. Maybe there was some way he could get to Shane, now that his da didn't protect him. Maybe Shane would do something stupid.

Rupert backed away. He'd known it for years, but it finally sunk in. He was no longer his father's favorite. If it wasn't Shane who took his place, it would be one of the others. Maybe even one of the shits.

Long ago, when they'd held the party for being underground one year, Da had hugged Rupert in front of everyone, and kissed his cheeks. He had praised him and said that he would be the new headman. Ru had rested in that promise.

Now it didn't seem certain.

People milled around his da and his new family. Shane headed toward a storage room. He came back with a bunch of boxes and smiled his beautiful smile with his white teeth. Everyone made way for him, smiling more.

"We can play here!" Shane announced, setting the boxes on a table.

Ru knew what they'd do next; they played chess almost every day. His da's new kids sat in the middle of the hall with chessboards, smilin' like they were a club nobody else could join. Shane would play all his brothers at once, running from table to table. He'd beat all o' them.

An' then he'd play Da. He'd beat him, too, but he'd have to work for that. He and Da would crouch over the table, rubbing their chins. They sat like statues, with that black-and-white board between them, loaded with chess pieces Rupert couldn't name.

Da had tried to teach him chess, but Rupert couldn't remember the names of the pieces and the ways you could move them. He'd tried as hard as he could, but just couldn't do it. He finally told him, "Ah gotta go check the fields, Da. Don't have time for this."

When his da finally kicked the kids and the whoor out, things had gotten better. Da had paid attention to him. He took him out to the fields to discuss the crops and where the irrigation should go. He put his hand on Ru's shoulder and gripped it. He had begun to think his da loved him best again.

Now that they were back together, things had gone back to the way they'd been. Shane had stolen his da. He'd stolen everything that was his. Ru wanted to slit that stinking bastard's throat. If he could get away with it, he would do it. He ground his teeth together. A time would come.

He looked at the chess players. Shane was playing Josh. His da was off to the side. The brown shits stood around looking. One of them held da's hand. He could see a couple more of the brownies standing around the hall. His da should have killed Arthur instead of crippling him.

The injustice struck him like a hammer. Rupert wanted to run through the hall slashing with his knife. But he held himself in. Someday his da wouldn't be there to protect them.

Suddenly, it felt as if a hot iron pierced his right eye, sending showers of sparks inside his head. Rupert gasped and put his hand over his eye. His head had been throbbing all day. Being angry made it beat harder. Everything had fuzzy, bright edges around it. He ducked his head to get away from the light. Pain made him bend over and clutch his belly. He felt like he might puke. Sound was so loud it hurt. He bent forward, barely able to keep from sobbing.

Clutching his right eye, Rupert dashed for his room. He barely made it to the crapper before all he'd eaten came up. He puked and puked, falling to the floor next to the toilet. He lay gasping.

The pain on the right side of his head hurt so much, all he could do was hold on. Lights flashed and brilliant blobs filled his vision. Ru crawled to his bed and collapsed, gasping as he tried to ride out the anguish. He knew what it meant, and that horror almost matched his agony.

His mother had had headaches like this before the disease took her. He'd cared for her from the time he was a child, bathing her head with water and comforting her. And then he'd had to clear out, because she got too dangerous. They put chains on her and locked her in the stone house. She'd spent years in there, locked up like an animal. His ma.

But they'd had to lock her up because she killed people. When Em'ly had cut her down, Ru had thought it was for the best.

Rupert wept bitterly. The headache meant he would get the disease. They would lock him up. He would never be headman. *Shane* would be the headman, and everyone would say it was for the best. His father would foock Em'ly till he dropped dead from it.

64

"Ru, ye OK?" Cooty Gill stuck his head in the door. Rupert groaned. He'd forgotten to lock it.

"Saw ye run outta the hall like ye were ailin'." Cooty looked at Ru sprawled on his bed. "Looks like yer in a real bad way." Cooty had been the barrel maker back in the village. He also had been the biggest grower of weed in the Hamptons. These days, he achieved distinction as Janelle's father.

Ru couldn't speak. His stomach threatened to heave up whatever was left in it. The lights flew around in his head and Cooty sounded as if he were screaming in his ears. "Huh," Ru said, picking up a pillow and holding it over his head.

"I got somethin' here'll help ya." Cooty, his missing teeth and patchy hair making him look older than he was, fished some limp leaves and seedpods out of his pocket.

"What is it?" Exploding rings of light now seemed to circle Cooty's head.

"It's somethin' the boys an' ah happen to grow. Actu'lly, it grew itself," he chuckled. "If ye chew it, it makes what's hurtin' ye go away."

Ru held out his hand, peering at the vegetation. "Looks like them beans we eat all the time. Soybeans."

Cooty bent close. "That's the beauty of 'er, Ru. Looks so much like 'em, even yer da can't find 'em. Grew up where they tore out the weed that Les and Ronny was growin'. The weed bred with the beans for somethin' total' new."

"Is it weed?" Rupert's eyes widened. He'd seen what weed had done to many in the village's older generation. Vacant eyes. Mouths babbling nonsense. Rages. Death.

"Nah. Ain't the same. We been chewin' it for a year 'r two." Cooty ducked his head when he realized he'd let out a secret. "Ye seen any dif'rence in us?"

"Who?"

"Most all o' us, Ru. Ain't easy bein' down here with nuthin'. We actin' any diff'rent?"

The pain in his head made thinking hard. Everyone seemed like they always had. "No. Ye seem the same."

"That's because the beans an' the weed mellow each other out." Cooty used his hands like he was shaping a figure. "Ain't nothin' like with the old weed."

"What does it do?" Rupert was ready to take anything.

"Makes the pain go away Ah mean, away. *Gone*. An' it makes ye feel good, an' it makes ye think better."

"It's na' the weed? Ye don't get sick or crazy?"

"We been chewin' a long time, Ru. Maybe more 'n a couple o' years. Nobody's ragin' 'r fightin'. We's all gettin' our work done. Makes things better, Ru. That's why ah brung it to ye."

Rupert took the leaves and pods. "Wha' do ye do?"

"Jus' chew 'em. When they's all chewed out, ye can eat what's left, or spit it in the crapper. Ah'll let ye be, an' come back to check ye in a while."

Rupert chewed gingerly. Tasted like soybeans. He'd never tried weed, being afraid of what it did. Maybe these leaves were a little different than soy, but nothing much. He chewed the wad and then swallowed it.

Warmth spread from his belly and he relaxed. The next thing he knew, he was opening his eyes and yawning. He felt like he'd slept for hours. Cooty Gill was sitting on the edge of the bed.

"How's yer head?" he said.

Ru rubbed a hand over his head. The pain was gone. So were the lights, his roiling guts, and sound being too loud. "Ah'm fine. Total' fine."

It seemed like a miracle. If the headache came again, he could stop it with the leaves. No one had to know he had them. Maybe they'd stop the disease from coming, too. He sat up.

"Keep it our secret, Ru. Just for the village people. Yer da don't have to know. He'll burn it like he did the weed. He don't understand that the people need a little somethin' now an' again. He don't know how some of us don't cotton to the new ways, an' the Commands. Can't do 'em, even tryin' harder an' hard."

That was true. No one knew how hard he'd tried to learn to read. The letters seemed to wiggle around and change directions. He didn't understand why there had to be so many of them, or so many words. He was stupid; Rupert knew that. All the others, even the young children, could read better than he could. *Especially* the children—*hers* and the brown babies.

Rupert stuck his chin out pugnaciously. "Yeah, Cooty, there's a dif'rence between us from the village true and the outsiders. Seems like they's taken over my da."

Cooty looked frightened by the criticism of Sam. "Well, now . . ."

"It's OK, Cooty. Ye can tell me. Ah understand. Tell me how the people think."

Ru sat back and listened. The people saw no need for the Commands, no need for most of the changes his da had made. A smile spread across his face. This is where he would get his power. Rupert Baahuhd might be stupid, but he wasn't dumb.

"Some changes is gonna happen, Cooty. Let's jus' go along an' let my da an' them think we love the new ways. An' ah'll make it easy on ye and work on gettin' things back to the way they was. Like the *real* village!"

Cooty smiled, looking relieved. He dropped his voice and bent closer. "Me an' the boys found a secret place, Ru. A place no one could ever find. It's a place where a man might have a still. Might make some fine hooch there. Wouldna ye like a taste again?"

A mighty thirst came upon him. "Yeah, Cooty, ah'd like a taste. Sure would be fine to take a swaller. But don't tell me nothin' about this place or where it is or what's goin' on. Ah sure would appreciate a cup, now an' again."

"Well, ah won't say more about 'er, Ru. But there is somethin' else we could talk about." He handed Rupert another handful of leaves, like he might need them. "Chew on this while ah explain.

"Say there was a beautiful girl who fell in love with someone she had no bus'ness fallin' for. Say he helped her along with that, makin' advances, foolin' with her 'til she was crazy wantin' to do it, tho' she's virgin an' all. An' then say he walks away, goes back to his whoor of a wife, leavin' her crazy with want, an' angry for what he done." Cooty looked at him appraisingly.

Rupert sat bolt upright, swallowing a hunk of leaves. He was talking about Janelle. "He never laid with her?" he choked.

"Oh, no. She told all them stories 'cause she was so mad an' wanted to get back at him. Hurt him bad like he done her."

"She never done it?"

"Never, ah swear. She's virgin, pure as can be. Waitin' for the man o' her dreams to take her." He looked at Rupert, as though gauging his readiness. "She wants ye, Rupert Baahuhd. She wants to open her sweet self and give her love to ye. Would ye have her, or hurt her like that other man?"

Heat surged through Rupert. "But ah'm married. What abou' Jennie?"

"Yer the headman, Ru, soon as Sam pops off, which could be any time. The headman has always had as many wives as he wanted, *always*, until we got stuck down here. Ye can do 'er, Ru. Jus' do 'er. Jenny don't care. She's dried up an' done. She can come live with us."

Cooty leaned closer. "Yer the headman ever'body wants. An' yer the man Janelle wants, Ru. She wants ye to be the headman, and she wants to be yer wife. She wants to have yer babes, Ru. Lots of 'em. She can have babies, Ru. Art'ur never put one o' them things in her." The villagers had figured out by themselves what Art had done to their women.

Rupert let out a huge sigh. His da would never agree.

"Ye can have her secretlike, Ru. Give her a babe, an' yer da won't say no. He'll marry ye. She's virgin, Ru. Ye'll get the firs' taste."

"The firs' and only taste," Rupert said. "She'll na have another but me." He swallowed the rest of the leaves. Something about them gave him strength. "Yeah, ah'll take 'er. Ah'll give her what my da didn't."

"Would ye like 'er now, Ru? She's waitin' outside, hopin' ye'd say yes."

The heat rose through Rupert again. "Yeah, ah'll take her. Ah'll take her right now." He was hard before he finished saying the words.

Cooty stuck his head outside the door. "Come on in, ye sweet babe. Here's a man gonna treat ye right."

Janelle walked in wearing the short skirt she'd worn to perform. The blouse showed even more of her titties than he remembered. Her hair swayed softly when she moved. Her eyes were wide and a little scared, as a virgin's should be.

"Come here, girl, ah got somethin' for ye." Ru smiled hard. The worst day of his life was turnin' out to be the best.

65

"Sam. Sam. Ah need ye." The voice was so soft, he could hardly hear it over the intercom. Sam sat up in bed. It was the middle of the night.

"Sally, is that you?"

"Yeah, Sam. Ah'm sick. Real bad."

"Ah'll be right there." Sam jumped out of bed and threw on his clothes. "Em, you stay here. Ah'll be back soon as ah can."

He dashed down the darkened corridor to Sally's room. Her skin was mottled red and white and she was as hot as anyone he'd ever felt. "Are ye painin', Sally?"

"Ye, right here. For a coupla' days." She indicated the right side of her abdomen.

"Why didn't ye call me?"

"Ye were havin' yer party an' getting' back together with yer family. Ah thought it was old lady's pains, is all. Would clear up by 'er self." He looked grave and gently felt the place she had indicated. She cried out.

"It's not old lady's pains."

"Can ye help me, Sammy?" Sally's eyes glittered feverishly.

"Yeah, though were better ye called me earlier. But ah can do 'er. It'll take a while."

"But that's the thing, Sam. We don't have a while." She sat up a little and grabbed his arm. "Ah don't know where the boys are. Yesterday, ah was fevered up. Ah don't remember much. They came in an' went out. Ah don't think they was back last night . . ."

"An' ye didn' call me to help ye?"

"Ah was sick, Sammy. Fevered an' not thinkin'. Thing's been goin' on ah didn' know. Billy Sam is turnin' bad like his ma. He's not mindin' me, an' he's hangin' out in the hall. Took Shane with him. They may even be doin' the new kinda weed. You gotta find them. Ah think they might try to get Shane hooked. Some people in this place would love t' ruin your boy."

Sam jerked. "Why?"

"Lotsa whys, havin' to do with what ah told ye the other day, about roosters running around and makin' people mad. Ye made enemies, Sam. The kind that don't forget. There's Art'ur and Em'ly, too. Ye na' takin' yer revenge on 'em for so long made some think yer weak.

"Shane walked right into their hands. He's been so mad with both of you. Ah heard he hardly had a thing to do with you at the party yesterday. Billy Sam's been stirrin' him up more.

"Billy Sam tol' Shane that Em'ly killed his ma and brothers an' all those others back at the beginning. Yer Voice kept people from rememberin' clear for all these years, but some're rememberin' now an' talkin' about it. Billy Sam tol' Shane. It was a shock t' him. Shane hates Em'ly for it, an' he's still mad with ye. He's mad enough to do anything."

Sam rose halfway, and then sat back. "Ah can't go find him, Sally. You'll die. It's about to burst in there."

"I'll find them. Don't worry." Emily stood in the doorway in her bathrobe.

"Are ye up to it, girl? There's some bad sorts out there."

"I'll be fine, Sally. Where do you think they are?"

She shook her head. "The fields are big, Em'ly, but ah think Cooty's got a hideaway beyond the last big pillar, just before the orchard."

"Em'ly, can you handle 'er?" Sam looked worried.

"For Shane? I could handle an atomic bomb." Her voice was sharp. "Find me when you're done, Sam." She disappeared up the hallway to get dressed.

Sam looked after her and then bent over Sally. The healing trance took both of them in an instant.

"It's not so bad, Shane. Yer da an' ma brainwashed ye. They probably never done nothin'." Billy Sam grinned. "Course, back in the village, yer da was laid out on his face mos' nights, drunk."

"He was not!" Shane barked, incensed.

"Oh, ask anybody. They'll tell ye. Biggest grot-head and cunnie-hound in the Hamptons. An' him tellin' everyone to be faithful to their hubby or wife. He's had ev'ry woman in the village, Shane. Didn't you know that?"

Shane didn't know. He pulled Billy Sam around. "That's not true."

"Sure is. Come with me out to the fields. The fellas is out there. They'll tell you. He went with their wives."

"I don't believe you."

"Come an' see, Shane. Your da ain't all playin' chess an' readin'. Ah wouldna be surprised if yer ma got the idea to do what she did with Art from him."

"Shut up!"

Billy Sam laughed. "Come on. Try a little an' ye'll see she's not so bad. Yer brainwashed. Yer da probably done weed, too. He's done ever'thing else. Come on. They're waitin' for us. They think yer ready to be a man."

Shane followed him, reeling from what he'd found out.

They walked a long way. A concrete path surrounded the fields, and a low cement wall enclosed the topsoil. Lights were attached to the walls, but they barely illuminated the area around each fixture. Billy Sam and Shane had to feel their way along.

Huge concrete and steel supports held up the ceiling like ribs of an ancient monster. It was chilly, and the echoes were worse here than anywhere else in the underground. Shane was scared, though he'd rather have died rather than admit it.

"When will we be there?" He felt bad about not telling Sally where they were going, but he couldn't very well say, "Auntie, I'm going off with Billy Sam to do drugs. Don't worry."

His parents would be having shit fits if they knew where he was going. It had been so fun refusing to play chess with Da after the dinner. His stricken expression had been beautiful, and this would be even better. Shane, their perfect son, was going to get loaded. He knew the others would want him to get high. He was the headman's son. A great prize. Maybe he'd become a dealer. Sell it to the little kids.

He swaggered and put his hands in his pockets. He'd make his parents sorry.

Tears came to his eyes when he thought of what he'd learned from Billy Sam. His mother was a killer and his da . . . Shane couldn't even think about what his da was.

Billy Sam grabbed his jacket and pulled him behind a pillar.

"Hi, Shane! Good to see ya!" It was Cooty Gill, two of his sons, and three other men he'd seen around but didn't know. A fourth came out of the shadows. Seven of them, eight counting Billy Sam. Shane didn't like the odds.

"Ye decided to grow up and join the men?" Cooty smiled, the empty holes between his teeth gaping. "'Bout time. They been keepin' ye a little girl." The others laughed. "We're gonna show you what bein' a man is about."

Cooty dropped his voice and leaned forward, shielding his mouth with his hand. "Ah heard there was a certain girl ye liked waitin' for ye o'er there, yon. In the orchard. She wants ye to bring her a sample, an' then give her a sample." The others erupted in riotous laughter.

"Shh! Shh! Ye numb brains. Ye'll have Sam out here in a lick, tryin' to prevent his boy from doin' what he done to ev'ry one o' our wives." Cooty's smile became a grimace. "Not that we got any hard feelin's, mind."

He pulled out a pack of leaves, and then fished deeper in his pouch for something else. "Ah got some o' the new stuff here"—he indicated the leaves—"but ah got somethin' over here that's better than cunnie." He smiled. "True an' fair. Men get on this an' don't want nuthin' else. That lil' girl will get lonesome if ye try this, but ye won' care." Cooty held out a gnarled root the size of Shane's palm. "Course if ye do this much, you'll go singin' wi' the angels. Just a nip; that's all ye need. Try 'er."

Shane pulled back. This wasn't what he had expected. He thought they'd meet some kids. Or just Cooty. Not all these men.

"You know, I think I'll pass on this one. I'll see you guys. I won't tell my da or anyone, Cooty."

They surrounded him before he could move.

"Oh, no, Shane boy. That ain't how this here's gonna go. Ye won't tell yer da because you'll be on the root. Ye'll suck my cock to get more, if ye try it once. An' yer gonna try it right now."

They grabbed him from all sides. One shoved a rag in his mouth and the others dragged him down.

"Well, Shane, when yer da sees ye shamblin' around, a grin-nin' idjit, ah hope he thinks of ma Dolly. He fancied her fine back in the village. An' these fellas' wives, too. Thing is, *we* didn't like it so much." The others nodded their heads grimly. Shane couldn't struggle free.

"What d' ye think, boys. About this much?" Cooty held out a piece of root the size of his thumbnail.

"That'll see him into next year, Cooty. Ye wanna hook 'em, na kill him." But the voice was laughing.

"This won't kill him, Jakie," Cooty said. "It'll make him higher than anybody ever been, but he'll live. Mostly. Open up his mouth now; we'll shove it down his gullet."

They pried his mouth open while he fought as hard as he could, but it was eight to one and he was twelve years old. Billy Sam held his head.

"OK, Cooty. We got 'em open. Drop 'er in."

"That's enough." The cold voice stopped everything. Shane stopped struggling as the men turned around.

"Who's that? Come out. Ah can't see ya." Cooty stowed the root in his pouch.

"I can see you." The voice was a few feet from him. It was a woman's voice, but no one recognized it. The voice had an edge that was scary. But Shane couldn't see her; her voice had materialized from a moving shadow.

"Ma'am, we's just having a little fun. Don't take it wrong."

"I am taking it wrong, Cooty."

One of the men took off running.

"Stop. That's your warning." He didn't stop. A red light shone on the back of his head; then it blew off his shoulders. White goo, bone chips, and blood splattered the floor and wall.

"That was Justin. What did ye do?" Cooty cried.

"That's how *I* have fun." A loop of red light came from a little box the black figure held. They hadn't been able to see the box until the red came out of it. She was standing so close, she could have touched them. The woman had a mask on; her face was solid black. Shane didn't know who she was. The red loop hovered and then dropped around them as if it were a lariat, then stayed, still red, suspended but not touching them. She attached the black box to her belt.

"I wouldn't touch that if I were you." She indicated the light nonchalantly.

"Let that stupid boy up and out here." They let Shane loose and he clambered under the red line, standing near the woman. "Don't you touch the light either, Shit-for-Brains," she said to Shane. "And don't go anywhere. We're not done." The men laughed.

"You think that's funny?" She spoke sharply. "Getting kids hooked? What is that root? Some sort of psychedelic? Magic mushrooms with a kick? Something that would turn his mind to mush?"

Cooty grinned stupidly and nodded his head. "All o' that. Brought it from home, but it grows good down here. An' it don't show from the top. That's the beauty of 'er. We're about to start sellin' it. If ye want, ah can can cut ye in for a share."

Her laugh said she'd as soon kill them as spit. "A share? I want all of it."

"That's not fair. Ye never done nothin' to grow 'er. We done the work, ma boys and me." He indicated two scrawny hulks on each side of him with a nod of his head.

"Are these your sons? They look just like you." Cooty nodded cautiously. "Which one is your favorite?"

"Uh. It's Milt." He pointed to the guy to his left.

Another red light flashed and the man to Cooty's right crumpled in a bloody heap. Cooty shrieked, "Oh, ye killed ma Bob. Ye killed ma best boy." When Cooty stooped to embrace his son, his hat touched the red lasso encircling them. A loud zap caused him to jump back. The hat's brim sizzled where it had touched the light. The part that had made contact fell off.

"I knew that even you weren't stupid enough to give up your favorite." The woman held up another black box. "It's really handy having two of these," she said conversationally. "I wish I'd had them when I was in the field. Then I had to use baseball bats and tire irons.

"I've got a whole bunch of stuff like this on my belt. Russian technology. The best." She looked down at her waist, smiling. Her belt bristled with small rectangles and guns and other menacing-looking things, all matte black. "So much fun!

"You do understand that, if you leave here alive, it will be after you've given me what I want." She paused and seemed to listen to something in the darkness, then whipped the black box she was holding in a wide arc behind her. The red beam lashed through the gloom, cracking like a bullwhip and leaving a trail of screams and explosions in the fields behind. Cooty's friends had been trying to sneak up on her.

"I count three down. Is that what you get, Cooty?"

He nodded furiously. "Yeah. They were three waitin' there."

"This suit is so neat. It's got sensors all around. I can see 360 degrees. But your idiot friends probably have figured that out by now. I doubt they'll try to rescue you again.

"You're fucked, guys." She laughed. "Let's get to work. Where's the weed? Where's the root? Tell me."

Cooty and the others remained silent and defiant.

She moved the black box again. The red light traced a line along the floor, then halted between Cooty's legs and moved up, hovering about two inches from his crotch.

"I'm getting good at this," she crowed. "You're about to become a capon, Cooty. Where's the root?"

"It's over there, under the big beam and three feet from the next pillar."

"I sure hope it is. Let's go on over." She began to move and the deadly red lariat took the group with her, the red light hovering in front of Cooty's pants as they walked.

"Scared, Cooty?" She looked at his pants. A wet stain had appeared on their front. "I guess you are. I would have thought more of you would have pissed yourselves. But we're just getting started. Where are your tools? You must have shovels around here."

"They're over there, hidden."

She indicated Shane. "You. Shit-for-Brains. Dig where he says."

Shane began digging, wondering when she would cut him down. He couldn't imagine who this stranger was.

He came up with a big pile of roots.

"Throw all that crap over here." The red light nipped a square out of Cooty's trousers. He shrieked. "Is there any more? Here? Anywhere else?"

Cooty had root growing in three more locations.

"The weed. Where is it? What is it?"

"It's all natural. Growed by itself out here in the fields. It's the soybeans crossed with the weed Les and them brought in at the start. Ah didn't make it. Ah just chewed on a coupla leaves and noticed what it did. Don't hurtcha. It's not like the old weed."

"So it could be crossbreeding with all the soybeans, contaminating our food source."

"Ah never thought of that." The whites of Cooty's eyes showed in the dim light.

"How do you tell it from the beans?"

"The color of the flower's different, an' the beans is bigger."

"That's all?"

"Well, ye can chew 'er and see what happens."

"Fuck. Where's the highest concentration?"

"What?"

"Where does the weed grow most?"

"Mostly here and there, and over there." Cooty indicated about a third of the growing field.

She shot him in the foot.

"Aw." He wailed. "That hurts bad."

"You don't even know what hurting bad is, Cooty. Do you know what I used to do, before coming down here?"

"No, ma'am."

"I was a fed, Cooty. A breaker for the FBI. Do you know what that is?"

Cooty and the others shook their heads.

"I pulled pieces off people until they gave me what I wanted. I'm really good with a knife." The red dot hovering in front of Cooty wiggled. "But I'm good at everything. Electronic stuff. I loved using drugs on my clients. And I love to kill. I had to give up my work when I came down here. And, you know, I miss having a professional identity."

"She's crazy, Da," Cooty's remaining son whimpered.

"I'm not crazy. I'm a psychopath," she replied sharply. "It

wouldn't bother me that much"—she snapped her fingers—"to kill all of you."

"Please let us live, ma'am. Ye've shown us our errors."

She chuckled. "Where's the still?"

"It's right over there, ma'am. There's a ledge back there up on top of that pillar Doesn't show from here."

"Let's go." They marched over, the men still held within the loop of light.

"Oh, I see. Right up there. OK." She handed the second black box to Shane. "The lasso will probably keep them where they are, but, if one of them tries to make a break, shoot him. Try it out: point it into the beans and pull the trigger." Shane did. Shooting it was easy.

"Good, you can do it. Now, if you start feeling merciful, Shit-head, remember what they were going to do to you. You'd have been lucky if you could find the toilet after eating that stuff. Think you can hold them, commando?"

Shane nodded vigorously. He'd do anything she wanted; he didn't want her chasing him down afterwards. Or now.

She tossed an anchor with a line on it onto the ledge and climbed up. She looked over. "This is a still all right. Is this the only one you've got?"

"Yeah." Anguish played on Cooty's face.

She threw something into the opening and rappelled down. A little poof! came from the ledge and metal fragments showered around them.

"Ma still!" Cooty looked as if he might cry. The others groaned.

"You got anything else you want to tell me?" She had some-thing in her hand, a long stick. "Tell me or I'll start playtime."

Cooty and the others began to talk and she learned a lot. "Shit-for-Brains, you getting this down? You're going to have to tell your father all of it. And you just made up with him, by the way. Love and kisses all around, and you won't give him any mouth."

"Yes, ma'am." Shane nodded.

"Ma'am, are you gonna let us live?" Cooty asked.

"Well, that depends upon when Sam gets here. If he's quick, probably. If he takes too long, I'll kill you.

"You have to understand that you've hit a sore spot with me. I used to be an addict; I'll admit it. I liked packies. Do you know about them?"

They nodded furiously. "Oh, yeah, ma'am. That's a *real* high."

"Sure is. Getting high is a blast, but detoxing is a killer. In fact, it almost killed me. I don't like people who get kids hooked on drugs. It pisses me off. When I get pissed off, I do this."

She swung the truncheon so fast, none of them saw it coming. It struck every man in the face, rippling down the line like a finger popping down a washboard. Broken teeth and spurting blood followed its path. Then she waded in, swinging so fast Shane couldn't see the stick. The men screamed and groveled.

"Don't do that, please," Shane begged. She turned on him. Shane cowered, then screamed when she nailed him in the ribs, faster than he could see. "Please, don't hit me."

"Baby!" she snorted. "Hasn't anyone beaten you before? Jesus Christ, we got this before breakfast where I grew up. Now this will hurt." She spun the stick and jammed the end of it in the soft area at the back of his elbow. He shrieked. Shane had never felt so much pain. He grabbed his elbow with his other hand, trying to keep from blubbering.

"Remember that, Shithead." He cradled his head in his arms while she yelled at him.

"You stupid, stupid jackass. Why did you need drugs? Asshole!" The nightstick kept moving all over him. Her feet left the ground every time she hit him. Shane pissed himself, as did all the others who hadn't done so already.

"Don't you ever, *ever* let me catch you doing drugs. Don't let me catch you *thinking* about doing drugs. Do you get it? Because there are people in the world who can fuck you up so bad, you'll pray for hell. I am one of them. I will put you there if you do *anything* like this again."

Stopping to shake out her hand, she said, "I'm getting tired. I think I'll kill you." She pulled out some kind of long gun and primed it, then aimed at Cooty.

"Before I kill you, I need to clear something up. You people call me a whore, and a bitch, and a slut. Maybe I'm the last two, but I'm not a whore."

They could see her now, a barely visible black form, cloaked in darkness. Her feet were spread, and she looked as powerful as the strongest man.

"You should be afraid of what I *am*, not what I'm not. I am the *devil* and I will put you in *hell!*"

She aimed at Cooty.

"VALERIE! STAND DOWN!" Sam grabbed the gun from her.

She glared at him. "Sam, you always stop my fun."

Shane recognized her voice. It was his ma's.

"Ma?" Shane sat up on the floor. "Is that you?"

66

The ceiling lights flooded the fields. Sam got the village up in the middle of the night to begin the cleanup. Everyone who could walk was out picking over the plants. Only Sally and the little kids and Arthur were missing.

"Rupert, check over here," Sam called. "Have your men dig for root right there. Check all the beans to see if they're hybrids."

Valerie had removed the hood and mask from her commando suit, but still wore the catsuit that made her almost invisible. She looked like one of the deadly black combat helicopters the general had flown over the estate.

"She's *bad*, Sam," Cooty stuttered. "She's doin' the same as she done all those years ago, killin' people without reason. She jus' killed five more, includin' ma Bob. No reason atall. She's crazy."

"I told you I *wasn't* crazy," Valerie said sharply.

"What you did was worse than what she did, Cooty," Sam answered. "Ye put ev'ry one down here in jeopardy. If the beans mix with weed—an' they will, for that's why it's called *weed*—we won't have anythin' to eat. We'll die."

"Ye can eat 'er. Ye jus' get high is all." He pointed at Valerie. "She tormented us. She beat her own son. She was gonna cut off my wanger for no reason."

"Da, we got another bunch o' root over here," Rupert called out. "Wasn't where Cooty tol' Em'ly. It's a new place."

"There's more than what he said?" Valerie exclaimed. She swung toward the old man, glaring.

Sam leaned toward Cooty. "Yer in trouble, Cooty. Ye shoulda told 'er all of it."

"Ah did. That mus' be a wild bunch. Ah tol' her all ah knew."

"Em'ly, persuade him to talk," Sam stepped aside.

"No! Not her! Ah'll talk."

Cooty talked, but not enough. Sam and Valerie could tell he was holding back.

"Go ahead, Em'ly."

"Here? Don't you want me to do it privately?" she asked.

"No. Do it here. Ah don't want any more of this." Sam turned to the fields and yelled. "It's gonna get noisy, everybody. As ye listen, jus' think of how yer never gonna grow weed or do anythin' bad. Think on what happens to those that do. Ah could use the Voice to get what ah want, but ah don't want to." Sam glared at Cooty. "Ye shoulda left ma son alone, Cooty."

"I'm disappointed in you, Cooty," Valerie said, moving in. "I thought you were being straight with me." She pulled something off her weapons belt. "I wonder what this does?"

There were two more stills, another section of the hybrid weed, and some pure weed Cooty had been growing out by the animal pens. Plus five more caches of root. Cooty's screams left Sam shaking. Valerie got even more out of Cooty when she worked on Milt, his remaining son.

"I think that's about it, Sam," Valerie said. Cooty was slumped on the ground, cut up, but alive. "I can work on some of the others if you want."

"Nah. That's enough." Sam was sickened by what he'd seen her do. "Ye betrayed me, Cooty, ye an' all yer men. Ye coulda killed us.

Ah am the headman. By the village ways, an' by the Commands, an' by what Jeremy the Great Tek said, ah have the right to kill any an' all of ye. For any reason. Ah got plenty o' reason with you.

"Em'ly, kill 'em all. An' those over there." He indicated a group in on the drug and hooch production, plus the remaining men who had tried to hook Shane on root. "Ah want 'em dead. Now."

Valerie knocked down the outlying group, then picked her way through those who had threatened her son. One young man kicked up a racket when she got to him.

"Da! Da! Please! Ah didn't know wha' they was gonna do. Ah didn't know!" Billy Sam pleaded. Sam looked at him and nodded at Valerie. She cut his head off.

Cooty was last. He groveled, sobbing and begging for mercy. She toyed with him for a while, as his screams ricocheted from the concrete bulwarks. Rupert and a small crowd of villagers watched. Everyone else huddled, facing the other direction and holding on to each other.

Valerie leveled her weapon at Cooty. As she squeezed the trigger, her head jerked. She fell to the floor. The gun went off. Pulses of red light slammed into the ceiling's concrete. Chips fell on the floor. Valerie lay on the cement deck, unmoving.

"Valerie!" Sam jumped toward her. "Val! What's the matter?" She was unconscious. He picked her up and headed for their room. Cooty took off like a gut-shot racehorse. "Ru, finish Cooty."

Rupert moved without hesitation.

"Sam. Ru's on the wee—" Cooty called. Rupert broke the old man's neck before he could get the word out.

67

Sam ran to their room, stripped the bloody suit off Valerie, and laid her on the bed. She was dying, but he couldn't figure out why. No wounds. She wasn't sick; she was disappearing. Not her body, but Valerie. He got a wet cloth and wiped her face.

"Don't go, Val. Ah love ye. 'Member us an' all we got. Don' leave."

Her eyelids fluttered. "Sam? Are you here?"

"Ah'm here. What's happenin'?"

"It's so hard, Sam."

"What's hard?"

"It's so hard to come out and stay. It's time for me to leave. I can't . . ." Her eyes rolled backward and closed. He slapped her cheeks lightly. She opened her eyes a bit, chest rising and falling. He thought she was dying.

"I don't like what I just did, Sam," she whispered. "Killing those people. Hurting them. It was wrong. I *do* feel remorse; what I told them wasn't true. You saved me—I know what I did was bad and I'm sorry for all of it." Her eyes filled with tears.

"Nah. It was right, Val. They tried to kill Shane. They could have killed all of us if the weed took over. What you did was right."

She shook her head, whispering. "It was wrong. They should have had trials."

"We'd be dead by the time we had a trial, Val. Nothin' wrong with what ye did." He caressed her cheek with the back of his fingers. "What do ah need to do to make ye well?"

She reached up and took his hand. "You made me well, Sam. You saved me in every way. You healed me. Now that I'm really healed, I can't do what I did anymore. And I can't come out like this. I have to leave."

A sob escaped him.

"Don't be sad. I'm ending up the way I'm supposed to." A sad smile.

"Where are ye going, Val?"

"I don't know. I think I'm melting into Emily. We'll be one person. Maybe. I don't know if I'll exist." Tears ran down the sides of her face. "But isn't that what everyone wants to be? Just one. You gave that to me. You healed me so I could be like everyone."

He started to speak, but she touched his lips. "Sam, tell the kids about me. Tell Shane. He needs to know now. He's confused. Tell him all about me, and tell the others when they're old enough. Promise me. Tell him everything. How you saved me. Tell how we met and about our meadow and how much we love each other.

"Shane is mine, Sam. I was in the body when he was conceived. I carried him and I birthed him. He's my baby, not hers. Tell him."

"Val, don't leave. Ah love you."

"I love you more than anything on earth or anywhere else. But I have to go. You and Emily need to be together. You need to heal. And I'm tired, Sam. It's hard being two. It's time for me to go." She caressed his cheek.

"I'll come back if you or the kids really need me. No matter where I go, I will come back if you need me. I will protect you and the children."

"What's goin' to happen?"

"I don't know." She looked very weak. "Sam, come close. I need to ask you something." She whispered in his ear.

"Ye want that?" He was incredulous.

"One more time while I'm in this body." She nodded, looking frail and fragile.

"Ah'll give ye what ye want, Val." Sam stripped off his clothes and got into bed with her.

"What d' ye want, chitlin'?" He stroked her belly. "What will make ye feel the way ye always wanted to feel?" He knew. He'd made her feel that way so many times. Sam kissed her softly, around the throat, down her chest. Taking her nipples in his mouth and rolling them with his tongue. Working downward, down to the opening that defined her, that was her in her depths.

She reached out and surrounded him with her hand, moving it the way she knew he liked. "Is it good, Sam? Is that what you want?" He groaned. "Hurry, Sam. I need you now." Sam rolled on top of her and sank into her at once.

He felt like a massive root pushing into the earth. A force. The image filled his mind. He was long and thick and rounded at the end. Blazing with color and light. Halos exploded from him as he pushed into the soil. Such deep soil. Deeper and truer than anything. It was thrown aside, throwing off prisms of light as it went. Yellow, sage green, light brown. Colors of the spring soil . . . spring when new life started. Brilliant, exploding from his core into her horizon. Through all and in all.

"I want a baby, Sam. Give me a baby. Let part of me stay here." Her head arched backwards and she thrust herself onto him, joining with what was hers.

The living, growing root plunged into the soil. The loam moved aside, but just barely, holding the shaft gently and with great power. They were one, the root and the earth. Eternally.

"Sam, I love you."

He flooded it all, the whole meadow and the world inside her and him. They felt the way they'd always wanted to feel.

Sam struggled to a sitting position. Valerie was lying there, deep in sleep. Or was it Emily? He took her in his arms. He was embracing a shell.

"Oh, Gawd, don't take her away." He held her to his chest. "Don't leave me! Oh, Val. Don't leave me alone."

68

Shane saw Da racing toward his room with Ma in his arms. He ran after them, though his feet would barely do what he told them. He hurt everywhere. He'd never been beaten before. This was a terrible day. He'd found out his da was a scumbag. Then Billy Sam, the guy he'd thought was his best friend, set him up to have his brain fried.

All the rest banged around in his head, too. The terror of being grabbed by Cooty and his gang. The terror of being rescued by that maniac commando, who had turned out to be his mom, but using the name Valerie. Then watching her torture and kill people he'd known all his life.

Something was choking him and making his eyes hurt. He rubbed them as he ran faster. Shane wanted to be with Da. Right next to him. Touching him. He was moving back home, too. He *needed* his da. Being on his own wasn't what he'd thought it would be.

Shane tried the door to his parents' room. Locked. He didn't have the lock's code, so he let himself into the kids' room from the hallway. He looked around the room he'd lived in all his life, as if he'd never seen it before. It was a total mess with all the kids living in it, but Shane thought it was wonderful. How could he have thought he could live anywhere else?

Shane changed his pants. He'd wet them when Valerie was beating him. Who was Valerie? Maybe she was someone he'd never met who happened to look like his ma. No. No strangers existed in the underground. He wanted Da badly.

The door to his parents' room from the kids' room was locked from their side. He knew what that meant. He'd better cool it for an hour or so. Shane sat on his bed. Such a nice bed. Sally's was nice, but this was home. He lay down.

He was dozing when he heard it. A roaring, choking sound coming from his parents' room. It had to be loud, because you really couldn't hear anything through the cement. The steel-clad door separating the rooms was almost as soundproof. He punched the code into the door's lock. Didn't work. They'd changed it.

No problem. Shane had been working on a few other skills. He picked up Josh's computer, logged onto his own network, then held the computer up to the lock so the wireless was close enough. Ran a program he'd written. Bingo. The door opened.

He pushed back the door and tiptoed into the closet. Peeking out, he saw his da wrapped around his ma. Broken sobs came from his da, wrenched from somewhere so deep Shane hadn't known it existed. Ma and Da were naked. He mostly saw his da's back. His head, the curve of his back and buttocks. His legs. Shane froze. He'd never seen his da naked. The sight shocked him. Da was beautiful.

The noises kept coming. He crept into the room, close to the bed. "Da?" he said, his voice faltering. "Did she die?"

Da jumped and looked up, confused. He turned and saw Shane, then tried to cover himself and Ma. "Shane . . . go . . . this is not . . ."

Shane threw the spread over them. "Is she dead, Da?"

"Nah. I don't know what she is. Sleepin', maybe. I don't know."

He buried his face in her neck and sobbed again. He couldn't hold it back. Finally, Da pushed himself up. "I . . . I . . ."

"Da. I'll be in our room. Come and talk to me when you can."

Shane went back to his room and called Sally on the intercom. "Are you all right, Sally?"

"Oh, ah'm fine. Yer da brought me back from the devil's mouth, but ah'm fine."

"What?"

Sally told him what had been going on with her while he was being abducted. "Appendix something. Yer da saved me just in time."

"Oh." Shane hadn't known. He'd been so intent on getting loaded with Billy Sam he'd forgotten about Sally. "Oh."

"Ah heard all about what happened in the fields, Shane. Ah've got a good mind to take my mixin' spoon to ye. But ah expect it can wait. What do ye want?"

"Can you take care of the kids? Da and I need to talk."

"Ah'm sure you do. Ah can take care of the kids. Your da cured me complete. Ah can handle a few younguns. The kids're already here. How's yer ma?"

"Uh . . . she's sleeping."

"Yeah. Killin' that many must be tiring. Ye talk as long as ye like."

Shane wondered what his da was doing. The sounds continued, but they were softer now. He'd never heard his da cry. Didn't know it was possible.

The room was dim. Must still be night. Shane wrapped a blanket around himself. He was trembling. Da, please come in here, he thought. Please. Shadows piled up in the corners. In them, he could see the darkness of the fields. Cooty grabbing him. The others throwing him down. Cooty's hand with the root getting closer. His mouth forced open.

She had saved him. Valerie. Or Ma. No, it wasn't Ma.

By the time his da walked into the room, Shane's body was shuddering, out of control. Da's face had been scrubbed free of tears, but it was still blotched and red.

"Da!" He jumped up, forgetting all the things he had intended to say. He threw his arms about his father.

"Oh, Da." That's all he could say. Sam hugged him back. He kept hugging and Shane soaked it in. His father was doing something to him. Shane could feel something coming from his heart and penetrating his skin. Da was healing him. The pain from the beating lessened. He started sobbing.

"Da. I was so scared. They said I'd be an idiot."

"I know, darlin'. I know what they wanted to do to ye. She saved you. I knew she would, too."

"Valerie."

"Yeah. Your mother."

Shane's brows knit and his cheeks scrunched up. "What?"

"I didn't know myself. She told me before she left. She told me to tell you it was her, not Emily, who had you. She told me to tell you all about her." Sam went silent, but looked as if he were carrying on a conversation with something invisible. He jerked and said, "Did you hear that? It was clear as day."

"What, Da?" Shane didn't know what was going on with his father.

"It was God telling me what to do. You remember me talkin' about Him out in the hall. About what God has done for me and the real commands he gave us? To make a good life and do good things?"

Shane nodded.

"All the time I've been cryin' over Valerie, I've been asking God, 'What is happenin'? How do I fix it? What do I do now?' I call that prayer, Shane. It's strum nice, because ye can sandwich it in when you're doin' other things. Like holdin' Val for the last time." Sam's eyes filled. He rubbed them with the sleeve of his black Russian uniform. Not something Ma had made.

"Ye didn't hear that a moment ago?" Da asked. "God said, 'Tell Shane about his mother.' It was a command, clear as when He talked to me out in the meadow on earth's last day. I'm to tell you all of it."

So Sam told Shane all about his mother, starting with the meadow and her holding a gun on him. Sam told him everything, right up to her killing Cooty and the rest, and then disappearing.

"She just *left*?" Shane could barely absorb what he was hearing. Plus he ached from where Valerie had hit him. He squinted and stared at his da.

"She said she couldn't handle being two. And to tell the truth, Shane, I think there were more than two. A bunch of babies and kids. But mostly it was her and Emily. She couldn't handle being two, and, after being in the background a long time, it was hard for her to come out and stay out like she did to rescue you. She had to leave.

"She didn't like what she just did, killing all them. She said she wasn't a psychopath any more because she felt sorry." He tossed his head in the direction of the fields. "I like what she did. That's why I had *her* kill them. I knew she'd hurt them more than I would. She did a good job, don't you think?"

"Yeah." Shane said. His father had never discussed torture and killing with him before.

Sam smiled. "It's a side of me you've not seen. I'm a killer, Shane. I don't mind doin' it an' I don't mind war. Just haven't done it much down here. Valerie was a killer, too. A soldier, an' a fighter. That's what made Val and me love each other so. We were alike." Sam heaved a huge sigh.

"I loved her, Shane. More 'n Emily, most likely. Em is beautiful and fun and dresses nice. She did a lot of nice things. Like teachin' me to read. So many things. But she doesn't have the spark Val had. We don't go to the deep places where Val and I did. I saved both of 'em and healed 'em, but Val needed it most and loved me back most.

"Val said she was melting into Emily. She did. I can't find her inside whoever's sleepin' in there. I don't know who will wake up, or what, or if that person and I will get along. I don't know if it will be just Em, or Val and Em mixed. I don't know what will happen now. I thought our family was back together and everything would be fine, but now I don't know."

He ran his hand through his hair. His stomach gurgled, then released an enormous growl. Sam listened to it as though it were coming from someone else. "I guess I'm hungry. You want some soup or somethin', Shane? We got some left over from the feast." Da said abruptly. "I'll go get it."

Returning with a pot of soup, Sam said, "No change. She's still sleepin'."

"I'll heat it up, Da." Shane hustled around their little kitchen. Making the snack kept him from feeling crazy thinking about what his father had revealed. His ma was two people? Or more? His real mom was Valerie, a murderer and torturer?

"Val never was unfaithful to me, Shane. That was Emily. Valerie kept me from going crazy all those years. She'd come and hold me and . . ." Sam didn't say any more about their life together.

"You're hers. She was using the body when we made ye, and she stayed there when ye were inside her, and she pushed you out."

Shane spilled the soup while setting it on the table.

"We've had a night, haven't we, son?" he asked. "Let me ask you somethin'. Assuming it's Emily wakin' up, should I tell her what I told you? Or just some of it? Or none of it? I don't know. Emily doesn't remember much of her past. Maybe she should know."

"I don't know, Da. It would be kind of a shock, don't you think, knowing you did all that? About her real parents? About Valerie?"

"You're right Shane. I think I'll make out she's been sleepin' a lot today an' not tell her anything."

"But the people out in the hall saw her killing all those people. That's going to be hard to explain."

Sam sucked in his breath. That and all the fields torn up and the drugs all over. How would he explain that? He needed to do it right now. "Shane, I gotta go out in the hall an' talk to people. You stay here in case your ma wakes up."

"But, Da. There's more I need to talk to you about really badly."

"I know, Shane. Sayin' ye weren't mine was the worst thing I've done. I was stupid all those months Em'ly and I were split. I'm so sorry. I didn't mean it and I'll ne'er do it again. An' I'll never tell you to leave again."

"You better not, because I'll find Valerie's gun and shoot you." Shane glared at his father. "I'm not kidding."

Sam laughed. "You *are* Valerie's boy! That's what she'd do!"

"That isn't all I meant, Da. There's other things. Bad things."

"Like?"

"Billy Sam said you had sex with every woman in the village, even having four wives. He said you did that all over the Hamptons. And that you passed out drunk in the streets."

Sam rubbed his chin and waited a while before speaking. "Well, Shane, nobody's perfect." He raised his eyebrows and nodded at Shane. "We all have our weak points."

"He wasn't *lying*?"

"I'd like to say he was, but he wasn't. Now, the drinkin' part was worse the last year before the atomics blew everything up." He told Shane about the feds tracking down the headmen by their brainwaves and him staying drunk to fool them.

"So it was a cover, Da?"

"Yeah. But, Shane, I loved my cover. An' I loved what I did while I was drinkin.' Which was the other part you brought up." He cleared his throat. "I never thought to be discussin' this with my twelve-year-old son, but I need to say somethin' to ye." He studied Shane. "Yeah. Just what I noticed when you were playin' your horn at the party." He grabbed Shane's shoulder. "You're gonna have the same problem I did."

Shane scowled. "Not me, Da. I'm getting married. I'll never have an affair. I'll never be like mom and Arthur. Or you."

Sam didn't answer for a moment. "I love women, Shane. An' I love doin' it. That's all I can say." He bent his fingers into a circle and then moved his hand up and down like he was pumping a cylindrical object. "I better give you some advice if you just want one wife: Say no and run *before* they get you. Once they've grabbed a hold, thinking is hard. Saying no to a woman who's got her hand on your dick is impossible. You're a good-looking boy, and they *will* come for you. Village girls ain't shy, Shane."

"They came after you?"

"Of course. While we're talkin', there's something I need to ask *you*. I've been thinkin' about it a lot. Would you like to be the headman when I die?"

"NO!" Shane shouted. "I do not want to do what you do. I'm not good at patching things up with people. I don't have the Voice or the Power."

"Yes, you do. I can feel it. A little."

"Da, I went down to the rabbit pen and tried my Voice on the bunnies. I couldn't get them to do anything. *Bunnies* don't pay attention to me. How could I make the villagers do what I say? I can't heal anything. I'm not friendly and inspiring. I don't know anything about crops and agriculture—and I don't want to learn.

"I like to play chess. I like to play my sax. But I really like this, Da." He picked up Josh's computer. "This is Josh's. Mine is better; I've done a lot of overrides and added stuff." He pulled a screen up. "I'm on my computer now."

"Where is it?"

"In Sally's room. This isn't the underground's surveillance system; I set this up myself." Another screen flashed. And another. "Wanna see what Arthur's doing now? They moved next door because it had more room for his wheelchair." Sam blinked. "Here. God, look at him, Da. You really messed him up." The screen showed Arthur trying to get out of the chair with Winnie's help. He could barely do it. Another screen change.

"What is that?" The screen showed a corridor with rounded metal walls, more modern than anything in the underground.

"It's the last of the giant space stations, Da, the one that's storing all Jeremy's data," Shane said excitedly. "Tomorrow I'm going to look up what Ma has, and see what I can find out about it. Look, this is the camera panning down the central aisle of the station."

Sam gaped. "Where is it?"

"Orbiting a few hundred miles over earth." Shane showed more images. Inside the space station. Shots of planets and space. They kept switching.

"You did this?"

"Yeah. We had a lot of time on our hands when you kicked us out. I was already into programming, so I did it more. Cool, huh?" Shane grinned. "I love to write code."

"You're like Jeremy."

"Oh, I don't know. Some of his code sucks. I've had to redo parts of it."

"Here, for the underground?"

"Yeah. The sewage system was about to crash. Not good. So I tinkered a little. Da, this is what I like to do. Fix things. Program. I love it. Wait until you see what I can do. I'm just learning."

"You're a Tek." Sam put his hand to his mouth. "Arthur said that your grandparents were geniuses." He looked at his son, awestruck.

"*Please* don't make me be headman, Da."

"OK. You don't have to be headman. I won't ask you. You're a Tek." Sam looked toward the door. "Shane, I've got to get to the hall. They're probably about to start brawlin'. Can you watch your mom? If she wakes up, call me." He indicated the pager on his belt. "I'll come no matter what."

"I will. Da, can you do something when you get back?"

"What, Shane?"

"Heal me. She hurt me." He curled up on the chair, chin quivering. He felt as if he might cry. His da saw it, too.

"Let me heal you right now." Da put his hands on him and Shane felt a dreamy feeling. He still hurt, even in the dream world. But not for long. His da took away the pain and healed the bruises. "Is that better, son?"

"Yeah, Da."

Shane watched his da walk out the door. That's when he did begin to cry. His tears fell on his trousers. He felt like a baby, but couldn't stop.

69

The people in the fields were as close to exploding as Sam had expected. No one had left. The fields were torn up to hell and back, piles of contaminated bean-weed hybrid all over, along with good plants yanked out by mistake.

Men stood in knots, growling as they looked at the savaged bodies of Valerie's victims. They glared in the direction of Sam's room. "She's a witch. Prob'ly come back an' eat 'em . . . We need to get 'er an kill 'er . . . Shoulda done it when Maddy said . . . Lookit poor Cooty o'er there . . . What'd he do to get that?"

The women clung to each other, howling and sobbing, and shaking as though a witch were indeed among them. Hysteria and mob violence were a breath away. Sam needed to change that as fast as possible, or the villagers were going to fixate on Val torturing and executing people and forget about the drugs and the drugs' threat to their lives and to Shane. Val would become the target rather than Cooty and his friends. Sam needed to plant a different reality in their heads. He didn't want them to remember that Val had been there at all.

"Ma friends!" He raised his arms over his head. "MA FRIENDS! A terrible thing has happened to us this night! A terrible,

terrible thing. Listen while ah tell ye the truth of it." He used the village brogue and his most powerful Voice, backed up with all his Power.

"We've seen somethin' so horrible that no man or woman or chil' should hafta see 'er. We seen our own lyin' on the ground, screamin' in agony. Tell me what ye saw!" Sam adopted the snake men's cadence, hoping he could better the best of them in effect. "Tell me!"

"It were horrible!"

"They was screamin'!"

"Blood ev'rywhere."

"Poor Cooty—"

Sam cut it right there. Nothing about "poor Cooty." He didn't have any plan at all, but he knew he needed to perform a miracle. He improvised as he went.

"Yea! Yea! We been wounded! We been hurt! Folks been killed. An' look aroun'. Our fields are ruined. Wrecked! We may starve! A fiend attacked us. That's it! That's it! The devil hisself has been here to the underground, out to get us." He grabbed the theme he wanted.

"Sit, ma people, an' let me tell ye what has happened this night." He motioned them to gather before him on the ground. "The devil has come."

Sam described the vision he'd had when the bombs were falling and he'd first entered the underground. He described— in great detail, with the Voice—how the beast had torn out his heart and flown off with it. Now people were crying out as much over his description as they had over the stacks of savaged bodies. The growing fields grew dark and empty, shadowed. Echoes of Sam's voice fought each other.

"The devil wants to carry us off, outta here, to *hell*! To real hell! What does the devil want?" He held his hand to his ear, asking for the call and response as the snake men had in their gatherings in the hollow. The villagers were conditioned to follow him. "Why did the devil come?"

"To carry us to hell! Hell an' damnation! Fire an' hell! For what we done! We'll get what we got comin.'"

"Why does the devil want us? What are we? Ye know! Tell me?"

"We are *sinners*! Sinners to the *bone*! Fornicators and thieves!"

"That's right, ma friends. We are down here in this hole because we are evil. That's how we got here instead of going up with the angel Eliana to the golden world. We're down here till we prove that we *deserve* somethin' better than a hole in the ground. We gotta prove ourselves."

The Voice was having the desired effect. The group sat clutching each other, but in fear of what might be coming, not what had happened and what they had seen.

"Now, you saw a lot a things tonight. You saw people ye know screamin' and yellin' an' bleedin.' What did you see?"

"Screamin'! Yellin'! Terrible things! So bad! Blood and . . . oh, ma Gawd, terrible things! Innards all over!"

"Yes! We have had a terrible lesson this night. Terrible lesson about what the devil can do when he comes down to people who aren't waitin' and ready for 'em. Ye know what happened tonight?"

"Noooo!" The word rang around the vast dome housing the fields. "Ah don't know what happened . . . It were awful, but ah don't know . . . What happened, Sam? Ah can' remember . . . Was bad an' there was blood."

"What ye saw is DRUGS! People takin' drugs! Brought down here by our own people." He stopped, then said coldly, "By Cooty Gill."

Their eyes got wide. They grabbed each other's hands and pulled away from Sam.

"We all know that Cooty grew the weed. We knew that, didn't we? *Didn't we?*"

"Yeah. Yeah. Yeah." The replies were loud, but rather sheepish.

"An' we knew that he hauled it around all over the Hamptons in his barrels. That maybe he made the barrels just so he could tote the stuff. We knew that. Tell me!"

"Yeah. We knew." They ducked their heads in shame.

"Did you know that he brought the weed down here and was growin' it in our fields? An' that it was breedin' with our good beans so they'd be so mixed we couldn't tell one from the other? They'd be so mixed that, if we ate 'em, we'd be so high, we couldn't work, we couldn't do nothin' but eat weed. Cooty was plannin' on killin' us, pure an' simple. The devil had took him an' he planned our murder!" Sam glared around at everyone. No one would meet his eyes. He kept battering them with the Voice.

"And Cooty did more 'en that. He brang somethin' new to the underground. He brought *root*." A pile of it sprawled in front of Sam. "That's root. There's enough there to kill all o' us ten times over. An' he got more 'en that all over this place." Sam made a great show of pulling out a handkerchief and picking up a hunk of root with it, keeping his skin from touching it.

"This here. This is *root*. This little bit would kill all of us. You hear of it?"

"No." They looked just as they did watching one of those horror pictures they sometimes played in the hall. About ready to jump out of their skins.

"Cooty brought it down here to kill us. He got enough planted to kill the whole world. But y' know who he was goin' to start on?"

Sam stood over them, eyes bulging in rage. "Ma son! Ma son Shane, the smartest fella the village has ever made and who will do so many good things for us. Cooty was gonna make him into a droolin' idjit. Y' know how ah know? Ask me!"

"How'd ye know, Sam?"

"Because ah was watchin'. Not out there"—he pointed to Cooty's hideout, which he expected most of the villagers knew about—"where it happened, but in ma room, where Jer the Tek set up a screen so ah can see anywhere down here. Ah saw what Cooty did an' heard his word. Him an' his two boys and Billy Sam, ma own son! Ma son! Fixin' to kill Shane." He shook his head.

"One thing ye should know about Shane. He's a Tek, jus' like Jeremy the Great Tek. He'll make great things for all o' us to make our lives better. An' Cooty wanted to kill him.

"This is what happened tonight. If you heard screamin' an' yellin', if you heard people cryin', that was Cooty an' them. You see him right here—torn apart. That's not from a witch. That's not from a fight or torture or anything like that. It's from this here *root*."

Sam approached a few people in the crowd. "Frannie, tell me what happened tonight."

"They took the root and it tore out their insides."

"And what did Cooty want to do, Jake?"

"Kill Shane an' all the rest of us."

"How, Jimmy?"

"With the root."

"What will happen if you eat it, Connie?"

"Ah'll die an' look just like that." She pointed at Cooty.

"Now we're going to clean it up. Rupert, ah need your help. Ah need help from a few of you. We're gonna get the dollies and wheelbarrows and wagons. We're gonna load up all this poison root and the plants. An' we're gonna load up Cooty an' all the others that killed themselves with poison this terrible night—a terrible night—an' we're gonna incinerate them. Let's go!"

Sam charged off to get one of the big, wheeled containers.

They were loading body parts and weed into the incinerator. He thought a dozen people had been killed. He'd work it out in the morning. Rupert was working along with him, doing more than his share. Sam loved to see Ru doing well.

"Rupert. My good son." Sam patted his shoulder and Rupert beamed. The pager on his belt buzzed. He looked at it. Shane had messaged, "She's awake." Nothing else. Not, "She's fine. She's crying. She wants you."

"Ru, ah've got to go. Can you handle the rest of this for me?"

"Sure, Da. Ah'll burn 'er all up. Ah'll finish on the fields, too."

Sam grabbed him by both shoulders and hugged him, "You're

such a good son." Then he was off to his room and whatever awaited him there.

The feel of his da's hands on his shoulders and that brief hug stayed with Rupert. Warm, like baked bread or chestnuts. "You're a good son." What he'd wanted to hear since his dad had had those other brats.

Maybe Shane woulda been better an idjit. Ru laughed to himself, but then took it back. He would do such a job that his dad would remember him as his *good* son forever.

Ru set himself to cleaning out the rest of the hybrid and replanting the beans that had been pulled up by mistake. He kept the men of the village going beyond the time they wanted to quit.

"Come on now. We need to get this cleaned up." Ru had the Voice, too. Not like his da, but he could get people to hustle.

He incinerated it all, cleaned the blood off the paths, and looked around. This was as good as it could be made right then.

"OK, everybody. Ye can go home an' to bed. Ye did a fair an' fine job!"

When they were gone, Rupert looked around carefully. The fields were empty. He walked to the end by the animal pens. Winnie kept a flower garden there. Not a big one, but she'd always liked flowers. It was gone to hell since Arthur had gotten so busted up, though he deserved it an' shoulda got it earlier. Ru got out a hoe and a shovel and began to work Winnie's garden.

When he reached the middle of the plot, he looked around again. He was alone. Opening his shirt, he pulled out a bunch of plants. Working with gentle fingers, he'd removed them from the soil as carefully as possible, their roots intact. Rupert quickly transplanted them among Winnie's flowers, the one place his da wouldn't suspect and dig up. People would think he was doing a good thing if he took care of Winnie's flowers, since she couldn't leave poor Arthur.

This new weed didn't hurt you. It helped you. It stopped his headaches. It would keep him from getting the disease. When he was chewing weed, he thought better and was smarter. He could be a good headman if he had the weed.

He had plans, too. Rupert knew how to do everything with plants. Grow 'em to be bigger, smaller, or different colored. He could make them look like flowers. Over time, he could change the weed plant, making it mellower and stronger at the same time. Wait till his da saw what he could do then. He just had to go slow and keep it secret.

"You're such a good son." Recalling his father's words, Ru smiled happily. He headed for Janelle and bed.

70

Shane was waiting in the hallway outside his room, pacing frantically. "Da!"

"What is it, Shane? Is she all right?"

"Yes. It's just that . . . I don't know who she is."

"What?"

"She's not Ma and she's not Valerie either."

"Are you sure? Does she look like them?"

"She looks the same, but she's not the same."

Sam started to open the door.

"She asked me to stay outside while she got dressed."

The way a mother, or a decent woman, would act. He paused, then pushed the button on the intercom. "Are you OK, Em'ly? It's me, Sam."

"Just a moment, Mr. Baahuhd." Her voice was melodious and cultured. Not Val's or Em's. And Mr. Baahuhd?

She buzzed them in. They walked down the corridor made by the cement wall and the backs of the armoires. Sam's heart was beating harder than it had when he'd been speaking to the people. "We're here, Em'ly."

He pulled around the corner and saw her. The big light on the ceiling shone behind her, shadowing her face. She wore a long white dress that flared at the bottom. It had long sleeves that also flared. The neckline sketched the bones below her throat. Barely an inch of her skin showed. Even seeing her in shadow, Sam knew she was beautiful—and angelic.

She reminded him of something. Light beams filtering through trees. Radiance behind them. A small girl's figure before him. She had piercing eyes and seemed as if she could understand anything. He had been healing Emily when he'd seen her. He recognized her and gasped.

"I am Shira Asher. We met years ago." Her voice was soft and sweet, yet the voice of a woman.

This was the little girl who didn't die. The child who was taken from her parents when she was six. Emily and Valerie's true identity. All grown up. Sam's mouth fell open. He couldn't close it.

"Uh . . ." He stood there, speechless.

"I feel quite the same way, Mr. Baahuhd. I awakened here, in this body. I recognize this place, but I've never been here."

"Ye never been here?"

"No. I usually live far away. I can barely see or feel this place. This is where my fragments lived, my separated selves. You knew them as Emily and Valerie. Now I'm here." She put her hand to her cheek. "It's startling."

"Sit down, lass." Sam led her to the sofa, Shane following at a distance. Sam sat next to her, but not too closely. She didn't like people close; he could feel it. Or maybe she wasn't used to it.

"Where are Emily and Val?" he asked. "Are they comin' back?"

"I'm afraid not, Mr. Baahuhd."

He felt his throat closing up. He put his hand over his mouth to stifle a sob.

"Oh! I'm so sorry. I didn't mean to upset you. They're in a good place. I can feel them."

Sam's head swiveled toward her. "Where did ye come from? Where are they? Why are ye here?"

"Oh." She sat up straighter. "As to where I came from, I've never tried to put it into words. There is a place that exists before words. It's very bright and good. It's full. Something fills it up. A wonderful, good, kind something fills it. That's where I lived. My parents were there."

"Were ye in heaven?"

"No. Well, maybe. My parents were there and I was happy. They showed me things and taught me everything they knew. It was very quiet, except for the singing and the bells and instruments."

"Were there a lot of gold people around? Really tall?" Sam thought she'd gone to the golden planet.

"No. Just my parents and me." She closed her mouth and pursed her lips. "This is hard to talk about. When they took my parents away from me in the physical realm"—her eyes filled—"I split. Part of me stayed with my parents in the deep world, and part rose higher, away from the good place. The part that rose was in this body. When the pain came, all of me felt it, the body and the split parts of me. All that time, part of me was in the deep good place and part in the pain. More things happened. Bad things, very bad things. I won't say what they were."

But Sam could see them floating all around her. He'd seen them when healing Emily and Val. Shira held the deepest memories.

"So we split and split and one of us was always in this body. The others fell into the depths, but not the good depths. They fell screaming with no hope, knowing that no one would come. Do you understand that other world, the bad one caused by pain? And why we split?"

"I get an idea sometimes, but I don't know," Sam said.

"It was about hiding. Hiding from everything that could hurt you by going deeper and deeper until you don't feel anything. You barely exist, but you're alive. Everything is hidden and locked away. You won't talk about what happened, because you'd die if you did. They'd kill you. So you stay quiet and hidden." Her hands lay in her lap. Tears fell on them like pearls.

"When ah found ye, lass, ye were screamin," Sam said softly.

"Yes. Sometimes nothing could stop the pain and I screamed. I still see the pink room. I think I always will. And all the rest."

"Ye know what happened to ye?"

"Yes. You healed us, Mr. Baahuhd. When you saw me that first time, you started healing the parts of me that were damaged. I'm very grateful, Mr. Baahuhd."

Sam blushed. "Ye got to call me, Sam, lass. I'm *Sam*."

"That's hard, Mr. . . . Sam. You worked on Valerie and Emily for years, but you worked on me, too. When they were well, I was sent forward."

"Because ye need healin'?" That's what this was? A switch for damaged goods?

"No." She lowered her eyes. "Because I'm the one you've wanted all your life."

He rocked backward. How could this be? He loved Emily. He loved Valerie. How could Shira, the little girl, replace what they had? She was the same size as Val and Em, but looked smaller and younger. Her face was radiant, more than beautiful. She was intelligent and kind, but not either of his wives.

"So Em and Val got kicked out so you could come here?"

"No. They left because their journeys were complete. They left because you were complete."

"Ah was complete?" Sam touched his chest. "Ah've always been complete. Ah'm the headman. The greatest headman ever. Nothin' in me to fix."

"You have had sexual intercourse with every woman in the village. That, despite having four wives. Even in the underground, while supposedly following the Commands, you had two wives, my alters. You once were a serious alcoholic. You've killed many men. You stole from Mrs. Edgarton by giving her false accounts of crop yields. You lie whenever you want. You followed village customs so blindly that you hurt your son, Shane."

"Stop!" He cut her off while she was taking a breath. "How d' ye know all that?" Color flashed in his cheeks. He looked at Shane, who had an approving smile on his face.

"I know everything about you, Mr. Baahuhd. I lived in Emily and Valerie's depths. I am them, though they could only touch me. I am prior to them. Do you understand?"

"No." What was this creature?

"I'm from a deeper level, as if of the ocean. I come from the golden place; I come from the source of everything in the universe."

"You're from *God*?"

"In a way. I'm from the place where people experience God directly. From that most intimate, joined place. That's what my captors and torturers did to me. They drove me to my depths. Something exists beyond all this." She indicated the room about them but a larger world also. "You pray to it often, Mr. Baahuhd. It answered you. I am its answer.

"It's time you grew up and had one wife, a wife who will satisfy you fully. It's time I grew up and left the golden realm of bliss and learned to be a woman and wife. So Valerie and Emily left and I'm here."

"Ye say ye're *better* 'n them?" Sam was outraged.

"Yes. I have fewer imperfections than Valerie or Emily. I don't kill people, for one, nor would I have an affair with your best friend or anyone else. I do have many imperfections, though."

"What?"

"I know nothing of children. I've never held a baby. I have never comforted a sick child. I've never lived in a community such as this one. I don't know how to cook or sew. Or clean. I know almost nothing of the world—"

Sam was so flummoxed, he said the first thing that came to mind. "Well, that's very nice. I'm going to bed. I'm bushed."

"Certainly, Mr. . . ."

"Call me SAM!"

"Sam. I will disrobe for the night."

He covered his head with his hands. "Not t'night, lass. Ah have a headache."

She looked at him knowingly. "That is a phrase commonly used by women to avoid sexual intercourse."

"An' men, sometimes. Shane, you better go sleep in the kids' room. Leave the closet door open."

When he woke up, she was lying on one side of him, sleeping hard and clutching him as if she'd die if she let loose. She was wearing a nightgown made of heavy flannel that covered everything but her head and hands. Where she'd gotten it, he didn't know. Shane was burrowed into his other side, wrapped in a blanket he'd loved since he was a baby. Looked like the doings of the previous day had been a little much for him, too.

Sam lay on his back, laughing silently. He felt great. Whatever insanity was happening, he hadn't felt so good since . . . well, ever, that he could remember. Lying next to the girl made him smile. Shira meant poetry. She was more than that; she was a gift from God.

"Well, Lord, if you sent her to me, ah guess ah'll take 'er. Much obliged. Ah'd be grateful if ye kept an eye out for Em and Val." Saying that caused his eyes to sting. "And stay with me, too. Ah've never had an angel for a wife."

He felt like the whole universe had turned a corner and things were gonna be good for a real long time.

PART III
THIRTY-THREE YEARS UNDERGROUND

71

S am sat with his back against the tree trunk. Looking up, he could see pointed leaves dark against the bright white of the skylights. The light couldn't pass through the mature vegetation, but the new foliage on the branch tips lit up golden-green. He could almost see through it to the sun outside.

In moments like this, Sam felt as he had in the orchards of the estate in the old days. Living greenery surrounded and filled him. The trees in the underground were full grown now, reaching up twenty feet and more. Oranges and lemons, peaches, avocados. Many more.

He slipped into the orchard sometimes and lost himself. Sometimes the visions he had of the past seemed more real than the life around him. Memories came easily at his age. Sam smiled. He was seventy-four years old. He had thought he couldn't live a day in the underground, but he had lived there thirty-three years. So far.

Emily had told him people in New York City regularly lived into their hundreds. "Almost everyone gets into his high nineties," she had said. He figured that was how long he'd live. Once Sam had gotten over the idea he was going to die any day, aging was nothing. Years passed.

The wrinkles on his face were deeper. His hair was white and had moved back on his head. He kept his beard trimmed and his hair short. He was thin. They all were, thanks to the mostly vegetarian diet. His skin seemed to have grown; it puckered all over him.

He looked more like someone from the city than the village. Shira kept him dressed in nice clothes. He wore those glasses with the line across the middle all the time. He usually walked around with a book or a reader in his hand.

Shane and he played chess almost every day, as they had since his son had been a child. Now Shane was thirty-two. He'd married one of Arthur's daughters by one of the marauder women. They were happily expecting a baby.

Sam liked to discuss God and things that he read and thought about with the villagers. Well, members of his extended family. The rest weren't interested. But he and those who were interested would meet in the hall and talk for hours about what life meant and what was important. Shira joined them; often she led them. She knew more about everything than anyone he'd ever known. "My parents were both professors, Sam. Don't forget. They taught me."

Shira *was* a gift from God. Everything about her made him happy. They'd had a few rough weeks when she first had appeared. But once they'd settled in and gotten to know each other, that changed. For twenty years, his house had been a place of love and contentment. He felt connected to Emily and Valerie through Shira, but she was the person he'd wanted all his life. Her love carried none of the pain the other two had brought him. She'd given him two children, Valerie and Shira.

She could not be more different from Emily or Val, yet no one seemed to notice. His only problem was remembering to call her Emily, when they were out of their room.

Sam went to the animal pens. "Come here, darlin'," he called. A light brown bunny separated herself from the bunch and hopped toward him. He smiled at her, beginning a familiar ritual.

They had changed the composition of the livestock over the years. Jeremy had made up a formula based on oxygen consumption—so many sheep, chickens, and rabbits. They'd stocked the underground as he'd said.

However, the sheep had turned out to be a bung idea. Took up too much space, shit too much, and didn't provide enough meat. They took too long to reproduce, too.

Chickens were certainly the best food source, since they produced both eggs and meat. They also reproduced and grew quickly. Got sick a lot, though. That was their bad side.

Overall, then, rabbits turned out to be the winners. Babies popped out of them like seeds from weeds, they didn't sicken, and they made good meat. Plus, they did something else no one had anticipated.

Sam reached over the pen's side and picked up his favorite. The rabbit's body was covered by light brown hairs intermixed with dark. She had dark brown ears and legs. She didn't struggle in his arms, cuddling into his chest the minute he pulled her close.

"That's a nice lil' girl," he said, whispering in the village brogue, his habitual speech those days. He took the rabbit and entered the orchard again. He didn't go in as deeply as he had before, just enough so no one could see him. He didn't want anyone to know that the headman liked to pet a bunny. The workday was over; no one was likely to be out there.

He leaned against a tree and stroked the rabbit. His hand moved by itself. The animal's soft coat reminded him of other animals he had touched.

Memory opened and he was back in the village standing by Oned. The world was green and gold, with brilliant skies and clear air. The stallion stood proudly, allowing Sam to groom him. He ran his hand over the horse's dark coat. Slick and glossy, the hair down his shoulder and along his body grew tightly in one direction. Over and over Sam had caressed the horse, talking to him constantly.

He combed the tresses growing from the crest of Oned's neck. Some of the lady's thoroughbred horses had manes like human hair, fine and smooth to the touch. Oned's was coarser, as befitted a villager's horse. He liked that better than the race-horses' silky locks.

Then he was riding Oned, racing across the meadow, shirt off, arms spread wide. He was young! The earth was alive! Anything was possible!

Memory turned. He was with Winnie the first time. She was twelve and he was nineteen. She was pink and white and delicate as a flower. He loved Winnie. He had loved her for years, but the ways of the village had covered it up. He hadn't known what she meant to him.

Her face was before him again, an older Winnie beseeching him close to twenty years ago. "Sam, please. Heal him." She had kneeled before him and begged, "If ye leave him as he is, he can't do anything. Sam, please, heal him the rest of the way."

He had healed Arthur after he'd beaten him, enough to keep him alive. His injuries were severe; he'd ended up in a wheelchair.

But, eventually, Winnie had come to him. "If ye ever loved me, Sam, heal him. Ah want my husband back. Please."

The desperation on her face had moved him. She wanted to live out her life with a real husband. And maybe Art would be that, now he and Emily were done.

So Sam healed Art so he could again be the commando he once had been. He didn't heal everything, but enough so Winnie wouldn't be mad at him. She had been pink and white with corn silk hair. He had healed Arthur because he had once loved Winnie.

The rabbit moved and brought him back to the present. He looked at the animal and smiled ruefully. He was an old man petting a bunny and dreaming of the past. The truth was that the world was dead and he was stuck in a hole. But the rabbit made it all right.

That was what no one had anticipated with the bunnies. Their fur comforted people. It took all the old villagers back to the days aboveground. And it let the new ones feel something that didn't exist elsewhere in their world: an animal's soft coat. Children touched the rabbits in wonder. Parents explained how dogs and cats had felt, and cattle and pigs and horses. They described textures the little ones would never know.

Sam stood up straight, still petting the rabbit, and took a step toward the livestock pens to put her back. Shouting and cursing made him stop. Someone was heading toward the orchard, making a racket. Sam stood hidden inside the tree line, watching.

Rupert was shoving a young boy toward a low concrete wall. "Ye filthy brown shit." He smacked the kid across the back of the head so hard, the boy flew off the ground, landing in a heap. "Ah'll give ye somethin' to remember, ye brown cunnie. Ye're not to play with yer betters. Yer good for nothin' but this." Rupert tore the child's pants down and threw him over the wall.

"Please . . ." The boy struggled, trying to get his knees under him.

Rupert slapped the child across the buttocks. "Shut 'er or ye'll make me mad." He tugged at the opening of his pants. "This is what ye brown whelps need. Yer good for nothin' else."

Sam was about to step out and intervene when Shane shot across the open space and pulled Rupert around. "What do you think you're doing?"

"What're *ye* doing, whoorson?"

"Leave Alex alone!"

"Alex! Alex! Ain't that a fine village name. Ye don't know who ye are. Or maybe ye do. Yer *hers*, the whoor's whelp."

Shane slapped him across the face.

"Ah!" Rupert erupted. "The lil' girlie wants to fight me, does she? Ah'll fight ye. An' none o' yer pansy friends wi' help ye."

Rupert was the same size as Sam, six feet eight inches. He and Janelle were the only people in the underground who were fat. Rupert wasn't rolling fat, but heavy enough to outweigh Shane by fifty pounds.

Shane was small by village standards, like all Emily's children. He was a couple of inches over six feet, but he was fast, and he knew how to fight.

Rupert swung on him, broadcasting his intentions like a lighthouse. Shane wasn't there when the punch flew by, but he was there to land a right uppercut on Ru's jaw.

"Fight like a man, ye hogswart! Ye fight like a girlie."

"You bugger little boys."

"Them brown shits is all o'er the place, put there by that fornicator, Art'ur. Ah'm gonna catch him an' tear off his balls! The vil' is *white. JUST* WHITE! No other color. Never been no other way. Them brown bastards are a' affront to ma *white* ancestors."

"Wow, Rupert. You used lots of big words: 'fornicator,' 'affront,' 'ancestors.' Can you spell them? Or do you have to ask little brown boys to do it for you?"

Ru and Shane stood facing each other, fists clenched, stalemated.

"This don't matter none." Rupert threw up his hands and then pointed at his chest. "Ah will be the headman! When ah am, ye will do everythin' ah say for the rest o' yer stinkin' life. What happens now is nothin'. It's what happens when ma da packs 'er in. It's the Commands."

"The Commands aren't so clear, Rupert. If you could read, you'd know that. Lots could happen before Da dies."

"That skinny ol' man been keepin' me from what's mine. Ah'm fifty-seven years ol'. Almos' daid maself an' ain't got what's mine. Ah can hardly suffer the time 'til he's daid."

"Fuck you, Rupert. *Fuck* you," Shane screamed. "You would be the worst headman in the world."

Rupert lunged for Shane and caught him around the neck. "See if ye ever get t' be headman, dung shit." Shane kneed Rupert in the balls, then jumped away when he doubled over.

"That's enough." Sam put the bunny down and walked over to the two men. Shane might be able to take Rupert in a fair fight. But a fair fight was hard to come by in the village.

Shane backed off, but Rupert didn't, grabbing the smaller man by the neck again.

"AH SAID, STOP!" Sam said in his most powerful Voice. They stood up straight and spun to face Sam. "Well, ah got to see ma son in action." He indicated the boy shivering on the floor. "Changed yer style, Ru? Ye don't like takin' virgin girls anymore? Now ye're after the boys? Pretty soon, the bunnies'll be scared." He said everything in the Voice.

"Ah'll tell ye, Ru, ain't certain atall who's gonna be headman. But that don't matter, because ah ain't dyin' for twenty years. NOW GET OUT OF HERE." Sam's face was mottled red as he pointed back to the main hall. He could see a gaggle of Rupert's people standing by the opening to the hall. Shira and his own clan were grouped a bit away.

"Think on that, ye bastards! Yer headman ain't dyin' for twenty years. Then we'll talk on who's next." He screamed at the crowd. They jolted when the Voice hit them. Everyone had forgotten how powerful Sam's Voice was.

"Get outta ma sight, ye baby buggerer," Sam said to Rupert. Rupert turned without a word and walked away. Sam called the little boy to him and put his arms around him, healing him.

"Ye gotta be tough," he said to the child. "But ye gotta live to grow up, too. Go to Arthur; he'll keep ye safe."

"Shane, go back to the corridor and get everyone together. We need a council right away. Take this boy to Arthur. Tell him to watch him better."

"What about you, Da? Aren't you coming?"

"In a while, Shane. Ah need to think on all this. We'll have a council when ah get back."

"You're sure you're OK out here?"

"Shane, ah got the Power an' ah got the Voice. What does Rupert have that can hurt me?"

72

Sam sat down heavily on the low wall, incredulous. He couldn't go back to the hall until he made some sense out of what he'd seen. How had it come to this? Rupert was going to rape a little boy and he wished his da were dead. Then Ru planned to do God-knew-what when he was dead. Sam's heart did a little bobble, but he paid it no mind. It did that all the time. He rubbed it with his hand.

When Rupert was young, he had been Sam's favorite, a mild boy who did what his father wanted without question. A good boy who would make a good headman. He wouldn't make a brilliant headman, but a good one.

He always remembered Rupert as that wide-faced, innocent boy with trust in his eyes. That's what he saw every time he looked at his son. But that wasn't who Rupert was now.

"Oh, Gawd, tell me what ah did wrong," Sam cried, dropping his face into his hands. As though waiting to be unleashed, images exploded in his mind: pictures, voices, words, feelings—all poured out of him. He couldn't stop them, control them, or ignore them. Everything he'd refused to admit came back.

"Sam, I'm not going to teach him anymore." A young Emily had burst into their room. "He tries to grab me every time we're alone."

"Sam, I'm doing my best, but I don't know if I can teach Rupert to read." A concerned Arthur had spoken, his face still unlined and his hair black. "I think he's got a learning disability. Or maybe . . . it could be his IQ." Arthur had looked worried. "I'll do what I can."

Long ago, Rupert had moved his family out of their room on the VIP corridor and into the small rooms along the edge of the hall. That had been the beginning of the division of the village into the hall and the corridor. Ru could be close to the villagers that way—his people.

A turning point was that horrible night when Cooty Gill had tried to kill Shane, and Valerie had destroyed so many of them.

Slowly at first, and then more rapidly, Rupert had begun to change. He'd held court in the hall and his rough voice boomed as he boasted. He swaggered. Sam had seen all this, but not seen it. He'd seen his boy, troubled, but still the child he'd loved.

When Sam had walked into the hall in recent years, clusters of men would look around furtively. Their hands shook and their eyeballs twitched. Mushrooms and weed. Hooch. They were in the underground, against the Commands and his orders. Rupert was in the middle of it.

It had been going on for years.

He'd seen it; why hadn't he acted? The coarse laughter continued.

In their early years underground, Sam had been involved with healing and lying with Emily and Valerie. He was in love, grinning like a fool, missing everything that happened outside his bedroom. Shane was born. Beautiful Shane, kissed by God. He was as stunning as Valerie and as self-assured as Sam, even as a tot.

Sam had sat in the hall with Shane on his knee, bouncing the babe up and down. Shane's laughter rang out, reverberating against the hard walls. Sam's laugh joined Shane's. Rupert had looked at them with murder on his face.

Sam hadn't seen. He hadn't seen. But he had.

The parade of unnoticed warnings continued. When Emily was with Arthur, Sam stormed through the concrete halls swinging his sledgehammer, looking for blood. Beating the pillars. Digging all night. So obsessed with Arthur and Emily that he hadn't seen. Rupert's men were there, rolling in drunken laughter, disappearing like shadows when he passed.

That had been Cooty's doing—the hybrid weed, and hooch. He'd been the kingpin. But the drugs hadn't disappeared after Valerie killed the offenders and then disappeared. Cooty and his friends had been destroyed, but someone had brought the drugs back. Where was the still? Where did they grow the weed and mushrooms? Sam had torn up the underground and not found them.

Pictures, images, memories. He remembered the party he'd given for Emily when he'd introduced Arthur's children as his own. The kids played their instruments. He'd turned and seen Rupert, again with a look of murder on his face. Ru hated the brown children Sam had adopted; he would do them harm if he could. Was that when Rupert passed a point of no return? Or had he been past it for years?

"Them is Art'ur's kids, not yours, Da. Don' ye know it?" Rupert clung to the thickest village tongue. "Ye should kill him, Da, for dishonerin' ye and fornicatin' wi' yer wife. An' kill them babies, too."

Sam had looked at his son. "No, Rupert. Ah'll not do that. And no one else will, either. They're *my* children."

"They got *brown* skin, Da. None but Art'ur has that. They're *his*. The fornicator. Ye should divorce her, too. She's a . . ." Rupert never called Emily a whore to Sam's face, but the hall buzzed with the word. "Ye should divorce her. Give her to me. Ah'll fix 'er. Keep 'er home."

Sam had walked away.

For years, Sam had walked through the hall in the fine clothes Emily had made him. Short hair and beard, holding a book. He could have come from New York City. He could read anything. He could use a computer as well as Arthur. He talked about books and films in the hall with the people.

But they weren't his people. The underground was split into Rupert's people and his. The main hall and the VIP corridor.

He could see the bright, eager faces of his people: the kids and grandkids of his second wife, Sally. Arthur and Winnie and their kids. Shira and their eight. Later, their children and grandchildren. His family had had very few kids and grandkids; they followed what Arthur had said about having babies. Sam visualized all the brown-skinned children. Sam had known what Arthur was doing and why. He hadn't interfered.

His group contained the smartest people in the underground. They were also a minority.

Rough voices raised in toasts. Brawling. Men and women coupling in the field, men and women who weren't husband and wife. Rupert had come to him about Janelle years before.

"She's got a babe, Da. It's mine. She was virgin, Da. Ah know— she was bleedin' after. Please marry us." He looked sweet. Sam's little boy, his firstborn. How they tricked him into thinking that hussy was a virgin, Sam would never know. He married them, insisting that Rupert divorce Jennie first.

"Oh, yeah, Da. It's OK with Jen. She's livin' by hersel' an' is happy." A month later, Jennie was living with Janelle and Ru. Rupert had a second wife, against the Commands. Now Rupert and Janelle had had eight kids, none authorized by him. All carrying the disease Rupert's mother had borne. Janelle looked like a nasty pig after bearing eight children. How could Janelle and Ru get fat? Where did they get the food?

More scenes rolled out, as vivid as if they were happening again. Scenes from years ago, the old village. Mollie was walking with the waddling gait that said the disease was coming soon. Her legs and feet stuck out to the side, and her head was thrust forward. Her voice was deep and strident. Her face was screwed up in a mask of rage.

She was chopping kindling with the other women. Janie Bougarht was smiling and laughing with the others. She bumped into Mollie, "Oh, ah'm sorruh—"

Mollie had swung the ax and taken off Janie's head. Then she kept going, wading into the other women. Mollie ran through the village when she was done at the woodpile. She killed three people that day, injured nine others.

Sam and four other men caught her and took the ax away. After that, they kept her in chains whenever she started to change. He let her live because he remembered their early days together.

How could he have forgotten the disease? Rupert must have eighteen kids now, between Jennie and Janelle. All of them carrying the disease.

Sam gasped, holding his chest, as the images unspooled. Five years before, the alarm had gone OOO-GAH! OOO-GAH! OOO-GAH! They really hadn't needed an alarm as most people were already lying on the floor, clutching their chests, gasping. A recorded message in Jeremy's voice had come on.

"The air-purifying system is in red alert. Go to your nearest first aid station and obtain an oxygen mask and tank. Certified technicians will reboot the system shortly. You will have sufficient oxygen in your tank to survive the emergency."

They hadn't had any certified technicians. They were with the scientists who hadn't come.

People had managed to drag themselves to the metal doors marked with a cross and pull out the oxygen setups. They'd fumbled, trying to put them together, trying to get them on. He and Shira and their kids figured out how to put the masks on first and then helped the rest. The villagers wheezed in panic.

Shane ran to Arthur. "I've got the plans and my computer. Let's go."

They'd sprinted to the equipment room which housed the air scrubbers and the rest of the air recirculation system. Shane ran through the computers and machines, taking readings from the gauges and comparing them to his computer output and the manuals.

"It's not here." He looked up. "It's up there." A hatch in the ceiling led to an area they'd never explored. He and Arthur clambered up. Sam stuck his head through the opening and watched. A huge metal-clad box almost filled the space.

"Jesus, it's a super-CPU. It runs everything. I've only read about them. Where did Jeremy get this?" Shane's voice was muffled by his oxygen mask. He got to work. "Read the printout to me, Art."

Arthur read and Shane tinkered. Sam tried to breathe as little as possible. How could Shane fix something he'd never seen, from a *book*?

They went from one end of the device to the other. More little doors than Sam had ever seen covered the box. Shane took something out of each, stuck it into his laptop. Nodded or frowned, and stuck it back, then went on. "We've got a bad chip or a piece of faulty programming," he said, and kept working. Arthur stood there, looking worried and reading entries. He was clearly over his head.

Time passed. Sam could feel his breathing becoming heavier. He felt sleepy.

"Sam," Shira called through the intercom, "people are passing out. We've found more tanks, but I don't know how long we can last."

"Just a little longer," he lied. Sweat ran down his face.

Finally, Shane found it. His mask was fogged up, but Sam could see his son's grin as he held up the tiny metal square. He stuck the chip in his computer and nodded, sitting down on the floor, fingers flying. "I just have to reprogram it and we're home free." As Shane typed, Sam could see a black computer screen with white writing and lines in various bright colors.

"It was a couple of bum lines of code," Shane said as he reinserted the chip into the machine. "Should start up now." He punched a button, and the supercomputer hummed. Soon the air scrubbers were vibrating.

"Let's get out of here. It's going to get noisy."

Sam, Arthur, and Shane had climbed down. Shane was exuberant. "*Jeremy* wrote some bad code!" He couldn't stop laughing. "I fixed *Jeremy's* code. Um, though, of course, anyone could make a mistake."

Shane should be the next headman, although he still refused every time Sam asked him. Shane had everything they needed in a leader. And he was thirty-two years old—a perfect age to take over. But he didn't want the job, and didn't want anyone else to know he'd refused.

Sam's chest rose and fell as he considered his next move. "God, you've been pretty quiet the last few years, but ah feel you with me. Tell me what to do." Should he kill Rupert, or just make Shane the new leader? What about all those babies carrying the disease? What about the way Rupert and his men flouted the Commands while saying they were following them?

Sam had eased up on how he enforced some of the Commands, but he hadn't budged on some. He insisted on fidelity and following his orders. He banned drug and alcohol use, for all the good it did him. He didn't tell anyone he was enforcing his interpretations of the Commands, not the Commands themselves. If they guessed, they didn't say anything. *He* ran the underground, which was as it should be.

Sam had wanted to make a good world. He wanted learning and cooperation and love. He'd found those with his people. He'd found it with Shira. But peace had never been the way of the village.

He closed his eyes; he had to, something was pulling him inward. The inner screen of Sam's mind was black and empty. Then red flames flashed across it, seamed at the middle, creating a horizon of scarlet, red, and orange. The inferno blazed, burning forever but consuming nothing. Sam ducked, shaken and awed by the sight. His head bowed.

"Oh, Gawd, what should ah do?" he cried.

Letters appeared in the blackness above the flames. Thick white letters that, somehow, allowed the darkness to shine through.

White letters outlined in effervescent blue. Sparkling, startling blue. The letters spelled: W A R. They spread from one side of the horizon to the other.

W A R

Sam stood up, feet parted, hands clenched. It was time for his people to pull out their weapons. He needed to trust Arthur and unleash him. It was time to kill anyone who didn't obey the Commands. Anyone who bore the taint of the disease. It was time for his people to destroy Rupert and those who followed him. It was time to make a good world, no matter what they had to do to achieve it.

God called for war.

Breathing hard, Sam turned toward the hall. Shane would have gathered everyone by now. All *his* people. They would plan for war against Rupert and his goons. His people were righteous warriors. They would win, even though they were a minority. He would lead them.

The solution to the succession flashed through Sam's mind. Sam would appoint Joshua, his second-born with Emily, his successor. He would make Arthur his second in command. Arthur had been a trained commando. It was time he became that again. Sam needed to take back control of the underground. The three of them could handle Rupert and his thugs.

Feeling as powerful as he ever had been, Sam turned to go back to the corridor. He took a long stride. Something fluttered inside him, and then gave way. He bent over, clutching his chest. Sam crumpled, falling to the floor. His heart felt as if something was wringing it. He was drowning in pain. He tried to call out. Maybe he did. The pressure strangled him, crushing his upper body, running down his left arm. He tried to crawl. Couldn't. Lights sparkled inside his head.

"Shira . . ."

73

Sam sat up. He was in a golden meadow like the one where he and Valerie had once made love. A beautiful place. As he watched, the scene formed up, becoming real. Real trees with leaves and hanging branches swayed in the wind. There was wind! He hadn't felt wind in so long.

And grass! Sam sat on real grass. He stood up. It was the meadow around the village. The sun was shining, warmer and more beautiful than he remembered. Birds sang, trilling and chirping, making his soul dance. He could hear the river in the background, slipping like silk. All of it was real!

He turned around and studied the area. It was the meadow, but the big house wasn't there. The village wasn't where it had been. Nothing was there.

"Hello? Is anyone here?" The place was deserted, but he didn't feel alone. He felt the presence he'd come to know well, something that held him up and made things turn out right. "God?"

"Yes, Sam."

"Where am ah?"

"Don't you recognize it, Sam?"

"It's the village. But no one's here."

"They'll be here, by and by. Just wait awhile."

Sam heard a sound he could never have forgotten. The three-beat cadence of a galloping horse. The creature hove into sight. The magnificent dark beast shot toward him, mane flying, hooves pounding. His white legs and the long feathers of hair on them flashed and rippled as he ran.

"Oned!"

The stallion slid to a stop next to him, standing proudly with his neck arched and coat glistening. He looked at Sam out of the kind, dark eye closest to him. It was so full of intelligence that Sam gasped.

"Ye're alive! Ye made it through the war!"

The horse pushed him in the stomach with his nose.

"OK. Let's go." Sam reached up to grab Oned's mane and withers so he could swing on. He froze. His shirtsleeves were rolled up. His forearms were tanned, their muscles stout and bulging. Reddish brown, sun-lightened hair curled on his arms and the backs of his hands. Most amazing was his skin. It had shrunk to fit again. He looked at his arms in wonder.

"Ah'm *young*. Ye made me *young*." He looked at himself. He was wearing clothes like those Emily had made him, but nicer. "Oned, what happened? Where are we?"

And then he knew what had happened and staggered back, beginning to sob.

The presence comforted him.

"In just a while, Sam, they'll be here. You can begin again."

"But ah didn' make a good world, like ye said. Ah failed." The language of the village came out of him without a sense of guilt. This was a place where the way a man talked didn't matter at all. High or low didn't exist in this realm.

"You did, Sam. For those who could see it, you made a perfect world. You are my beloved."

Sam could feel a smile bigger than the universe surround him. "Ah did OK?"

"You did very well, my faithful friend."

Sam swung up on the horse. "Let's go!"

Oned leapt forward, covering ground as he never had before. The forest rushed toward them. Sam raised his hands high over his head and shouted as the stallion coursed across the brilliant plain.

He had found a perfect world.

74

Arthur sat in a dank concrete room, his portable computer balanced on his lap. He was suited up in commando gear, wearing his weapons belt. The laser sword was under his right hand. He typed fast, face grim.

> This is Arthur Romero. I'm writing in the idiotic belief that, maybe, somehow, someone will get out of here and tell our story.
> That's really crazy when you're locked in a hellhole three hundred feet beneath the ground with a gang of maniacs. None of us knows if we'll live another day.
> I want to set the record straight. This is the truth.
>
> Sam and Emily lived happily ever after until Sam died a year ago. He was seventy-four. They got back everything they'd lost in their marriage and loved each other so much that it hurt to look at them. I expect they'll go down with the great

romantic figures of history. I saw them that way, as legends.

Sam Baahuhd had been headman for fifty-five years. He died the oldest headman the village had ever had, and the best.

When Sam passed, all the shelter's life-support systems were working fine. The fields made enough food for everyone, the place was clean, and the people were as happy as they could be stuck down here. The shelter's population was one hundred. We had held the line, barely. We had been living underground for thirty-three years. I was sixty-five years old. Emily was fifty-seven. Our kids were grown and had big kids of their own.

Rupert has told the story of Sam's death differently, but this is what really happened.

Sam had a heart attack out by the orchard. We all thought Shane should have been the next headman. Sam had never mentioned this as a possibility, I don't know why. We could have made Shane the headman anyway, if we'd been ready. Even though the Commands named Rupert, and Sam had given him his blessing publicly years ago, another man could have taken over.

Sam had told me the transition was always a dogfight. He'd had to kill four men after his dad died. He'd had to fight down coup attempts most of his life. The position of headman was earned, not given.

What happened between Emily and me messed things up. Sam never totally forgave me. He no longer discussed anything important with me. I could see a showdown with Rupert screaming toward us, but I couldn't convince Sam to listen to me. It was as if Rupert had been his favorite and he couldn't bear to see his faults. Or think about favoring one son over another. Or get it together to announce, "Shane's my choice. Tough shit, Rupert."

Sam might have had something like that in mind right before he died. Shane told us the horrible story of Rupert trying to rape Alex, and Sam stopping it. Sam had called for a meeting. Maybe he was going to declare war and announce a successor. We'll never know.

When Sam died, it was the hall vs. the VIP corridor. The VIP corridor held the people with education and intelligence. Sam's followers were his kids and grandchildren, my kids and theirs. Sally's bunch. Twenty-eight people out of a hundred.

Rupert led the "back to the real village" movement in the hall. Everybody out there spoke the old village dialect exclusively. They were making hooch somewhere, too. And growing mushrooms. And weed. Ru and his friends rolled around loaded half the day, laughing their asses off. It was the old village, all right.

Years ago—I don't know when—Rupert and his cronies had started an Aryan brotherhood thing, with no opposition. He made a big deal over the fact that my kids were brown, and that I was brown. My kids and I are the only people of color in the underground.

Since I'm baring my soul, I might as well bare all of it. A bunch of brown babies popped up. My kids. I treated the infections of the three hostage women and bred them. I picked out the women with the most variant genetic structures and bred them. It was the worst, most disgusting thing I've ever done. But I did it. I'd had it planned from the beginning; I didn't give those women birth control implants.

Winnie knew what I was doing. She didn't like it any more than I did, but we could see it was necessary. We took my babies and raised them. Their mothers didn't want them, once the Aryans started yapping.

I'll quit stalling and tell you what happened.

I can remember exactly what people said. I can hear their voices and remember what they wore. I know who stood where.

Sam collapsed next to the orchard. That was the place he liked best. We were gathered for the meeting he'd called, so I got out to the orchard with Shane and some of our boys pretty fast. I had them take the stretcher to his room, rather than the sick bay. I knew there was nothing I could do the minute I saw the color of his face. His skin was bluish and his eyes were dilated. They put him on the bed.

Emily was waiting. She ran to him, crying, "Oh, my God. Oh, God. Sam."

He reached for her hand, but he died with his eyes locked on mine. I knew what he was saying: Take care of her. Take care of them all. I was the only one who could save the underground. Sam finally had forgiven me.

Emily threw herself on Sam's body, wailing.

"Emily, you know what's going to happen," I said. I didn't want to push her, but I had to. "Rupert will be here soon. You have to get out of here." Winnie came in. I took Emily by the shoulders and pulled her off Sam. "You have to go; it's not safe." I handed her over to Winnie, who was staring at Sam's body, eyes rimmed with tears.

"Take her, Winnie. Lock everything down. Full alert."

The kids arrived, all Emily's eight and the two Winnie had had with Sam, plus the two Winnie and I had. And Sam's kids with his second wife, Sally. And some grandkids. I ran to the laptop and sent its contents to the main computer, then set it to erase when the download was done. Everything of any importance would be in the lab. I had the only access to that. Rupert would not be able to run the shelter from here the way Sam had.

We had done a couple of smart things. Sam had had his boys seal and disguise the secret doorways that led to the labs and the munitions bays. Even an expert couldn't tell the doors were there. I looked around the room frantically, wondering if I had forgotten anything.

I heard Rupert and his mob coming long before they arrived.

"Ma da is daid! Ma da is daid! Aw, Jaysus, ma da Is gone!" Rupert howled dramatically.

"'Tis all right, Ru. Is a good day comin' for us all. Yer da was a good man, but yer better. Buck up, boy. Is a strum fine day!" Rupert's friends made Sam's death sound like a reason for celebration. They sounded happy. "Lemme in, Art'ur," Rupert bellowed. "Get out o' the way. Ma da is daid!" He shoved his way into the room.

Rupert looked down at his father, his face contorting. "Oh, Da. Oh, Da. He's daid." He fell to his knees and grasped Sam's hands. "He's still warm!" Rupert turned on me. "Ye bastard! Why didn't ye save him? Ye have the med'cine." He stood up, towering over me and clenching his fists.

"I couldn't save him, Rupert. He was seventy-four. No headman ever has ever lived that long."

"An' don't I know it, waitin' all ma life for ma chance. Livin' like a whoorson while she had the good room. An' him! She turned him again' me, the stinkin' bitch." Rupert turned toward his father's corpse. "Ah've wasted ma life waitin' for him to get outta this world. This is ma time! An' ah'll make it good for all o' us. Ah am the headman!"

Rupert's friends shouted triumphantly.

Shane asserted himself. "My father had the right to this room as long as he lived. And don't talk about my mother that way."

"He's ma da, too, chicken guts. Ma father. He'd been ma father for much longer than he been yers. Ah'm the new headman!" More cheers.

"Not necessarily," I cut in. "I've read the Commands carefully. They say that the headman will be the old headman's oldest son—" Rupert's supporters cheered.

"Ev'ryone knows that." He swaggered toward me.

"The difference is in what Jeremy ordered the headman to do. It wasn't automatic. Jeremy charged Sam with doing anything he needed to do to keep the place running. That includes changing the successor. Naming someone else if his oldest son wasn't fit. You've broken all the Commands, Rupert. You don't live the way Jeremy said the headman should. You have two wives. You use drugs—"

The floor shook from the noise that came out of Rupert. His face turned red. He looked as if he were going berserk. His men crowded in, shoving against me and Shane and the rest of the kids. Ruperts' friends jammed the doorway.

"Shuddup, ye brown monkey! Ye shit-faced forni-cator! Ye didn't stop with the whoor, did ye? Ah see brown faces all over. Ye foocking . . ."

He rushed at me, but I'd had the sense to grab my weapons belt. I had my stick in my hand. I didn't want to hit him, but I raised it. That was enough to stop him cold.

"Ye gonna beat the headman, brownie? Try it an' see how ye like bein' strung in the hall by yer thumbs."

His buddies growled agreement and sort of low-ered down a bit, ready to spring. While not armed for war, all of them carried big hunting knives.

"Wait a minute." Shane stepped in. "This isn't right. We just lost a great headman and our father. We should decide this after his funeral. We should have a meeting and examine The Book."

Rupert looked at him, sneering. "We jus' had our meetin'. Ma da ne'er told nobody nuthin' about me not bein' the headman. He's the one that has to say. An' that's what it says in the Commands an' ever'wheres else. Ah can read, y' know. Ma da's daid an' ain't said nuthin' to no one 'bout nuthin'.

"Get out, ye shits. Both o' ye. Get outta ma room. Clear all this out." Rupert waved his hand at the tat-tered but still luxurious room. "Get all her dirt outta here. Me an' ma wives is movin' in.

"Nah. Wait. We'll take 'er all. Livin' with all this will be fine." He changed his mind abruptly and waved his hand to indicate the frayed ostrich plumes on the corners of the bed's canopy. "Strum fine. Like bein' a king. Le' her live like a . . ." He couldn't think of the right word.

"Like a whoor, Ru. What she is!" Rupert's gang piped up.

"Yeah. Like a whoor." He glared at me, daring me to say something.

"She's not a whore, Rupert," I said.

"Oh, she be a whoor an' don't you know it." He turned to his friends, who pulled closer together, scowling. "Where is the whoor? Ah got somethin' for her." Rupert laughed and grabbed at his crotch.

"Emily is grieving," I told him. "She was your father's wife, Rupert. Have some respect."

"Ma Ma was ma Da's wife. Ma Ma an' the village-born was his wives. She killed ma Ma." Rupert noticed the young people behind me. Well, they ranged from their late teens to forties—young to a sixty-five-year-old like me. "Ye bring yer brats? What d'ya think they'll do again' us men?"

They'd do very well, I hoped. I'd trained them into first-rate warriors, in the gym anyway. I remained silent.

As though realizing what he was up against, Rupert turned to his father's body. "Get this dead trash outta here. Ah been waitin' for this day for years and years. Get rid of it."

"No." I said. "Sam was the greatest headman the village has ever had. He'll have a proper funeral. The people will have a chance to pay their respects."

Sam's body was laid out in the main hall. Most trooped past it, kissing his hands and face, sobbing and crying out. But some stood off with Rupert and his wives, laughing.

How did we fall apart like this, I thought. Where did we fail?

One person didn't show her face. Emily was sequestered in the VIP corridor. It was the only safe place for her.

Winnie and I took Emily into our room after Sam died. We actually took Emily into our bed. I don't want you to get any funny ideas about that. We were like a brother and sisters by then. We kept her so close because we didn't know what she might do.

Emily fell apart. Just shattered. She had changed so much over the last twenty years, I wouldn't have recognized her as the Emily I knew. She dressed like a nun, didn't show an inch of skin. She was quiet and sweet. Scholarly. Didn't work out hard the way she used to. Whatever happened to her, Em and Sam were the happiest couple I've seen. They glowed.

And when he died, I've never seen anyone as depressed as she was. She curled up on her side and seemed to shrink. She started to look like one of those ancient mummies they're always finding in the mountains somewhere. Dried out, fragile. Dead.

Then she changed. One day, she got up and went to the gym. She started eating more, making sure she got enough protein and vitamins. We thought that was good. She started spending all day in the gym, making up what she'd lost in physical condition when she was depressed. She got her weight and strength back.

Great, we thought. She still didn't talk and wasn't interested in anything but working out, but at least she wasn't lying there like she was dead.

Boy, were we wrong.

"Get the kids in here. They've got to get ready." She commandeered all the "kids," the younger generations, and started sparring with them. I suited up and joined them. I'd always liked sparring with Emily. I'd worked on turning the kids into soldiers for years, but they didn't seem hard enough mentally really to fight.

"Get in there and fight or you're going to get your balls ripped off!" Emily bellowed louder than any drill sergeant. "If you aren't tougher than that, you are going to get fucked up! Handle it, soldier! Do you want to cry? Is mommy being hard on you?"

She fought with them. It wasn't sparring, it was real fighting. All the time she was in the gym, she spewed obscenities.

"I KNOW WHAT'S COMING, SOLDIER! BE PREPARED OR BE DEAD! FIGHT OR DIE! FIGHT OR DIE!"

She tore the kids apart. We had a broken arm, strained ligaments, bruises, knocked-out teeth. Emily was pushing fifty-eight years old at that time, but as tough as they come. She took them on two and three at a time and was only satisfied when they knocked her out. That's no exaggeration; she got a concussion in one session.

"Now we're getting somewhere," she said, then pointed out the two who had rendered her senseless. "Those two know how to fight. The rest of you pussies are going to get screwed. Fight or die!"

All this time, I had kept locked down the part of the corridor where our people lived. Sam had dug a secret access from the VIP corridor to the fields years before. His digging proved to be useful, we were finding. We could get to the food relatively safely. Once we were out in the fields, we were at risk, but we were fast and tricky. I changed the combinations on the control panels two or three times a day.

Rupert's reign was creating insanity in the main hall, but we were relatively safe. Rupert could bellow all he wanted from Sam's old room, but we could ignore him. Inside our rooms, we couldn't hear him at all.

Rupert had always had the Voice and the Power. Not like Sam, but to some degree. His Power ratcheted up when Sam died, which was normal when a new headman took control. We still could withstand it; we weren't compelled to do what he said. We were used to this kind of limited power; all Sam's kids had it.

There was a big difference between Rupert and his father. While Sam used his Power to heal and make the community come together, Rupert used it to punish and intimidate. He had the main hall jumping to his tune. He worked on me when he could. I got it worse than any of our people; Ru called me out every day to monitor the controls for the shelter's systems. I got banged up a bit. No, that's bullshit. They beat the crap out of me whenever they could catch me. Rupert and his buddies didn't seem inclined to learn about how the shelter worked as long as they had me.

Almost a year passed in a low-key state of siege.

In the twenty-four hours before it happened, I had changed the codes on the control panels four times. No one could get into our area without knowing the latest combination.

I woke up in the pitch dark. Emily wasn't there. That wasn't unusual; sometimes she started working out that early and kept at it all day. But this day was different. I had a bad feeling.

I shot to my feet and put on my clothes. "Winnie! Call the kids. Have them come to the gym."

Bright light flooded into the corridor from the gym. I ran into the room. There were seven of them, including Rupert. Village giants, all of them way over six feet tall. Rupert was talking to her in the Voice. She was frozen stiff, stuck like a bug with a pin through its belly.

"Ye'll be ma wife. Ma third wife, after Janelle. Ye'll do what ah say, an' what ma wives say, too." And he told her exactly what he expected her to do for him. "Ah'm gonna split yer ass! Yer gonna suck me night and day. Yer gonna be the bitch ye always was."

"Hey," I barged in. Ru turned to me and I felt as though I'd been struck by a wall. His Voice was as powerful as Sam's had been. I couldn't move.

"Whatcha doin' here, computer man? Wanna see how a real man treats a whoor?"

"Stop it, Rupert." I could talk, but not move. Shane came running in with the rest of the kids behind him. They got into the room and were also frozen by Rupert's Voice. They looked around wild-eyed.

"Looks like yer brats need to learn a lesson!" Rupert laughed. "Ah been practicin', computer man. Ah got the Voice like ma da. Things'll be different now." He turned back to Emily.

"Come on, darlin'. Gimme a taste." He moved toward her, wagging his tongue from side to side.

"I'd rather die than be your wife," she screamed. "Sam said you were a *stupid*—"

The instant she said his father's name, Rupert went berserk. He leaped at her and tore her to pieces. He yanked out his knife and went to work. He used the blade, but also his teeth, his hands.

Even his boots. We stood watching, screaming and crying, but couldn't help. Ru's goons crowded closer, excited by the metallic smell of blood and the stench of her ripped-open organs. Excited by the grunting noises Rupert made as he pulled her apart.

I don't think she suffered long—he ripped out her throat first.

When he was done, Rupert turned drunkenly, blood covering him from his mouth to his feet. His hands and forearms were glossy red. He saw Shane standing frozen and helpless. Rupert reached him in three strides and cut his throat.

Rupert has been telling all sorts of stories. He said Emily killed herself in grief over Sam. Then he said that she had agreed to be his wife. He also said she already was his wife and had been before Sam died. The best one was that she isn't dead; she's hiding in a secret place in the shelter, where she meets him. They're lovers.

He's been saying that Shane got the spots—what they called pox—and died. I didn't vaccinate him properly. Or that he slit his own throat in grief over his mother's death.

Insane nonsense.

I thought the talk about Emily committing suicide was bullshit until I found a letter on my computer. Here it is:

Dear Arthur,

Rupert wants me. He's wanted me as long as I've known him. Eventually he'll get powerful enough to come for me. You'll fight him. You and Shane and the kids.

There's more of them than us, Arthur. We could lose. I don't want a war over me. And I don't want anyone to die for me.

Please forgive me.

It's not just because of Rupert. I can't live without Sam.

When Sam died, I felt like all the protection I had disappeared. I've remembered who I was. I was Valerie Zanner, a federal agent. I've killed more people that I can count. I remembered the pink room where the man who adopted me kept my sisters and me. I remember what he did to us. Sam must have kept it from me somehow.

Valerie Zanner is taking over—I'll end up being her. She could kill all of you.

I can't let that happen.

Good-bye, my love. You were my love, Arthur. But Sam and I always had a spark between us. That won out.

Take care of yourself. Make sure the kids know how to survive. Try to see that people remember me the way I really was.

Emily Baahuhd

Did she let Rupert in that morning? I thought that maybe one of the kids, overwhelmed by Rupert's Voice, opened the door. But was it Emily? Did she set it up? Or did Ru's viciousness and lust find a way past Jeremy's security?

We'll never know. All I know is that I saw the love of my life torn to pieces. I saw the finest young man I've known slaughtered.

Emily got it right when she was leaning on the kids. It's fight or die. I'm going to fight.

I'm the bad guy in this story. I'm the man who lusted after another man's wife. I'm the guy who broke up the king and queen and caused pain and chaos all over my world. I'm not going to whitewash what I did or excuse anything.

Before you judge me, I'd like you to imagine what it is like to live in a concrete mausoleum that echoes even if no one's making a sound. Imagine seeing the same, mostly uninteresting people every day and eating the same lousy food. And knowing that's it for the rest of your life.

Imagine knowing that at any minute, a life-support system could fail and you could be without air, or water, or food.

Imagine never going for a walk on the beach again.

Or petting a dog.

Or seeing your parents and family.

Smoking a cigar.

Having a barbecue.

Taking a trip.

Going for a swim.

Drinking a beer.

If you can imagine living like that, you will know that a person could get seriously, seriously fucked up in the head. I fell in love with Emily. That wasn't crazy, but acting on it was.

How did I feel about betraying my best friend? Like crap. I felt so guilty all those years that I had to force myself to look *anyone* in the eye. And I still was in love with Emily. The only time I didn't feel guilty was when I was with her. I was glad Sam practically killed me with that beating. I deserved it.

I lost my best friend. From the minute Em and I started up, Sam didn't speak to me unless he had to. He never trusted me enough to work with me on the succession or anything that mattered.

I lost Emily. She wouldn't come near me. Either she didn't want to get Sam aggravated or she didn't want to start anything up again. Or I disgusted her.

My relationship with Winnie took a major hit. She'd been Sam's wife. Before he came down here and started following the Commands, he ripped and ran more than any New York hipster. So Winnie knew about being cheated on. But what I did with Emily broke the bond we'd had. We got most of it back, but that took years.

I lost my kids with Emily. The minute Sam started paying attention to them, it was no contest. As a dad, Arthur Romero couldn't hold a candle to Sam Baahuhd. They dumped me flat and Sam encouraged them.

And, of course, Sam never fixed my face. When he beat me up, he made sure that I wouldn't run off with any other man's wife. I'm not my mama's pretty baby boy any more.

That's what I did and that was the price.

Emily and Sam are gone and I'm in charge of keeping our children alive and this place afloat. Rupert's hunting down our kids—the kids Sam and Emily had, my boys with her, and my boys with Winnie. All the others associated with us. My kids are easy to spot— they're brown. They'll be targeted first.

Rupert's voice is irresistible. If he catches us, we're dead. I don't know how long we'll last. Or what will happen next.

It's time to open up the parts of the underground that only I know about. We're going into the depths of the earth. I will do everything I can to make sure that my children and theirs survive. I won't allow everything we created and suffered for down here to die.

I want you to know our story. It may be all that endures.

Arthur Romero

Arthur saved the document he had created, encoded it, and then directed the electronic packet to 186A-Beta, the data collection satellite specified by his military commanders. He would never know if anyone downloaded it.

"It's time to go. We've got to get out of here," Joshua whispered.

Art stowed the computer and moved down the dark tunnel to where Sam's kids waited. "OK. Let's rock. Josh, you take the left tunnel . . ."

EPILOGUE
A FINAL NOTE FROM SAM GOOD MAN

Arthur did save most of our kids in his time. He taught those he saved to be tough, to endure, and to find safety where we could. He taught us stealth. He educated us. The Arthurs and Emilys and Sams from our lines—the lines without the disease—became the scribes and scholars. Enough of us lived in each generation to keep us going for one more round. That wouldn't have happened without Arthur Romero. He died a hero.

Arthur taught us how Sam spoke and thought, and he taught what he knew about Emily. Those of us from the line of Emily passed down her story in its fullness—but to each other, only. Arthur told us about himself and Rupert and Winnie. He made sure we could tell the story to the next ones in line. And that's how it went for 105 generations. We carried Art's legend in our heads and hearts. And now I've told our history to you, and made it into a book. A book of the truth, a book Arthur would have loved.

Arthur took us deep into the underground, to secret places only he knew. We learned you can run and hide, but only for so long. Eventually, Rupert and those who came after him found our hiding places and pulled us out.

We suffered. We endured terrible things. Most of us died.

Of the line of Emily born underground, only I am left.

I'm laughing as I write this. We've been sitting on this rock ledge for years. In that time, the lady and I have had three children. I'm so happy, I can barely stand myself.

Lady Grace and I are in love and our babies are beautiful and strong. In loving the lady, I get to have what Sam Baahuhd once wanted so much.

Except that she was always intended for me.

I can feel Emily's joy and that of all my ancestors when they remember the hard times and all they went through. We came out on top at the story's end. And—by and by—we all end up with Sam in his perfect world.

The line of Emily continues.

Sam Good Man

ABOUT THE AUTHOR . . .

SANDY NATHAN

Sandy Nathan writes to amaze and delight, uplift and inspire, as well as thrill and occasionally terrify. She is known for creating unforgettable characters and putting them in do-or-die situations.

She writes in genres ranging from visionary fiction to juvenile nonfiction to spirituality and memoir.

"I write for people who like challenging, original work. My reader isn't satisfied by a worn-out story or predictable plot. I do my best to give my readers what they want."

Mrs. Nathan's books have won twenty-one national awards, including multiple awards from oldest, largest, and most prestigious contests for independent publishers. Her books have earned rave critical reviews and customer reviews of close to five-star averages on Amazon. Most are Amazon bestsellers.

Sandy was born in San Francisco. Sandy grew up in the hard-driving, achievement-orientated corporate culture of Silicon Valley.

Holding Master's Degrees in Economics and Marriage, Family, and Child Counseling, she was a doctoral student at Stanford's Graduate School of Business. Sandy has been an economic analyst, businesswoman, and negotiation coach, as well as author.

Mrs. Nathan lives with her husband on their California ranch. They bred Peruvian Paso horses for almost twenty years. She has three grown children and two grandchildren.

www.sandynathan.com

THE HEADMAN & THE ASSASSIN
EARTH'S END 3

A note from author Sandy Nathan—

People ask me where I get the ideas for my books. I use a technique I call "literature through disaster." That's a cheeky way of saying that many of my books are my soul's way of making sense of my personal tragedies. The Earth's End exists because of a painful loss.

A few years ago, my brother died suddenly. I was heartbroken—he was my only sibling and adored baby brother. On the outside, I looked calm, but on the inside, grief fought with memories, creating a contained despair.

Perhaps three months after my brother's death, I had a dream. A shining, golden light hovered above me as I lay in bed. The light was a conscious being radiating goodness. I would call the apparition an angel, except that she was just a hovering light. No wings or halo or so on. (But maybe those are human add-ons.)

The light lowered itself onto my body, finally merging with me. The bliss was enormous. Indescribable. For several hours, I enjoyed the state of that beatific creature.

That dream was the inspiration for the angelic Eliana in the first book of the Tales from Earth's End. My creative process turned my experience into an angelic alien sent to earth on a vitally important mission.

The rest of the book's plot was revealed to me during the next week. *The Angel & the Brown-Eyed Boy* occurs hours before a nuclear war destroys the planet. The story describes the attempts of an ensemble of people to escape the conflagration. I introduce the gigantic underground bomb shelter on the Piermont estate.

When I finished the draft for *The Angel & the Brown-Eyed Boy*, the characters were as real to me as people I know in daily life. My mind kept churning, turning out two sequels in record time.

The second book, *Lady Grace*, tells what happens when the radiation clears. It chronicles the attempts of the survivors to create a new world. Some of the characters come from *The Angel & the Brown-Eyed Boy*; some are new. *Lady Grace* is a romance as well as a thriller, with more twists than a politician's cover story.

My mind/heart/psyche/word generator was still stoked when I finished *Lady Grace*. The character of Sam Baahuhd from *The Angel & the Brown-Eyed Boy* captivated me. Sam is the headman of the village—the community composed of the staff and workers of the Piermont estate where the action in The Angel ends up.

Sam is huge, almost a giant, and as tough as they come. He's a seasoned fighter and defender of the estate, as well as an agricultural expert and top manager. He's been stunted by the serf-like conditions in which the villagers live.

Sam Baahuhd fascinated me so much that I wrote *The Headman & the Assassin*. *The Headman & the Assassin* is a love story that takes place in the bomb shelter below the Piermont estate. It's a passionate and sometimes dangerous romance that lasts a lifetime.

A fourth book in the series is shaping up in my mind and is partially written. Book four will pick up where *Lady Grace* ends. No title yet. This book will not be released for a while.

That's because I've got two series in play. The characters in *Lady Grace* are visited—involuntarily on their parts—by Bud Creeman and Wesley Silverhorse from my other collection, the Bloodsong Series. The Bloodsong Series tells the story of the richest man in the world, Will Duane, meeting a great Native American shaman, Grandfather.

Numenon, the first book in the Bloodsong Series, takes place in 1997, as Silicon Valley billionaire Will Duane and his employees travel to New Mexico to attend Grandfather's final spiritual retreat.

When Bud and Wes drop into *Lady Grace,* they're leaving their world in 2015. Eighteen years have passed since *Numenon* and much has happened in Will Duane's world. You need to know what went down.

Several Bloodsong Series books must be released before the fourth book from Earth's End can come out and make sense. When completed, The Bloodsong Series and Earth's End will cover more than half a century in our time--and span thousands of years in the world of Earth's End.

It's a spectacular journey that may take a lifetime. I invite you to make it with me.

Sandy Nathan

From award-winning author Sandy Nathan—

THE ANGEL & THE BROWN-EYED BOY
EARTH'S END 1

Tomorrow morning, a nuclear holocaust will destroy the planet. Two people carry the keys to survival: Jeremy, a 16-year-old, tech genius; and Eliana, an angelic, intergalactic traveler.

Welcome to a future world only heartbeats from our own.

By the late 22nd century, the world has become a police state. A ruined United States barely functions. Government control masks chaos, dissenters are sent to camps, and technology is outlawed. War rages while the authorities proclaim the Great Peace.

It's New York City on the eve of nuclear Armageddon.

Join Jeremy and Eliana on a quest to save two doomed planets … and find each other.

THE ANGEL & THE BROWN-EYED BOY
EARTH'S END 1

ISBN-13: 978-0-9762809-0-3 (Trade paperback)

From award-winning author Sandy Nathan—

LADY GRACE
& THE WAR FOR A NEW WORLD
EARTH'S END 2

First there was *Numenon* of the Bloodsong Series, a 20th century tale of spirituality and mysticism. Then came *The Angel & the Brown-Eyed Boy*, which took readers to the edge of a planet's extinction. Now Jeremy, Eliana, and their friends are joined by Bud Creeman and Wesley Silverhorse in exploits that bridge times and realities.

In this world of the future much time has passed—but has it been enough to create a better world?

LADY GRACE & THE WAR FOR A NEW WORLD
EARTH'S END 2

ISBN-13: 978-1-937927-02-8 (Trade paperback)

www.ingramcontent.com/pod-product-compliance
Lightning Source LLC
Chambersburg PA
CBHW030541260626
47157CB00006B/2133